Thomas Dick Lauder

Tales of the Highlands

Thomas Dick Lauder

Tales of the Highlands

ISBN/EAN: 9783337174255

Printed in Europe, USA, Canada, Australia, Japan

Cover: Foto ©Andreas Hilbeck / pixelio.de

More available books at **www.hansebooks.com**

TALES of the HIGHLANDS

BY

SIR THOMAS DICK LAUDER, Bart.

*Author of " The Moray Floods," " The Wolf of Badenoch,"
"Lochandhu," "Royal Progress in Scotland," &c.*

WITH SIX ILLUSTRATIONS

LONDON: HAMILTON, ADAMS & CO.
GLASGOW: THOMAS D. MORISON

1881

DEDICATION.

TO HIS GRACE JOHN DUKE OF ARGYLL.

My Dear Duke,

The permission which you have so kindly given me to dedicate this volume to you, affords me a double source of gratification.

In the first place, it recalls and strengthens the recollection of the first formation of that which may now be called an old friendship between us; from the continuance of which I have, from time to time, derived so much valuable scientific and general information, as well as so much rational recreation of mind, and which has, moreover, produced some of the happiest hours of my life.

Secondly, I am thus allowed to attach to my Highland Legends the name of Mac Chailein Mhòir, which is certainly of all others, that most fitted to be associated with Highland story.

With my best thanks, therefore, and with every wish for your Grace's health and happiness, as well as for those of all you hold dear, I beg that you will always believe me to be, with the highest respect and regard,

My Dear Duke,

Most sincerely and affectionately yours,

THOS. DICK LAUDER.

NOTE EXPLANATORY OF THE ARGYLL PATRONYMIC
OF MAC CHAILEAN MHOIR.

THIS patronymic of the noble family of Argyll has been strangely changed by Sir Walter Scott, and others, into MacCallum More. The true orthography and reading of it is Mac Chailein; that is, the son or descendant of Colin. Mòr signifies great; and when used in the genitive case as above, it is written Mhoir—pronounced Vòr, or rather Vore —having much the same sound as More in English.

Mac Chailean Mhoir, the son of the Great Colin, or Mac Chailean, is synonymous in Gaelic with Argyll; and Mòr, *great*, makes it, in fact, the Great Argyll.

Calain Mòr—so called from his stature or his actions—was the eighth knight of Lochow of the name of Campbell. He commanded the right wing of the Scottish army at the battle of Largs, in the year 1263. His father Archibald was in life at the time, though Colin led on the men of Argyll. Colin Mor was knighted by Alexander III. in the year 1280. He was killed in a fight with John Bachach (that is, Lame John) MacDougald of Lorn, about the year 1293, in forcing a pass called the Ath-dearg, or the Bloody Ford, in Lorn. His remains were carried to Kilchrennan, on Lochow side, and interred in the parish churchyard, where his tombstone is still a conspicuous object. From him the family of Argyll have the patronymic of Mac Chailean Mhoir, or, as generally pronounced, Mac Calain Mòr.

The author has to thank the Rev. Dr. Norman Macleod of Glasgow for having afforded him the information which has enabled him to give this explanation, and he is the more grateful for it from the interest he personally takes in the memory of the heroic Sir Colin, from whose great grand-daughter, Alicia, he has himself the honour of being descended.

CONTENTS.

PREFACE.

THIS collection of Highland Tales is published in continuation of that which appeared in 1837, and in pursuance of a plan—long cherished by the author—of collecting and preserving in print all the more interesting of the traditional and local histories of the Highlanders that yet remain, but which, to the regret of all antiquaries, are fast melting away. Not a year passes over us that does not see some ancient Seanachaidh, whom perhaps we may have known as the venerable historian of the district where he lived—to whose tales of love, strife, or peril we may have often listened with eager attention—borne to his silent grave in the simple churchyard of some lonely Highland parish, where his snow-white head is consigned to its parent earth, and there left to moulder into dust and oblivion, together with all the legendary lore which it contained. The author has always had great pleasure in availing himself of every opportunity that occurred to him of conversing with those living records of the glens, and he has never failed to write down whatsoever curious matter it may have been his good fortune to gather from them. By such means, as well as by the assistance of many kind friends, he has been enabled to make a very considerable collection of these traditions from all parts of the Highlands of Scotland; and, like all other collectors, he has become only just so much the more insatiably avaricious to increase his store the larger that he sees the heap becoming.

Such legends are not only curious and interesting in themselves, but they will often prove to be helps to history, from the little incidents which they furnish, that may throw light upon it. But, however they are to be estimated in this respect, they must always be considered as having some value, from the pictures which they afford of the manners of the times to which they belong.

It is quite possible that many of these traditions, in the course of their long descent through successive ages, during which they have been distilled and redistilled through the poetical imaginations of so many narrators, may have undergone considerable alteration, and even, perhaps, in some instances exaggeration. To many fervid minds such an effect produced by their antiquity may not render them one whit less palatable, whilst people of a less romantic and more common-sense cast will always be able to winnow out for themselves the more solid grains from the glittering but empty chaff. But anyone who, from the apparent improbability of some of their attendant circumstances, should assert that such legends have no foundation in fact would fall, it is apprehended, into a very grievous error. The author thinks that no legend, however improbable, can have been created without having had some foundation in reality—some germ, in short, from which it had its origin—and perhaps he cannot better illustrate this observation, or prove its truth, than by narrating a circumstance, with the particulars of which he was favoured by his friend the Venerable Archdeacon Williams, which shows this connection in the strongest light. What he has to tell, it is true, belongs more particularly to the Principality of Wales, but it only furnishes a more than ordinarily curious and striking example of a class of which many similar samples might be easily produced from the Highlands of Scotland, as well as from many other parts of the world.

Some of the Welsh legendary historians tell us that in the year 500 there flourished a renowned chief called Benlli Gawr. His usual residence was where the present town of Mold now stands, and his hill-fort, or place of strength, was erected on the highest of the Clwydian range, nearly due west from Mold, and about half-way between that place and Ruthin. The hill on which the remains of this fortalice still exists is called Moel Benlli, or the conical hill of Benlli, and it presents a conspicuous object from Mold, Ruthin, and Denbigh. An immense *carnedd*, or cairn of stones, which was still to be seen some years ago in an entire state in a field about half a mile from the town of Mold, was supposed to have been the place of this hero's interment; and if we may believe what we read in the Welsh verses on the graves of the warriors of the Isle of Britain, his son's place of sepulture was in a spot about eight miles distant, and is thus noticed in the following rhymes :—

> " Pian y bedd yn y Maes Mawr,
> Balen a law ar ei larn awr :
> Bedd Beli ab Benlli Gawr."

That is—

> " He who owns the grave in the large field,
> Proud his hand on his blade :
> The grave of Beli, son of Benlli Gawr."

But to return to the great Carnedd of Benlli himself in the field near Mold. It was always called Tomen y r Ellyllon, or the Tumulus of the Goblins, and for this reason that from time immemorial it was believed that the grim ghost of Benlli, in the form of a knight clad in splendid gear, and especially wearing a Celain Aur, or golden corselet, appeared after sunset standing on the cairn, or walking round it, and that there he continued to maintain his cold post till the scent of the morning air or the crowing of the cock drove him to the necessity of retiring from it to some more comfortable quarters. This legend had for generations so terrified the people that no bribe could have tempted anyone to have passed by that way after nightfall. Yet, though nobody went thither, and that every possibility of having anything like direct evidence as to what the spectre knight's personal appearance and dress really were, had been thus precluded by the circumstance that everyone shunned his dreaded presence, the most wonderful and incredible accounts of his stern countenance and terrific bearing, together with the most fearful stories of their effects upon people who had beheld them, continued to be propagated, although no one could specify the individuals who had seen them, or been so affected by them.

Towards the end of the year 1833 it happened that the occupier of the field where the carnedd stood took it into his head that the stones of which it was composed might be of use for the construction of a road, or for filling drains, or for some such rural purpose. It was with some difficulty that he could procure workmen bold enough to make such an assault on the very castle of the goblin, even although it was to be carried on during the hours that the blessed sun was abroad. But having at last succeeded in obtaining these, he proceeded to work, and soon drove away some four or five hundred cart-loads of stones from the cairn, when at last the workmen came upon something of a strange shape, which was manifestly constructed of some sort of metal. It was with no little dread that they ventured to touch it, but their observation having led them to believe that it was some old brass pot-lid or frying-pan, it ceased to be an object either of dread or of interest in their unlearned eyes, and they threw it carelessly into a hedge, where it lay all night neglected.

Some person of education having come to the spot next morning, who had heard of such a thing having been found, was led by curiosity to examine it, when, to the astonishment of all who heard of it, the brazen frying-pan was discovered to be a lorica, or corselet of gold.

The metal was found to be of about the same degree of purity as our present coin. It was so thin, that it weighed altogether no more than sixty sovereigns, and therefore it appears evident that it could not have been used as armour of defence in combat. It is more than probable that it must have been worn merely as an ornamental piece of armour on occasions of state or parade, in which case it was, very likely, originally lined with leather. It was embossed all over it, of a simple pattern, but it was not perforated.

The obliging correspondent through whose kindness, and that of his friends, I have become possessed of these very remarkable facts, amuses himself by calculating the immense value which such a piece of dress must have had in the time of Benlli-Gawr, its wearer, that is, in the year 500. "This," says he, "may be done by referring to the ancient laws of Wales, now publishing under the Government Commission. In these laws, the average price of a cow was five shillings, and allowing for the difference in the value of money, a cow would now cost about ten pounds. Then one pound at that time would buy four cows, and the ten pounds would buy forty cows, and the sixty sovereigns would be the value of two hundred and forty cows, or two thousand four hundred pounds sterling."

This curious and highly valuable *morceau* of antiquity was immediately claimed by the Honourable Edward Mostyn Lloyd Mostyn as lord of the manor, and by Colonel Salusbury of Gallbfarnan as the possessor of the field where it was found, and the law having determined that it should belong to the former gentleman, it is now in his possession. It is gratifying to the Author to think, that it should have fallen into the hands of Mr. Mostyn, with whom he has since had the honour of becoming acquainted, during the Welsh Eisteddvod, held at Liverpool, where, as President of that body, his high attainments—his courteous manners—and his ardent devotion to the cause of the preservation of Welsh literature and antiquities, gave universal satisfaction to

all present, and afforded a sufficient assurance for the safety of the
interesting relic, of which an account has been given.

This is certainly a very powerful instance of the soundness of the
proposition, that legendary tales, however incredible many of their
circumstances may be, have always some foundation in truth. It
appears to be by no means difficult to speculate reasonably enough
on the probabilities of the matter in this case; and it would seem
that they have in all likelihood been these :—In the year 500 or
thereabouts, the renowned hero, Benlli, died, and in obedience to
his own last instructions, or of those of his son, Beli, or of some
other relative or friend, he was buried in the tumulus with his
golden corselet on, and then the Carnedd was heaped up over his
remains. To prevent the risk of any avaricious follower or serf, or
any other promiscuous pilferer, uncovering his body during the
night, in order to possess himself of the glittering prize, his surviv-
ing friends circulate the story that his ghost, frowning fearfully, as
such ghosts are wont, is seen nightly to guard the tumulus, girt in
the golden armour. Terror fills the superstitious minds of the inhabitants of the district, and no man for his life will venture
to approach the Carnedd after sunset. This lie protective is thus
very naturally and innocently handed down from one generation
of the superstitious people of the neighbourhood to that which
succeeds it, and implicitly believed; and so the story is traditionally
preserved for about fourteen hundred years, until it is now at last
unravelled, in our own time, by the removal of the Carnedd
of stones, and the discovery of the golden corselet itself.

Let not anyone refuse then to give credence to the main circumstances of these, our Highland legends, because they may perhaps
be somewhat overlaid with circumstances of a romantic or doubtful
nature, but let the judgment rather be exercised to discover, and to
discriminate, between the thread of the true and original history,
and those adventitious filaments of later manufacture which have
from time to time been introduced and interwoven with it. This
will generally be found to be no very difficult task, and there are
many by whom it will be considered rather as an agreeable amusement, than as an irksome occupation.

TALES OF THE HIGHLANDS.

STRATHDAWN.

We left the Highland village of Tomantoul after an early breakfast, and proceeded to wend our way slowly up the pastoral valley of Aven. The scenery as yet had nothing peculiarly striking about it, but our faces were turned towards the Cairngorm group of mountains, and the closing in of the hills forming the termination of our present view, already excited interesting expectation regarding those higher regions which arose beyond them. This was especially the case with my fellow-travellers, who had not previously visited this elevated district. A certain air of tranquil repose that hung over everything around us, and gave an indescribable charm to the simple features of nature, rather disposed our minds to quiet and passive enjoyment, so that we walked leisurely along for some time, less inclined to talk than to ruminate each within himself. Our young friend Clifford was the first to break silence.

Clifford.—What a beautiful little plain! How animating the clear river that waters it, with its stream sparkling under the bright morning sun! And see how appropriate the few figures that give life to it. Those cattle there, so agreeably disposed, cropping the fresh herbage, with that boy so intent upon plaiting a cap of rushes for the innocent little girl who sits beside him. It would make a subject for a Cuyp or a Paul Potter. What a scene of simple happiness, contentment, and peace!

Dominie Macpherson.—It is indeed a quiet enough scene at this moment, sir. But peaceful as it is at this present time, it hath not been always so, for it hath more than once had its green turf trodden into black and dusty earth by the thundering hoof of the neighing battle-steed. The day has been, Mr. Clifford, when, as Maro has it—

> "Agmine facto
> Quadrupedante putrem sonitu quatit ungula campum."

2

Here it was, sir, that Montrose encampit with his army in 1645, after having defeated the godly sons of the Covenant in the bloody field of Auldern, and before marching to glut his cruel spirit by massacring more of them at Alford on the Don. And, as if the soil of this fair spot had not been thus sufficiently polluted, it so chanced that, in June 1689, the bloody Clavers also cumbered it with himself and his followers on his way to the Pass of Killiecrankie, where, on the 16th July thereafter, praise be to the Lord, his wicked existence was at last put an end to.

Grant.—Ha! These historical recollections do indeed give a new interest to the scene.

Clifford.—Only fancy the motley troops, in the varied military costume of the time, drawn up here in their lines, the tents and huts stretching along yonder in regular order,—the mingled sounds arising from the busy camp followers,—the trumpets clanging,—and the bold Dundee scampering across the plain on his gallant black charger! What a contrast to the figures which are now before us!

Dominie.—Aye; and if all tales be true, he was but an uncanny beast that black horse of his. But, my certy! the beast and the man were well matched.

Clifford.—You seem to have a great distaste at the Viscount Dundee, Mr. Macpherson, and yet he was followed by the great mass of your Highland clans.

Dominie.—That may be, Mr. Clifford; but that makes no odds to me, sir. I am in no ways answerable for the deeds of my forebears. If they turned out to support popery and yepiscopacy, that is not what I would have done. I reverence the manes of those sainted heroes who drew their good broadswords for God and the Covenant, and who suffered all manner of tortures and all kinds of cruel deaths rather than abandon so glorious a cause,—a cause, let me tell you, with all due respeck to you, Mr. Clifford,—a cause in which I should be proud to die at this moment.

Clifford.—Your enthusiasm is not only excusable, but honourable to you, Mr. Macpherson. But will you tell me the name of this spot, that I may endeavour to remember it?

Dominie.—It is called Dell-a-Vorar, or the Lord's-haugh, a name which it got from one, or may be from both, of these two lords I have named, though it is more probable that it was from Clavers, seeing that the place in Braemar to which he marched from here has ever since borne the same name.

Grant.—I know there is a place in Braemar so called.

Author.—By the bye, Mr. Macpherson, does not the dwelling of Willox the wizard lie somewhere in this neighbourhood?

Dominie.—Yes, sir, it does. Gaulrig, as the place is called, lies up beyond yon hollow in the hill on the right side of the glen which you see before us yonder, dipping into the valley of the Aven from the north.

Clifford.—Let us visit the old fellow by all means, Mr. Macpherson.

Dominie.—We may easily do that, sir, for the house is not much out of your way, and we are pretty sure of finding him, for he is too old now to be often or far from home.

A walk of some couple of miles brought us to the place where we found the residence of this extraordinary man, standing on the sloping side of the northern hill, immediately below a small tributary ravine, which ancient popular superstition has very appropriately consigned to the dominion of the fairies, and other beings belonging to the world of spirits, and in which there is one of those green artificial-looking knolls called *shians*, from their being supposed to be places of especial fairy resort. His cottage hangs on the edge of the bank facing the Aven, is of the most primitive architecture, composed of drystones and sods, and forms, with its humble outhouses, two sides of a small square. Near one angle of the house there is a rude stone, on which the old warlock is in the habit of sitting to enjoy the sun.

Understanding that Willox was at all times rather flattered by a visit from strangers, we made no scruple in requesting an interview with him; and, accordingly, he soon appeared from the door of his dwelling. Notwithstanding all that Mr. Macpherson had said to the contrary, I had found it a difficult matter to persuade myself that I was not to see a vulgar countenance, strongly marked with that species of sordid cunning, which one might suppose sufficient to enable a knave, of the lowest description, to impose on the most ignorant class of rustics. The figure of the man, indeed, who now showed himself, had nothing about it to do away with this preconceived notion of mine. He was rather under the middle size, and was dressed in the ordinary *hodden grey* clothes, which have now so generally usurped the place of the gayer tartans, and more picturesque highland dress. But I at once perceived that his low stature was to be attributed to the decrepitude of old age, for he was probably above ninety. The moment he put forth his head from the threshold, and perceived those who sought for an interview with him, an inconceivable expression flashed from his eyes, which, I might almost say, threw over him a

certain light of dignity. We were all of us at once convinced
that this was no common man, and our regard was riveted
upon him. It seemed as if the native lightnings of an un-
educated, but naturally very powerful mind, were bursting
through the obscurity of those grey orbs, which had been
dimmed by the gathering mists of many a long year. The
half dormant spirit appeared to have been suddenly summoned
to the portal of the eye, by this anticipated interview with
people whom he had never seen before, just as, in the olden
time, the jealous captain of a fortress might have been brought
to its barbican by the bugle call of some knight of doubtful
mien who wished to hold parley.

As he advanced to meet us, I was struck with the corselike
paleness of his face, to which the glaze of his eyeballs, and the
grizzly and tangled locks that strayed from beneath his bonnet,
gave an inexpressibly ghastly effect. A transient gleam of
electric fire shot from within his eyeballs into each of our
countenances individually, as he was introduced to us in
succession. We felt as if it had penetrated into the inmost
recesses of our very souls. It appeared to us as if he had
thereby been enabled, from long practice in the study of mankind, at once to read our several characters and thoughts, like
so many lines of the great book of nature hastily skimmed
over. To each of us in turn he bowed with a polished air, and
a manner liker that of a faded courtier of the age of Louis
Quatorze, than the inhabitant of so humble a dwelling, in the
simple and pastoral valley of Strathdawn; and strangely indeed
did it contrast with the coarseness and poverty of his dress,
and the squalid *impropreté* of his whole personal appearance.

After the usual preliminary salutations were over, I expressed a wish to see the far-famed magical kelpie's bridle and
mermaid's stone, for the possession of which he is so celebrated
in all the neighbouring districts.

" You shall see them both, sir," said he, after eyeing me for
a moment with a searching look. " To such gentlemen as
you, I cannot refuse a sight of them, though they are hardly
to be seen by vulgar eyes, and never to be handled by vulgar
hands;" and, with a marked politeness of manner, he returned
into the cottage to bring them out.

" Now," said I to my companions, " you must keep him in
talk, whilst I endeavour to steal a sketch of him."

" Here are the wonderful implements of my art," said he,
as he returned, holding them up to our observation.

" They are very curious," said I; "perhaps you will have

the goodness to allow me to make a hasty drawing of them. I hope it will have no effect in taking away their virtues.

"Their virtues cannot be taken away by human hands," replied Willox, gravely. "You are welcome to draw them if you please, sir, and I shall hold them for you so that you may best see them."

I thanked him, and proceeded instantly to my work. My friends followed my injunctions so well as fully to occupy his attention in replying to their cross fire of queries, whilst I was myself obliged to interject a question now and then, in order to get him to turn his countenance towards me. The wonderful expression I have already alluded to appeared even yet more striking, on these occasions, by his ghost-like features being brought so closely and directly opposite to my eyes. I then looked in as it were upon his spirit,—and it was manifestly a spirit which, in ancient days, when superstition brooded as much over the proud castle of the bold baron, as it did over the humble cot of the timid peasant, might well enough have domineered over the minds of nobles and princes, nay subjected even crowned heads to its powerful control.

I did make sketches of the *mermaid's stone* and the *water-kelpie's bridle*, the two grand instruments of his art. As already described to us by Mr. Macpherson, we found the stone to be a circular and flattish lens, three inches diameter, of semi-opaque crystal, somewhat resembling, in shape and appearance, what is called a bull's eye, used for transmitting light through the deck of a vessel into its smaller apartments below. The water-kelpie's bridle consists of a flat piece of brass, annular in the middle, and having two lobe-like branches springing from it in two curves outwards, the wider part of each lobe being slightly recurved inwards, so that they present the appearance of two leaves when they are held flat. Attached to the ring part, but loose upon it, are two long doubled pieces of flat brass, and, between these, a short leathern thong is attached by a fastening so intricate that it might have rivalled the Gordian knot. It has not the most distant resemblance to any part of a bridle, and none of us could guess to what purpose, either useful or ornamental, it could have ever been applied. Willox's own account of the acquirement of these two wonderful engines of his supernatural power, elicited by our repeated questions, was nearly as follows :—

THE WATER-KELPIE'S BRIDLE AND THE MERMAID'S STONE.

MY grand-uncle Macgregor, was so much devoted to the study of that mysterious and unpronounceable art which gives man control over the world of spirits, that he ultimately became a powerful adept in it. He lived on the banks of the river Dulnan, in Strathspey, and his fame went so much abroad, that his name was never mentioned without reverential awe. Whilst involved in the pursuit of these studies, he was much used to take solitary walks, during which it was believed that he held high converse with beings rarely brought within the reach of human communing.

He was walking one evening on the lonely shore of Loch-an-dorbe. The sky was calm, but the air was hot and sulphurous, and the sun went down in a blood-red haze, that the gifted eye of Macgregor knew to be portentous. Wrapped in his plaid, he leaned against a huge stone, and stood earnestly gazing at the sinking orb till it had altogether disappeared. He read therein that some mighty deed was to be achieved, and he wound himself up to encounter whatever adventure might befall him.

Suddenly the black waters of the lake began to heave from their centre without any seeming cause. Not a breath of wind stirred them, yet they came boiling outwards, so as at once to dash their waves on every part of the surrounding shores. A dark object was seen to bound forth upon the beach at no great distance from the spot where Macgregor stood. A less strongly fortified heart would have quailed with fear, but his was armed with potent spells. He stretched his eyeballs towards the object, when, less to his astonishment than delight, he beheld a black horse, of immense size, and of beautiful proportions, approaching him through the lurid twilight. On he came, prancing proudly along the strand, pawing the ground from time to time, and neighing aloud with a voice of thunder, while blue lightnings were ever and anon darting from his expanded nostrils, and his eyes were shining like stars. It required not Macgregor's skill to know that this was no ordinary horse, but his superhuman knowledge made him at once aware that it was the water-kelpie himself, and he watched his coming with a heart beating high with hope. Well instructed as to the measures which it now became necessary for him to adopt, he stood aside behind the large stone, and employed certain charms which he knew would aid in his concealment; and as this terrific incarnation of the spirit of the waters was curvetting grandly past him, he sprang suddenly out upon him, and, seizing his bridle with his left hand, he raised aloft his gleaming claymore with his right, and cut it out of the water-kelpie's head at one blow. In an instant the terrible spirit was metamorphosed into the shape of a man of huge and very formidable appearance.

"Give me back my bridle, thou son of earth!" cried he, in a voice like the roaring of a cataract.

"No!" said Macgregor, boldly; "I have won it, and I shall keep it."

"Then," roared the enraged spirit, "you and it shall never enter your house together!"

Macgregor stayed not to hear more, but ran off in the direction of his home, from which he was then distant a good many miles. The enraged spirit came roaring and howling after him. Ten thousand floods pouring down over the rocky ridge of Ben Nevis could not have created so appalling a combination of terrific sounds. The hot breath of the fiend came about Macgregor as he flew, as if it would have threatened suffocation. Lucky was it for my grand-uncle that the kelpie, in losing his bridle, had also lost with it, for the time at least, the power of becoming a horse, else had his chance of escape been small indeed. As it was, however, it seemed as if Macgregor had suddenly acquired a large proportion of those racing qualities which were derived from that magical virtue so strongly inherent in the bridle which he bore; for he appeared, even to himself, rather to skim than to run over the vast extent of moors, hills, and bogs that lay between him and his own home, scarcely bending the heather tops in his way, so lightly and rapidly did his feet fly over the ground. But great as was the supernatural speed he had acquired, that of the water-kelpie was so little short of it, that the wicked spirit was close at his heels when he reached his own house. With a presence of mind, and an adroitness, which no one but an experienced and expert adept in the management of a contest with powers naturally so superior to man, could have commanded or exercised, he avoided entering by the door, although it stood yawning temptingly wide to receive him. Luckily a window was open. "Hulloo!" cried he hastily to his wife, whom he happily observed within, "catch this in your apron!" And, throwing the bridle to her through the window, he cunningly avoided the denunciation which the kelpie had uttered against him.

No sooner did the kelpie perceive that he was thus out-witted, than he shrieked so loud that all the hills of Strathspey re-echoed again.—Yes, you need not stare, gentlemen ; I tell you that the mountains echoed again, as if the lofty Craig Ellachie had rent itself from its foundations, and rolled itself into the river Spey. The water-kelpie disappeared, and, what is strange, he has never since been seen by mortal man. But my grand-uncle Macgregor had his bridle, which, as you see, afterwards descended from him to me.

The story of the acquirement of the Mermaid's Stone is no whit less extraordinary than that of the bridle. The stone came to me from my maternal grandfather, who gained it by the superhuman powers which he possessed ; for in my veins two most potent streams of necromantic blood have united themselves, though it would ill become me to say that I have ever equalled my ancestors. After having made frequent visits to the sea coast, my grandfather at last found out the spot where a beautiful mermaid was wont to sport amid the shallows, and sit on a rock, to comb her long hair, and to sing the most exquisite melodies. Long and anxiously did he watch her motions, till he perceived her one day combing her lovely tresses over her face and bosom, altogether unconscious that she was observed. Arming himself with certain spells which he possessed, which gave him superhuman powers, he crept into the sea from the rocky point where he lay concealed, and wading silently towards the stone where she sat, he came behind her, and clasping her eagerly in his arms, he held her fast, and, in spite of all her wailings, her lamentations, and her struggles, he succeeded in carrying her on shore. When fairly on land, she became exceedingly helpless, so that he had no farther trouble with her, and, delighted with his fair prize, he brought her home in triumph. There he made a soft bed for her upon the rafters of the house ; and although he was un-willingly compelled by prudence to make sure of her by sub-jecting her to the restraint of tying her to the couples of the roof, he in all other respects lavished the utmost kindness upon her.

So very much, indeed, was my grandfather taken up with his new acquisition, that my grandmother began to grow jealous of his attentions to the fair sea nymph ; and, more out of spite, perhaps, than from any real wickedness, she began to encourage the visits of a young man who had been formerly attached to her. Now, strange as it may seem, it is no less true, that, great as were my grandfather's powers in the art magic, he was yet unable thereby to discover the fact, that his wife received the visits of this lover, on certain occasions, when his trifling affairs required his absence from home. Now, it happened one day that my grandfather returned so suddenly, and so unexpectedly, that his wife was compelled to conceal the youth hastily behind a bed. The lady was in a terrible taking, you may believe; but she so far subdued her agitation as to receive her husband with every possible appearance of kindness and affection.

"I dreamed a strange dream last night," said she, after fully recovering her presence of mind, and smiling gaily. "I dreamed that I put both my hands over your eyes, and yet you saw as well as if they had not been there."

"Come try, then!" replied her husband sportively, taking what she said as the mere prelude to some little innocent matrimonial frolic; "come try then, my dear. I believe I can see as far into a millstone as most people."

"No doubt you can," said his spouse, laughing outright, and approaching him with a merry air, she clapped her hands so firmly over his eyes that he was completely blindfolded, "now can you see?" exclaimed she.

"No!" replied the husband, "not one whit."

"Stay a little," cried his wife, laughing heartily again, "depend upon it this miraculous light will come to you at last!"

"Aye, aye!" cried he, struggling till he escaped from her hands, and then kissing her heartily, "I see now well enough." But, alas! my grandfather's vision had come too late, for the lover had availed himself of this brief opportunity, so cunningly afforded him, to make his escape.

The mermaid, who was seated on the rafters above, laughed aloud with an unearthly laughter, as she witnessed the trick that had been played to my grandfather. To divert her husband's attention from a mirth that at first appalled her, the lady, with great presence of mind, threw down the girdle-stone, a flat stone, which in those primitive times was used for firing the oaten cakes, instead of the iron plate of that name, which now forms so important an article of furniture in the kitchen of every Scottish cottage. The stone was broken to pieces, and the lady's loud lamentation for this apparently accidental misfortune, quickly diverted her husband's attention from the mysterious merriment of the mermaid, and having

thus effected her purpose, she threw the fragments of the stone
out on the dunghill.

The poor mermaid pined and sighed for her native element,
until she wrung the heart of her captor to pity.

"Take me but down to the sea," said she with her sweet
voice, "take me but down to the sea, and put me but into the
waves—but three yards from the shore—and it shall be better
for thee than all the good thou can'st gain by keeping me here."

Softened to compliance at last, my grandfather did take her
down from the rafters, and carrying her to the coast, he waded
into the sea with her, the three yards she had specified, and
put her gently down amid the waves, near the very stone
where he had originally caught her. The joy of this beautiful
marine spirit in finding herself thus again bathing in invigorating waters of her own native ocean, after having been so long
hung up, as it were, on the rafters of a Highland cottage, to
be smoked like an Aberdeen haddock, or a kipper salmon, may
be easily imagined. But, although wicked people might perhaps impute her parting speech more to that natural love of
scandal which is said to belong to her sex, than to any strong
feeling for my grandfather, yet we must say, that her words
and her counsel showed that her gratitude was no less abundant
than her joy. Turning to him who had treated her so com-
passionately, she passed her taper fingers gracefully through
her long silken tresses, and thus addressed him with her siren
tongue:—

"Travel not so oft nor so far from home again! Ill luck
attends that home whence the master often wanders. Dost
thou remember my loud laugh on that day when thy wife
broke the girdle-stone? It was because she made a fool of
thee by blinding thine eyes that her lover might escape unseen.
Be wiser in future, and never leave home ; and when you go
back now, look among the straw where the broken bits of the
girdle-stone were thrown, and you will find that which will be
a treasure to you and to your children for ever."

With these words she dived among the breakers and was seen
by him no more. My grandfather returned home rather chop-
fallen ; but on searching where the mermaid had indicated
him, he found that very stone, which has now, for three
generations, been the agent in performing so many wonders.

THE DOMINIE DEPARTS.

Soon after quitting the dwelling of the Warlock, we were doomed to lose the company of one, with whom we were all much more unwilling to part.

Dominie Macpherson.—I can hardly bring myself to tell you, gentlemen, that I must now—sore against my will—take my humble leave of you. My road to my brother's house lies north over the hill there. But ere I go, I am truly glad to have it in my power to put you under the guidance of my good friend, Serjeant Archy Stewart. I sent him a message last night to come and meet us here; and there is the very man coming over the knoll, with his Sabbath-day's jacket and bonnet on.— How is all with you, Serjeant? My certy, I need not ask, for you look stout and hearty.

Serjeant Archy Stewart.—Thank ye, Mr. Macpherson, I cannot complain. I am a little the worse for the wear—but my old legs, such as they be, are fit enough for the hill yet. I am glad to see you well back in the country again.

Dominie.—Thank ye, Serjeant. Now, my good man, these are the three gentlemen you are to guide. Three better gentlemen you never fell in with in all your travels. You must do all you can for them; and, above all things, be sure to give them plenty of your cracks. They like to hear all manner of auld-warld stories; so, as you must put on a budget of their provisions on your back—which, by the bye, will be like Æsop's burden, always growing less,—you may e'en lighten yourself as you go of as many of the auncient legends which you carry in your head as may help to ease your travel.

Serjeant.—Uh! I'll not be slack at that, Mr. Macpherson, I promise ye, if it be the pleasure of the gentlemen.

I shall not attempt to describe the scene of our parting with the worthy schoolmaster. It threw a gloom over us all. As for the good man himself, his voice trembled—his lip quivered —and his eyes filled with moisture, when he pronounced that most unpleasant of all words—farewell—and gave us the last cordial shake of the hand, pouring out his best wishes and blessings upon us. He then put his stick firmly to the ground, as if to help his failing resolution, and, as he took his way over the hill, he turned and waved—and turned and waved, twenty times at least, e'er he disappeared from our sight.

Our attention was now directed towards Serjeant Archy
Stewart, who was cheerfully occupying himself in shouldering
a portion of our necessaries.   He was a veteran of about sixty
years of age, of middle size, and of a hardy, wiry, though not
very robust frame.   His fresh coloured countenance was lighted
up by a pair of small, grey, and very intelligent eyes ; and its
bold forehead, aquiline nose, high cheek-bones, and prominent
chin and lips, exhibited traits of a very undaunted and indomitable resolution, which his whole appearance showed had been
well tried by hardships.   All this, however, was tempered and
sweetened with so perfect an expression of courtesy and good
humour, pervading every line of his weather-beaten features,
that he instantly gained the golden opinions of our party.
After adjusting the wallet to his back, he pointed his hazel
stick to the grass, and led the way before us with an activity
much beyond his years.

Clifford.—Capital fishing hereabouts, no doubt Mr. Stewart?

Serjeant.—Just grand, sir—no better in this, or any other
country side.

Clifford.—You know the river well, I suppose ?

Serjeant.—Few should know it better, sir—for I've known it
ever since I could look out over the nest.

Clifford.—You are a native of these mountains, then ?—
Come ! we have been told that you are full of their legendary
lore, and we look to have much of it out of you ere we part.

Serjeant.—I am sure your honor is welcome to as much as
you can take and I can give you.

Clifford.—Come away then—you shall begin, if you please,
by giving us your own history.

Serjeant.—Oh troth, sir, my history is little worth ; but,
such as it is, you shall have it.   I was born in this very glen
here—for I am come of the Clan-Allan Stewarts, who were
the offspring of Sir Allan Stewart, who was said to have been
a natural son of the Yearl of Moray.

Author.—What Earl of Moray was that, Archy ?

Serjeant.—Really and truly I cannot tell you, sir.   But this
I know well enough, that them Clan-Allan Stewarts were a
proud, powerful, domineering race, and always reported to
have been very troublesome customers to those who happened
to have any feud with them.   I've heard say, indeed, that
while they bore sway here away, fint a man of any other name
dared to blow his nose throughout the whole of Strathdawn
without their leave being first asked and granted.   Wild
chields they were, I'll warrant ye.

Author.—That may be, Serjeant; but I shrewdly suspect that you are not altogether right in your genealogy. My belief is, that it does in reality go somewhat farther back than you suppose.

Serjeant.—Do you think so, sir? Well it may be so.

Author.—I am inclined to think that you must be come of the old Stewarts, Earls of Athol.

Serjeant.—Aye, aye!—Yearls of Athol!—that would be strange. But what makes you think that, sir?

Author.—Why, we know that it was through the marriage of Alexander, third Earl of Huntly, with the Lady Johanna Stewart, daughter of one of these Earls, in 1474, that Strathdawn first came into the family of the Gordons, with whom it still remains. It is therefore clear that Sir Allan, your ancestor, must have come here considerably before that period; and if your forefathers, the Clan-Allan Stewarts, were such hard-headed, knock-me-down, domineering fellows as you would seem to say they were, it is by no means improbable that they may have managed, by the use of their swords, to bear sway here for many a long day, after the lands were chartered to the Gordons.

Serjeant.—I have little doubt that your honor is perfectly right; and now I think on't, I remember an auncient legend of the Stewarts of Clan-Allan, in which a speech of the old Lord of Cargarf strongly supports the very view of the matter which you have so well explained. I never could very well understand it before—but now, when I put that and that together, I see the truth as clear as day light.

Clifford (taking out his tablets and writing.)—I shall put you down for that same legend, Mister Serjeant; but in the meanwhile proceed with your own history, if you please.

HISTORY OF SERJEANT ARCHY STEWART.

WELL, Gentlemen—as I was telling you, I was born in Strathdawn here—as pretty a glen as there is in all Scotland. Oh, what a bonny glen it was in my young days! You see plain enough, without my telling you, that there are no trees now in it to speak of—none, indeed, but a parcel of straggling patches and bushes of aller and birch and hazel about the bit water-runs and burnies, or hanging here and there on the brae sides. But when I was a boy, the hills were all one thick wood of tall trees, that gave shelter to great herds of deer in the winter. Now, alas! the trees have fallen, and the deer, annoyed and persecuted by sheep, shepherds, and sheep-dogs, have longsyne retreated to the upper mountains and valleys of the Cairngorms, save may be, at an *anterin** time, when severe weather on the heights, may drive an odd few of them down upon us for a short season.

Well, gentlemen—not to detain you with my school-boy days—(for I *was* at school, gentlemen—and not so bad a scholar neither)—when I grew up to be a stout lad, I left the glen, with six others of my own age, to go and seek for work in the south country. I shall never forget that day that we left it. We went off full of life and joy—for we thought but little of leaving our friends or the scenes of our youth, since we trusted that the same firm legs that were carrying us away could at any time bring us back to them the moment we had the will to return. We panted to see the world, and it was now opening before us. All the fanciful dreams of our boyhood were, as we thought, now about to be realised. Light, I trow, were our hearts, and full were we of hopes, as we made our way across the Grampians, and in a few days these hopes were realised, by our finding ourselves busily employed, and working hard, though at good wages, in a quarry near Cupar in Fife.

There we continued for some time perfectly contented with our labour, as well as with the price of it, till John Grant of Lurg, grandson of the famous Robert of Lurg, well known by the nick-name of *Old Stachcan*, or the stubborn ——

Clifford (breaking in on the Serjeant's narrative).—What! the fierce looking fellow whose picture we saw at Castle Grant with a pistol in his hand?

Serjeant.—Just exactly—the very same, sir—he has a pistol in his hand in the picture, and well, I promise you, did he know how to use it when he was in the body. Well, it was his grandson, John of Lurg, who, some how or other, smelt us out in the place where we then were in Fife; and as he was at that time raising men for a company, you may well believe that his joy was not small when he thus came, like a setting dog, to a dead point on such a covey of stout young Hillantmen in a quarry. He soon contrived to get about us altogether, and with a hantel of fair words, and mony a bonny speech about our Hillant hills —Hillant glens—Hillant waters—Hillant lasses—and, what was more to his purpose at the time, about Hillant deeds of

---

* Accidental, and rarely occurring.

arms—all of which, observe ye, gentlemen, were made over a reeking bowl of punch that you might have swum in, he very soon succeeded in stirring up the fire of military ambition within our souls, until he ultimately so inflamed us that, with all the ease in life, he quickly converted us, who were nothing unwilling, from hard-working quarriers, into gentlemen sodgers, by enlisting us, all in a bunch, into the ninety-seventh regiment, or Inverness Highlanders.

I need not tell you all the outs-and-ins of adventures that befell me while I was in the ninety-seventh, in which corps I remained about two years and a half. But I may mention to you, that I was serving with it when I got my first wound—I mean this bit crack here, gentlemen—(and he pulled up his trews, and showed his right leg immediately below the knee, which was shrunken up to half the thickness of the other, from having had the greater part of the muscles utterly destroyed). —Some way or another, they took it into their heads to put us on board of the Orion, one of the ships of Lord Bridport's squadron, to act as marines—an odd sort of duty truly for Hillantmen, and one, I'll assure you, that we by no means liked over much, seeing that, on board of a ship, we were obliged to stand to be peppered at like brancher crows on a tree, without the power of having our will out against the villains, by charging them with the baggonet, as we should have done had we been opposed to them on dry land; and, indeed, we soon felt the frost of this, when we came to be engaged in the action fought with the French fleet on the 23rd of June, 1795.

On that day, the French had twelve line-of-battle ships, besides a number of frigates and other smaller vessels. From all their manœuvres it was very clear that they did not wish to face us—for they stole off in a very dignified manner, never looking over their shoulders all the time, as they were fain to have made us believe that they never saw us at all, or that we were quite beneath their notice. But it was no time for us to stand upon ceremony. We after them full sail, and we soon made them condescend to attend to us. In spite of all they could do we brought them to action in L'Orient Bay. There we lethered them handsomely, and we very speedily took from them three great ships—the Alexander, the Formidable, and the *Tigger*; and, if it had not been for the batteries on shore, there was no doubt that we should have had every keel of them. Well, you see, gentlemen, a large splinter of oak—rent away from the ship's side by a cannon shot—took me just below the knee, and demolished the shape of my leg in the ugly fashion I showed you this moment.   But I was young then, and hearty, and no very easily daunted or cast down, so that I was soon out of the doctor's list, and on duty again.

But what was far worse than all the wounds that my body could have suffered, though it had been shot and drilled through and through like a riddle, was that which befell me at Hilsea barracks after we returned to Britain.   You know very well, gentlemen, that the Bible says, "a wounded speerit who can bear?"   Now, you may guess what were the wounds of my speerit, and, consequently, what were my sufferings, when I and some of my Hillant comrades were told that we were to be immediately drafted into the ninth, or East Norfolk—an English regiment!

It was with sore hearts, and no little indignation, that we heard of the odious order for this cruel separation from our beloved native regiment—a corps in which we had all been like bairns of the same family in the bosom of our common mothers—where our officers had been more like elder brothers than superiors—cracking with us, at times, in Gaelic, over all our old Hillant stories—and enjoying, as much as we did, our Hillant songs and Hillant dances—and many of them, having known sundry individuals among us when at home in boyhood, were as familiar and easy with us, at any ordinary bye-hour, as you, gentlemen, are pleased to be with me at this precious moment—and yet the de'il ae bit was our discipline any the waur o' that, whatever his Grace the gallant Duke of Wellington may say against such a system—and, for aught I know, he may be right enough as to the English, who have not been brought up as we were in the allowance of such liberties,—but, as for us, when the parade hour came, or the time for duty, all such familiarities ceased, and everyone filled his own place, like the wheel of a watch, to be turned at the will of him who was above him.   You may easily conceive, then, that banishment, or even death itself, would have been better to us than the being thus torn from such a regiment for the express purpose of being joined to a corps composed of Englishmen, with whom we could neither crack of our homes, nor of our Hillant hills, nor sing Gaelic songs, nor tell auncient stories, nor speak about Ossian, nor hear the pipes play, nor dance the Hillant-fling. And then, instead of the kind and brotherly correction of our Hillant officers, the very slightest sound of whose word of reproof brought the blush of shame into our cheeks, and was as effectual a punishment to us as if we had been brought to the halberts—think what it was to us to be snubbed by some cross tempered upsetting Sassenach, who could know nothing of our nation's temper or disposition, and who might perhaps, of a morning, order our backs to be scored, with as little remorse as he would order a beef-steak to be brandered for his breakfast. Oh it was a terrible change! Our very speerits were just altogether broken at the very thought of it, and we actually ceased to be the same men.

But, gentlemen, if this was the effect produced on our minds by the mere anticipation of this most bitter change in our fate, what think ye was the misery of body which we sustained, and, especially, what think ye was my misery, when I, who never wore aught else but a kilt from the day I was born till that accursed moment, was crammed, in spite of all I could say or do to the contrary, hip and thigh, into a pair of tight regimental small clothes! Aye, you may laugh indeed, gentlemen —but if anybody was to tie your legs together with birken woodies, as they have tied the fore-legs of yon pouny that you see feeding yonder in the bit meadow at the foot of the brae, and if you were then to be bidden to climb up the steepest face of Ben-Machduie, you could not be more helpless, or more ill at ease than I was. As for drilling, you might as well have set up a man in a sack to march.

"Step out!" cried they eternally—"why the devil don't you step out?"

But it was just altogether ridiculous to cry out any such thing to me, for fint a step could I take at all, unless they had letten me step out of my breeks.—I was in perfect torture with them.—The very circulation of my blood was stopped— my nether man was rendered entirely numb and powerless. Nay, had I been built up mid man into a brick-wall I might have stepped out just as well.

Now, I would have you to understand, gentlemen, that especially and above all things, the confounded articles grippit and pinched me most desperately over the henches. The joints of my henches were so bound together in their very sockets by their pressure as to be rendered altogether useless; and the torture I endured in these quarters became so great, that I felt I could bear it no longer. I sat down, therefore, to hold a consultation with myself what was best to be done; and, after as cool and calm a consideration of my lamentable case as my extreme state of misery would allow, I came, in my own private council of war, to the determination, that I had only three things to choose from, and these were,—to desert—to cut my

3

throat—or to cut my breeches; and, after having much and duly weighed these different evil alternatives, I finally resolved to adopt the last of them.

Having come to this resolution, I then began, like a skilful engineer, narrowly to examine the horrid instruments of my sufferings, in order to ascertain how and where I could most easily make a breach in them, and one that was most likely to give the greatest ease to myself. A little farther thought and observation soon convinced me, that, as the parts most grievously afflicted, were those which your masters of fortification would have called the *sailliant* angles of my henches to right and left, and especially as on these hinged much of the motion of the whole man, it was clear that the proposed attempt to work myself relief should be first tried in those two points. I lost not a moment, therefore, in carrying my plan into execution. I immediately borrowed a pair of shears from a sodger's wife; and, sitting down regularly before my breeches, like an experienced general about to besiege a fortress, I fairly attacked the two *sailliant* angles of the bastion, and carried them by storm; and having, with the greatest nicety, cut out a round piece of the cloth of three or four inches in width, directly over each hipjoint, I ventured to thrust my limbs within the very garrison of my breeches; and really, gentlemen, the ease I obtained in consequence of this bold operation is not to be described.

So innocent was I, and so utterly unconscious of even a suspicion that I had done any thing wrong, that when the drum beat, I went off to the private parade of the company I had been attached to, with my heart almost as much eased as my henches; nay, it was absolutely bounding with benevolence, and brimful with the earnest desire and intention of spreading the blessed discovery I had made, and making it widely known among my Hillant comrades, so that all of them who might be in the same state of misery as I had been, might forthwith proceed to benefit themselves, as I had done, by the bright discovery I had made. Rejoicing in my ease, therefore, I strode across the barrack-square, with a step so much wider and grander than any I had lately been able to use, that I felt a pride in the excellence of my invention which I cannot possibly describe. I halted for a moment—stretched out, first my right leg, and then my left, just as I have seen a fowl do upon its perch—and then, clapping my hand upon the new made hole on either side of me, I chuckled for joy.

"Hah!" cried I; "breeches do they call you? By my faith, then, but I have made you more like your name by these well-imagined breaches of my own contrivance, which I have so ingeniously opened through your accursed sides."

I then bent myself down, and made a spring into the air ; after which, being quite satisfied that a paring or two more off the edges of the round holes would make all nearly right, I walked on with an air of dignified self-satisfaction that was not to be mistaken. But I had not come within ten yards of the spot where the company was falling in, when I heard the serjeant exclaim:—

"My heyes! look at that ere Ighland savage! I'm damned if he arn't been cutting big oles in his Majesty's rigimental breeches!"

A loud horse-laugh burst out from among the men, and the serjeant joined heartily in it. But it was no laughing matter to me; I was cut to the soul. All our horrible anticipations of English officers, halberds, and cat-o'-nine-tails, came smack upon me at once. I was overwhelmed—I grew dizzy—and, before I had well recovered myself, I was marched off to the guard-house under the charge of a corporal and a file of men, and a written crime was given in against me in these terms—

"Privut Archbauld Stewart of Captain Ketley's compnay, confined by order of Sargunt Nevett, for aving cut two big oles in the ipps of a pair of riggimental britches belonghing too is Magesty King George the Third."

Well, gentlemen, there was I left in the guard-house for some hours a prisoner. But if I was confined in one way, I took good care to put myself very much at my ease in another; for I pulled off my tormentors altogether, and sat quite coolly and comfortably without them. But I was sore enough at heart, for all that; for, independent of the fearful prospect of the unrelenting punishment that awaited me, the disgrace of confinement to which I had thus, for the first time in my life, been subjected, and that so unjustly, stung me to the very heart. For a good hour or more I could do nothing but grind my teeth with absolute vexation and rage ; but at length I began to gather some command of myself, and to think of the necessity of making up my mind as to what was to be done. I recalled the three evil alternatives, from which I had already made that which had now proved to be so unfortunate a selection, and as that had so miserably failed me, I continued for sometime swinging backwards and forwards, like a bairn in a shuggy-shue,* between the two that yet remained to be tried,

* A swing.

and I had not yet made up my mind on the subject, when the serjeant appeared, and ordered me to put on my breeches and follow him. I obeyed like a man who gets up from his straw to go out and be hanged. But there was one great difference between such a poor wretch and me, very much in his favour, for as his fetters in such a case are taken off, I was on the contrary condemned to buckle on mine.

I did follow the serjeant as he bade me, but notwithstanding the outlets I had made in the breeches for the joints of my hench bones, and the comparative ease I had thereby formerly enjoyed, yet the few hours I had had in the guard-house of a freedom of limb resembling that which I was wont to enjoy in my old kilt, made me feel so strange upon thus recommitting my joints to the thraldom of the accursed garments, that I went shaughling along after him, as if they had undergone no improvement at all. He took me directly to Captain Ketley's quarters, and whilst I was on my way thither, I was compelled to bring my doubts to a hasty conclusion, and so I resolved that of the two plans now only remaining for me to choose from, desertion should be first tried, seeing that if it should fail me, I might cut my throat afterwards, for that if I should cut my throat first, I should not afterwards find it an easy matter to desert. I had no more time than just enough to settle this point with myself, when the serjeant rapped at our captain's door.

"Come in!" cried Captain Ketley, in what sounded in my ear like a tremendous voice.

"Privut Archbauld Stewart and his cut breeches, your honour!" cried the serjeant, ushering me without ceremony into the middle of the room.

There I stood with my head up, and in the military attitude of attention, the which, as you will naturally observe, gentlemen, was, of all others, out of all sight the most convenient and best chosen attitude for me at the time; for, as you will understand, the palms of my two hands were thus exactly applied to the two holes I had made, though the size of the holes themselves was so great that I could by no means entirely cover them. But if I could have done so, this well conceived manœuvre of mine would have been of no avail.

"Stand at ease!" cried the serjeant, giving me at the same time a smart tap on the back with his rattan cane.

"Serjeant," said I impatiently, "you know very well that it's not possible for me to stand at ease in thir fashious breeks of mine."

I saw that Captain Ketley had a hard task of it to keep his gravity.

"What is this which has been reported to me of you, sir?" demanded he with as stern a look as he could possibly assume; "how comes it that you have taken upon you to destroy a pair of new regimental breeches in that manner?"

"Captain," said I, now quite brought to bay, and making up my mind to go through with it, whatever the consequences might be; "Captain, if your honour will but hear me, I will speak."

"Speak on then," said Captain Ketley, provided you say nothing that as an officer I may not listen to. Serjeant Nevett, you may retire."

"You need not fear that I shall offend you, Captain Ketley," said I, "I have been over long accustomed to speak to officers to forget the respect and duty I owe to them as a sodger, and since your honour is so kind, I will be as short as I can. I enlisted, you see, to serve in the Inverness Highlanders, and in so doing I covenanted to fight in company with my own countrymen, and in the freedom of a kilt. Now, against all bargain—against all manner of justice—against my will—and against the very nature of a Hillantman, I have been thrust, first into this English regiment, and then into this pair of English small clothes—well may they be so called, I'm sure. Captain Ketley, all this is most unreasonable. You might as well put a deer of the mountains into a breachame, and expect to plough the land with him, as to put a Hillantman into such cruel harness as thir things, with the hope that he can do his work with them; and, although I am as wishful as any man that serves King George can be, to spend the last drop of my blood, as some of it has flowed already in the cause of his Majesty, God bless him! and for our common country, yet I will just tell your honour plainly and honestly—though with all manner of respect—that I will not stay in this Ninth Regiment to be kept in the eternal torture of thir breeks, though I should see the men drawn out to shoot me for trying to desert—for death itself is desirable rather than that I should longer endure such misery as this. So I say again, that although I am quite willing to serve King George in any regiment he may be pleased to put me into that wears the kilt, yet I will take the first moment I can catch, to run away from such disgraceful and heartbreaking bondage as this to which I am now subjected."

"No, no, my good fellow," said Captain Ketley, who had

all this time had his own share of trouble in keeping himself from laughing, and who now gave way and laughed outright; "you must not run away from us, Archy. We cannot afford to lose so good a man. We must do all we can to put you at your ease with us. Your complaints are certainly not altogether unreasonable. But you should not have cut holes in your breeches—you should have come and stated your grievances to me. Remember in future, that you will always find me ready to listen to any well-founded complaint you may have to make. Meanwhile,—see here," said he, taking a pair of old loose trowsers out of his chest, and tossing them to me,—"wear these for a few days, till your limbs get somewhat accustomed to the thraldom of small clothes, and until we can get you fitted with a better and easier pair of your own. I shall see about your immediate release from confinement, and that you and your Highland comrades be excused from duty until you are more at home in your new clothing. If you behave yourself well, you shall always find a friend in me."

"God bless your honour!" cried I, with a joyful and grateful heart, and, if you will believe me, gentlemen, almost with the tears in my eyes; "your honour has spoken to me just like one of our kind Hillant officers of the Ninety-seventh. I'll go all the world over with you, though my breeks were of iron!"

Well, gentlemen, Captain Ketley was as good as his word—he was a kind and steady friend to me as long as he lived. He inquired of me whether I could read and write; and finding that I could do both—aye, and spell too—and that somewhat better, as I reckon, than Serjeant Nevett,—and, moreover, that I was not a bad hand at counting,—he got me made a corporal in less than a fortnight, and, very soon after that, a serjeant. But woe's me! a few months had hardly passed away when Captain Ketley died. Many were the salt tears I shed over his grave, after we had given him our parting volleys, and no wonder, for he was one of the best friends I ever had in my life. I cannot think of him, even yet, without regret. Willingly would I have given my life for his at any time. But what is this miserable world, gentlemen, but a valley of sorrow?

Well, I got fond enough, after all, of the Holy Boys, as the old Ninth lads were called.

Clifford (interrupting.) — How did they get that name, Archy?

Serjeant.—Oh, I'll tell you that, sir.—You see, when they

came from the West Indies, as a skeleton regiment, they were made up again with growing boys. Colonel Campbell of Blythswood tried to do them some good by getting them schoolmasters and Bibles. But the young rogues had been ill nurtured in the parent nest, and they used to barter their Bibles for gin and gingerbread. The Duke of York used to say of them, that they were everything that was bad but bad sodgers—ha! ha! ha!

And now, gentlemen, I believe I have little more to tell you about myself, except that I got my jaw broken in two places by a musket ball in Holland, on the 19th September, 1799. See what a queer kind of a mouth it has made me in the inside here. You see I had been out superintending the working party in the redoubts, and I had returned, tired as a dog, to the barn where the light company were quartered, and had just laid my head on my wife's knee to take a nap—for I was married by this time—when a terrible thumping came to the door, and Corporal Parrot ran to see who was there. Now, it happened that one of our serjeants was sick, and the other had been killed.—It was Adjutant Orchard who knocked so loud.

" Where is Serjeant Stewart?" demanded he, in a terrible hurry, the moment he entered the place.

" Can't I do instead of him?" replied Corporal Parrot; " for he is just new out of the trenches."

" No!" replied the Adjutant; " if he was new out of hell, I must have him directly."

" What's ado, sir?" demanded I, jumping up.

" You know as much as I do," replied the Adjutant; " but, depend upon it, we are not wanted to build churches. Get you out the light bobs as fast as you can."

Well, I hurried about and got out the light company with as little delay as possible; and no very easy matter it was to get hold of the poor fellows, knocked up as they were. Some of them I actually pulled out of hay stacks by the legs, as you would pull out periwinkles from their shells. The troops marched fifteen miles without a halt. We found the French and Russians hard at it, blazing away so that we could see the very straws at our feet as we marched over the sand. The balls came whistling about us like hail as we advanced, First came one, and knocked away the hilt of my sword; then came another, and cracked off the iron head of my halberd.

" If you go on at this rate, you villains," said I, " you'll disarm us altogether."

Then smack came another, whack through my canteen, and spilt all my brandy.

" Ye rascals ! " said I, trying at the same time to save as much of it as I could in my mouth, " that is most uncivil. Ye are no gentlemen, ye scoundrels, to spill a poor fellow's drop of comfort in this way."

By and bye, half a-dozen of balls or so went through the blanket I carried on my shoulders.

" By my faith," said I, " it's time now that I should return you my compliments for all your civilities, you vagabonds."

I stooped to take a musket from a dead Russian for my own defence. The piece was a rifle, and it was yet warm in his hand from the last discharge.

" By your leave, my poor fellow," said I, " I'll borrow your firelock for a shot or two, seeing that you have no farther use for it at this present time."

But dead as he was, the last gripe of departing life had made him hold it so fast, that I was obliged to twist it round ere I could make him part with it. I took off his cartridge-box by pulling the belt over his head. He had fired but two cart-ridges, and eighteen still remained. I loaded and fired twice ; and I was just in the act of biting off the end of my third cartridge to fire again, when a musket ball took me in the left cheek, and knocked me over as flat as a sixpence on the ground. The captain of the company looked behind him, and seeing that I was still able to move my hands, he very humanely ordered a file of men to carry me to the rear. They lifted me up from the ground, and the whole world seemed to be going round with me. They supported me under the arms, and I staggered along like a drunk man. They took me to a barn, where I lay insensible for some time, until coming to myself somewhat, as I lay there, I saw two surgeons employed with the wounded. " You will have little trouble with me, gentlemen," thought I within myself; " I shall be dead before you get at me." Just at this moment I heard one of the surgeons say to the other,—

" I believe I shall die of hunger."

" I am like to faint from absolute want," said the other.

" I could not speak, but I beckoned.

" By and bye," said one of the surgeons, shaking his head.

" Your turn is not come yet," said the other.

I beckoned again, and pointed to the wallet at my side.

" Oh ho ! " said the first surgeon crossing the place, and rapidly followed by the other,—" Oh ho ! " I comprehend you now. Let's see what you have got in your larder."

" He put his hand into the wallet, and found some balls of oatmeal, which my wife, honest woman, had made by rolling them up with water, and then giving them a roast among the ashes. The two gentlemen devoured them with great glee. They then looked at my chafts, put some lint into the wound, and bound it up.

" Well," thought I to myself, "a leaden ball made the wound, and a ball of oatmeal has doctored it. Many thanks to my worthy wife, God bless her ! "

After the doctors left us, the place, which was pitch dark, became hot and pestiferous, and the groans that came from some of the poor wretches put me in mind of pandemonium. I was for some time feverish and restless. I tried to stretch myself out at length, but I felt some one at my feet who would not stir all I could do. Though I could not speak, I was not sparing of my kicks, but still the person regarded me not. Next to me was Serjeant Wilson with a broken leg, and he was pressed upon by some one at his side. But the Serjeant had the full use of his tongue.

" Sir," said he to his neighbour, for he was noted for being a very polite man, "will you do me the favour to lie a little farther over, and take your elbow out of my stomach ?"

His civil request was disregarded, and there was no reply.

" Oh ! " said the serjeant, " perhaps the gentleman is a furreiner ; but all them furreiners understands French, so I'll try my hand at that with him :—Moushee wooly wous have the goodness to takee your elbow out of my guts. Confound the fellow, what an edification he has had that he does not understand French. I've heard Ensign Flitterkin say that it is the language of Europe. Pray, sir, may I ax if you be a European ? No answer,—by my soul then I may make bold to say that you are anything but a civilian. "Sir," continued the serjeant, beginning now to lose patience altogether, and to wax very wroth, " I insist on your removing your elbow. I say, rascal ! take your elbow out of my stomach this moment !"

And so the serjeant went on from bad to worse, till he swore, and went on to swear, at the poor man more and more bloodily the whole night. But neither his swearing, nor my kicking, could rid either of us of our troublesome companions. And it was no great wonder indeed—·for when the day-light came, we discovered that they were two dead Russians !

" This is a horrible place ! " exclaimed the principal surgeon when he came back in the morning. " As near as I can guess, one hundred and fifty-two men have died in this wretched barn since last night!—we must have the wounded out of this."

Thanks to my wife's oatmeal balls, which the grateful surgeons had not forgotten, my wounds were dressed the very first man. We were soon afterwards carried on hand-barrows by a Russian party down to the flat-bottomed boats, and so we were conveyed to the Texel. I bore the bullet home in my chafts, and it was cut out by an English doctor in Deal hospital. I was discharged on the 23d of June, 1800. But my pension was granted before pensions were so big as they are now-a-days, so that I am but ill off compared to some who have come home from the late wars. But, thank God, I am contented, since I cannot make a better of it.

GALLANTRY OF THE SEVENTY-FIRST HIGHLAND LIGHT INFANTRY.

Clifford.—How little known are the miseries to which the brave defenders of Britain's glory are subjected!—and how meagre is their reward, and how poor is their harvest of individual fame!—Our Nelsons and our Wellingtons, to be sure, are as certainly, as they are deservedly, destined to immortality of name. But is it not most painful to think that so many of our bravest hearts have gallantly fallen, to sleep in undistinguished oblivion? Your scene in the old barn, Serjeant, reminds me of an anecdote which I had from an officer of the Ninety-first Regiment.—It has never yet appeared in print, though it well deserves to be so recorded, as being worthy of that distinguished corps, the Seventy-first Highland Light Infantry, to which it belongs.

The circumstances took place in 1813, during the Peninsular War. The Seventy-first were at that time stationed with the Fiftieth and the Ninety-second, at St. Pierre, on the main road between Bayonne and St. Jean-pied-de-Port.—This was the key of Lord Hill's position on the rivers Adour, and the fire of musquetry brought against its defenders on the 13th December, was such as the oldest veterans had never before witnessed. The corps under Lord Hill, indeed, were on that day attacked by Soult's whole force. But so nobly did those fine regiments perform their duty, that the late Lieutenant-General the Honourable William Stewart, next day gave out an order, which I remember treasuring up in my memory as a masterpiece of soldier-like diction. I think the very words were these :—" The second Division has greatly distinguished itself, and its gallantry in yesterday's action is fully felt by the Commander of the Forces, and the Allied Army."

And well indeed had they merited this highly creditable testimonial of their good behaviour. But the carnage was great, and there were many who, alas ! did not survive to participate in the honour conferred by it. Several of the wounded belonging to the respective corps, were huddled together in the lower storey of an old house, that stood upon the very ground on which the thickest part of the contest had taken place. Now it happened, that certain officers from different regiments had taken shelter in a room in the floor above, where they were refreshing themselves, after their fatigue, with such food and other restoratives as they could command, and among them was that officer of the Ninety-first who told me the facts to which he was an ear-witness.

The conversation of these gentlemen, though mingled now and then with many regrets for lost companions, had a certain temperate joy in it—a joy arising from a conviction that they had behaved liked men—and which was tempered by strong feelings of gratitude to a kind Providence, who had preserved them amidst all the perils of the fight. Suddenly their talk was put an end to by the most heart-rending groans and shrieks of agony, that came up from the room below, through the old decayed floor. What mirth or joy there was among them, was altogether banished by the frequency and intensity of the screams, that betokened the mortal sufferings of a dying man. They sat for a time mutely, though deeply sympathizing, with the poor unfortunate from whom they came. At length they distinctly heard another faint, and apparently expiring voice, say, in a tone of rebuke,—" Haud your tongue, James, and bear your fate like a man. We'll soon be baith at ease.— But, in the mean time, haud your tongue, for there are folk aboon us that may be hearin' you ; and if you have no respect for yoursell, recollect what you owe to the gallant Seventy-first Hillant Light Infantry, to which we baith belong."

This appeal had the desired effect. All that could now be heard, in the stillness of the night, was a low murmur. A surgeon, who was of the party, immediately went to administer what relief he might to the wretched sufferers. But in one short hour these heroic men had ceased to exist, and no one can now tell even the name of either of them.

Author.—A most touching anecdote!—What magnanimous fellows!

Grant.—Their names should have been written by the hand of Fame herself, in letters of the purest and most imperishable gold!—Yet they have been allowed to sink into the sea of forgetfulness, and,

> " Like the snow-falls in the river,
> A moment white, then gone for ever,"

they have melted into oblivion—so far, at least, as this world is concerned.

Clifford.—Yes; they sleep unremembered, whilst every lily-livered cobbler, or tailor, who has handled his awl, or his bodkin, with no more peril to his person than may have lain on the point of one or other of these formidable weapons, has his tombstone—his death's head and cross-bones—and his attendant cherubims—as well as his text and his epitaph.

Serjeant.—Very true, sir—very true. What have such chields as these to do with fame? But for all that, we see fame arise to the silliest men, and from the most trifling causes.

Grant.—Right, Archy. For instance, I remember a certain Highlander, who gained his fame in a way that may perhaps make you envious—for it is the tale of your unwhisperables that has brought him to my mind.

Serjeant.—Aye, sir!—What was his story?

Grant.—Why, the hero was a certain Rory Maccraw, who, despising the kilt which he had worn all his life, resolved, at all risks, to figure in a pair of those elegant emblems of civilization called breeches. At the present day, one may travel from the Tweed to the Pentland Firth without seeing such a thing as a kilt; but at the time of which I am now speaking, anything in the shape of breeches was just as rarely to be seen as the kilt is now. Rory had a pair made for him in some distant town, where, as they would say in Ireland, he had not been by when his measure was taken, and having put them on, he left his glen to go to a market. It was observed by his neighbours, that he never before took so long a time to walk the same distance, and, from his strange and stately manner of strutting, they attributed this circumstance to the pride he felt in his new garments. Arrived at the market, the expectation he had indulged in, that he was to excite the wonder and envy of all the people there, did not deceive him. He was followed, and stared at, and admired, and questioned wherever he went. If a dancing bear had waddled through the fair, he could not have had half the number of people after him. But like most of those who envy the lot of their neighbours, these good folks only saw the outside of things, and knew not the misery which was covered by this fair external show. In the midst of their admiration, poor Rory was in torture. He would have given all he was worth, unmentionables and all, to have got rid of the admiring crowds that followed him; and at last, long before he had done half his business in the market—for as to pleasure, he could taste none of it—he, the envied, the observed of all observers, watched his opportunity to steal hobbling away down a back lane, whence he went limping in agony into the country. There, seating himself by the public way-side, regardless of what eyes might behold him, he pulled off the instruments of his suffering, and hanging them on the end of his staff, he placed it over his shoulder, and so trudged his way homeward, in defiance of the taunts, gibes, and laughter of the crowds which he fell in with by the way. But his fame was established; and ever afterwards he went by the name of Peter Breeks.

Clifford.—Capital!

Author.—Well, Archy, to return to your own story, and the disappointment you have met with in the arrestment of your career of glory, I would fain comfort you with the old proverb, that a contented mind is better than riches.

Serjeant.—This is very true, sir; and I am very thankful that I am blessed with that same. And although I got but little in the army but hard knocks, yet I would take them all over again, rather than that I should not have seen the many things I did see, as well as the heaps of queer human beings I met with during the few years I served. What is man, gentlemen, unless he gets the rust of home, and the reek of his own fire-side rubbed off him by travel? He can never be expected to speculate on any thing but the ducks in the dubbs, or the hens on the midden-head. Though I had a tolerable education for the like of me, what would I have been had I never been out of this valley? Not much better, I trow, than one of the stirks that are bred in it. Bless you, sirs, I saw a vast of human nature in my travels.

Grant.—And thought much and well on it too, Archy, if I mistake not.

Serjeant.—May be I did, sir,—and a very curious nature it is, I'll assure you. But, gentlemen, we must cross the water at this wooden bridge here.

Author.—If you had not seen so much by going into the world as you have done, Archy, I have great doubts whether that curiosity, which has since made you pick up that great store of your native legends which you are said to possess, might not have lain entirely dormant.

Serjeant.—Oh, bless your honour, I should never have thought of such things. It was the seeing so much that roused up the spirit of enquiry within me. And so it happened, that after I came back from the sodgering trade, this spirit could not rest till I had gathered up all the curious stories I could get. And then I fell tooth and nail upon books, so that, when I was not working, I was always reading histories, *novelles,* magazines, newspapers, and such like, so that I am not just altogether that ill informed. But stop a moment, gentlemen ; do you see yon bright green spot in the hollow of the hill-side yonder above us ?

Grant.—Yes ; but what is there wonderful about that, Archy ?

Serjeant.—There is nothing very wonderful about itself, indeed, but it is worth your remarking for all that. It is what we call in this country a *wallee*, that is, the quaking bog out of which a spring wells forth.

Clifford.—Tut, Archy ! There are few grouse shooters who have not experienced the treachery of these smooth-faced, flattering, but most deceitful water-traps.

Serjeant.—Smooth-faced, flattering, and deceitful, indeed, sir ; I've heard them compared by some to the fair sex, beauteous and smiling outside, and cruelly cold-hearted within. But I think any such comparison is most unjust, for my old woman never deceived me ; and, as I have told you, if it had not been for her oatmeal balls I verily believe I should not have been here at this moment.

Clifford.—It would ill become you, indeed, to slander the fair sex, Mister Serjeant, and depend upon it, you will not catch me doing so.

Serjeant.—But about the wallee yonder ; I was saying——

Clifford.—Aye, the wallee ; I shall never forget the first cold-bath I had up to the neck in one of them. It was all owing to the spite of a cunning old moorcock, which I had severely wounded. Out of revenge, I suppose, for the mortal injury I had done him, he chose to come fluttering down into the very middle of what I conceived to be a beautiful surface of hard green-sward. Being but a young sportsman at the time, and very eager to secure my bird, who sat most pro-

vokingly *tock-tock-tocking* at me, as if he had bid me defiance,
I ran down the bank, and made a bound towards him. In I
went souse. I shiver yet to think of it—my very senses were
congealed—and for a moment I verily believed that I had
been suddenly transformed into the North Pole, and that the
cock-grouse that fluttered around me was Captain Parry come
to explore me. And, i' faith, if it had not been for the light
foot and strong arm of the gilly who was with me, I believe I
might have been sticking upright there, preserved in ice till
this moment. There was a *moorish* bath for you !

Serjeant.—They are most unchancy bits for strangers; that
is certain, sir.

Clifford.—Unchancy indeed ! But if that is all you have to
tell us about yonder place in the hill-side, Mr. Archy, you may
save yourself the trouble of attempting to astonish me with
your information; for, Sassenach though I be, I promise you
that I have been long ago initiated into the full depth of the
mystery.—Nymphs and Naiads of the crystal Aven, what a
beautiful stream there is for fishing!

Serjeant.—'Tis very good, indeed, sir. But yon wallee that
I was speaking about would swallow a horse, with you on the
top of it. Many a time have I thrust a long pole down into it
without reaching anything the least like firm ground. It would
swallow that fishing-wand of yours, sir.

Clifford.—(Already employed in putting his rod together.)—
Plague choke it, I should be sorry indeed to see my rod go in
any such way. It is one of the best Bond ever made; and
though adapted, by means of these different pieces, to any size
of stream, it was never intended for such deep-sea fishing as
you would put it to. I shall apply it to another purpose, my
good serjeant. With this sky, the trouts there will take a
grey mallard's wing with a yellow silk body, in great style.

Serjeant.—But the wallee up yonder is worth your notice,
because of an auld auncient monumental stone that once stood
on the dry bank beside it.

Grant.—Ha ! a monumental stone !—let us hear about that.

Serjeant.—It was about seven feet high, sir, and the tradition
regarding it is that it was set up there in memory of a sad
story that is connected with it.

Author.—A story, said you ?

Clifford.—Then, my good fellow, Serjeant Stewart, just have
the kindness to sit down there, and tell us the particulars of
your sad story, while I give a few casts here over this most
tempting stream.

Serjeant.—With all manner of pleasure, sir; I shall be happy to tell your honours all I have gathered about it. It is the very legend for which Mr. Clifford marked me down in his book.

Clifford immediately began to fish. Grant and I seated ourselves on the daisied bank of the river, one on each side of the serjeant. The gilly stretched himself at length on the grass, and was soon asleep—the pony with the panniers grazed as far around him as the length of his halter would let him, and my Newfoundland dog Bronte sat watching the trouts leaping, whilst Archy proceeded with his narrative, as nearly as I can recollect, in the following words; but if not always precisely in the serjeant's own language, at least I shall give it with a strict adherence to his facts.

LEGEND OF THE CLAN-ALLAN STEWARTS.

FROM the important correction which your honour has made upon my genealogy, I think I may now venture to say, with some confidence, that the time of my legend must be somewhere about the fifteenth century—how early in it I cannot say; but it is pretty clear that my ancestor, Sir Allan Stewart, must have lived about that period. As I have already told you, the whole of this country, hill and glen, was then covered with forests, except in such spots as were kept open by the art of man for pasture or for tillage, but of the latter, even of the rudest kind, I suspect there was but little hereaway in those days. I take it for granted that the chief of the Clan-Allan must have had his stronghold at the old tower of Drummin, though I do not mean to say that it was identically the same building that now exists there. It stands, as some of you perhaps know, gentlemen, a good way down the country from where we now are, on a point of table land considerably elevated above the valley, which is there rendered wider by the junction of the river Livat with the river Aven, and just in the angle between these two streams. When the noble old forests waved over the surrounding hills, leaving the quiet meadows below open in rich pasture, it must have been even yet a more beautiful place for man to dwell in than it is now; and, let me tell you, that is saying a great deal.

My history begins towards the end of the life of Sir Allan Stewart, whose term of existence had been long, and no doubt

boisterous enough, as you may very well guess. He was by
this time so old as to be confined to his big oak chair, which
was generally placed for him under the projection of the huge
chimney of the ancient fire-place, or *lumm*, as we call it in
Scotland; and there he sat, propped up with pillows, crooning
over old ballads, and muttering old saws from morn till night,
as if he now cared for nothing in this life but to drone away
the last dull measure of his time, like the end of some drowsy
ill-composed pibroch, if such a thing there can be. But the
lively interest which he took when any stirring event occurred,
which in any degree affected the honour or welfare of himself,
his family or clan, sufficiently showed that all his martial fire
was not extinguished; for then would it flash out from beneath
his heavy eyelids—his bulky form would move impatiently on
his seat, and he would turn his eyes restlessly towards his
broadsword and targe, that hung conspicuously among the
deers' heads, wolfs' skins, and the numerous warlike weapons
that covered the walls, with an expression so animated, as very
plainly to speak the ardour of his decaying spirit, which still,
like that of the old war-horse, seemed thus to snuff up the
battle from afar.

Sir Allan had two tall strapping sons by his first marriage—
Walter and Patrick, both of them pretty men. To Walter, as
the elder of the two, he looked as his successor, and, accordingly, he already acted in all things, and on all occasions, as his
father's representative. After the death of their mother, Sir
Allan had married a woman of lower degree, by whom he had
a third son, called Murdoch, whose naturally bad dispositions
had been fostered by the doting fondness of his old father.
Murdoch's mother, at the time we are speaking of, was what
we would call in our country phrase a handsome boardly-look-
ing dame, of some forty years of age or so, whose smooth
tongue and deceitful smile covered the blackest and most
depraved heart.

"See, father!" said Walter Stewart to old Sir Allan, as he
and his brother Patrick entered the hall one evening, followed
by some of their people, with whom they had been all day
engaged in the pursuit of a wolf, whose grinning countenance,
attached to his shaggy skin, was born triumphantly on the point
of a hunting spear. "See here, father! we have got him at
last. We have at last taken vengeance on the villain for his
cruel slaughter of poor Isabel's child. Look at the spoils of
the murdering caitiff who devoured the little innocent."

"Hath he not been a fell beast, father?" said Patrick, hold-

4

ing up the hunting spear before Sir Allan, and shaking the
trophy.

"Ah!" said Sir Allan, rousing himself up, "a fell beast
indeed!—aye, aye—poor child, poor child!—bring his head
nearer to me, boy! Would I could have been with you! Aye,
aye—dear me—age will come upon us. But I have seen the
day, boys—aye, aye—och, hey!"

"Ho, there!" cried Walter Stewart, "what means it that
there are no signs of supper? By St. Hubert, but we have
toiled long enough and hard enough to-day with legs, arms,
spears, spades, and mattocks to have well earned our meal!
Where is brother Murdoch?—where is the Lady Stradawn?"

"Aye, aye," said the querulous old Sir Allan, "it is ever
thus now-a-days. I am always left to myself—weary, weary is
my life I am sure—and I am hungry—very hungry. Aye,
aye."

"'Thou shalt have thy supper very soon, father," said Patrick,
kindly taking his hand; "and Walter and I will leave you but
for a brief space, to rid us of these wet and soiled garments."

The two brothers then hastened from the hall to go to their
respective chambers.

"Whose draggle-tailed beast was that I saw tied up under
the tree beyond the outer gateway as we came in?" demanded
Walter of his attendant, Dugald Roy.

"I have seen the beast before," replied Dugald. "If I am
not far mista'en, it is the garron the proud Priest of Dalestie
rides,—and a clever beast it would need to be, I am sure, for
many a long, and late, and queer gate does it carry him, I trow."

"How came the animal there, Dugald?" demanded Walter
quickly.

"If by your question, *how* the animal came there, you would
ask what road he took Sir Knight," replied Dugald, "I must
tell you that the man that could answer you would need to deal
with the devil, for no one but the foul fiend himself could
follow the Priest of Dalestie; for, unless he be most wickedly
belied, his ways follow those of the Evil One, as much as our
good father, Peter of Dounan, is known to travel in the path
of his blessed Master."

"Nay, but I would know from thee, in plain terms, where
thou judgest that the rider of the horse may be?" said Sir
Walter, impatiently.

"With your lady mother, the Lady Stradawn, I reckon,"
said Dugald, sinking his voice to a half whisper.

"Call her not my lady mother!" said Sir Walter, angrily,

" my lady step-mother, if thou wilt, or my step-mother without
the lady, for that, in truth, would better befit her, disgrace as
she hath been and still is to us all.—Here, undo this buckle !
—But what, I pr'ythee, hath she to do with the proud Priest
of Dalestie, as thou hast so well named him ?"

" Nay, nothing that I know of, Sir Walter, unless it be to
confess her," replied Dugald.

" Why, the good old father, Peter of Dounan, was here but
yesterday, was he not ?" exclaimed Sir Walter, " might he not
have shriven her ?"

" Father Peter was here sure enough," replied Dugald, " but
it would seem that he is not to the lady's fancy."

" Beshrew her fancy !" cried Sir Walter, bitterly,—" Where
could she, or anyone, find a worthier confessor than Father
Peter of Dounan ? He is, indeed, a good and godly man,
and, frail as he is in body, we know that he is always ready
to run, as fast as his feeble limbs can carry him, wherever
his pious duties or his charities may call him.—Moreover, he
is at all times within reach, what need, then, hath she to send
so far a-field for one whose character is, by everyone's report,
so very questionable—give me my hose and sandals, Donald.—
Now thou may'st go.—By the Rood, I like not that pestilent
and ill-famed fellow coming about our house ! He hath more
character for arrogance, and self-indulgence as a glutton and a
toss-pot, than for sanctity.—It was an ill day for this country
side when it was disgraced by his coming into it."

After muttering this last sentence to himself, Walter quickly
descended the narrow stair, and approached the door of the
lady's bower in another part of the building.—It was partially
open.—He tapped gently, and, no answer being returned, he
pushed it up, and great were his surprise and disgust at the
scene which he beheld. The Lady Stradawn was sitting, or
rather reclining, in her arm-chair, with a pretty large round
table before her, covered with good things.—A huge venison
pasty occupied the centre of it, and around it stood several
dishes, in no very regular order, containing different dainties.
Two well-used trenchers, showed that someone else had assisted
her in producing the havoc that appeared to have been wrought
in the pie, and among the other viands—and a black-jack half
full of ale—and a tall silver stoup, which, though now empty,
still gave forth a potent odour of the spiced wine which it had
contained—together with two mazers of the same metal, which
bore the marks of having been used in the drinking of it,
proved that the guest, who had just left the lady, must have

been a noble auxiliary in this revel, which, judging from the
fact of an over-turned drinking horn that lay on the floor, and
one or two other circumstances that appeared, must have been
a merry one. The deep sleep in which the lady lay, and her
flushed countenance, left no doubt in Sir Walter's mind that
she had enjoyed a full share of this private banquet. By the
time he had leisure to make himself fully aware of all these
particulars, the lady's bower-woman appeared at the chamber
door. She started, and would have retreated—but Sir Walter
seized her by the wrist, and adroitly put a question to her before
she had time to recover from her confusion.

"When did the Priest of Dalestie go forth from hence,
Jessy?" demanded he.

"I have just come from seeing him to horse, Sir Knight,"
said the woman, trembling.

"Well, Jessy, thou mayest go; I would speak with thy
mistress in private," said Sir Walter, seeing her out, and shutting the chamber door; and then turning to the Lady Stradawn,
and shaking her arm till he had awakened her. "Madam,"
said he, "what unseemly sight is this?"

"Sis—sis—sis—sight, Sir Priest?" replied the lady, with
her eyes goggling; "sis—sight! What mean ye, Sir Priest?
he! he! he!"

"Holy Saint Andrew grant me temper!" said Sir Walter.
"Madam, Sir Allan waits for thee to give him his evening
meal: he is impatient. Sir Allan, I say!"

"Tut! hang Sir Allan," cried the lady, still unconscious as
to whom she was addressing, and taking him by the arm;
"hang Sir Allan, as thou thyself said'st but now, thou most
merry conditioned mettlesome, Sir Priest. He! he! he!
Hang the old stobber-chops, and let's be jolly while we can.
Come; sit down—sit down, I say. You need not go yet. Did
I not tell thee that Jessy keeps the door?"

"I am not the priest, vile woman!" cried Sir Walter, with
indignation, whilst, at the same time, he shook her off with a
force and rudeness that seemed almost to bring her back to her
senses. "Did'st thou not now, alas! alas! to our shame, most
unworthily fill that place once occupied by my sainted mother,
and that thine exposure would prove but the greater dishonour
to our house, by the holy Rood, I would call up everything that
hath life within these walls, down to the very cat, that all eyes
might behold thy disgrace, and then should'st thou be trundled
forth, and rolled into the river, that the fishes might gorge
themselves on thine obscene carcase!"

Bursting from the apartment, Walter hastily sought the hall; and the evening meal having been by this time spread, he called to the retainers to be seated, and hastened to busy himself in attending to his father, in supplying him with the food prepared for him, and with such little matters as he knew the old man most liked—feeding him from time to time like a child.

"Aye, aye, that's good," said old Sir Walter. "Thanks, thanks, my boy; you are a good boy. But where is Bella? where is the Lady Stradawn? Och hey, that's good,—but she is often away now; seldom it is, I am sure, that I see her. Aye, aye, Walter, boy, that is good—that is very good."

When his father was satisfied, Walter seated himself at the board, and ate and drank largely, from very vexation and ire, and in order to keep down the storm of rage which was secretly working within him. This, as well as the cause of it, he privately determined to conceal, even from his brother Patrick, with whom he had been, upon all other occasions, accustomed to share his inmost thoughts. For the rest of the night he sat gloomy and abstracted, and at an earlier hour than usual he hurried off to his chamber. There, having summoned his attendant, Dugald Roy, he questioned him more particularly as to all he knew regarding the visits of the Priest of Dalestie to Drummin, and having then dismissed him, with strict injunctions to maintain a prudent silence, he threw himself into bed, to pass a restless and perturbed night.

The next morning saw the Lady Stradawn glide into the hall, to preside over the morning meal, gaily dressed, and covered as usual with chains, brooches, and rings of massive worth, which she procured no one knew how. Her countenance beamed with her wonted smiles, as if nothing wrong had happened, or could have happened on her part. Walter and Patrick saluted her with that cold yet civil deference, which they had always been in the habit of using towards her, as the wife of their father, and in which Walter took care that neither his brother, nor anyone else, should perceive any shadow of change upon the present occasion. The manner of her salutation was as blythe, kind, free, and unconcerned as it ever was before.

"Wicked rogue, Walter, that thou art!" said she in a tone of merry raillery, "fie for shame on thee! to steal into thy lady mother's bower to catch her asleep in her arm-chair! In sooth I was not altogether well last night, else had I joined thee at the festive board, to rejoice with thee over the spoils of that grim gaffer wolf, whom they tell me thou hast so nobly slain."

"Thou did'st indeed seem somewhat indisposed, madam," said Sir Walter with a peculiarly significant emphasis, and with a penetrating look which she alone could understand.

"I was very much indisposed as you say, Walter," replied she, as if quite unconscious that he had intended to convey to her any covered meaning; "that foolish old woman, Nancy, the miller's wife, took it into her wise head to come a plaguing me, to reckon with her about the kain fowls she had paid into the castle since last quarter-day; and she talks—Holy Virgin, how the woman does talk!"

"Truly the woman does talk marvellously," replied Walter, biting his nether lip to keep down his vexation.

"As thou say'st, son Walter, she does e'en talk most marvellously. Her tongue seems to have learned the art of wagging from the clapper of old John's mill. I protest I would as lieve sit listening to the one as to the other. My head aches still with the noise of her clatter."

"I wonder not indeed that thy head should ache," replied Sir Walter.

"And then, forsooth, I behoved to call up meat for the greedy cummer," continued the lady,—"Holy Mother, how the woman did swallow the eatables and drinkables!"

"She must have swallowed enough of both sorts," said Sir Walter, with a meaning in his mode of speaking, that he began to suspect he might have made almost too plainly marked; and, hastening to change the subject, "Madam," continued he, "I fear you have forgotten Sir Allan this morning."

"Holy Saints, but so I have!" cried she, starting up from her seat,—"what have I been thinking of? My poor Sir Allan!" continued she, as she hastened to him with a covered silver dish, that contained the minced food the old man was wont to take; and, after making of him, with all the fuss and phrase she would have used to an infant, she put a napkin around his neck, and proceeded to feed him.

"Where is Murdoch this morning?" demanded Patrick of his brother.

"I know not," replied Walter, as he sat musing with a clouded brow.

"He was not at supper last night," observed Patrick again; "nay, I know not that I have seen him for these three days bypast."

"He was not at supper," said Sir Walter, still absorbed by his own thoughts.

"Murdoch is an idle good-for-nothing," said the Lady

Stradawn, joining in the conversation, from the place where she stood by the side of Sir Allan's chair. "Though he be mine own, I will say that for him, that it would be well for him to take a pattern by his elder brothers, and be killing wolves, or doing some such useful work, and not be staying out whole days and nights this way, at weddings and merry-makings, without ever showing us his face. I wish you would give him a good word of your brotherly advice, my dear son Walter."

"Chut!—tut!" cried old Sir Allan,—"let the boy alone!—aye, aye—let the boy alone. The lad is young.—I was a wild slip myself once in a day—that I was. But old age will creep on—hech, sirs!—aye, aye—what days I have seen!—Och, hey!"

"Here, take this, my dear Sir Allan," said the lady,—"take this, dearest—'tis the last spoonful."

"Where art thou going, brother?" said Patrick, rising to follow his brother Sir Walter, who had left the table and was moving towards the door.

"Up the glen to look for a deer," replied Walter.

"Then have with thee brother," said Patrick.

Sir Walter would have fain shaken himself free from his brother, for that morning at least; but he felt that he could not do so without a certain appearance of unkindness, which the warm affection that subsisted between them could not allow him to use, or that otherwise he must have given him an explanation, which he was conscious that he could not have given him consistently with those designs which he then privately cherished in his bosom. He was therefore compelled silently to assent to his accompanying him. They both accordingly assumed that humble garb, which they usually wore when bent upon the pursuit of the deer,—in which, but for their carriage and bearing, they might easily have been mistaken for the humblest of their party, and, after such preparation, they sallied forth.

They were hardly gone when the Lady Stradawn, leaving the old Sir Allan to entertain himself with his own dreamy musings and vacant thoughts, climbed to the bartizan of the tower to look out for her son, Murdoch. It was yet early in the morning—but as her two step-sons had a walk of a good many miles before them ere they could reach the place where they proposed hunting, they and their people were seen toiling up the valley, at a pace which corresponded with the violence of those feelings which then possessed Sir Walter, who was stretching away at the head of the party.

"Curses on ye both !" cried the lady, with intense bitterness, after having followed them with her malignant eyes till they had wound out of sight behind a projecting spur of a wooded mountain that flanked the valley.—"Curses!—black and withering curses on ye both, vile spawn that ye are, that stand between my boy and his prospects!—I fear that Walter—my especial curse upon him!—for, with all his fair words, he is stern and ferocious as a wild cat when he is roused.—But, wild cat though he be, the wily viper may yet wind its folds silently around him, and sting him to the death ere he may have time to unglove his claws.—What can make my darling boy tarry so long.—He has now been absent for more than three days.— Much as he hath enriched me with money and jewels, I like not the risk he runs.—But he will not be forbidden.—Nature works in him, and perhaps it is as well that he should thus render himself hardy, seeing that he must one day—aye, and that soon too, if I have any cunning left in me—command the proud Clan-Allan. Stay, did I not see tartans yonder, and arms glittering in yon farther lawnde, in the vale below, beyond those nearer woods? That must surely be Murdoch and his men. The foolish boy will not surely bring them within nearer ken of the Castle? Ha!—I see one figure separate from the rest, whilst the main body seems to take to the woods on the hill-side. In sooth, there is no prudence lacking in the youth, nay, nor any cunning neither, as I well know, from the trouble it hath cost me to lull his suspicions regarding the Priest of Dalestie. But if Murdoch hath cunning, he hath it from me, his mother; and it will be hard indeed if mine cannot match it. Ah!—there he already bursts from the wood—I must hasten to meet him in my bower, that I may learn what luck he hath had."

The lady hurried down to her bower—quickly found some errand on which to despatch her woman—and then she sat waiting impatiently, turning over the bunch of antique keys which hung at her girdle, until she heard her son's step in the passage, and his gentle tap at her door.

"Come in !" said the Lady Stradawn in a subdued voice— "come in, my son !"

"Ha!—I am glad that thou art here and alone, mother," said Murdoch, a slim, handsome, dark-eyed youth, who, after cautiously entering, shut the door behind him, and carefully turned the huge key that locked it. "I am glad that you are here alone, for I have such treasure for you."

"Hush, hush, my darling," said the lady, almost in a whisper

—"speak lower, I entreat you, lest any eaves-dropper should hear you.—Quick!—how sped ye?—and what have you got?"

"We have been all the way to Banff again this time," replied Murdoch. "Seeing that we sped so well the last time we made thither, as thou well knowest we did, we thought we should try our luck there once more. We heard that there was a market in the Brugh, and we sent a clever-witted spy among the packmen, to gather who among them might be best worth holding talk with. Two of them we learned were to travel together for company's sake—fellows who dealt in gold-smiths' work. But, marry! they travelled not far from the town-end till we met them, when, like good-natured civil fellows, we eased them of their heavy loads, under which they seemed to sweat so grievously; and that they might not trouble us here, and at the same time being loth to part two such friends, we set them both a travelling together on a journey to the next world."

"Speak not of the next world, Murdoch!" said the lady, shuddering. "But they were sickerly sent thither, said'st thou?"

"As surely as we shall one day go there ourselves, good mother," replied Murdoch.

"Speak not of our going there, boy," said the lady. "'Tis time enough yet. But there is little crime I wot, after all, in ridding this world of such cheating gangerels as those you tell me of."

"Crime!" replied Murdoch. "Why, mother, there is an absolute virtue in such a deed. Have we not put an end to their rapacity and knavery? And have we not thereby saved many a foolish maiden from being cheated by them! By Saint Nicholas, but the doer of so good a deed deserves to be canonised!"

"But come, boy, thy treasure," said the greedy and impatient dame. "Quick,—what hast thou got to show me? Haste thee to feast mine eyes with the spoil of these miscreants."

"In the first place, then," said Murdoch, "as at a feast we should always begin with the solids,—here is a small bag of broad pieces, which might well satisfy many a hungry man. Secondly, here are your curious cates and delicacies, enow to bedizen out a dozen of lordlings' daughters!—See what a chain! —how exquisite the workmanship!—Behold these rings,—see what sparkling gems! Every one of them set, too, most rarely in a different fashion! Here is one, for example, which would seem to have a curious posey in it; some ready-made love verse, I suppose. Let me see,—' *Feare God and doe no evyle*,' —eh! ha!—that—that is a good advice, which the last owner, as I take it, was too great a knave to profit by; but you and I, mother dear ——"

"Have done with thy foolery, Murdoch," said the lady, impatiently; "have done with thy foolery, and give me thy booty, without farther nonsense. Now, leave me for a while, and go talk with the old man, whilst I bestow the treasure in a place of safety. Thou knowest it will all go to deck thy bride, when thou canst find one."

"Leave me alone for that, mother," said Murdoch significantly. "I promise thee, I have mine eye on a good man's daughter, whom I shall have by foul or by fair means ere I die. But that is a secret I shall keep to myself till the time comes; so good day, good mother."

"What can he mean?" said the Lady Stradawn, after he was gone. "But 'tis nothing, after all, but his wild talk. No, no; I must have my say with him when it comes to that!"

Now that the lady found herself alone, she doubly locked and bolted the door. She then spread the gold and the jewels on the table before her, and glutted her eyes for a time with the glittering sight. Applying her keys to a cabinet which stood against the wall, she opened the leaves of it, and so exposed the front of a set of secret drawers, shallower above and deeper below. Selecting other keys from the bunch, she began to open and to examine the drawers, one by one, from above downwards—her eyes successively surveying the riches they contained, whilst, with scrupulous attention, she from time to time selected articles from among the spoils on the table, and deposited them among the rest, as fancy led her to sort and arrange them, carefully locking each drawer ere she proceeded to open the next; and thus she went on until she found that she had disposed of the whole of the trinkets.

"'Twas no great things, after all," said she, musing; "I wonder when they will go forth again? But let me count the money.—Aye, that is pretty well; and yet it might have been more for the death of two men. But there are other two men I know of, whose lives would be worth more!—Hush!—did I not hear a noise?—Quick—let me huddle the gold into this drawer in the cabinet, where I bestowed the broad pieces in the hurry I was taken with when the Priest came in last night. —What!—nothing there!—Ha!—can the man who—can the villain have robbed me?—Yes; it could have been no one else.

—I see clearly how it was. He asked me for money—I gave him two pieces from that very drawer. His greedy eyes saw what it contained, and, whilst my back was turned, he must have cleverly helped himself to the whole. It could have been nobody else, because I well remember that I carefully closed the leaves of the cabinet, locked them, and put the keys into my iron strong-box, before I called Jessy to bring the refreshments.—What a consummate knave!—But what could I expect better of such a reprobate—a priest who glories as he does in his wickedness? It would have been well perhaps for me that I had never seen him.—And yet—but his share of his crime is his own.—Wretch that he is, he might have had it all for the asking.—Weak woman that I am, I could have refused him nothing.—Well, I must e'en let it pass, and be more careful again.—But I shall look better after this bag of broad pieces. It shall be added to the heap I have here," continued she, unlocking a drawer of deeper and larger dimensions. "Aye!" said she, eyeing the treasure it contained with avaricious delight,—"that is all safe; go thou, then, to increase the store, and may my darling boy soon fetch me other bags to bear these company in this their prison-house."

I must now return to the two brothers. Walter, who usually directed everything in all their expeditions, never halted until he found himself far up on these very mountains now before us. He sought for deer, it is true; but, whilst he did so, or rather, whilst he allowed his brother and his people to do so, his mind seemed to be occupied with something else than hunting. It was towards evening, when he and the rest of the party were still tracking their way through the forest without success, when they at last found themselves in that part of it which then covered the hill that hangs over the haugh of Dalestie, some miles above this. Partial breaks among the trees there gave Sir Walter, now and then, a view downwards into the valley below; and, as he walked and ruminated within himself, as if oppressed with some weighty matter, his secret musings were suddenly broken by the distant toll of the bell of a small chapel, which, if I am rightly informed, then stood near the bottom of the hill. The sound came mellowed over the intervening woods, and Sir Walter started as it reached his ear. He became deeply moved; but his emotion was not like that movement of piety which the note of the church-going bell should awaken. It more resembled that which, when the hoarse trumpet has sounded, or the shrill pipes have struck up, I have myself seen convert the godlike countenance of man into that of a demon. Sir Walter Stewart stamped upon the ground.

"Dugald !" cried he aloud; "what ho, Dugald Roy, I say. Does that bell call to evening mass ?"

"It does, Sir Knight," replied Dugald.

"Then, get thee down through the wood," said Sir Walter; "get thee down through the wood ere it hath ceased to sound, and tell the proud priest of Dalestie, that I, Walter Stewart of Clan-Allan, am upon the hill, and that, if he dares to mumble a word, yea, or a syllable, before I come, his life shall pay for it."

"Stay, stay," cried Patrick Stewart, eagerly; "stay him, dear brother ! What sudden fit is this that hath seized thee ? A priest !—how canst thou think of sending such a message as this to a priest ?"

".Dugald Roy, begone, and obey thy master's bidding !" cried Sir Walter, sternly. "Brother, I forgive thee this thine interference, though I cannot allow myself to be swayed by it. Trust me, I have mine own good reasons for so acting, though this be no fitting time for making thee aware of them."

Patrick, whom affection, as well as habit had long disposed to show implicit deference and obedience to his brother Walter's will, said no more, but followed his solemn footsteps down the mountain path that led to the chapel. They had not gone half the way till the bell had ceased to toll. And they had not gone two-thirds of the way till Dugald Roy met them.

"Thou hast not sped on thine errand, then ?" said Sir Walter, with an expression in which more of satisfaction than of disappointment might have been read. "Speak, Dugald; how did the arrogant caitiff receive my message ?"

"Since I must say it, Sir Knight," replied Dugald, with some hesitation,—"he received it very scurvily.—'Tell the proud Stewart,' said he, 'that though he may be lord of the land, I am the king as well as the priest in mine own chapel.' —And so he straightway began the holy service, but rather, methought, as if he had been dighting himself for single combat, than for prayer, and in a manner altogether so irreverent, that the few people who were there, with faces full of dismay, quietly arose and left the chapel, as if some wicked thing had ta'en up the priest's surplice in mockery."

"By the Rood, but they were right if they so thought !" cried Sir Walter, quickening his pace—"He is a vile obscene wolf that hath crept like a thief into the fold.—But I'll speak to him anon."

The rate at which Sir Walter now strode down the hill, kept his astonished brother Patrick and the whole party at their full bent. The trees grew thinner as they came nearer the level valley, and by and bye they ceased altogether, so that a full view was obtained of the haugh at the bottom. There the Priest of Dalestie was seen leaving the chapel to go homewards.

"There he goes!" cried Sir Walter—"there he goes stalking along with an air and a gait, that might better befit a proud prince of the earth than Heaven's humble messenger of peace, as his profession ought to have made him.—What, ho, Sir Priest!—I would speak with thee."

The Priest started—looked suddenly back—halted, and drew himself up—then turned again, and moved a few paces slowly onwards, as if irresolute what he should do. Again he halted, and again he moved on, whilst Sir Walter's footsteps were hurrying fast up to him.—At length, he seemed to have made up his mind to abide that parley which he now saw he could not escape, and, turning sharp round to face the Stewart, he planted himself firmly in the way before him.

"What would'st thou with me, Sir Knight?" demanded he, in a haughty and determined tone.—"After the rude and unwonted message which thou hast just dared to send to me, a holy minister of the Church, methinks that thou canst dare to approach me now, for no other purpose than to sue penitently for pardon and absolution at my hands."

"A holy minister of the Church!" exclaimed Sir Walter.—"A minister of the holy Church, if thou wilt—but thyself most unholy.—My sins, God pardon me!—are many.—But albeit that I am at all times ready to kneel in confession, and in humble penitence, before that true and godly servant of Christ, the good and pious father, Peter of Dounan, or any other such as he, I will never bend the knee before one whose wickedness has been the dishonour and reproach of the district, ever since it hath been cursed with his presence, and who yet profanely dares most impiously to approach the holy altar."

"Brother! brother Walter!" cried Patrick Stewart, endeavouring to moderate Sir Walter's growing ire; "what madness is this! Think of the sacred character he wears, however little common fame may give him credit for supporting it. Think how——"

"Silence, I say, Patrick!" cried Sir Walter, in an authoritative tone, which he had never before assumed to his brother.

"Again I say, thou knowest not the secret reasons which move me at this moment. That foul swine, whose sensual snout hath been in every man's dish, and who hath uprooted that very vineyard which hath been confided to his care, must be forthwith cast out. He must be no longer permitted to live. Seize him and bind him!"

"Lay not a hand on me, good sirs, if you would avoid the thunders and excommunications of the Church," cried the priest, now no longer proud, but trembling, and in an humble tone.

"Seize him and bind him, I say," cried Sir Walter. "If there be any one man among the Clan-Allan here—if there be one Clan-Allan Stewart, I say, who in his conscience believes that he doth not deserve to die by fire, that man hath my leave to sit apart, and bear no faggot to the pile that is to consume him. Who among you is there that doth not know his misdeeds? Not a man answers. Then is he condemned by all. Let each man, then, get him to the wood, and bring a faggot of the driest fuel, and let him forthwith be brent, and his ashes scattered to the winds, so that the earth may be no longer polluted with his carcase, and that even the very memory of him may perish!"

"Brother, brother!" cried Patrick Stewart, in a tone of entreaty; "do not bring upon yourself the terrors of the Church. His fame, indeed, is none of the best; but, whatever be his sins, bethink thee that 'twere better to let him be tried by that sacred tribunal to which he is naturally amenable."

"By the holy Rood, which this traitor to his crucified Master has so wickedly profaned, he shall not live an hour," cried Sir Walter, rising in his rage. "I am but the executioner of God's justice on him; and he shall die, be the consequences what they may. See!—see how busily the fellows toil! Their hearts are in the work. The labour is a pleasure to them. Not a man hath stood aloof from it, far less hath any one dared to speak in his cause. Why, then, shouldst thou speak, brother Patrick? Though thou knowest not all, thou knowest quite enough to know that he hath well earned the fate I have awarded him. But though thou art ignorant of all that now impelleth mé, I tell thee that I have enough to satisfy bishop or pope, if need were, that I am now doing the Church good service. But, be that as it may, I trust the time will never come when the chieftain of Clan-Allan shall not dare to deal with all within the bounds of Stradawn, whether churchman or layman, as his pleasure may dictate. Ha! see,

"Mercy, most noble Knight," cried the wretched man.—Page 47.

the pile is already heaped high, and now they are preparing to set fire to it; that shows no want of good will; and see, of their own accord, they prepare to drag him to it!"

"Then, brother, though I am the younger, I must needs interfere," cried Patrick Stewart, rushing forward to throw himself between the men of the clan and their terrified victim; "such a deed as this must never be done by thee, my brother."

"Patrick, dispute not mine authority," cried Sir Walter, his rage now beginning to get the better of him; "my father's weakness hath made me thy chieftain. Stand back, I tell thee! Stand back! place thyself not between me and my just vengeance, or even the name of brother shall not hinder me from dashing thee to the ground."

"Nay, stand you back!" cried Patrick, covering the priest with his body, whilst the clansmen retreated from the prisoner at his word. "Walter, I would save this wretched man for another and a calmer tribunal; and, in thus saving him, I would save thee, my brother, from——"

"Stand from before his polluted carcase!" cried Sir Walter, collaring Patrick, and casting him from him with a force that threw him several yards away from the spot where they were contending, and prostrated him headlong on the ground. "Now, Clan-Allan! now do your duty to your chieftain! I'll see that my sentence—aye, and your sentence, is duly carried through!"

"Mercy, most noble knight!" cried the wretched man, as they dragged him along to the pile, deadly pale, and quailing with fear—his pride all gone, and the terrors of a horrible death upon him. "Mercy! O spare me! spare me, most noble Sir Walter Stewart! I confess that I have deeply sinned against you and yours; I confess that——"

"Silence, caitiff!" cried the stern Sir Walter, loudly and hastily interrupting him; "I am no priest—I want none of thy confessions. Confess thyself inwardly to thine outraged Maker. Thou shalt have time for that. Down on thy knees! confess thy sins in secret to Him, and pray to Him for mercy in the next world, for here all laws, human and divine, tell me that thou shouldst have none; and thou shalt have none from me."

The miserable wretch, trembling, haggard, and conscience-stricken, knelt down at a short distance from the great heap of dry and decayed timber which they had prepared. By this time it was lighted, and it soon began to blaze up so high as widely to illuminate the broad faces of the wooded hills on

both sides of the valley, arousing them from that gloom which
had been already gradually deepening over them into shadow,
since the sinking of the sun.   Neither his countenance nor his
eyes were directed heavenwards; yet his lips moved, more like
those of some one uttering an incantation, than of a penitent
seeking of Heaven to be shriven of his sins.   Full time was
allowed him.   But the stern Sir Walter Stewart stood over
him, as if jealous lest his fears or his agony of mind, might
goad him on to utter some secret aloud before the clansmen,
which he wished to see consumed, and for ever annihilated
with all that was mortal of him who held it.   And when he
thought that he had given the wretched man enough of licence,
he waved his hand—turned himself aside for a moment—heard
one piercing shriek—and when he looked again the myriads of
brilliant sparks that were rising into the air from the fall of a
heavy body among the fuel, sufficiently proved to him, that the
miserable object of his wrath had been thrown into the very
midst of the burning heap.   Another, and a fainter cry, made
Sir Walter again turn involuntarily towards the pile.   There
the head appeared, with the face contorted with torment, and
fearfully illuminated.   The body reared itself up for a moment,
as if by one last struggling effort of life, and these half-stifled
words were dolefully heard,—

"WALTER STEWART!—THY GRAVE IS NEAR!"

The Clan-Allan men stood appalled.   Again the figure
sank.   More broken and decayed wood was thrown on the
pile, and they continued to heap it up until all signs of a
human form were obliterated.   Then it was that Sir Walter,
calling his followers into a ring around him, swore them
solemnly, on their chieftain's sword, to eternal secrecy; and
then, sick at the thought of the work they had done, chieftain
and clansmen slowly, and silently, left the place, and began to
wend their way down the glen.   Sir Walter thought of his
brother Patrick as he went—he halted, and blew that bugle
sound, which was well known as a private signal between
them.   But there was no note of reply.   Taking it for granted,
therefore, that the stern act of justice, which circumstances had
compelled him to see done on the Priest, had been too much
for the sensitive mind of Patrick even to contemplate, and
that, therefore, he had hurried away to avoid witnessing the
horrible spectacle, Sir Walter pensively and moodily moved
homewards.

But the cause of the muteness of Patrick Stewart's bugle,

was very different from that which his brother believed it to be. At the time that he had been dragged from before the Priest, and thrown so violently to a distance, Sir Walter had been too much excited by rage to notice how he fell, or indeed whether he fell at all. Nor in the fearful work in which they were all so intently, and with so much good will engaged, did any of the Stewarts of Clan-Allan once think of him more. Had Sir Walter known that his beloved brother had been stretched bleeding, and senseless, on the ground, by his rash hand, and that he was now leaving him to perish without help, his mind, during his homeward journey, would have been even less tranquil than his reflections on the past event permitted it to be. The truth was, that Patrick Stewart's bonnet, having been driven off by the furious force with which Sir Walter had hurled him from him, his unprotected head came into contact with a large stone, that projected out of the surface of the meadow-sward, with a sharp point, from which he received so severe a cut, and so rude a shock, that he never moved after it, but lay there as if he had been dead, in the midst of a pool of blood that flowed from the wound. How long he had remained in this situation, he had no means of guessing, but when his senses returned to him, he found himself seated, with his back leaning against the trunk of a great tree, near a fountain that welled out from the side of the hill. By the blaze of a bit of moss fir that a man held in his hand, he perceived that there were several people around him, who seemed to be busied in administering to him. One especially was anxiously supporting his head, staunching the blood that was still discharging itself from the cut in his temple, and holding a cup to his lips.

"How fares it with thee now?" enquired this person eagerly; "how fares it with thee, my dear friend?"

"Arthur Forbes of Curgarf!" said Patrick faintly.

"Holy St. Macher be praised that thine eyes are opened, and that I once more hear thy voice!" cried Arthur Forbes, "I had mine own fears that thou wert done for. What, in the name of all that is marvellous, hath befallen thee? Hast thou chanced to come into the hands of the Catteranes, who are said to harbour sometimes among those mountains?"

"Where am I?" said Patrick, turning his eyes around him, his brain still swimming in confusion. "Ah! that fire yonder!"

"Aye, that fire!" said Arthur Forbes eagerly, "what knowest thou of that fire?"

5

" Nay nothing," replied Patrick shuddering.

" By the Rood, but it brent boldly when we first saw it from the far hill-side yonder," said Arthur, " though it hath now fallen somewhat lower.   Knowest thou at all who kindled it ? We heard a bugle blast come faintly up from the bottom of the valley, as we came first within sight of it."

" It was not burning when I fell," replied Patrick guardedly.

" How did you fall, I pray you ?" demanded Arthur Forbes.

" As I was hurrying through the haugh," replied Patrick, " my foot tripped in the twilight against something in the grass, and I was thrown forward, with so much force, that it is no wonder I was stunned."

" Your head must have struck upon some sharp stone," said Arthur Forbes, " that gash in your temple is a very ugly one, and it still bleeds considerably.   Let me bathe it for you."

" The ice-cold water is most reviving to me," said Patrick, sitting up ; " I am much better now.   I think I am almost strong enough to walk."

" Shall we help thee down to the Priest's house ? " demanded Arthur ; " that, as thou knowest, is the nearest dwelling."

" The Priest's house !" said Patrick, with an expression of horror which he could not restrain.

" Nay, 'tis no wonder that thou should'st shudder at the very mention of that reprobate," said Arthur Forbes ; " he is a scandal to the very name of priest."

" I would rather go anywhere than to the Priest's house," said Patrick Stewart.

" Nay," said Arthur Forbes, " it is a thousand to one that we should find him abroad on some of his unseemly nocturnal pranks ; but you might at least repose thee for a time in his dwelling."

" I should find no repose under the Priest's roof," said Patrick Stewart quickly.   " I would rather try to make the best of my way to Drummin."

" Thou shalt never essay to go to Drummin to-night," said Arthur Forbes.   " And, now I think on't, why should you not go over the hill with me to Curgarf?   My sturdy fellows there shall carry you.   And then, when you are there you know," continued he, sinking his voice to a whisper into Patrick's ear, " my sister Kate shall nurse thee."

" Your proposal is life to me," replied Patrick, in the same tone.   " I gladly accept your kind offer.   But as to loading your poor men with the weight of my carcase, there will be no occasion for that.   Now that my head is bound up, I feel quite strong, and I know I shall get better every step of the hill I travel."

" I thought that Kate's very name would be a potent balsam for thy wound," whispered Arthur Forbes again. " Thou wilt be better in the hands of Kate, my friend, than in those of the Catteranes. Lucky was it for thee, truly, that those knaves did not find thee in thy swoon. They were the people, no doubt, who kindled yon rousing fire, from which they were probably driven away by our first appearance on the hill. Thou were lying scarcely half a cross-bow shot from the very spot where they must have been making merry, and if they had but stumbled on thee by accident, their cure for thy wound would have been a dirk-point. Holy Saint Michael, what an escape thou hast made!"

The way to Curgarf was long and tiresome enough, for they had to cross over the very summit of the mountain-ridge—that, I mean, which now divides us from the water of Don. But Patrick Stewart bore the fatigue of the walk better than any, one could have expected, and there was no doubt that the prospect of seeing Catherine Forbes very much improved his animal powers. He was already known to his friend's father, who received him hospitably, though rather haughtily. The old Lord of Curgarf's coldness of carriage towards him was to be attributed to the suspicion he entertained of that which was in reality true, that a secret attachment existed between Patrick Stewart and his only daughter Catherine. This he did not wish to encourage for many reasons. The Clan-Allan Stewarts—to say nothing of what he considered their questionable origin—were a new race in the neighbouring strath; and although he had never been actually at war with them, there had yet been many petty grievances and heart-burnings between them and his people. These had not in the least shaken the friendship that had accidentally arisen, during their boyhood, between Patrick Stewart and Arthur Forbes; and you all know, gentlemen, that the affections of a woman's heart are but little swayed by any such circumstances. The bonny blue eyes of Catherine Forbes sparkled, and her bosom heaved with delight, when she saw Patrick Stewart enter the hall of Curgarf, though she was compelled to keep down her emotions, and receive him as a mere acquaintance. Certain stolen glances did, however, pass between them; and when Arthur mentioned the accident which had led to his bringing his friend to the castle, and made him exhibit his wound, Catherine had an opportunity of giving way, in some degree, to her feelings, without the risk of being chargeable with anything more than that compassion naturally to be expected from a lady, even towards a perfect stranger, who came under such circumstances. Patrick was by this time satisfied that the wound was of no great moment. But his love for Catherine, and the opportunity which it thus happily afforded him of being under the same roof with her, made him very cautious in contending that it was not severe, and he had no objection to admit, when he was much pressed, that the pain he suffered from the contusion which his head had received, was very considerable.

Patrick retired to his chamber that night, his mind filled with the lovely image of Catherine Forbes, his eyes having done little else, during the evening meal, than carefully to collect and treasure every minute beauty of her fair countenance, and graceful person, so as to deepen the lines of that portrait of her which had been for some time engraven on his heart. But fond as he was of dwelling upon so much loved an object, he felt it difficult to keep possession of her image, or to prevent it from being driven from his memory, by the frequent recurrence of that horrible scene, of which he had witnessed so much, previous to his being rendered unconscious, as well as to overcome the distressing recollection of his brother Walter's violence towards himself, and he found it a very difficult matter to control his mind so far as to prevent his imagination from sketching out the revolting circumstances of the catastrophe that followed, with a degree of detail, and in colours, scarcely less appalling than those of the dreadful reality.

Patrick was next morning blessed with a short private interview with Catherine Forbes. It was short indeed, but it was long enough to give time for the ingenuity of lovers to arrange a plan for a more satisfactory meeting. It was agreed between them, that they should separately steal out in the evening, to a grove of ancient pine trees near the Castle, where, if I mistake not, they had met with one another before, with the sanction of Arthur Forbes. There they hoped for leisure and privacy enough to enable them more fully to open their hearts to each other, and to talk of their future hopes and fears. Contented with this arrangement, Patrick submitted to the confinement which was imposed upon him in his character of an invalid, and spent the day in basking silently in the sunshine of his lady's eyes, in conversing with his friend Arthur as the confidant of their loves, and in doing all that in him lay to thaw the icy politeness of the old Lord of Curgarf. An earnest desire to make one's self agreeable to another, will generally succeed, in some degree, in the long run; but Patrick's success with the old Lord was much beyond what he could have believed or expected.

"Truly thou art a pretty fellow, Patrick!" said Arthur Forbes jocularly to him, at the first private moment which he chanced to catch. "Judging by the proximity of the place where you were found lying last night, to the fire which had been kindled by the Catteranes, there can be no doubt that you must have fallen among thieves. This being the case, I, like the good Samaritan, pick thee up by the wayside, bring thee here in thy wretchedness, pour wine and oil into thy wounds, and see thee well fed and lodged; and how dost thou repay me, I prythee? Why, not contented with carrying off my poor love-sick sister's heart, thou art likely to run away with the old man's too."

"I rejoice to hear that I have any such chance," replied Patrick; "I had feared that thy father's coldness towards me was invincible."

"Nay, promise me not to interfere with my birthright, by taking away half my father's lands with Kate, and I will tell thee what he said of thee but half an hour ago."

"I should be too happy to have thy treasure of a sister, with nothing but the sandals her fair feet tread on," said Patrick, with enthusiasm.

"Tush, man!" replied Arthur Forbes, "be assured thou shalt have her some day or other; aye, and a bit of land, and some good purses of broad pieces with her to boot. But hear what the Lord of Curgarf said,—'Arthur, do you know that friend of thine hath a mighty pleasant manner with him; yea, and his discourse is more worth listening to than a young man's talk usually is: moreover, he hath a certain noble air withal. I remember that, when I was a child, I was once taken to visit the old Earl of Athol. His appearance made so strong an impression on me, that I think I see him yet, and that Patrick Stewart is the very image of his progenitor.' There is for you, my gallant friend! As to finding thee agreeable, I marvel not much at that; for other people, both men and women too, have been before him in making that wonderful discovery; and then, seeing that thou didst listen so well to his talk, and agree with him in everything he propounded, his finding that your conversation was good was all natural enough. But to discover that you bore so strong a resemblance to the old Earl of Athol—a person whom he is ever ready to cite as the pattern of everything that was graceful and pleasing in days long gone by, and now never to be matched again—ha! that was something indeed to give thee a great stride into the citadel of his affection."

"Be the breach through which I may be allowed to march in thither, produced how it may," said Patrick Stewart, "I am not sorry at thine intelligence. But, much as I love the good Lord of Curgarf's converse, I must freely tell thee that I would fain slip away from it, for some half hour or so, before supper to-night, unperceived by him, to exchange it for that of thy sweet sister. We have not had above five words of private conference together since I entered the Castle. So pray have the charity to keep thy worthy father in talk, while the Lady Catherine and I are out, for a brief space, on an evening walk."

"A pretty use thou wouldst put me to, truly!" said Arthur Forbes, laughing. "But to pleasure thee, thou shalt be obeyed."

The lovers waited with no little impatience for the hour which was to yield them the desired meeting. When it at length arrived, they stole out at different moments, and went by different ways to the trysting spot. No one but a lover can fully estimate the delight of such a stolen interview as this was. They felt it deeply; and the only difficulty they had was in estimating the lapse of time. The surly-toned bell, that pealed from the tower of the Castle at some distance, warned them to separate, ere, by their calculation, they had been more than a few short minutes together.

"Must we then part so soon?" said Patrick, fondly. "How swiftly the moments have flown!"

"I dare not tarry one instant longer," said the Lady Catherine; "my father, you well know, ——"

"Alas! I do know," interrupted Patrick; "yet have I now some hopes of working my way into his good favour. But I shall tell you more of this anon. We shall meet again to-morrow night, shall we not?"

"Yes, yes!" replied Catherine, hurriedly.

"At the same hour and place?" said Patrick. "Alas! till then I must be contented with such converse with thee as our eyes may yield us: and blessings on thine for the intelligence they convey to me."

"I hope my father may not be able to read them so readily," replied Catherine. "But I must go now."

"Stay for one moment, my sweetest heart," said Patrick. "Ere you go, let me fix thine arryssade more firmly over thy bosom." And, as he said so, he took from his sporran a golden brooch, formed of two entwined hearts, set with garnets.

" Wear this trifle for my sake over thy heart. And now may I say, what I dare not utter in thy father's hall—Farewell, my love—my dearest Catherine ! "

"Farewell! farewell! my dearest Patrick!" replied she, with a throbbing heart. "I shall never part with this thy gift whilst life or sense endures; and I shall wear it ever thus, as thou sayest, over this heart, which beats but for thee alone."

Thus they at last parted, with lingering reluctance; and each took a different and circuitous way to return to the Castle.

As Patrick entered the hall, a significant nod passed between him and Arthur Forbes. Soon afterwards, the retainers came crowding in, and the evening meal was placed on the board by the serving men. The piper had played his accustomed number of turns upon his walk, in the open gallery over the court-yard. All were ready to sit down. But there was one most important personage wanting; I mean the fair Lady Catherine Forbes. The fashion of the house, as well as of all well fashioned houses of the time, forbade their sitting down till the lady appeared. The Lord of Curgarf grew impatient.

"Go!" said he at length to one of the attendants; "go, and send some of the women to knock at the Lady Catherine's chamber door, to tell her that supper is served, and that we wait for her presence."

Again the company remained standing for some time. The old Lord of Curgarf arose from his arm chair, and took two or three turns on the large hearth before the fire place. Meanwhile, Arthur Forbes stole an enquiring glance at Patrick Stewart, but could gather nothing in reply. At length the Lady Catherine's bower woman entered the hall, pale and trembling.

"What wouldst thou say, girl?" cried the Lord of Curgarf. "What of my daughter? Thy looks are ominous! She is not ill?"

"No, my Lord," replied the girl, "my Lady is not ill; that is, she was quite well little more than an hour ago—but—but——"

"But what?" cried Arthur Forbes, anxiously; "cannot the girl speak out?"

"Tempted by the balmy evening," replied the girl, "my Lady threw her arryssade about her, and walked forth beyond the castle walls, as her custom sometimes is, to breathe the air a little while."

"Run!—fly all of you!—take lights, and search for her everywhere?" cried the Lord of Curgarf. "How provoking this is! How often have I tried in vain to cure her of this most foolish and pernicious custom! And then to go without an attendant too! and beyond the walls!—how very imprudent!"

The two friends were among the first to hurry out, in obedience to these orders from the old man. Both were extremely agitated; and, so far as this example went, it would have been difficult to have, from it, determined the question whether the affection of a loving brother or a tender lover, should be accounted the greater. Arthur Forbes was eager for some explanation from Patrick Stewart as to what he knew of the Lady Catherine. But, alas! Patrick could give him no information beyond that which I have already detailed to you. Leaving the crowd of the retainers to examine every hole and corner, bush and brake, immediately around the castle walls, Arthur and Patrick, from their knowledge of circumstances, pushed their search farther; and as they secretly knew the way that Catherine had taken from the pine grove homewards, they looked diligently for her all along the path. Of her, or anything belonging to her, they discovered nothing. But at last, in one place, where the path ran through a thicket, where the ground was soft, they were struck with the appearance of numerous newly impressed prints of footsteps. On examining these more closely by means of a torch, they observed, among those of many a rude brogue and sandal, mixed and mingled together, and pointing in all directions, as if those who wore them had been engaged in hurried action—among all these, I say, they observed one tiny and delicate footprint, which was here and there perceptible, and which Patrick Stewart at once declared, could have belonged to no one but to the Lady Catherine Forbes. Wild with dread and alarm, they returned to the castle. On questioning the warder, he admitted that he did remember having heard something like a woman's shriek, that came faintly from some distance in the direction of the thicket, but as it was immediately drowned by the first drone of the piper's warning, and had been heard by him no more, it had passed away altogether from his thoughts. Not a doubt now remained in their minds, that the Lady Catherine had been carried off by some villains, who had been lurking about the castle. The old Lord of Curgarf was inconsolable. He was quite unmanned, and unable to give an order as to what should be done. His son Arthur, the Master of Forbes, lost no time in acting for him. The retainers were hastily armed, and commanded to prepare for instant pursuit; and, being divided, at Patrick Stewart's request, into two bands, the

friends determined each to take the command of one of them,
—and accordingly, with such hasty refreshments as the men
could snatch, and carry with them, they took leave of one
another, and started off, each upon such a line of country as
he, in his quickly summoned forethought, judged to be the
most likely to bring his expedition to a successful termination.

As we have already learned from the conversation of the
Master of Forbes, when he first met Patrick Stewart after the
accident which befell him near Dalestie, it was pretty generally
known in the country, at this time, that a gang of Catteranes,
or free-booters, from the west, were occasionally harboured
somewhere among the neighbouring mountains, but no one
could precisely tell whereabouts they most commonly secreted
themselves. On this point, however, Patrick Stewart had some
general suspicions, though he knew nothing that could lead him
to guess—even within miles—as to the exact spot where their
lurking place might be. He took his way directly over the
mountain that separates the upper part of the river Don from
the Aven, and he descended towards the valley of the latter
stream, through that precipitous ravine, that affords a course for
the little tributary burn of Cuachan-Seirceag, down the face of
the white cliffs that almost overhang the small house of Inchrory, which, if we be all spared gentlemen, we shall see this
night before we sleep. There is not a tree there now; but, at
that period, the ravine was thickly shaded by such timber as
could find footing or nourishment among the rocks, and it
therefore formed a good and well-known place of shelter.
Having fixed on it as the point of rendezvous, Patrick took his
way up the valley of the Aven for some little distance, and then,
dividing his people into two parties, he sent one of them off by
the pass leading in the direction of Loch Builg, whilst he
continued to lead the other up that which is more properly
called Glen Aven, by the Lynn of Aven, where the river throws
itself over the rocks in a fine wild fall. Having then ascended
the mountains, he began, by break of day, to march, and
countermarch, over and across them, visiting, and carefully
examining every retired nook or corner that he thought might
be the least likely to be chosen, by such villains, as a hiding-
place, until mid-day came without bringing him the least clue to
the object of his search. Then it was that he unwillingly
halted his party in a hollow by the side of a spring, that the
poor fellows might refresh themselves with food, and rest for a
time.

THE SERJEANT HALTED FOR REFRESHMENT.

Clifford (Interrupting the Serjeant).—Gentlemen, I beg to remark, that I think it would be quite proper that we should refresh ourselves with food, whilst Mr. Patrick Stewart and his party are engaged in doing so. We shall thus save time, as must be self-evident to all, seeing that the action of the story is thus brought, for a little while, to a state of repose. Of bodily rest we have had enough, in all conscience—thanks to the length of Mister Archy's yarn.

Grant.—I beg to second the motion of our worthy secretary, which, in my mind, is most sensible.

Clifford.—Methinks, then, that a slice or two from that cold round of beef, which I saw so carefully bestowed in the right hand pannier on the pony's back, would come well in as an episode to Serjeant Stewart's story. Here Davy, untruss, if you please.

Grant.—Spread the cloth before us here on the grass, and then lay out the eatables.

Clifford.—Now, methinks, we can more readily sympathise with Patrick Stewart and his people at their luncheon. But come, Davy ; we must have something potable too.

Author.—Bring us one of those bottles from the pannier on the other side of the pony.

Clifford.—Aye, that's right ; something to wash the dust out of the serjeant's throat would considerably improve his voice. What say you to my prescription, Archy?

Serjeant.—Troth, sir, you're an excellent doctor. Well, here's wishing all your good healths, gentlemen !

Author.—By the way, Clifford, how many trouts have you caught?

Clifford.—None of your jokes, my good friend. Why, you know very well that I have never made a single cast. Before I had time to give one throw over the stream, Archy hooked me here with the thread of his discourse, and here he has been reeling me out such a line, that I can plainly see it will be some time ere he can wind it up again so as to land me. Fish !—no, no, I may as well put up my rod at once, that we may all hear his Legend quietly to an end.

Author.—I think so, indeed.

Grant.—Well, Archy, when you think that your Patrick Stewart and his party have had their luncheon, and that you have satisfied your own hunger and thirst, we shall all be ready to listen to you.

Serjeant.—I am well served now, sir, and quite ready to proceed.

Clifford.—Spin away then, my gay fellow.

LEGEND OF THE CLAN-ALLAN STEWARTS CONTINUED.

WITH a view of multiplying the chances which might still remain of effecting the anxious object of his expedition, Patrick Stewart had no sooner started again from the heather where they had been seated, than he subdivided his party into several sections, under certain intelligent leaders, and having given to each of them such instructions as he deemed necessary for their guidance, he sent them off in different directions, with orders to meet together again, by nightfall, at the ravine of Cuachan-Seirceag. There they were all to wait till he should join them, unless in the event of the Lady Catherine being recovered by any of them, in which case they were to proceed in a body, without tarrying, to carry her straight to Curgarf, leaving one of their number behind them to certify him of the agreeable intelligence. For his own part, he took with him a single attendant only, one of the Curgarf retainers, called Michael Forbes, with whose superior sagacity and activity, some former circumstances had led him to be more particularly acquainted.

After all the others had left them, Patrick and his companion began a most particular and persevering search through the forest, and among the mountains, of that part of the country which he had especially marked out and reserved for himself, leaving no spot unexplored that had anything the least suspicious connected with it. But the wilderness through which they wandered was so wide, and, in many places, so very thickly wooded, that they might have been employed for days in the same way, without his being one whit nearer his object. It is not wonderful, then, that the evening began to manifest its approach, whilst he was yet actively engaged in laborious travel, yet still he bore on with unremitting exertion, altogether unconscious of the wane of day.

The wild scenery by which he was surrounded was beginning to grow dim in the increasing obscurity, when he arrived at the edge of a deep corry or ravine, in the steeply inclined side of a mountain. It was a place, of the existence of which, neither he nor his companion had ever been aware, well as they were both acquainted with the mountains. The precise position of it has been long ago forgotten; and indeed, if it could be guessed at, it is probably now so altered, and blocked up, by the fall of the mountain masses from time to time, as to be no longer in such a state as might admit of its being identified. But it was one of those rugged places of which there are plenty of examples among these mountains. The elevation on the mountain side was not greater than to have allowed Nature, at that time, to have carried the forest partially up around it, and the wood, that in a great measure concealed it, was chiefly composed of the mountain pine. The trees, which were seen struggling against the wintry tempests that prevailed around the summits of the cliffs above, appeared twisted and stunted, yet they grew thickly and sturdily together, as if resolved, like bold Highlanders in possession of a dangerous post, to put shoulder to shoulder for the determined purpose of maintaining their position, in defiance of the raging elements. Their foliage was shorn, not thinned by the blast. On the contrary, it was thickened by it, from that very clipping to which the storms so continually subjected it, so that the shade which was formed by their tops overhead, was thereby rendered just so much the more dense and impenetrable. The narrow and inclined bottom of the immense gully below, was composed of enormous fragments, which had been wedged out by time and frosts from the faces of the overhanging crags, and piled one over the other to an unknown depth, whilst the ground, that sloped rapidly down into it, from the lower part of the abrupt faces of the precipices on either side, was covered with small and lighter materials of the same sort, mingled with a certain proportion of soil. There some scattered trees had been enabled to grow to a huge size, from the uninterrupted shelter which the place afforded; but whilst few of these had altogether escaped injury and mutilation from the frequent descent of the stony masses, many of them had been entirely uprooted and overturned, by the immense magnitude of some of those falling rocks which had swept down upon them, and there lay their enormous trunks, resting upon their larger limbs, or upon one another, the whole being tossed and tumbled together in most intricate confusion, so as to cover the rocky fragments beneath them, with one continued and almost impervious natural *chevaux-de-frize.*

Patrick Stewart halted behind the bole of a tree, and, resting against it, so as to enable him to lean forward over the precipice, he surveyed the gulf below, as accurately as the evening twilight, and the intervening obstacles permitted him to do.

He and Michael Forbes then stole slowly and silently along the very verge of it, in that direction that lay down the mountain side, using their eyes sharply and earnestly as they went, and peering anxiously everywhere, with the hope of discovering some track which might tend downwards into the ravine. While so occupied, Patrick became suddenly sensible of the fresh smell of wood smoke. From the manner in which it was necessarily diffused, by the multiplied network of boughs through which it had to ascend, he looked for it in vain for some time, till he accidentally observed one or two bright fiery sparks mount upwards from below, such as may be often seen to arise from a cottage chimney top, when new fuel has been thrown upon the fire by the people within. Marking, with great atten- tion, the spot whence these had proceeded, he commenced a more narrow examination of the edge of the ravine, until he at length discovered a perforation in the brushwood, so small, that it might have been easily mistaken for the avenue leading to the den of some wild beast, but which, a closer inspection persuaded him, might have been used by human creatures, there being quite enough of room for one man at a time to creep through it in a stooping posture. At all events he was resolved to explore it, and accordingly, having first stationed his attendant, Michael Forbes, in a concealed place, near to its entrance, that he might watch and give him warning if any one approached from without, he bent himself down, and began his strange and hazardous enterprise.

Creeping along, with his bonnet off, and almost on his hands and knees, he found that the track, which inclined gently at first over the rounded edge of the ravine, became, as he pro- ceeded, nearly as steep as an upright ladder, but it was less encumbered with branches than the first part of the way had been, though there was still enough of growth to aid him in his descent, and to take away all appearance of danger. It went diagonally down the face of the cliff, dropping from one narrow ledge of footing in the rock, to that beneath it, with considerable intervals between each. But to one accustomed, as Patrick Stewart was, to scramble like a goat, the difficulties it presented were as nothing. All his anxiety and care was exerted to guard, if possible, against surprise, as well as against making any noise that might betray his approach, to any one who might be harboured in the ravine below.

Having at last got to the foot of the precipice, he found it somewhat easier to descend the rugged slope that inclined downwards from its base, and, upon reaching the bottom, he discovered that the track continued to lead onwards under the arched limbs of an overthrown pine, the smaller branches and spray of which, appeared, on a minute examination, to have been evidently broken away by frequent passage through underneath it. This circumstance he had some difficulty in discovering, as the increasing darkness was rendered deeper here, by the overhanging shade of the rocks and trees high above him. Bending beneath the boughs of the fir, he advanced with yet greater caution, and with some difficulty, over the rugged and angular fragments, until he suddenly observed something that made it prudent for him to halt for a moment, that he might well consider his position. This abrupt stop was occasioned by his observing a faint gleam of light, that partially illumined the broad side, and moss-grown edge, of a large mass of stone, a little way in advance of the place where he then was. He hardly breathed, and he tried to listen—and, for a moment, he fancied he heard a murmur like that of human voices. Again he stretched his ear, and again he felt persuaded that he heard the sound of the voices coming hollow on his ear, as if from some cavity, somewhere below the surface, at a little distance beyond him. Resolving at last to proceed, he moved on gently, and upon a nearer approach to the great stone, on the broad edge of which the light fell, he found that it formed one side of a natural entrance to a passage, that led upwards under the enormous superincumbent masses, that had been piled up over it, in their fall from the shattered crags above. Pausing again for a moment, he drew himself up behind a projecting part of another huge stone, that formed the dark side of the entrance, that he might again listen. He was now certain that he distinctly heard voices proceeding from within, though he was not yet near enough to the speakers to be able to make out their words. The smell of the wood smoke was exceedingly powerful, and his heart began to beat high, for he was now convinced that his adventure was drawing to a crisis.

He plucked forth his dirk, and stooped to enter the place. He found the passage to be low, narrow, gently ascending, and running somewhat in an oblique direction, from the illuminated stone at the mouth, for a few paces inwards, till it met with another block of great size. The edges of this block glowed with a brighter light, that seemed to come directly upon it, at a right angle, from some fire, not then visible, but which was evidently blazing within, and which was again reflected from the side of this stone towards that of the stone at the entrance.

Having crept onwards to this second fragment of rock, where the passage took its new direction, he discovered that it led into a large, and very irregularly-shaped chamber, which was within a few feet only of the spot which he had now reached, but he had no accurate means of judging of the full extent of the cavern. He could now see the rousing fire that was burning in a recess in the side of the rocky wall of the place, the smoke from which seemed to find its way upwards, through some natural creyice immediately over it, for the interior of this subterranean den was by no means obscured by any great accumulation of it. By the light of the fire, one or two dark holes were seen, apparently forming low passages of connection with other chambers. How many living beings the place might then contain, he had no means of knowing or guessing. All that came within the field of his vision, were two persons, which he supposed were those whose voices he had heard. One of these was a slim youth, who was employed in feeding the fire from time to time with pieces of rotten wood and branches, and in attending to a large pot, that hung over it by an iron chain, depending from a strong hook fastened in the rock above. But the youth and his occupations were altogether disregarded by Patrick Stewart, in the intense interest and delight which he experienced in beholding the Lady Catherine Forbes, the fair object of his toilsome search, who sat pensively and in tears, on a bundle of heather on the farther side of the fire.

You will easily believe, gentlemen, that it was difficult for him to subdue his impatient feelings, so far as to restrain himself from at once rushing forward to snatch her to his arms. But prudence whispered him that her safety might depend on the caution he should use. Ignorant as he was of the extent of the subterranean den, or how it might be tenanted, he felt the necessity of exerting his self-command, and to remain quietly where he was for a little time, until he might be enabled to form some judgment, from what he should see and hear, as to the probable force he should have to contend with, as well as to determine what might be his best plan of action.

"If thou wouldst but listen to my entreaty," said Catherine Forbes, addressing the youth in an earnest tone of supplication, whilst the tears that ran down her cheeks roused Patrick's feelings to an agonising pitch of intensity—"If thou wouldst but fly with me, and take me to Curgarf, my father would give thee gold onough to enrich thee and thine for all thy life."

"I tell thee again that it is useless to talk of it, lady," replied the youth. "I have already told thee that I pity thee, but it were more than my life were worth to do as thou wouldst have me. And what is gold, I pray thee, compared to such a risk?"

"Methinks that, once out amidst these wide hills and forests, the risk would be but small indeed," said Catherine.

"That is all true," replied the youth. "The hills and forests are wide; but the men of the band well know every nook and turn of them. Nay, they are everywhere, and come pop upon one at the very time when they are least looked for. Holy Virgin, an' we were to meet any of them as we fled!—My head sits uneasily on my neck at the very thought!—By the Rood, but there would be a speedy divorce between them! and where would your gold be then, lady?"

"Then let me go try to explore mine own way without thee," said the Lady Catherine.

"Talk not of it, lady," replied the youth, impatiently. "My head would go for it, I tell thee. It would go the moment they should return and find that thou hadst escaped. They may be already near at hand, too, if I mistake not the time of evening. Therefore, tease me no more, I pray thee."

"Spirits of mine ancestors, give me strength and boldness!" cried the Lady Catherine, starting up energetically, after a moment's pause, during which she seemed to have taken her resolution, and assuming a commanding attitude and air as she spoke. Let me pass, young man!—give me way, I say!—or I will struggle with thee to the death, but I will force a passage!"

"I have a sharp argument against that," said the youth, drawing his dirk, and planting himself in the gap before her. "Stand back!—or thou shalt have every inch of its blade."

"Out of the way, vermin!" cried Patrick Stewart, no longer able to contain his rage, and dashing down the youth before him as he entered.

"Patrick!—my dear Patrick!" cried the Lady Catherine, flying into his arms with a scream of joy.

"My dearest, dearest Catherine!" said Patrick, fondly—"this is indeed to be rewarded!—Wretch!" cried he, grappling the youth by the throat, and putting the point of his dirk to his breast, as he was in the act of rising from the ground, apparently with the intention of making his escape—"Wretch! our safety requires thy death."

"Oh, do not kill me, good Sir Knight!" cried the terrified youth piteously, and with a countenance as pale as a corpse.

"Spare him!—spare him!" cried Catherine,—"his worthless life is unworthy of thy blade."

" Oh, mercy, mercy ! " cried the youth again. " Spare me !
—oh, do not kill me ! "

" If I did kill thee, it would be no more than what thou hast
well merited," said Patrick. " But, as thou sayest, Catherine,
my love, such worthless blood should never wantonly soil the
steel of a brave man ; and if I could but make him secure by
any other means, I should be better contented."

" Bind me, if thou wilt, Sir Knight ; but, oh, do not !—do
not kill me ! " cried the youth.

" Well then, I will spare thy life, though I half question the
wisdom of so doing," said Patrick.

Casting his eyes around the cave, he espied some ropes lying
in a dark corner. Catherine flew and brought them to him.
He seized them, and quickly bound the youth neck and heel,
in such a manner as to make it quite impossible for him to move
body or limb, and then, lifting him in his arms, he groped his
way with him into the farther end of one of those dark recesses
that branched off from the main cavern, and there he deposited
him.

" Now, let us fly, my love ! " cried he, hastily returning to
the Lady Catherine. " Every moment we tarry here is fraught
with danger. Follow me quickly !—I grieve to think of the
fatigue you must undergo. But cheer up, and trust for your
defence, from all danger, to this good arm of mine. Above all
things, be silent."

" With thee as my protector I am strong and bold," said
Catherine. " Thanks be to the Virgin for this deliverance ! "

Patrick now led the Lady Catherine forth into the open air.
But before he ventured to proceed, he listened for a moment
to ascertain that there was no one near. To his great horror,
and to the lady's death-like alarm, they distinctly heard a
footstep slowly and cautiously approaching. Pushing Catherine gently behind the dark mass of stone at the entrance, he
placed himself before her in the shadow, that, whilst concealed
by it himself, he might have a perfect view of whosoever came,
the moment the person should advance into the light, that was
reflected on the wall-like side of the rocky mass opposite to
him, and fell on the ground for a little space beyond it. He
listened, with attention so breathless, that he seemed to hear
every beat of his own heart, as well as of that of his trembling
companion. The footstep was that of one person only, and he
felt as if his resolution was quite equal to an encounter with a
dozen ; but he knew not how many might be following, and
he was fully conscious of the importance, as regarded the lady,

6

of avoiding a conflict, unless rendered indispensable by circumstances. The step came on, falling gently, at intervals of several moments, as if the individual who approached was unwilling to make the least unnecessary noise. The dim figure of a man at length appeared, under the arched boughs of the fallen pine tree. He advanced, step by step, with increased caution. A dirk blade, which he held forward in his outstretched hand, first caught the stream of reflected light that came from the mouth of the cavern. The next step that the figure took brought his face under its influence; and, to the great relief of Patrick Stewart, displayed the features of Michael Forbes. Patrick gave a low whistle. Michael had at that moment stopped to listen, with a strange expression of dread and horror, to the complaints of the youth who was bound in the innermost recesses of the cavern, whence they came, reduced by its sinuosities, into a low wild moaning sound, that had something supernatural in it, so as to be quite enough to appal any superstitious mind. The whistle startled him.

"Michael!" said Patrick in a low tone of voice, "why did'st thou desert thy post?"

"Holy virgin, is that you, Sir Knight?" said Michael, in a voice which seemed to convey a doubt whether he was not holding converse with a spirit.

"What could make you desert your post?" demanded Patrick, angrily, and at the same time showing himself.

"Holy saints, I am glad that it is really you, Sir Knight," replied Michael. "I crave your pardon, but your long delay led me to fear that something had befallen you, and that you might lack mine aid."

"Had an accident befallen me, Michael," said Patrick, "thine aid, I fear, would have been of little avail. But we have lost much time by this thy neglect of mine orders. Quick! let us lose no more, and give me thy best help to aid thy mistress, the Lady Catherine."

"The Virgin be praised!" exclaimed Michael, as Catherine appeared; "then the lady is safe!"

"But so far only," replied Patrick Stewart. "We have yet much peril to encounter; but our perils are increased every precious moment that we loiter here. Get thee on quickly before us to the top of the path where it quits the ravine,—the spot, I mean, where I left thee, and see that you be sure to give me good warning, shouldst thou see or hear anything to cause alarm."

Michael obeyed; and Patrick, having led Catherine out from under the boughs of the fallen pine, began to assist her in ascending the path. He had some difficulty in dragging her up the wild-cat's ladder that scaled the side of the cliff; but, by the assistance of his strongly nerved arm, she reached the summit without danger. She then forced her way through the narrow passage in the brushwood that grew over the top of the crags, until she had at length the satisfaction of being able to stand erect, to receive the cooling mountain breeze on her flushed cheek and throbbing temples. But this was no place for them to rest. Patrick whistled softly, and Michael appeared.

"Catherine, my love," said he, "this is no time for cere-mony. Give one arm to Michael, and put the other firmly into mine—so. Now take the best care you can of your footing, and lean well upon me as we go down the mountain side. Oh, how I long to talk to thee! But, dearest, we must be silent as death, for we know not whom we may meet."

After a long, rough, and slippery descent, they came at length into a narrow glen, where the trees grew taller and farther apart from each other. This was so far fortunate for them; for as the shadows of night became deeper here than they had been on the mountain side, they were compelled to move slower; and it required all the care of the Lady Catherine's supporters, to save her from the injuries she might have sustained from the numerous fallen branches, and other obstacles lying in their way.

They had nearly reached the lower extremity of this lesser tributary glen, where it discharged a small rill into the wider glen and stream of the Aven, when Patrick Stewart suddenly halted.

"Stop!" cried he; "I hear voices on the breeze, and they come this way too. We must up the bank, Michael. Courage, my dearest Catherine! let me help thee to climb. Trust me love, thou hast nothing to fear."

"I fear nothing whilst thou art by my side," replied Catherine, exerting herself to the utmost.

"Now," said Patrick, after they had half carried her some thirty or forty paces up the steep slope; "we have time to go no farther. Hark! they come! Stretch thyself at length among this long heather, Catherine, and let me throw my plaid over thee. Nay, now I think on't, Michael's green one is better, the red of mine might be more visible. There; that will do. Now, Michael, draw thy good claymore, as I do mine. Here are two thick trunks which stand well placed in front of us. Do thou take thy stand behind that one, whilst I post myself behind this, so that both of us may he between the lady and danger. They cannot come at her but by passing between us. And if they do! But see that thou dost not strike till I give thee the word. Hush! they come!" ·

They had hardly thus disposed of themselves, when the voices drew nearer, and the dusky figures were obscurely seen moving up the bottom of the little glen. They came loitering on, one after another, in what we of the army used to call Indian files,—man following man along the track, where they knew that the footing was likely to be the best. This plan of march necessarily made them longer of passing by, but it relieved those who were lurking in the bank above from any great fear of being discovered by any stray straggler. Two individuals of the party, who had probably some sort of command over the rest, were considerably in advance. These lingered on their way, and halted more than once to give time for those that followed to come up, so that Patrick Stewart caught a sentence or two of the conversation that fell from them.

"He must be as cunning as the devil," said one of them to the other, in Gaelic.

"Thou knowest that she has not yet seen his face," replied the other: "so that, when he comes to act the part of her deliverer, she will never suspect that it was to him she was indebted for her unwilling travel last night, and her present confinement. And then, you see, he thinks, in this way, to make his own, both of her and her old father, by his pretended gallantry in rescuing her from——"

Patrick Stewart in vain stretched his ears to catch more, for on came the rest in closer lines, gabbling together so loudly about trifles, and with voices so commingled, that it was not possible to gather the least sense out of their talk. These all passed onwards; and, a little way behind them, came four other men, who walked very slowly, and stopped occasionally to converse in Gaelic, like people who were so travel-worn, that they were not sorry to halt now and then, and to rest against a tree for a few moments.

"What made Grigor Beg stop behind Allister?" demanded one.

"Hoo! you may well guess it was nothing but his old trick," replied the other. "The boddoch would have fain had me to tarry for him, that I might help him, by carrying a part of what load he might get. But I was no such fool. My shoulders ache enough already with carrying the rough rungs of that accursed litter last night, to let me wish for any new burden."

"If thou hadst not been carrying the bonny lassie for another's pleasure, methinks you would maybe have thought less of it," said a third man.

Whilst attentively listening to this dialogue, Patrick Stewart observed some ill-defined object, coming stealing up the slope of the bank, in a diagonal line, from the place a little way down the glen, where the four men had halted. It came on noiselessly, but steadily pointing towards the spot where Catherine lay. It stopped, and uttered a short bark, and Patrick now saw that it was a large, rough, Highland wolf-dog. Again, with its long snout directed towards the plaid that covered Catherine, it barked and snarled.

"Dermot, boy!—Dermot!"—cried one of the men from the hollow below. "What hast thou got there?"

As if encouraged by its master's voice, the animal barked and snarled again yet more eagerly, and seemed to be on the very eve of springing upon the plaid. The blade of Patrick Stewart's claymore made one swift circuit in the air, and, descending like a flash of lightning on the neck of the creature, his head and his body rolled asunder into different parts of the heather, and again Patrick took his silent but determined stand behind the tree.

"Dermot!—Dermot, boy!"—cried the man again from below.—"What think ye is the beast at, lads?"

"Some foulmart or badger it may be," replied another.

"Can'st thou not go up and see, man?" said a third.

"Go thyself, my good man," said the dog's master. "I am fond enough of the dog—aye, and, for that part, I am fond enough of travel too, but I am content with my share of fagg for this day without going up the brae there to seek for more. A man may e'en have his serving of the best haggis that ever came out of a pot. Trust me, I am for going no foot to-night beyond what I can help.—Dermot—Dermot, boy!—See ye any thing of him at all, lads?"

"The last sight that I had of him at all, was near yon dark looking hillock, a good way up the bank yonder," said another man.

"I'm thinking that the brute has winded a passing roebuck," said the fourth man, "I thought I saw something like a glimmer just against the light cloud yonder above, as if it had been the dog darting over the height, the very moment after the last bark he gave."

"Dermot! whif-hoo-if!" cried the dog's master, and, at the same time, whistling shrilly upon his fingers. "Tut! the fiend catch him for me! let him go! I'll be bound that he'll be home before us."

"Come, then, let's on!" said another. "I wonder much that Grigor Beg hath not come up with us ere this."

"Hulloah, Grigor!" shouted one of them. "No, no, we'll not see him so soon, I'll warrant ye."

"Come! come away, lads!" said another, moving on with the rest following him. "I'll be bound that the boddoch hath got a swingeing load upon his back."

"Awell!" said one of the first speakers, "rather him than me. But we shan't be the worse of it when it's well broiled, for all that. I'm sure I wish I had a bit of it at this moment, for I'm famishing. I'm dead tired to-night; I hope that we may have some rest to-morrow. Know ye ought that is to do?"

"I heard the Captain say that"—— but the rest of the dialogue was cut off by the distance which the men had by this time reached.

"Thanks be to St. Peter, they are gone at last!" said Patrick Stewart. "How my fingers itched to have a cut at the villains.—Catherine," continued he, lifting the plaid, and assisting her to rise, "art thou not half dead with terror? But courage, my love. There lies the murderous four-footed savage, whose fell fangs had so nearly been busied with the plaid that covered thee. If we may trust to what we have just heard, there is but one man to come; and, judging by the name of Beg* which they gave him, he ought to be no very formidable person. Michael, get thee on a few steps in front, and keep a good look out for him. Were we but out of this narrow place, and fairly into the wider glen of the Aven, we should have less to fear, and then we shall find means to carry thee."

"Thanks to the Virgin, I am yet strong," said Catherine. "Let us fly, then, with all speed."

A farther walk, of a few minutes only, brought them into Glen Aven, and they pursued its downward course, for a considerable length of way, until Patrick Stewart began to perceive something like fatigue in the Lady Catherine's step.

---

* Mòr, *great*, and Beg or Beag, *little*, are well known Highland cognomina, employed like Dubh, *black*, Ruadh, *red*, and Bàn, *white*, to distinguish different individuals of the same name.

He therefore halted, and made her sit down to rest a while. In the mean time, he and Michael Forbes contrived to hew down two small sapling fir trees, by the aid of their good claymores, and having tied their plaids between them, they, in this manner, very speedily constructed a tolerably easy litter for the lady to recline at length in. This they carried between them, by resting the ends of the poles upon their shoulders, Patrick making Michael Forbes go foremost, and reserving the place behind for himself. I need hardly tell you that the Stewart especially selected that position, for the obvious reason that he might be thereby enabled to cheer the Lady Catherine's spirits, and to lighten her fatigues, by now and then addressing a word or two of comfort to her as they went. In this manner they pursued their way down the glen, until the loud roar of many waters informed them that they were approaching the grand waterfall, called the Lynn of Aven. You will have ample opportunity of becoming intimately acquainted with all the details of this fine scene, gentlemen, as you go up the glen to-morrow. But in the meanwhile, I may tell you generally, that the whole of this large river, there precipitates itself headlong, through a comparatively narrow chasm in the rocks, into a long, wide, and extremely deep pool below.

The sound increased as the bearers of the litter drew nearer to the waterfall, and the rocky and confined passage, over which they had to make their way, compelled them to walk at greater leisure, and to select their footing with more caution. Fortunately they had now the advantage of the moon, which had been for some time shining favourably upon them, and they were already within a very few steps of coming immediately over the waterfall, when they were suddenly alarmed by a fearful and most unearthly shriek. It came apparently from the very midst of the descending column of water below them.

"Holy Virgin Mother!" cried Michael Forbes, halting, and backing like a restive horse, so unexpectedly, that the ends of the poles were nearly jerked from Patrick Stewart's shoulders, by the shock which was thus communicated to them. "Holy Mother, didst thou not hear that, Sir Knight?"

"I did hear something," said Stewart, not quite willing to increase that dread which he perceived was already quite sufficiently excited in his companion, and of which he could not altogether divest himself. "I did fancy that I heard something. But for the love of the Virgin take care what thou dost. Thou hadst almost shaken the poles from my shoulders by thy sudden start. Come! proceed, man!"

Again, a louder, and more appalling shriek arose from the midst of the cataract, piercing their ears above all the roaring of its thunder.

"For the love of all the saints, let us turn back, Sir Knight!" cried Michael. "It is the water-kelpie himself!"

"Nay," said Patrick Stewart; "back we may not go, without the risk of falling again into the very jaws of the Catteranes. They are no doubt hard on foot after us by this time. Forward then, and fear not!"

Again came the wild shriek, if possible louder and more terrible than before.

"For the love of God, Sir Knight, back!" cried Michael, now losing all command of himself, and forcing the litter so backwards upon Patrick Stewart, as to compel him, from the narrowness of the rocky shelf where they then stood, to retreat in a corresponding degree, to avoid the certain alternative of being precipitated over the giddy ledge into the boiling stream of the Aven. "For the love of God, back, I say! were it but for a few paces, till we have leisure to lay down our burden, and cross ourselves."

"Merciful saints! what will become of us?" cried the Lady Catherine, in great alarm.

"Now," said Patrick Stewart, after yielding a few steps, "now, we may surely halt here till thy courage return to thee, Michael. What a fiend hath so unmanned thee to-night? I thought thou hadst been brave as a lion."

"A fiend indeed, Sir Knight," replied Michael, as they were laying down the litter; "I trust that I lack not courage, at any time, to face any mortal foe that ever came before me. But," added he, eagerly crossing himself, "to meet with the devil thus in one's very path! Good angels be about us, heard ye not that scream again? Have mercy upon us all!"

"There is something very strange in this," said Patrick Stewart. "But this will never do. We cannot tarry here long without the certainty of being overtaken by the whole body of the Catteranes. By this time they must be well on their way in pursuit of us."

"Holy Virgin! what will become of us if we should fall into their hands?" cried the Lady Catherine, in an agony of distress.

"Fear not, my love!" said Patrick Stewart; "I will forthwith fathom this mystery. I will see whence these horrible screams proceed."

"Nay, Sir Patrick, tempt not thy fate," cried Michael. "If thou dost thou goest to thy certain destruction."

"Oh stir not, dear Patrick!" cried the Lady Catherine, starting up from the litter, and endeavouring to detain him. "Do not attempt so great, so dreadful a danger."

"Catherine, my dearest!" said Patrick, fondly taking her hands in his; "listen to reason, I entreat thee. The danger that presses on us from behind is imminent, and more than what two swords, good as they may be, could by any means save thee from. And since God hath given us strength to flee from it, he will not forsake me in a conflict with the powers of hell, should they stand in my way. I go forward in his holy name, then; have no fear for me therefore. Rest thine arm upon Michael, dearest—tell thy beads, and may the blessed Virgin hover over thee to protect thee! As for you, Michael, draw your claymore, and stir not a step from the lady till I call thee."

Patrick Stewart now crossed himself, and then strode slowly and resolutely along the narrow ledge of rock towards the roaring lynn, repeating a paternoster as he went. The moon was by this time high in the heavens, and its beams produced a faint tinge of the rainbow's hues, as they played among the mists that arose from the waterfall. The shrieks that came from below were now loud and incessant, and might have quailed the stoutest heart. But still Patrick advanced firmly, till he stood upon a shelving rock, forming the very verge of the roaring cataract, whence he could throw his eyes directly downwards, through the shooting foam, into the abyss below. Far down, in the midst of the rising vapour, and apparently suspended in it, close by the edge of the descending column of water, he could distinguish a dark object. New and more piercing screams arose from it. He bent forward, and looked yet more intently. To his no inconsiderable dismay, he beheld a fearful head rear itself, as it were from out of it; the long hair by which it was covered, and the immense beard that flowed from the chin, hanging down, drenched by the surrounding moisture, and the eyes glaring fearfully in the moonlight, whilst the terrific screams were inconceivably augmented. Appalled as he was by this most unaccountable apparition, Patrick was shifting his position, in order to lean yet more forward, that he might the better contemplate it, when the toe of his sandal grazed against something that had nearly destroyed his equilibrium, and sent him headlong over the rock. Having with some difficulty recovered himself, he stooped down to ascertain what had tripped him, when he found to his surprise that it was a rope. He now remembered that the feudal tenant of the neighbouring ground, who owed service to his father, Sir Allan, was accustomed to hang a conical creel, or large rude basket, by the edge of the fall, for the purpose of catching the salmon that fell into it after failing in their vain attempts to leap up.

"Ho, there!" cried Patrick Stewart, in that voice of thunder, which he required to exert in order to overcome the continuous roar of the cataract.

"Oh, help! help! help!" cried the fearful head from below.

"Man or demon, I will see what thou art!" cried Patrick, stooping down to lay hold of the rope, with the intention of making an attempt to pull up the creel.

"For the love of Saint Andrew, lay not a hand on the rope, Sir Knight, as thou may'st value thy life!" said Michael Forbes, who, having heard Patrick's loud shout, had been hurried off to his aid by the fears and the commands of the Lady Catherine.

"Why hast thou left the lady, caitiff?" demanded Patrick Stewart, angrily. "Did I not tell thee to stay with her till I should call thee?"

"We heard thee call loudly, Sir Knight," replied Michael, trembling more from his proximity to the place whence the screams had issued than from anything that Patrick had said.

"True, I had forgotten," replied Patrick; "I did call, though not on thee. But since thou art here, come lend me thy hand to pull up the basket."

"Nay, Sir Knight; surely thou art demented by devilish influence. For the love of all the saints!" cried Michael, quaking from head to foot; "for the love of ——"

"Dastard, obey my command, or I will hurl thee over the rock!" cried Patrick, furiously, and with a manner that showed Michael that it was time to obey. "Now, pull—pull steadily and firmly; pull away, I say!"

"Have mercy on us! have mercy on our souls!" cried Michael, pulling most unwillingly.

"What a fiend are you afraid of? Why don't you pull, I say?" cried the Knight again.

"Jesu Maria, protect me! that I should have a hand in any such work!" muttered Michael. "Oh, holy Virgin! to have thus to deal with the Devil himself!"

"Come! pull!—pull away, I tell ye—pull! aye, there!" cried Patrick Stewart, as the basket at last came to the top of the rock.

"Preserve us all!" cried Michael; "the water-kelpie, sure enough! Mercy on us, what a fearful red beard! what terrible fiery eyes! For the love of heaven, Sir Knight, let him down again!"

"Coward!" cried Patrick, "if you let go the rope, I'll massacre thee! Now, do you hear? pull the creel well out this way. Ha, that will do! Now I think it is safe."

"Oh, may the blessed saints reward thee!" said a little shred of a man, who now arose, shaking in a palsy of cold and wet, from the midst of at least a dozen large salmon, with which the creel was heaped up; "thou hast saved me from the most dreadful of deaths."

"How camest thou there?" demanded Patrick Stewart; "answer quickly, for we are in haste."

"Oh, I know not well how I got there," said the little man, shivering so that he could hardly speak. "I stepped aside from the path, just to take a look down to see if there were any salmon in the creel, when something took my foot, and over I went. Oh, what a providence it was that ye came by! Another hour and I must have been dead from cold and wet, and buried in salmon, for they were flying in upon me like so many swallows. I thought they would have choked me."

"Here," said Patrick Stewart, taking out a flask, "take a sup of this cordial; it will speedily restore thee."

"Oh, blessings on thee, Sir Knight!" said the little man; "I will drink thy health with good will. But tell me thy name, I pray thee, that I may know, and never forget, who it was that saved my life."

"I am Patrick Stewart of Clan-Allan," replied the knight carelessly. "Come now, Michael, we must tarry here no longer."

"Sure I am that I shall never forget the name of Sir Patrick Stewart," said the little man, whilst he was following them along the narrow path, as they retraced it towards the place where they had left the Lady Catherine; "and if ever I can do thee a good turn I shall do it, though it were by the sacrifice of my life."

Catherine's fears were soon allayed by the explanation that was given her. She was again put into the litter, which was quickly shouldered by her protectors, the little man lending them a willing helping hand; and Patrick and Michael proceeded on their way, whilst the half-drowned wretch went up the glen, pouring out blessings upon them. Without fear or interruption they now passed by the spot which had occasioned

them so much dread and delay, and they soon left the roar of
the lynn behind them, and at length reached the ravine of
Cuachan Searceag, where, much to their relief, they found the
whole of the party anxiously waiting for them. When the
Forbeses beheld Patrick Stewart, and, above all, when they
beheld their young mistress, the daughter of their chief, safe
and well among them, they rent the air with shouts of joy that
made the whole glen ring again.

" Aye," said Patrick Stewart, as they sat down to rest a little
while, and to take some hasty refreshment, " we may now
make what noise we list, for, if the whole gang of these accursed
Catteranes should come upon us, we have brave hearts and
keen claymores enow to meet them.   But, for all that, we have
too precious a charge with us to tarry for the mere pleasure of
a conflict ; so be stirring, my men, and let us breast the hill as
fast as may be."

You may all well enough guess, gentlemen, how Patrick
Stewart was received by the old Lord of Curgarf when he
entered his hall, leading in his fair daughter safe and sound.
The joy of the father was not the less, that his son, Arthur,
the Master of Forbes, had returned but a brief space of time
before, jaded, dispirited, and sorrowful, from his long, tiresome, and fruitless expedition.   Worn with anxiety, the old
man had counted watch after watch of the night, and the day
and the night again, until his son's arrival, and then he had
sunk into the most overwhelming despair.   After pouring
forth thanks to Heaven, and to all the saints, he now gave
way to his joy.   The midnight feast was spread, and all was
revelry and gladness in the castle, Patrick Stewart was now
viewed by him as his guardian angel.   Seeing this, Arthur
Forbes took an opportunity of advising his friend to profit by
the happy circumstance which had now placed him so high in
his father's good opinion.   He did so—and the result was,
that he obtained the willing consent of the old Lord of Curgarf
to his union with his daughter, the Lady Catherine, with the
promise of a tocher which should be worthy of her.

The happiness of the lovers was now complete, and the next
day was spent in open and unrestrained converse between
them.   The time was fixed for the wedding, and then it was,
after all these arrangements had been made, that Patrick
Stewart first had leisure fully to recall to mind, all those
afflicting circumstances which had taken place when he last saw
his brother Walter.   He thought of his father—he felt the
necessity of going immediately home, to relieve any anxiety

which his father, Sir Allan, might have, in consequence of his
unexplained absence, as well as to make him acquainted with
his approaching marriage. He accordingly took a tender leave
of his fair bride that evening, and, starting next morning, he
made his way over the hills to Drummin.

Patrick Stewart was already within sight of home, when his
attention was arrested by the blast of a bugle, which rang
shrilly from the hill above him. It conveyed to him that
private signal which was always used between his brother
Walter and himself. For the first time in his life it grated
harshly in his ear, for it immediately brought back to his
recollection those oppressively painful circumstances which had
occurred at Dalestie, which he had so studiously endeavoured
to banish from his memory. But the strong tide of brotherly
affection within him was too resistless not to sweep away every
feeling connected with the past. He applied his bugle to his
lips, and returned the call; and, looking up the side of the hill,
he beheld Walter, and a party of the Clan-Allan, hastening
down through the scattered greenwood to meet him.

"Thanks be to Heaven and good Saint Hubert that I see
thee safe, my dearest Patrick," said Sir Walter, hurrying towards him, and warmly embracing him. "Hast thou forgiven
a brother's anger and unkindness?"

"Could'st thou believe that I could for a moment remember
it, my dear Walter?" replied Patrick, returning his embrace.

"Where in the name of wonder hast thou been wandering?"
demanded Sir Walter. "Where hast thou been since that
night—that night of justice, yet of horror—when you disappeared so mysteriously? Since that moment, when I returned
home and found thee not, I have done little else, night or
day, but travel about hither and thither, anxiously seeking for
tidings of thee."

"Let us walk apart," said Patrick in his ear, "and I will
tell thee all that has befallen me."

"Willingly," said Sir Walter in the same tone; "for, in
exculpation of myself, I would now fain pour into thy private
ear all those circumstances which secretly urged me to execute
that stern act of justice and necessity, which then thou could'st
not comprehend, and against which thy recoiling humanity did
naturally enough compel thee so urgently to protest."

Arm in arm the two brothers then walked on alone, at such
a distance before their clansmen as might insure the perfect
privacy of their talk, and long ere they reached Drummin,
they had fully communicated to each other all that they had

mutually to impart. Old Sir Allan had been querulous and impatient about Patrick's absence, and he had been every now and then peevishly inquiring about him. But now that his son appeared, he seemed to have forgotten that he had not been always with him. He was pleased and·proud when the contemplated marriage was communicated to him, and he enjoined Sir Walter to see to it, that everything handsome should be done on the occasion. In this respect, Sir Walter's generosity required no stimulus; and if Patrick was dissatisfied at all, it was with the over liberality which his brother manifested, which, in some particulars, he felt inclined to resist.

"Patrick," said Sir Walter aside to his brother, with a more than ordinarily serious air, "I give thee but thine own in advance. One day or other it will be all thine own. There is something within me that tells me that I am not long for this world. The last words of that wretch, delivered to me, as I told thee, from the midst of those flames that consumed him, were prophetic. But, be that as it may, I have never had thoughts of marrying, and now I am firmly resolved that I never shall marry, so that thou art the sole prop of our house."

The entrance of the retainers, and the spreading of the evening meal, put a stop to all farther conversation between the brothers. Patrick had not yet seen either the Lady Stradawn, or her son Murdoch. On inquiry, he was told that Murdoch had gone on some unknown expedition on the previous day, and that he had not yet returned. A circumstance, so common with him, excited no surprise. As for the Lady Stradawn, she now came swimming into the hall, with her countenance clothed in all its usual smiles. Her salutation to her stepsons was full of well-dissembled warmth and affection. She hastened, with her wonted affectation of fondness, to bustle about Sir Allan, with the well-feigned pretence of anxiety to attend to his wants, after which she took her place at the head of the board. It was then that Patrick's eyes became suddenly fixed upon her with a degree of astonishment, which, fortunately for him, the busy occupation of every one else at the table left them no leisure to observe. To his utter amazement, he beheld in her bosom that very garnet brooch which he had given to Catherine Forbes! His first impulse was to demand from her an explanation of the circumstances by which she had become possessed of it; but a little reflection soon enabled him to control his feelings, though he continued to sit gazing at the well-known jewel, altogether forgetful of the feast, until the lady arose to retire to her chamber.

"My dearest Sir Allan," said she, going up to the old knight's chair to bestow her caresses on him ere she went; "My dearest Sir Allan, thou hast eaten nothing for these two days. What can I get for thee that may tickle thy palate into thy wonted appetite? Said'st thou not something of a deer's heart, for which thou hadst a longing? 'Tis a strange fancy, I'm sure."

"Oh, aye! very true, a deer's heart!" said the doting old man. "Very true, indeed, my love. I did dream—oh, aye—I dreamed, I say, Bella, that I was eating the rosten heart of a stag—of a great *hart of sixteen*,* killed by my boys on the hill of Dalestie—aye, aye—and with arrows feathered from an eagle's wing. As I ate, and better ate, I always grew stronger and stronger, till at length I was able to rise from my chair as stoutly as ever I did in my life—och, aye! that day is gone! Yet much would I like to eat the rosten heart of a deer; but it would need to be that of a great hart of sixteen."

"My dear father, thou shalt not want that," said Sir Walter; "thou shalt have it ere I am a day older, if a hart of sixteen be to be found between this and Loch Aven."

"Aye, aye, Walter boy, as thou sayest," said the old man; "a great hart of sixteen—else hath the heart of the beast no potency in't—aye, and killed with an arrow feathered from an eagle's wing—och, aye—hoch-hey!"

Though the two brothers were satisfied that this was nothing but the drivelling of age, they were not the less anxiously desirous to gratify their father's wish to the very letter. Accordingly, the necessary orders were given, and the trusty Dugald Roy† was forthwith summoned to prepare six arrows, which would have been easily supplied, with the small portions of feather which were necessary for them, from the eagle wing in Sir Walter's bonnet. But Sir Allan stopped him as he was about to tear it off.

"What, Sir!" exclaimed the old man testily, and in a state of agitation that shook every fibre of his frame like a palsy;—"What! wouldst thou shear the eagle plume of my boy Walter, thou ill-omened bird that thou art? Yonder hangs mine; it can never more appear bearing proudly forward in the foremost shock of the battle-field. Och, hey, that is true! Take that, thou raven! Thou may'st rend it as ye list. But,

---

* That is, having sixteen or more tynes upon his antlers.
† Or Ruadh, red.

my boy's!—the proud plume of mine eldest born boy!—thou
shalt never take that!"

"I crave your pardon, Sir Knight," replied Dugald Roy;
"and now I think on't, I need not take either, for I have some
spare wing feathers in my store that will do all the turn."

The next morning saw Sir Walter and his brother Patrick
early on foot, dressed in their plainest hunting attire, stretching up the valley at the head of their attendants. Each of the
brothers had three of the eagle-winged arrows stuck into his
belt; for, as both were dexterous marksmen, and as they had
resolved to use their shafts against nothing else but a great
hart of sixteen, they felt themselves to be thus most amply
provided to insure success. Fortune was somewhat adverse to
them, however; for although they saw deer in abundance, they
found themselves in this very part of the valley, when the day
was already far spent, without having once had a chance
of effecting their object.

"Look ye there, brother Walter!" at length cried Patrick
Stewart suddenly, as he pointed to a hart with a magnificent
head, which was crossing to this side of the river, at the ford
you see above yonder. "Look ye there, brother! there he goes
at last!"

"By the rood, but that is the very fellow we want," replied
Sir Walter. "Watch him! See!—he takes the hill aslant.
He will not go far, if we may judge from his present pace."

"I saw him walk over that open knoll in the wood high up
yonder," said Patrick, after some minutes of pause. "He has
no mind to go farther than the dip of the hill above. I think
that we are sure of finding him there. What say you,
brother?"

"Thou art right, Patrick," said Walter. "Then do thou
run on, and take the long hollow in the hill-side, beyond the
big pine tree yonder. I will follow up the slack behind us
here. Let your sweep be wide, that we may be sure of stalking well in beyond him, so that, if we fail of getting proper
vantage of him, we may be sure that we drive him not farther
a-field. Let us take no sleuth-hound, nor bratchet neither,
lest, perchance, we cause him alarm. You, my merry men,
will tarry here for us with the dogs."

Off went the two brothers, each in his own direction, and
each with his bow in his hand, and his three arrows in
his belt. In obedience to Sir Walter's directions, Patrick
hurried away to the great pine tree, and then began his ascent
through the long hollow in the woody mountain's side with all

manner of expedition. After a long and fatiguing climb, he began to use less speed and more caution, as he approached nearer to the somewhat less steep ground, where his hopes lay. Then it was that he commenced making a long sweep around, stealing silently from tree to tree, and concealing himself, as much as he could, by keeping their thick trunks before him, and creeping along among the heather, where such a precaution was necessary. Having completed his sweep to such an extent as led him to believe that he had certainly got beyond the hart, he was about to creep down the hill, in the hope of soon coming upon him, when he chanced to observe a great up-rooted pine, which lay prostrated a little way farther on, and somewhat above the spot where he then was, its head rising above the heather like a great green hillock. Thinking that he might as well have one peep beyond it before he turned down-wards, and wishing to avail himself of its shade to mask his motions, he took a direct course towards it. But it so happened, that the hart had found it equally convenient for the same purpose, as well as for a place of outlook, for it had taken post close to it, on the farther side. Descrying Patrick Stewart through an accidental opening in the foliage, and having no fancy to hold nearer converse with him, the creature moved slowly away. His quick and practised eye caught a view of it through the opening, as it was going away up the hill, as it happened in a direct line. Well experienced in wood-craft, he, in a loud voice, called out "*hah!*" As is com-mon with red deer when in the woods, the hart made a sudden halt, and wheeled half round to listen, and in this way he placed his broadside to the hunter's eye. This was but for an instant, to be sure; but in that instant Patrick Stewart's arrow, passing through the break in the foliage of the pine, fixed itself deep into the shoulder of the hart.

"Clumsily done!" exclaimed Patrick Stewart from very vexation as he saw the hart bound off. "I'll warrant me the arrow-head is deep into his shoulder blade. One single finger's breadth more behind it would have made him mine own, and with all the cleverness of perfect wood-craft."

Patrick, baulked and disappointed, now extended his sweep, and crossed and re-crossed the ground, with the hope of meeting his brother Sir Walter; but as he did not succeed in falling in with him, he followed the track of the hart for some distance up the hill, until he lost every trace of his slot upon the dry summit, after which he returned with all manner of haste to make his way downwards to the party in the valley

7

below. This he did, partly with the expectation of meeting
his brother Sir Walter there, and partly with the intention of
getting the dogs, that he might make an attempt to recover his
wounded hart.   There he found—not his brother Sir Walter—
but his brother Murdoch—who stood exulting over a dead
stag.   He was a great hart of sixteen, just such an one as he
himself had been after.

"Thou see'st that I have the luck," said Murdoch Stewart,
triumphantly.

"Whence camest thou, Murdoch? and how comes this?"
demanded Patrick.

"All naturally enough, brother," replied Murdoch Stewart,
carelessly.   "As I was wandering idly on the hill-side above
there, I espied the people here below, so I came sauntering
down to see what they were about, and to hear news of ye all.
But, as my luck would have it, I had hardly been with them
the pattering of a paternoster, when the very hart that thou
wentest after came bang down upon me—my shaft fled—and
there he lies.   Mark now, brother, is he not well and cleanly
killed?   Observe—right through the neck you see.   But, ha!
—it would seem that thou hast spent an arrow too—for these
fellows tell me that thou tookest three with thee, and methinks
thou hast but twain left in thy belt."

"I used one against the hart I went after," said Patrick, coldly.

"And missed him, brother—is't not so?" said Murdoch,
laughing.   "Well, I never hoped that I should live to wipe
thine eye in any such fashion ; for these varlets all say that
this is the very hart that thou went'st after."

"Nay, then," replied Patrick with an air of indifference ;
"if this be the hart I went after, I must have found another
great hart of sixteen the very marrow of him ; and him I have
so marked, that I'll be sworn he will be known again ; for I
promise you that at this moment he beareth wood on his
shoulder as well as on his head."

"The hart thou sayest that thou sawest may be like Saint
Hubert's stag for ought I know," said Murdoch ; "but it is
clear, from all that these fellows say, that there lies the very
hart that thou went'st forth to kill, and that is no arrow of
thine that hath fixed itself in his gullet."

"I did see a hart—draw my bow at a hart—and sorely
wound a hart," said Patrick, rather testily : and were it not
that the scent is cold, and the hour so late, I think that the
sleuth-hounds there, would soon help me to prove to thee that
he is as fine a hart of sixteen as this which thou hast slain."

"Cry your mercy, brother," said Murdoch; "I knew not that such great harts of sixteen had been so rife hereabouts, as that one should start up as a butt for thine arrow the moment that the other had been lost to thee. Yet it is clear that thou has spent an arrow upon something. Ha!—by the way— where is our brother Walter? They tell me that he went up the hill-side with thee."

"After seeking for him on the hill-side in vain, I reckoned on finding him here," replied Patrick. "But if he be within a mile of us I'll make him answer."

He put his bugle to his lips, and awakened the echoes, with such sounds as were understood between Sir Walter and himself; but the echoes alone replied to him.

"He may have met with a deer which may have led him off in pursuit over the hill," said Patrick.

"Aye," said Murdoch; "he may have fallen in with your hart of sixteen—yea, or another, for aught I know, seeing that harts of sixteen are now so rife on these hills."

"Fall in with what he might, he is not the man to give up his game easily," said Patrick, somewhat keenly.

"Whatever may have befallen him," said Murdoch, "we can hardly hope to see him hereabouts to-night."

"I hope we may see him at Drummin," said Patrick; "for as the night is now drooping down so fast, he will most readily seek the straightest way thither. So, as thou hast now made sure of a great hart of sixteen for Sir Allan, we may as well turn our steps thitherward without more delay."

On reaching Drummin, Patrick Stewart's first inquiry was for his brother Sir Walter. He had not returned home; but it was yet early in the night, and he might have been led away to such a distance as to require the greater part of the night to bring him home. The hart was borne up to the hall in triumph, and exhibited before Sir Allan, with the arrow still sticking in his neck. The old man's countenance was filled with joy and exultation when he beheld it. The Lady Stradawn could not contain her triumph.

"So, Murdoch," said she, "thou art the lucky man who hath killed the much longed for venison! Thou art the lucky man who hath brought thy father the food for which his soul so yearneth! There is something of good omen for thee in this, my boy!"

"A noble head!—a great hart of sixteen, indeed," said Sir Allan. "Aye, aye, that is a head, that is a head indeed! Yet have I slain many as fine in my time. Aye, aye,—but those

days are gone; och, hey! gone indeed. See what a cuach his
horn hath. Yet that which I slew up at Loch Aven had a
bigger cuach than this one by a great deal. As I live, you
might have slaked your thirst from the hollow of it the drow-
thiest day you ever saw. Yet this is a good hart—a noble hart
of sixteen,—aye, aye! hoch-hey! But, hey! what's this? A
goose-winged shaft? Did I not tell ye that my dream spake
of an eagle's wing? His heart will be naught after all—naught,
naught—och, hey! och, hey!"

"Nay, we shall soon convince thee to the contrary, father,"
said Murdoch, motioning to the attendants to lay the deer down
upon the hearth. "I will forthwith break him under thine
own eye, and thou shalt see, and judge for thyself."

Murdoch then drawing forth his knife, began to open up the
animal according to the strictest rules laid down for breaking a
deer, as this operation was called, and on proceeding to slit up
the slough, to the great wonder of every one, it was discovered
that the old man was right. The heart was indeed so very
small that it might very well have been said to have been
naught. Murdoch was dismayed for a moment at an omen so
very inauspicious, which, in his own mind, he felt was more
than enough to overthrow all the fair prognostics which his
mother had so evidently drawn from his success. The Lady
herself was equally disconcerted.

"Naught, naught!" whimpered Sir Allan. "'Tis an ill
omen for thee, boy. Thou shalt ne'er fly with an eagle's wing
—nay, nay! Aye, aye! Thou art ever doomed to gobble i'
the muddy stagnant waters like a midden-gander. Uch, aye!
och, hey!"

"The fiend take the old carl for his saying!" whispered
Murdoch angrily aside to his mother.

"Amen!" replied the Lady Stradawn bitterly, in the same
under tone. "But fear ye not, boy, thou shalt wear his eagle
wing, aye, and sit in his chair to boot, ere long."

This dialogue apart was unobserved by any one, and both
son and mother speedily recovered their self-possession. The
lady very cunningly set herself, straightway, to turn the weak
and dribbling stream of Sir Allan's thoughts from the subject
which then occupied them, to some other, which was to her less
disagreeable at the moment, and she easily succeeded.

Patrick Stewart's attention was attracted from all this superstitious trifling, as well as from what followed it, by again
observing the garnet brooch, which appeared in the bosom of
the Lady Stradawn. His thoughts were entirely occupied with

it, and his eyes were from time to time riveted on it. At length it seemed as if Murdoch had somehow remarked his fixed gaze, for a private sign appeared to pass from him to his mother, after which she pleaded a sudden faintness, and left the hall, to return no more that night, and her son soon afterwards followed her. Patrick Stewart's mind remained filled with strange speculations regarding the jewel, until the night wore late, and he began to think anxiously about his brother Sir Walter. Having done the last offices of attention to his father for the evening, he secretly desired Dugald Roy to follow him.

"Dugald," said he, "I am, most unaccountably, unhappy about thy master. Surely, if all had been well with him he should have been here ere this? I cannot rid my mind of the idea that there is something amiss with him. He rested not, as thou knowest, when I was missing, and it would ill become me to sleep when he is absent. Let us go seek for him, then, without delay."

Dugald Roy readily assented; and both of them having dighted themselves well up for turmoil, as well as for toil, they secretly left the tower of Drummin. All that night they travelled, and by daylight they had got into the range of mountains, and of forests, where they had reason to hope for tidings of Sir Walter. They searched through every part of the wooded side of that hill where he had last disappeared, and they visited every human dwelling within a great range around it, but all without obtaining the slightest intelligence regarding him. Disappointed, and disheartened, they had returned nearly as far as where the village of Tomantoul now stands, on their way home in the evening, when they met with Dugald Roy's brother Neil.

"What brought thee here, man?" demanded Dugald; "and what a fiend gives thee that anxious face?"

"Holy Saint Michael, but it is well that I have foregathered with you both!" replied Neil. "You must take some other road than that which leads to Drummin, Sir Patrick. Believe me, it is no place for you at this present time."

"What, in the name of all the saints, hath happened to make it otherwise?" demanded Patrick Stewart.

"Cannot ye speak out at once, ye Amadan ye, and not hammer like a fool that gate?" cried Dugald, impatiently.

"Patience! patience!" said Neil; "patience! and ye shall know all presently. In the first place, then, Master Murdoch says that Sir Walter is murdered."

"Murdered!" cried Patrick, in an agony of anxiety; "My brother Walter murdered? Where?—when?—how?—by whom? Oh, speak, that I may hasten to avenge him! But, no!—'tis impossible!—speak!—I have mistaken thee—surely it cannot be!"

"Master Murdoch says that it is true," replied Neil. "But the worst of all is, that he hath accused thee, Sir Patrick, of having done the deed, with an arrow, somewhere in the wood on the hill of Dalestie."

"Merciful Saints!" exclaimed Patrick; "can he indeed be such a villain? But who will believe so foul and unnatural a calumny? Oh, Walter, my brother, my brother! Heaven above knows that thy life was ten thousand times dearer to me than mine own!"

"Nay," replied Neil, "he hath called all the clansmen who were there to witness and to support the strong suspicions which he hath industriously raised against thee."

"What argument hath he against me?" cried Patrick Stewart impatiently.

"He says that the men who were present can testify that you and your brother, Sir Walter, went into the wood together," replied Neil; "and that Sir Walter hath not been seen since; and then, he contends, that the sudden flight which you made from Drummin, under the cloud of night, is enough to show that you have taken guilt home to your conscience."

"And is this all?" demanded Patrick Stewart.

"Nay," replied Neil, "there was more stuff of the same kind, by the use of which he hath contrived so to persuade them with his wily tongue, that they are all clamorous against thee. Nay, he hath even warped the feeble judgment of Sir Allan himself to the same belief."

"Serpent that he is!" cried Patrick Stewart. "But let me hasten home to confront this vile traducer. My brother!—my brother Walter!" continued he, bursting into tears. "My brother Walter gone!—and I accused of his murder! Oh, my brother!—my dear brother! Heaven above knows how willingly I would have laid down my life to have saved thine! Nay, how willingly would I now lay it down at this moment, were it only to secure to me the certainty that thou art yet alive! The very thought that it may be otherwise is agony and desolation to me. But let us hasten to confront this villany. Let us hasten to revenge! For the love of Heaven, let us hasten home, Dugald!"

"Nay, my good master," said Dugald, weeping, "for if this sad tale be true as to Sir Walter's death, other master than thee, I fear me, that I now have none. Neil says well that Drummin is no place for thee to-night, with so sudden and tumultuous a clamour excited against thee. Thine innocence will avail thee nothing. Even the innocence of an angel would naught avail against the diseased judgments of men, with minds so poisoned and so possessed. Be persuaded to go elsewhere, until the false, and weak foundations of this most traitorous accusation fail beneath it, and the mists drop from men's eyes. Who can say for certain that my beloved master, Sir Walter, is dead? I cannot believe in so great a calamity. What proof is there that he is dead? There is no news that his body hath been found."

"Nay," replied Neil, "he is only amissing as I said."

"Thou dost well advise me, Dugald," said Patrick Stewart · after a moment's thought. "There is, as thou say'st, no proof that my brother, Sir Walter, is dead. It is most reasonable to believe that this may, after all, be nothing but a foolish or malicious surmise. My best hope, nay, my belief is, that it is founded on naught else; and may Heaven in its mercy grant that it may prove so. I will take thine advice. I will not go to Drummin at present, but I shall straightway bend my steps towards the Castle of Curgarf."

"Then shall I and Neil attend thee thither, Sir Knight," said Dugald; "for the next to Sir Walter Stewart do I assuredly owe thee fealty and service."

Sir Patrick and his two attendants now turned off in the direction of Curgarf, and the day was so far spent that the sun was setting, as they were passing over the ridge of the country lying between the Aven and the Don. The trees of the forest there grew thinly scattered in little stunted patches. Sir Patrick was walking a few paces in front of the two brothers, musing as he went, when he was suddenly surprised by a shower of arrows falling thickly on and around him. One stuck in his bonnet, another buried itself harmlessly in the folds of his plaid, a third pierced his sandal and slightly wounded his foot; and, whilst a fourth struck fire out of a large stone close to him, two more fell short of him among the heather near him. In an instant his bow and those of his attendants were bent, and their eyes being turned towards the place whence the shafts had flown, they descried some men lurking beneath one of the straggling patches of dwarf pine trees. To have stood aloof with the hope of shooting at them successfully would have been fatal, for the archery of Sir Patrick and his attendants could have done nothing against men so ambushed, whilst the Knight and his people would have been a sure mark for their traitorous foes.

"On them, my brave Dugald!" cried Sir Patrick Stewart, drawing his sword, and rushing towards the enemy.

Dugald Roy, and his brother, Neil, were at his back in a moment. Before they could reach the point against which their assault was directed, several arrows were discharged at them. But so resolute, and so spirited an attack had been so little looked for by those who shot them, that they were too much appalled to take any very steady aim, so that all of them fell innocuous. Seeing Sir Patrick and his two attendants so rapidly nearing their place of concealment, the villains thought it better to turn out, that they might receive their onset on ground where they could all act at once. Six men accordingly appeared claymore in hand, and as Sir Patrick continued to hurry forward, he now took the opportunity of speaking hastily to Dugald and Neil, who were advancing to right and left of him.

"Draw an arrow each," said he, "and when I give you the word, stop suddenly, and each of you pick off the man opposite to you, and leave me to take my choice of the rest. —Now!"

The unlooked for halt was made just as the assassins were preparing to receive the on-comers on the points of their swords. The aim was sure and fatal. Three men fell—and on rushed Sir Patrick and his two people with a loud shout. The three, who yet stood against them, were panic-struck, and, ere they could well offer defence, they were also extended writhing among the heather, in the agonies of death; and the whole matter was over in less time than it has taken for me to tell of it. But, uncertain whether the partial covert of the pine-patch might not still shelter some more enemies, they rushed in among the trees, brandishing their recking blades. Up started a youth from among some low brushwood, and ran off like a hare. Neil was after him in a moment, and up to him ere he had fled twenty paces. Already he had him by the hair of the head, and his claymore was raised to smite him, when Patrick Stewart called to his follower to stay his hand. Neil obeyed, and granted the youth his life; but when he brought him in as a prisoner, what was the Stewart's surprise when he discovered that he was the same individual whose life he had spared in the Catterane's den.

" Ha !" exclaimed Sir Patrick ; " said I not well that I questioned the wisdom of sparing thy life when we last met, thou vermin ? What hast thou to urge that I should show mercy to thee now, Sir Caitiff ?"

" Oh, mercy, mercy, Sir Knight !" exclaimed the youth, piteously. " Trust me, I came not hither willingly. I had no hand in this treacherous ambush against thy life."

" Appearances are woefully against thee," said Patrick Stewart ; " yet would I not willingly do thee hurt, if thou be'st innocent. But this is no convenient time nor place to tarry for thy trial. So bring him along with thee, Dugald. We shall take our own leisure to examine him afterwards ; meanwhile, take especial care that he escape not."

Sir Patrick Stewart's reception at Curgarf may be easily guessed at. He told of the providential escape he had made from assassination by the way ; but he thought it better, as yet, to say nothing of the mysterious disappearance of his brother, Sir Walter, or of the traitorous accusations against himself, to which it had given rise. His resolve to be silent as to this matter was formed, because he had by this time reasoned himself into the firm persuasion that his brother's reappearance would speedily make his own innocence as clear as noonday.

He was next morning happily seated in the hall, now talking with the old Lord of Curgarf on one subject and again taking his opportunity of whispering to the Lady Catherine on another, when he suddenly recollected the brooch he had given her. It was not in her bosom.

" Where are the two twined hearts ?" said he to her, smiling. " Fear not, dearest—I am not jealous."

" Thou hast no cause for jealousy, dear Patrick," replied the lady ; " and yet, I grieve to say, that I have not the jewel. When the Catteranes hurried me off from here, and just as they stopped for a little time to make up a litter, that they might the more easily carry me, one who appeared to have a certain command over them, but whose face or person I could not see in the obscurity which then prevailed, snatched it from my bosom whilst affecting to fasten my arryssade more firmly around me. Nay, look not so serious, dearest Patrick ! surely thou dost not doubt me in this matter ?"

" Doubt thee, my Catherine !" said Sir Patrick, kissing her hand with fervour; "sooner would I doubt mine own existence; thou art pure virgin truth itself ! Think no more of it. Thou shalt have another and a richer one anon. But say, dearest !

why should we longer delay to set our own very two hearts in
that indissoluble golden knot, with which the sacrament of our
holy church may bind them together, so as to form a jewel, of
which neither robber nor Catterane can rifle us, and which
cannot be rent asunder savé by the iron hand of death? I have
thy father's permission to move thee to shorten that cruel
interval which thou hast placed between me and happiness."

In such a strain as this did he continue to urge his suit,
until it was at last successful; and, to his great joy, it was
ultimately arranged, with the consent of all parties, that the
marriage should take place on the second day from the time I
am now speaking of. The bustle of preparation began in the
Castle the moment the circumstance was announced; and it
immediately spread far and wide everywhere around it, and
went on incessantly day and night. Joy was everywhere as
universal among the clansmen as their devotion to the Lady
Catherine, the bride, and their admiration of the merits of the
bridegroom, could make it. The day at length arrived. The
Castle was crowded with all the friends and retainers of the
family, who came pouring in to witness a ceremonial so interesting to them all. The Priest had arrived; the Castle chapel
had been set in order; the bridal-chamber had been dight up;
and the feast prepared; and every soul was astir to contribute,
so far as in them lay, to the general felicity, as well as to share
in it. The old Lord of Curgarf seemed to have grown young
again. Arthur, the Master of Forbes, was all life and raillery.
Already had the whole company been assembled within the
hall. All the men-at-arms within the Castle had crowded in
thither. Even the old warden at the gate had lowered his
portcullis, and made everything secure with bolt, bar, and
chain, so that he might safely leave his post to the charge of
their stubborn defences. The blushing bride, arrayed in the
richest attire, had been led in, attended by her blooming
maidens; and the movement towards the chapel was about to
be made, so that the ceremony might go on, when suddenly a
shrill bugle blast from without the gate made the very Castle
walls resound again.

"Go some of ye, and see who that may be who summons us
so rudely," said the Lord of Curgarf.

"Murdoch Stewart and a party of the Clan-Allan are at the
gate craving admittance," said the messenger, on his return.

"Son Arthur," said the old Lord of Curgarf, "get thee down
quickly, and give Murdoch Stewart of Clan-Allan, the brother
of this our son-in-law to be, instant entry. Let the gate be

opened to him, aye, and to all his people, dost thou hear? It was kind in him thus to come, on the spur of the occasion," continued the old Lord, addressing Patrick, after his son had gone with his attendants to obey his will—"It was kind in thy brother to come thus unasked on the spur of the moment. Would that Sir Allan, thy father himself, could have been here."

The courtyard and the stair now rang with the clink of armed men, and Arthur, the Master of Forbes, entered, ushering in Murdoch Stewart, proudly attired, and followed by a formidable band of the Clan-Allan, whose flaring red tartans were strongly contrasted against the more modest green of those of the Clan-Forbes. To the no small surprise of his brother Patrick, he no longer wore that appearance of youthful carelessness and indifference, under the mask of which he had hitherto disguised his true character. His bearing was now manly and lofty, suited to the command of the Clan-Allan, which he now seemed to have assumed. His salutation to the Lord of Curgarf was grave, dignified, and courteous; and, as way was made for him, he advanced, with the utmost self-possession, into the middle of the hall.

"I rejoice that I have arrived thus, as it seems, in the nick of time," said he, looking around him, and bowing as he did so, but without once allowing his eyes to rest on his brother, who stood fixed in silent astonishment at what he beheld.

"So do we all rejoice," replied the old Lord of Curgarf. "Had we but known that our bridal might have been thus honoured by the house of Clan-Allan, on so short a warning, trust me thou shouldst not have lacked our warmest bidding, as thou hast now our warmest welcome."

"Welcome or not, my Lord," replied Murdoch Stewart, with a respectful reverence, "thou wilt surely thank me for this most unceremonious visit, when thou shalt know the object of it. I come to save the honour of thy house from foul disgrace: would, that in so doing, I could likewise save the honour of that which gave me birth! But although, in saving thee and thy house from dishonour, the good name of that of Clan-Allan must assuredly be tarnished, it shall never be said of me, that I preserved it by falsehood or infamous concealment."

"Of what wouldst thou speak?" demanded the Lord of Curgarf. "I do beseech thee, keep me, and keep this good company, no longer in suspense."

"Then, my good Lord," replied Murdoch, solemnly, "much as it pains me to utter it, and much as it must pain thee, and all present, to hear it, I must tell thee, that strong suspicions are abroad that mine eldest brother, Sir Walter Stewart, hath been most foully murdered, and that he on whom thou wert now on the very eve of bestowing thine only daughter, is the foul murderer, who took an elder brother's life to make way for the gratification of his own ambitious and avaricious desires. The circumstances are so strong against my unfortunate brother Patrick that all agree that no one else could have been the murderer."

" All !—all !—all !—all !" was echoed from the stern Clan-Allans, at the lower end of the hall.

" Holy saints defend us !" exclaimed the Lord of Curgarf, sinking into a chair.

" 'Tis false ! oh, 'tis all false, father !" cried the trembling Catherine Forbes, rushing forward to assist her father.

" Infamous traitor !" cried Patrick Stewart; "lying and infamous traitor ! Where are the proofs on which you found so foul and false an accusation ?"

" Would, for the credit of our poor house, that it were false !" said Murdoch, mildly. " But it is impossible to conceal that thou wert the last person seen in our poor brother Walter's company. Thou wentest up the wood with him, with three arrows in thy belt. Thou camest back shortly afterwards without him. One of thine arrows was gone. Thou gavest reasons for the want of it which proved to be false; and our dear brother Walter hath never been since seen."

" He is guilty ! He, and no one else, is the murderer !" cried the men of Clan-Allan, hoarsely.

" Woe is me !" said the distracted Lord of Curgarf, springing from his chair with nervous agitation; " the circumstances are indeed too suspicious !"

" Father !—father !—father, he is innocent !" cried the frantic Lady Catherine Forbes, holding the old lord's arm.

" Sister," cried the Master of Forbes, taking the Lady Catherine affectionately by the hand, and speaking to her with great feeling—" Dearest sister, this is indeed an afflicting trial for thee ; yet, be of good courage—I have no fears of the result. Patrick Stewart cannot be guilty of the foul and cruel deed of which he hath been accused. We must have the matter sifted to the bottom ; the truth must be brought out; and, as his innocence must be thereby established, all the evil that can happen will be but the short delay of your nuptials till he be fairly and fully cleansed from these wicked charges."

" I am sent by my father," said Murdoch Stewart—" I am sent by my father, and that most unwillingly, to demand his

"Hold!" cried Dugald Roy, in a voice like thunder.—Page 93.

son Patrick as a prisoner. Forgive me, my good Lord of Curgarf, for thus daring to execute his paternal order under your roof.—Men of Clan-Allan, seize and bind Patrick Stewart!"

"Hold!" cried Dugald Roy, in a voice like thunder— "Hold, men of Clan-Allan! Lay not a hand upon him, to whom, if my dear master Sir Walter be indeed gone, ye must all soon, in the course of nature, swear fealty as your chieftain. He is guiltless of my beloved master's murder, though murdered, I fear, he hath most foully been. But here is one who can tell more of this cruel and wicked deed. Come hither boy, and tell us what thou may'st know of this mysterious matter."

Dugald Roy then led forward the youth whom he had brought prisoner to Curgarf, of whose very existence Sir Patrick Stewart had lost all recollection, amidst the tumult of joy in which he had been so continually kept by his approaching nuptials. The Lady Catherine Forbes started with surprise when she beheld him ; but the countenance of Murdoch Stewart turned as pale as a linen sheet at the sight of him.

"What hast thou to say, young man, to the clearing up of this dark and cruel mystery?" demanded the Lord of Curgarf.

"My Lord, I saw Sir Walter Stewart of Clan-Allan murdered," said the youth in a tremulous voice. "I saw him shot to the death by the arrow of Ewan Cameron, one of the band of Catteranes."

"How camest thou to have been in any such evil company?" demanded the Lord of Curgarf.

"Trusting to have mercy at your hands, my Lord, I will tell my whole story as shortly as I can, if thou wilt but listen to me," replied the youth. "I was prentice to a craftsman in the town of Banff, a man who wrought in gold and silver. Being one day severely chidden by my master for some unlucky fault, the devil entered into me, and I resolved to be revenged of him. Having become known to the captain of a certain band of Catteranes, I stole my master's keys, and gave them to him, so that he and his gang were enabled to rifle the goldsmith's stores of all his valuables. In dread of punishment I fled with them to their den in the hills, where they afterwards kept me in thrall to do their service. The lady, thy daughter, can tell thee that I was there when she was brought in by them, and had not Sir Patrick Stewart left me bound when he spared my life, they would have certainly taken it on their return, in their rage and fury at her escape ; but, fortunately, I was lying quite out of their way at the moment, and was not discovered till they had somewhat cooled. Finding that their retreat had been found out, they hastily abandoned it, and dispersed themselves through the hills. On the day that followed after that we were all collected together to meet our captain, and after two days more a breathless messenger came early in the morning to tell him something which was kept secret from all else. There were but few of the band with him at the time, but these were ordered to arm on the sudden, and even I, who had never been called out on any expedition until that day, was commanded to arm like the rest.

"Our small party marched off in all haste, and about midday we were planted in ambush on the side of a hill above the Aven. Our captain seemed to be restless and anxious. He moved about from place to place, stretching on tiptoe from the top of every knoll, and sometimes climbing the tallest pine trees, in order to scan the valley below more narrowly. At length, as it grew late in the afternoon, he took a long look from one point, and then, as if he had at last made some discovery of importance, he suddenly moved us off into a thicket, which grew on the edge of a considerable opening in the wood on the hill-side; and I would know that opening again, for it had the green quaking bog of a well-head in the very midst of it.

"We had not stood long there, till a man in very plain attire, with a bow in his hand, came up from the thick wood below, and began to pass aslant the open space. 'There goes a good mark for an arrow,' said the captain of the band. 'Shoot at him, my men.'—'He is not worth a shaft,' replied some of his people. 'He is a poor fellow who hath nothing in his sporran to pay for the killing of him.'—'No matter,' said Ewan Cameron, 'he hath a good pair of sandals on him; and my brogues are worn to shreds—so, here goes at him.' And just as the man was passing along the bank close above the well-eye, the arrow fled, and pierced him to the heart. 'Well shot, Ewan!' cried the captain, in a strange ecstasy of joy; 'thou shalt have gold for that shot of thine.' So instant was his death, that he sprang high into the air, and his body fell headlong and without life into the very middle of the bog, with a force that buried it in its yielding mass, so high, that nothing was seen of him but his legs. Ewan hastened to the place, quietly took off the sandals from the dead man, threw off his own brogues, and put on the sandals in place of them, and then the captain himself ran eagerly to help him to force the corpse downwards into the bog; and this they did till the green moss closed over the soles of its feet. I then knew not who the murdered man might be,—and the deed was no sooner done, than our captain ordered us to make our way back, as fast as we could travel, over the hills, whilst he left us to go directly down into the glen.

"Early next morning, a messenger again came to us; and five picked archers were sent out under the orders of Ewan Cameron. I was directed to accompany them; and I marvelled much why I, who was so inexperienced, should be required to go on an expedition where they seemed to be so very particular in choosing their men. But Ewan Cameron soon let me into the secret. 'Thou knowest the person of Patrick Stewart of Clan-Allan, dost thou not?' said he to me.—'If that was he who took the lady from the cave, and left me bound,' replied I, 'then have I reason to remember him right well.'—'Then must I tell thee, that we are now sent forth expressly to hunt for him, and to take his life,' replied Ewan; 'and if thou would'st fain preserve thine own, thou wilt need to look sharply about thee, that thou mayest tell me when thou seest him.'—'Who covets to have his life?' demanded I.'—'He who made me take the life of his brother Walter, for those sandals which I now wear,' said Ewan—'What! our captain?' exclaimed I; 'that must be in revenge, because Sir Patrick Stewart took the lady from him.'—'Partly so, perhaps,' replied Ewan; 'but I am rather jealous that our captain's greatest fault to Sir Patrick Stewart is, that he, like his brother, Sir Walter Stewart, was born before him. Knowest thou not, that our captain is no other than Murdoch Stewart, the third son of old Sir Allan of Stradawn?' I was no sooner made aware of this, than—"

The youth would have proceeded, but the loud murmur of astonishment and horror that arose everywhere throughout the hall, so drowned his voice, that he was compelled to stop.

"Holy Saint Michael, what a perfect villain thou art!" exclaimed the old Lord of Curgarf, darting a look of indignant detestation at Murdoch Stewart.

"Thou wouldst not condemn a stranger unheard," said Murdoch, calmly.

"Nay," replied the Lord of Curgarf, "thou shalt have full justice. We shall hear thee anon. But let this youth finish his narrative, which would seem to be pregnant with strange and horrible things."

"I have but little more to say," continued [the youth. "Gratitude to Sir Patrick Stewart, for having spared my life, when his own security might have required the taking of it, at once resolved me against betraying him to slaughter. Ewan

Cameron marched us straight away to the hill, which rises above the track that leads from the little place of Tomantoul to the river Don, and there he kept us sitting, for some time, watching, till we espied three men coming along the way. Whilst they were yet afar off I knew one of them to be the very person whom the murderers were in search of. ' Is that Sir Patrick Stewart that comes first yonder?' demanded Ewan. —'I cannot tell at this distance,' said I ; ' but I think the man I saw in the cave was much taller than that man.'—' That is a tall man,' said Ewan ; 'take care what thou sayest, or thou mayest chance to have thy stature curtailed by the whole head.' —'I say what is true,' said I ; ' no man could know his own father at that distance.'—' Then will I assert that thou sayest that which is a lie,' said one of the party ; 'for great as the distance may be, I know that to be Sir Patrick Stewart. I mean that man who comes first of the three.'—' Let us down upon him without loss of time then,' cried Ewan ; 'and do you come along, sirrah ! Thou shalt along with us; and, when our work is done, we shall see whether we cannot find the means of refreshing thy memory.' Having uttered these words, Ewan hurried us all down to the covert of a small patch of stunted pines, that grew on the flat ground below. There we lay in ambush till Sir Patrick Stewart, and his two attendants, came within bowshot, and there, as is already known to most here, the six assassins were speedily punished for their wicked attempt, and I became Sir Patrick Stewart's prisoner."

"Now," said the Lord of Curgarf, addressing himself to Murdoch, "what hast thou to say in answer to all this? What hast thou to answer for thyself?"

"I say that the young caitiff is a foul liar!" cried Murdoch, violently. He is a foul liar, who hath been taught a false tale, to bear me down."

"He may be a liar," said the Lord of Curgarf; "but his story hangs marvellously well together."

"Who would dare to condemn me on his unsupported testimony?" demanded Murdoch, boldly.

"Here is one who is ready to support his tale," said Michael Forbes, pressing forward, and pushing before him a strange looking little man, with a long red beard, and a head of hair so untamed, that it hung over his sharp sallow features in such a manner, as, for some moments, to render it difficult for Sir Patrick Stewart to recognise in him, the man whom he had saved from his perilous position in the salmon creel, at the Lynn of Aven.

" Ha !—Grigor Beg ! " cried Murdoch Stewart, betrayed by his surprise, at beholding him; " what a fiend hath brought thee hither ?   But thou—thou can'st say nothing against me."

" I fear I can say nothing for thee, Murdoch Stewart," said the little man, darting a pair of piercing eyes towards him, from amidst the tangled thickets of his hair.   " Nor is it needful for me now to say all I might against thee.   But here, as I understand, thou hast basely and falsely accused thy brother Sir Patrick Stewart of murdering his elder brother Sir Walter. Now, I saw Ewan Cameron shoot down Sir Walter Stewart with an arrow ; and it was done at thy bidding too, for I was by, on the hill-side, when thou didst give to Ewan Cameron his secret order to slay thy brother, and when thou didst teach him to do the deed, as if it were an idle act, done against a stranger."

" Lies !—lies !—a very net-work of lies, in which to ensnare me ! " cried Murdoch.   " But who can condemn me for another's death, who, for aught that we know truly, may yet appear alive and well ?"

" Thou hadst no such scruple in condemning thine innocent brother, Sir Patrick," said the Lord of Curgarf; " yet shall no guilt be fixed upon thee, till thy brother's death be established beyond question.   Meanwhile thou must be a bounden prisoner, till the truth be clearly brought to light."

" Men of Clan-Allan ! will ye allow him who must be your chieftain to be laid hands on in the house of a stranger ?" cried Murdoch Stewart aloud.   " You are armed ; use your weapons then, and leave not a man alive ! "

" A thrill of horror ran through every bosom.   There were brave men enough of the Clan-Forbes there, to have made head against three times the number of Clan-Allans that now stood, armed to the teeth, and in a firm body, at the lower end of the hall ; but there was not a man of the Forbeses, who, if not altogether unarmed, had any weapon at all to defend himself with but his dirk.   Those who had such instruments were drawing them, whilst others were rushing to the walls, to arm themselves with whatsoever weapons they could most easily reach, and pluck down thence.   The noise and bustle of the moment was great, when, all at once, there fell a hush over the turbulence of the scene.

" Stir not a man of Clan-Allan ! " cried Sir Patrick to the Stewarts, who stood in their array, like a heavy and portentous thunder-cloud.   " Stir not, men of Clan-Allan !—Stir not a finger, I command you !"

"Sir Patrick Stewart is our young chieftain!" broke like a roll of Heaven's artillery from the Clan-Allans. "Sir Patrick Stewart is our young chieftain! Murdoch is a foul traitor and murderer! Bind him, bind him! Let him be the prisoner, and let us have him forthwith justified!"

"Nay, nay," cried Sir Patrick; "bind him if you will, but lay not your hands upon his life. This day, my Catherine," said he, turning to the lady, and addressing her tenderly and sorrowfully; "this day, that was to have been to me so full of joy, must now, alas! be the first of that doleful time, which, in the bereavement of my heart, I must devote to mourning for my beloved brother Walter. My first duty is to go and seek for his remains; and in following out this most sad and anxious search, I must crave thy presence, my Lord of Curgarf, and thine, too, Arthur, with that of such of our friends as may be disposed to go forth with us, to aid us in so painful a quest."

The wishes of Sir Patrick Stewart were readily agreed to. The nuptials were for the present postponed; and instead of the marriage-feast, some hasty refreshment was taken, preparatory to their immediate departure on their melancholy search. The treacherous Murdoch Stewart was now given in charge, as a manacled prisoner, to those very Clan-Allans, at the head of whom he had come, so triumphantly, to fix a false accusation on his brother Sir Patrick. With them too went the youth, and the little man, Grigor Beg, who had given their evidence against Murdoch. The old Lord of Curgarf's quiet palfrey was led forth; and he set forward, attended by Arthur the Master of Forbes, Sir Patrick Stewart, and a considerable following of those who were led to accompany him by duty, or from curiosity.

They first visited the scene of the attempted assasination of Sir Patrick Stewart. The spot where the six catteranes were slain, was easily discovered, by the flock of birds of prey that sat perched upon the tops of the dwarf pines, or that wheeled over them in whistling circles; whilst every now and then, some individual, bolder than the rest, would swoop down on the heath, to partake of the banquet which had been spread upon it for them. That some considerable share of courage was required to enable these creatures to do this, was proved to the party, who, on their nearer approach, scared away a brace of hungry, gaunt-looking wolves, who had been employed in ravenously tearing at the bodies, and dragging them hither and thither with bloody jaws; as well as an eagle, who had dared to sit a little way apart, to feed upon one of the carcases, in defiance of his ferocious four-footed fellow-guests. The spectacle was shocking to all who beheld it. But one object of their search was gained; for, on examination, Patrick recognised his brother Walter's sandals, which were removed from the feet of the corpse of Ewan Cameron, and taken care of—thus so far corroborating the testimony of the youth. Having completed their investigations in this place, they piled heaps of stones over the bodies on the spot where they lay, and the party then pursued their way, over the mountain, towards the alleged scene of Sir Walter Stewart's murder.

Providence seemed to guide their steps;—for, as they passed over the brow of the wooded hill that dropped down towards the Aven, they scared away two ravens from a hollow place in the heath; and, on approaching the spot, they discovered the well-picked bones of a deer. His head showed him to have been an unusually fine great hart of sixteen. An arrow was sticking so deeply fixed through the shoulder-blade, as to satisfy all present, that its point must have produced death, very soon after the animal had received it.

"As I hope for mercy, there is the very arrow that was lacking of Sir Patrick's three!" cried Dugald Roy, triumphantly. "See—there is the very eagle's feather which I put on it, with mine own hand! And, look—there is the cross, which I always cut on the shaft, to give them good luck. No shaft of mine, so armed, ever misses, when righteously discharged. But for foul or treacherous murther, I'll warrant me, that the most practised eye could never bring it to a true aim. But," added he, as he very adroitly dislocated out the shoulder-bone, as Highlanders are wont, and then possessed himself of the shoulder-blade, arrow and all—"I'll e'en take this arrow with me, with the bone just as it is, as a dumb but true witness in a righteous cause."

Led by the directions which they received from Grigor Beg, they now descended through the forest, till they came to that very well-eye you see yonder—for that was the very individual place, that both the old man and the youth had described as the scene of Sir Walter's murder. They had used the precaution to bring with them implements for digging; and, by means of these, a few sturdy fellows were soon enabled to make an opening into the lower end of the quaking bog, so as very quickly to discharge the pent-up water within it. The green surface then gradually subsided, and the legs of a human being, with hose on, but without sandals, began to appear, sticking out, with the feet upwards; and, by digging a little around it, they soon succeeded in bringing the body of Sir Walter Stewart fully to light. It was in all respects unchanged. The fatal arrow was deeply buried in his left breast; his bow was firmly grasped in his hand; and his three eagle-winged shafts were in his belt. The small unplumed bonnet which he usually wore, when dressed for following the deer, was fast squeezed down on his head, by the pressure which had been exerted to sink him. How differently were the two brothers, Patrick and Murdoch Stewart, affected by the harrowing spectacle which was now brought before their eyes! Murdoch shed no tear—yet his features were strongly agitated. He looked at the corpse with averted eyes, and shuddered as he looked; while his face became black, and again deadly pale, twenty times alternately. Sir Patrick Stewart, on the other hand, threw himself, in an agony of tears, on the cold and dripping body of his murdered brother, as it lay exposed on the bank; and, unable to give utterance to his grief, he clasped it to his bosom, and lavished fond, though unavailing caresses on it. In vain he essayed, with as much tenderness as if his brother could have still felt the pain he might thereby have given him, to pluck forth the arrow, deeply buried in the fatal wound. All present were overcome by this sad scene;—but poor Dugald Roy hung over them, and sobbed aloud, till the violence of his grief recalled Sir Patrick Stewart to himself again.

"Aye!" said Dugald Roy; "that is a murderous shaft indeed! A good cloth-yard in length, I'll warrant me; and feathered, too, from the wing of some ill-omened grey goose, that was hatched in some western sea-loch. This is no arrow of the make of Aven-side, else am I no judge of the tool. No cross upon this, I'll be sworn. No, no. By St. Peter, but it hath murther in the very look of it! Aye, and there are the true arrows of the cross in his belt! These are of my winging, every one of them. Little did I think, when I stuck them into my poor master's girdle, that this was to be the way in which I was to find them! Would that he had but gotten fair play! Would that he had but got his eye on the villains ere they slew him! If he had but gotten one glimpse of them, by the Rood, but every cross of these shafts would have been eager to have dyed itself red in the blood of their cowardly hearts!"

The body of Sir Walter Stewart was now wrapped up in a plaid, and fastened lengthwise upon two parallel boughs, and it was borne towards Drummin. Their movements were so slow, and so often interrupted, that it was dark night long ere they came to the place of their destination. Sir Patrick Stewart felt the necessity of preparing his father, Sir Allan, for the coming scene, as well as for the reception of the Lord of Curgarf, and his son, the Master of Forbes. He therefore resolved to hurry on before the party, that he might have a private meeting with the old Knight, before their arrival. But being fully aware that Sir Allan's mind had been already filled with those iniquitous falsehoods, which his wicked brother, Murdoch Stewart, had engendered against him, he thought it prudent to take with him Dugald Roy, and two other men of the Clan-Allans, that they might be prepared, if necessary, to support his justification of himself.

As Sir Patrick Stewart, and his small escort, approached the outer gate of the Castle of Drummin, they perceived that it was shut. Dugald had no sooner observed this circumstance, than he made a signal to the Knight to remain silent, and then he advanced quietly to the little wicket in the middle of the gate, and knocked gently.

"Who is there?" demanded the Warder, from within.

"Open the wicket, man, without a moment's tarrying," replied Dugald.

"Is that thee, Dugald Roy?" demanded the Warder.

"Who else could it be?" replied Dugald.

"It may be that any other might have done as well," replied the Warder, gruffly. "Thou wentst not forth with Murdoch Stewart;—Art thou of his company at the present time!"

"What matter though I went not forth with him, if I come home in his company?" replied Dugald, readily.

"Is he with thee, then?" demanded the Warder.

"To be sure he is," cried Dugald impatiently. "Come, man! he is close at hand, I tell thee. Come! art thou to keep us standing here all night? By all that's good, he is coming upon us;—and, if he be detained but the veriest fraction of a prod-flight, thou shalt surely have a cudgelling for thy supper. Come man!—open I tell thee."

The huge iron bolts were now withdrawn from their fastenings, the key grated among the rough wards of the lock, and the wicket was thrown back, whilst the Warder, peering through the opening, seemed as if he were inclined to know something more of those without, before he removed his own bulky person, that still blocked the passage. But Dugald, stooping his head, sprang through the low aperture, and throwing his skull right into the poor fellow's stomach, with the force of a battering-ram, he laid him sprawling on his back.

"Hech!" cried the Warder, as he fell. "Hech me!"

"Old fool that thou art!" cried Dugald, taking up the first word of quarrel with him; "who was to think that thou wert to be standing in the very midst of the way? Yet I hope I have not hurt thee, for all that. Thou knowest, Rory, that I had rather hurt myself than thee."

"Nay, nay," said the old man, with a surly sort of acquiescence, as he was slowly raising himself from the ground by means of Dugald's assistance, during which operation Patrick Stewart, wrapped up in his plaid, and followed by the other two men, had made good his entrance into the court-yard. "Nay, nay, I am not hurt. I'm no such eggshells, i'faith. Yet what a fiend made thee so impatient? I behooved to be careful who I let in, seeing that I was strictly charged to open to none but Murdoch Stewart himself there," pointing to Sir Patrick, who was standing a few paces aloof. "More by token, I required to be all the warier, seeing that there was none living within the walls, besides myself, save the old Knight Sir Allan, and the Lady Stradawn."

"How comes that?" demanded Dugald; "though so many went to Curgarf, there were still some left behind, surely."

"True enough, true enough," replied the Warder. "But I know not what hath possessed the lady. They have been all sent hither and thither, on some errand or another;—even the very women folk have all gone forth."

Sir Patrick Stewart stood to hear no more, but making a signal to Dugald and the others to follow him, he crossed the court-yard towards the door of the keep tower, where they stood aside, whilst he knocked gently, yet loud enough to be heard in the hall above. Soon afterwards, a timid and unsteady footstep was heard descending the stair.

"Open, good mother," said Sir Patrick.

"Oh, how thankful I am that thou art come!" said the Lady Stradawn, mistaking him for her son Murdoch, their voices being a good deal like to each other, and opening the door, pale and trembling, with a lamp in her hand, which the gust immediately extinguished. "A plague on the wind, my lamp is out! But oh, I am thankful that thou art come! 'Tis fearful to be left alone in the house with a dead man, and one too——Oh, 'twas fearful!"

"Dead!" cried Sir Patrick, with an accent of horror, which might have betrayed him, but for the agitation which then possessed her whom he addressed. "A dead man, saidst thou?"

"Aye!" replied the lady, in a·hollow tone, "aye! I saw that thou hadst yearnings. Yet, after all, it was but giving him ease, by ridding him of a lingering life of pain. It was kindness, in truth, to help him away from such misery. Yet, 'tis no marvel that thou, who art his very blood, should have some compunction. But thou mayst be at rest now, for he is gone beyond thy help, or that of any one else."

"Gone!" exclaimed Sir Patrick again—"Gone! how did he die?"

"Horribly! most horribly!" replied the lady, shuddering. "It was fearful to behold him in his agonies! Knowing, as I did, the potency of the poison, I could hardly have believed that the old man would have taken so long to die."

"Horrible!" exclaimed Sir Patrick, involuntarily.

"Aye, it was horrible!" replied the lady; "horrible indeed, as thou wouldst have said if thou hadst seen it. For a moment the poison seemed to have given him new strength, and he rose from his chair as if he would have done vengeance on me. 'Twas fearful to behold him!"

"Art sure he is quite dead?" said Sir Patrick again.

"Aye," replied the lady, "as dead as his son Walter; so dead, as to make thee surely the Laird of Stradawn, the moment thou shalt have made as siccar of Patrick, as we may now soon hope thou wilt be able to do. I did but help him, as I was saying, out of the pains and wretchedness of old age and dotage. Yet it was an awful work for me. And oh, his last look was fearful! I wish I may ever be able to get rid of it! Would that thou couldst have steeled thyself up to have done it thyself, Murdoch! But come in—come in quickly! Hast thou secured the prisoner?"

"I have," replied Sir Patrick, now exerting a certain degree of command over his feelings; "he will be here anon."

"That is well," replied the Lady Stradawn; "then all is thine own. His trial must be short, and his execution speedy. But come, we have much to do to make things seemly ere they arrive. He must appear to have died of a broken heart caused by the wickedness of his son. Everything suspicious must be removed from about him. I could not dare to touch him. Why stand ye so long hesitating? But 'tis no wonder, for I could not look upon him myself without fancying that the devil was grinning over my shoulder. 'Tis horrible to think on't!

But come," continued she, as she at last seemed to summon up resolution to climb the stair; "lock the door, Murdoch, and follow me up quickly, for we have no time to lose."

Sir Patrick Stewart made a signal to Dugald and the others, and then ascended to the hall after the Lady Stradawn. A deathlike silence prevailed within it. A single lamp was glimmering feebly on a sconce at the upper end of it; and there stood the lady, pale and trembling, at that side of the chimney which was farthest from Sir Allan's chair. Sir Patrick, in his agitation, moved hurriedly forward, and the moment the light of the lamp fell upon his features, the lady uttered a loud scream, and swooned away upon the floor.

The spectacle that now met his eyes harrowed up his very soul. His father lay dead in his chair, with his features and his limbs fixed in the last frightful convulsion, by which the racking poison had terminated his existence. His mouth was twisted, his tongue thrust out, and his eyeballs so fearfully staring, that even his tenderly affectionate son felt it a dreadful effort to look upon that which used to be to him an object of the deepest veneration and love. Beside his chair was a small table, on which he was usually served with his food. There stood a silver porringer containing the minced meat, which his extreme age required; and notwithstanding all that the Lady Stradawn had said to the contrary, the operation of the poison seemed to have been so quick, as to have mortally affected him, ere he had taken the fourth part of the mess that had been provided for him. Sir Patrick was overpowered by his feelings. He sank into a chair, and covering his face with his hands, he gave way to his grief, in which he remained so entirely absorbed, that neither the entrance of Dugald, nor the thundering which some time afterwards took place at the outer gate, nor the noise of the many voices of those who came pouring in, were sufficient to arouse him.

Dugald Roy had the presence of mind to hurry down to the court-yard, to prepare the Lord of Curgarf, and those who came with him, for the dreadful spectacle they were to witness. Thunderstruck and shocked by his intelligence, they crowded up to the hall, where the general horror was for some time so great, as to render everyone incapable of acting; but at length they gathered sufficient recollection to bestir themselves. The poisoned porringer was first carefully preserved; the Lady Stradawn was carried off in strong fits to her apartment; the body of Sir Walter Stewart was borne up into the hall; and there, after undergoing the necessary preparations used on such occasions, the father and son were laid out in state together, and the couches on which the bodies rested were surrounded by so great a multitude of wax tapers, as to exchange the melancholy gloom of the place into a blaze of light, which, reflected as it was from the various pieces of armour that glittered in vain pomp upon the walls, shone but to produce a greater intensity of sadness. The good priest of Dounan was sent for; and the appalling news having spread quickly around, the retainers began to swarm into the Castle, from all quarters, in sorrowing groups, full of lamentation. Meanwhile the Lord of Curgarf and his son, the Master of Forbes, occupied themselves in soothing the afflicted Sir Patrick Stewart, and in aiding and encouraging him to go through with those trying and painful duties which this most afflicting occasion demanded of him.

Food and wine had been carried to the Lady Stradawn, where she sat alone in her bower, so deeply sunk in remorse, and dejection, and dread, as to be quite unconscious of the entrance or departure of those who brought her these comforts. Those who were compelled to be the bearers of them, gazed on her with fear, and hastened from her with expedition, and no one else could be persuaded to go near her, even her woman refused to remain with her, as something accursed, so that she was left abandoned by all, as a prey to her evil thoughts. Had any one ventured to look in upon her, as she sat motionless in her great chair, with a lamp flickering on a table beside her, and throwing an uncertain light by fits and snatches on her face, now pale and fixed as marble,—and on her glazed and tearless eyes, and her dry and withered lips, he might have fancied that she was already a corpse; yet deep, deep was the mental agony that she felt.

The midnight watch had been set, and all had been for some time silent within the walls at Drummin, save the distant hum of the subdued voices of those who, according to custom, sat waking the corpses in the hall, when the door of the Lady Stradawn's bower opened, and her son Murdoch appeared. If the spirit of her murdered husband had arisen before her eyes, she could not have started with more astonishment, or recoiled with greater apparent horror.

"Murdoch!" cried she, in a loud and agitated voice, "Is it thee, Murdoch?" And then, sinking back into the same fixed and motionless attitude, whence she had been thus momentarily aroused, she added, in a faint, low, and feeble tone, "Murdoch! —would that thou hadst never been born!"

"Mother," said Murdoch, calmly shutting the door behind him, and taking a seat beside her chair. "I have heard all from Nicol, the playfellow of my boyhood, who chanced to be set to guard me, in the apartment below. I wished to see thee ere we die; and I purchased from the sordid wretch this midnight hour—this last hour of privacy with thee."

"Ha!" cried the Lady Stradawn, with a strange and sudden transition from the apathy and torpor of despair, to the most energetic anxiety of hope; "If Nicol did that for thee, why may we not bribe him to open a way for us through those who guard the gate? Quick!—quick!—quick!—oh, let us quickly escape!—oh, let us not tarry one moment longer! There are my keys; we have treasure in that cabinet, which may well bribe him, and yet leave us rich!"

"Be composed, my most worthy mother," said Murdoch Stewart; "there is not the shadow of a chance for us in that way. The door of the keep is doubly barred, and doubly guarded, and no one leaves it unexamined beneath the light of a blazing torch. The whole men-at-arms and clansmen within the walls, infuriated against us, are of their own free will engaged in vigilant watching. The portcullis is down, the gate barricaded, the barbican manned, and the walls surrounded by patroles. Mother, cast aside all such hopes as useless, for as the guilt of both of us must soon appear as clear as to-morrow's noonday, so that sun, which shall certainly arise to-morrow morning, shall as surely look upon our graves ere he sets."

The Lady Stradawn sank again into the chair, from which the sudden impulse of hope had so energetically raised her, and, groaning deeply, she relapsed into her former state of deathlike stillness, broken only by the long drawn sob that at certain intervals convulsed her whole frame.

"Mother!" said Murdoch Stewart, after a pause; "where are all the fruits of that career of crime for which thou nursed me as an infant, tutored me as a boy, and prompted me as a man? Have I not followed thy bidding through deceit, robbery, and murder, and where is now my reward? Thine is locked up there in that secret cabinet of glittering toys, which to-morrow thou must leave, to go out to be hanged by the neck on the gallows-tree, with the son, whom thou wouldst have had Lord of the Aven, grinning at thee like a caitiff cur from the farther end of its beam."

"Oh!—oh ho?" cried the agonised woman, shaken through every limb by the palsy of her fears; "is there no—no deliverance for us?"

"Yes," said Murdoch Stewart, calmly; "yes, there is a deliverance, and a speedy one too."

"Oh, name it!" cried the frantic woman; "oh, name it! and quickly let us avail ourselves of it!"

"Here it is," said Murdoch Stewart, quietly taking a small paper packet from his bosom; "here it is, mother. A few small pinches of this powder, mingled in a cup of that wine, will snatch us both from the torture of being made a disgraceful public spectacle to-morrow—of being gazed at by the vulgar eyes, and pointed at by the vile fingers of those wretched serfs, and their grovelling mates and spawn, whom, a little better luck and better fortune for us, had by that time made the abject slaves of our will. See! here it is mingled, already it is dissolved, and now the draught is potent. Good mother, I pledge thee," said he, drinking down half of what the goblet contained; "and now here is thy share."

"No,—no,—no!—I cannot!—no, I cannot!" cried the Lady Stradawn, with frantic horror in her averted eyes.

"Then do I tell thee, mother mine," said Murdoch Stewart sternly; "thou hast not trained me up to deal in deeds of blood and death for naught. I shall never suffer thy womanish fears to bring the disgrace of the gallows upon thee. I love thee too much for that. See here, good mother! 'tis but a choice of deaths. Here is a concealed dagger, look you. Say! wouldst thou bring one more murder—the murder of a mother—on my already over-burdened soul, to sink it deeper in that sea of torment to which these priests would fain have us believe that those who, like us, have used the wit and the strength with which they have been gifted, for bettering their own condition in this world, must hasten from hence? Drink! or by every fiend that suffers there, thou diest in the instant!"

The Lady Stradawn glared at her son with a vacant stare, as if all reason had fled from her. She took the cup mechanically from his hand, and drained it to the bottom.

"What hast thou done?" cried the man-at-arms, who had been brought to the door by the violent tone of some of Murdoch Stewart's last words, and who rushed in just as the Lady Stradawn had swallowed the poison.

"Do what thou wilt now, Nicol," said Murdoch Stewart, with perfect composure; "we are beyond thy power or that of anyone else within the castle of Drummin."

Nicol at once guessed at what had happened, and ran instantly for the Priest. The good Father of Dounan was deeply skilled in medicine as well as in divinity. He called for assistance, and antidotes were forcibly given to Murdoch Stewart, and passively received by his mother the Lady

Stradawn.   Their wretched existence was thus prolonged, though death could not be altogether averted.   They lingered on in great pain for many days, during which all judicial proceedings were suspended.   The pious priest lost not one moment of this precious time.   By exerting all his religious learning and all his eloquence he at length succeeded in bringing both of them to a full sense of the enormity of their guilt, as well as to an ample confession of all their crimes.   It is not for us to interpret the decrees of the Almighty in such a case as theirs ; but if the apparent deep contrition that followed was real and heartfelt, we may trust that the mercy as well as the benefit of the merits of that blessed Saviour, who died for us all upon the cross, even for the thief that was crucified with Him, was extended to them, dreadful as their crimes had been.

My legend now draws to a hasty conclusion.   The days of mourning were fully numbered by Sir Patrick Stewart for his murdered father and brother.   The kindness of the old Lord of Curgarf and his son Arthur Master of Forbes towards him was unwearied and most consolatory.   Nor were the delicate affections of the Lady Catherine Forbes less tenderly or unremittingly displayed, so that, in due time, by becoming her husband, he bound himself to both his friends by the closest and dearest ties.   In pious remembrance of his brother Sir Walter's murder, he erected the pillar of stone I spoke of as that which stood so long by the side of the well-eye where he was slain ; but he refrained from inscribing anything upon it, lest his doing so might have revived the recollection of Murdoch Stewart's atrocity.   He likewise ordered a stone to be set up where the proud Priest of Dalestie was burned, rather as a sort of expiation of the stern act of justice, which his brother Sir Walter had inflicted upon him than to perpetuate the detested memory of the depraved wretch who suffered there.

FATE OF THE AULD ANCIENT MONUMENTS.

Clifford (as we arose to pursue our journey).—And what became of these two monuments, Serjeant Stewart ?

Serjeant.—A certain gentleman, who was building a house somewhere in this neighbourhood (for I had rather not designate him too particularly), cast his eyes on the fine stone that stood by the well-eye, and perceiving that it would make an excellent lintel, he took immediate measures to get it carried off to his rising edifice. Having accomplished his intention, with no little difficulty, it was speedily employed in the building, where it promised to conduct itself with the same quiet and decorum which were observed by all the other stones of the edifice, after being put to rest, each in his separate bed of mortar. But no sooner did the house come to be inhabited than it began to be haunted by strange and mysterious noises. Some of these were quite unintelligible, for they resembled no earthly sound that had ever been heard before. Then long conversations began, and were continued, in small sharp clear voices; but although the words fell distinctly enough on the ears of those who heard them, the language was as a sealed book to them. And ever and anon the seeming dialogue would be interrupted by strange uncouth fits of laughter, as if of several persons together, or in different parts of the premises, that were so far from creating a corresponding disposition to mirth or merriment in the listeners that they froze up the very blood in their veins. But this was not all. The most dismal croaking of frogs arose in every part of the house. You would have sworn that the creatures were in the cupboards—the presses—the chimneys—in the beds—on the floors—nay, on the very tables, and among the dishes which the good folks of the family had set before them. It was as if the frogs that formed the great plague in Egypt had filled the house with their hoarse voices. One would begin as if he were the leader of the band, and then others would start off, one after another, till the doleful chorus, resounding from all quarters, made the concert loud and sonorous. It was no uncommon thing, during the dark and dreary watches of the night, for the voice of the leader, which had something peculiarly striking in it, to arise of a sudden, as if he that uttered it was sitting astraddle on the nose of the goodman of the house. In vain was the hand applied to the organ, to drive off what, in reality, appeared to be the organist. There was nothing there; yet the sound continued as if it had come from the deepest pipe in the organ loft of some cathedral, yea, of that of the great organ of Haerlem itself. The more he rubbed the more it grew, and the louder and more universal became the chorus. His very nose itself increased in size from the frequent and severe rubbings to which it was thus subjected, whilst he began to grow thin and emaciated in proportion, till his whole person at length appeared rather as if it had been an appendage to his nose, than his nose an appendage to his person. At last, being worn out in spirit, as he was very nearly in body also, he was fain to take out the stone from the building, and to carry it back to the hill-side again, and then, to be sure, he enjoyed perfect quiet.

Clifford.—A sensible man, truly. But what had evil spirits or fairies to do with a monumental stone?

Serjeant.—Nothing that I can see, sir, except that being guilty of so impious a deed as the removal of such a stone, he was for a time left unprotected by all good angels, and consequently he was altogether at the mercy of those evil ones.

Grant.—Very well made out, Mister Serjeant. But where is the stone now?

Serjeant.—Why, sir, I am sure you will hardly believe me when I tell you that a few years ago it was wantonly destroyed by another gentleman, who shall be also nameless.

Grant.—What a Goth he must have been! Why should you conceal his name, Serjeant? It deserves to be held up to public reprobation.

Serjeant.—I know my own interest too well to be the officious person who shall publish it though. Yet I must own that it would have served him right that it should have been so marked. What do you think he did, gentlemen? Happening to be in this part of Strathdawn, he, without rhyme or reason, and out of sheer wickedness, ordered his people to break both that and the *Clach-na-Tagart,* or the Priest's stone, which shocking pieces of barbarism he took care to see executed in his own presence, whilst he stood by, like a mischievous baboon, chuckling over their destruction.

Clifford.—The fellow deserved to have been plunged over head and ears into the Wallee in the first place, and after being thus well soaked, he ought to have been leisurely consumed at the Priest's stone, like a well watered sack of Newcastle coals.

Serjeant.—Why, sir, I must allow that he has been punished severely enough. The whole people of the country cried out upon him, and every one declared that it was quite impossible that the fellow could thrive, after having demolished two such ould auncient antiquities. And so in truth it turned out, for not long afterwards he lost the whole *fushon** of his side. As for the Clach-na-Tagart, the Roman Catholics, who form the chief population hereabouts, intended to have clasped it together with iron bands, but, (addressing author), as you know very well, sir, from having recorded the fact in your book, the great flood of August, 1829, saved them the trouble of doing so, for the Aven then carried the broken stone clean away, aye, and

---

* Power.

it swept off the best part of the haugh it stood upon into the bargain.

Grant.—But stay, my good friend Archy. What do you mean by quitting the level path to climb this confounded steep hill, as the direction of your nose, at this moment, would seem to indicate your present intention to be?

Serjeant.—I would fain show you an extensive prospect, gentlemen. It is only a bit start of a pull up here. A mere breathing for you after the long rest you had by the water side yonder. (Then addressing the gillie.)—My man, hold you on the road to Inchrory with the horse, and tell the gudewife there that we are coming.

Clifford.—'Tis a very stiff pull, Archy. But we shall be all the better for something of this sort to put us in wind. I calculate that we shall have some worse climbing than this before we are done with these mountains.

Serjeant.—Troth, you may well say that, sir; and as for this hill, we may be very thankful that we have not to climb it with a strong demonstration of the enemies' riflemen lining the ridge of it.

Clifford.—You are out there, serjeant. Depend upon it, if we saw an enemy lining the height, we should both of us climb it like roebucks, to be at them.

Serjeant.—I'm not saying but we might, sir; that is, if we saw that we were sufficiently well backed. But for all that, we might find our graves before we were half way up the hill; and then what the better should we be, of our comrades saying, as they passed by us, " Poor fellows, you are settled !" Would that be any consolation to us, as we lay writhing in the last agonies?

Grant.—Very small consolation indeed, Archy.

Serjeant.—I wot it would be little indeed, sir. Yet ought a man to do his duty for all that, simply because it is his duty. Many is the time I have heard my good friend Captain Ketley say that; and there were few words fell from his mouth that had not some good sense, or some good moral in them. And certain it is, that if we did not always keep this rule of our conduct in view, we should neither be good sodgers nor good Christians.

Clifford.—Right again, old boy.

Serjeant.—And yet, Mr. Clifford, as I reckon, there is some pleasure in coming out of the scrimmage in a whole skin, and with ears that can hear all the honest commendations that are bestowed upon your own brave and gallant conduct.

Grant (after reaching the summit of the hill).—That was indeed a breather; but now, Serjeant, for the prospect you promised us, I see nothing as yet but the bare flat, moist, moory hill-top.

Serjeant (leading us to the eastern verge of the top of the hill).—Come this way, then, gentlemen.   See here what an extensive prospect you have down the course of the river Don. It looks but a small stream there, especially from this height.

Author.—What old castle is that which we see below us there, near yonder clump of trees ?

Serjeant.—That is Curgarf Castle. That is the very spot to which so much of my legend referred, though I shall not pretend to say that the building you see there is precisely the same. But now, gentlemen, turn your eyes westward again. Is not that a fine mountain view ? See how proudly the Cairngorms rise yonder ! But, observe me—you don't see the highest summits as yet, because those big black lumps opposite to us there, hide the highest tops from our eyes.

Author.—It is a magnificent scene, notwithstanding, especially as viewed at present, under that splendid display of evening light, that is now shooting over those loftier ridges from the descending sun.

Grant.—A very grand scene indeed !

Clifford.—Aye, Grant, we shall have some climbing there, I promise you.

Grant.—There can be little doubt of that.   But tell me, Serjeant, what solitary house is that we see in the valley below.

Author.—I can answer you that question.   That is Inchrory, the small place, half farm-house, half hostel, where we are to sojourn to-night.   It is used as a place of rest and refreshment, by the few travellers who pass on foot or on horseback, by the rugged path which we left in the valley, and which goes hence southwards, up through the valley of the Builg—past the lake of that name,—so across what is there the rivulet of the Don, —and then onwards over the hills to Castleton of Braemar. That deep hollow in the mountains, that turns sharp westwards beyond Inchrory yonder, is what is more properly called Glen-aven. The river Aven comes pouring down hitherwards through it, and our way lies up its course.

Clifford.—I should be sorry if it did so this evening.   I am quite prepared to hail yonder house of Inchrory below, as a welcome place of refuge for this night.

Author.—Few places must be more welcome to a wayworn traveller than Inchrory, especially when first descried by the

weary wayfarer from Castleton, in a winter's evening, as the
sun is hasting downwards.

Serjeant. —You are not far wrong there, sir. A dreadful hill
journey that is, indeed, from Castleton to Inchrory, amid the
storms of winter. Not a vestige of a house by the way.
Many a poor wretch has perished in the snow, amidst these
trackless wastes. Not to go very far back, there was a terrible
snow storm about the Martinmas time in the year 1829. It
roared, and blew, and drifted so fast, that it was mid-day or
ever Mrs. Shaw of Inchrory ventured to put her head out
beyond the threshold of her own door, to look at the thick and
dreary shroud of white in which dead nature was wrapped, and
which covered the whole lonely scene of hill and valley around
her, and was in many places blown into wreathes of a great
depth. There was not a speck of colour, nor any moving
thing to vary the glazed unbroken surface, except on one
distant hillock, where a single human figure was seen, wandering to and fro, as if in a maze, like some one bereft of reason.
The male inhabitants of the house were all out looking after
the stock belonging to the grazing farm; and, as Mrs. Shaw
was in doubt whether the person she beheld might not in
reality be some one who was deranged, as his movements rather
seemed to indicate, she was afraid to venture to approach him.
But curiosity as well as pity made her cast many a look towards him during that afternoon, as he still continued to move
slowly round the hillock, and backwards and forwards, without
any apparent sense or meaning, and stopping now and then, as
if utterly bewildered. At length, as it was drawing towards
night, Mrs. Shaw observed that the figure had either fallen, or
lain down among the snow, and her charitable feelings then
overcoming all her apprehensions, she proceeded to wade
through the snow towards the hillock where he lay. Having,
with very considerable difficulty, made her way to the spot,
she found him lying on his back, as composedly as if he had
lain down in his bed. The intense cold had so benumbed his
intellects, indeed, that he did not seem to be in the least aware
of his own melancholy situation.—" Wha are ye? and what are
ye wantin?" said he, to Mrs. Shaw, with a faint smile on his
emaciated face, as he beheld her stooping over him with an
anxious gaze of inquiry. "I came to help you," replied Mrs.
Shaw; "Will you let me try to lift you up?"—"Thank you,
I can rise mysel'," replied he, making a vain effort to get up.
—"You had better let me help you," said Mrs. Shaw.—"Ou,
na, thank ye," replied he again; "I can rise weel eneugh

mysel'."—"Do so, then," said Mrs. Shaw, whilst at the same
time she prepared herself for giving him her best assistance
during his attempt.   In this way, a strong effort on her part
enabled her at last to succeed in getting the poor man on his
legs; and then, after the expenditure of so much time as might
have easily enabled her to have gone five or six miles, and with
immense labour and fatigue, this heroic woman was finally
successful in supporting him, or rather, I should say, in half
carrying him to Inchrory.   When she had got him fairly out
of the snow, and into the house, she had the horror to discover,
that not only were his shoes and stockings gone, but that even the
very flesh was worn off his feet.   When help arrived, they got
him into bed, and did all for him that charitable Christians
could do.   Food was brought to him, but it was some time
before he could be made to swallow any portion of it, and that
only by feeding him like a child.   The poor fellow turned out
to be a young man of the name of Thomas Macintosh, servant
to the Rev. Mr. MacEachan, the Roman Catholic priest at
Castleton, which place he had left on the Wednesday morning,
and he had wandered among the snow, without food or shelter,
and becoming every moment more and more bewildered, until
the Friday evening, when Mrs. Shaw's praiseworthy exertions
brought him to her house.   On the Saturday, the good people
carried him down the valley to the next farm, on his way to
the doctor.   But, alas! no doctor was ever destined to do him
any good, for he died that same evening.   Two one pound
notes and a few shillings were found in his pocket, which sum
went to pay the expense of his interment in the newly made
church-yard at Tomantoul, of which, as it so happened, he was
the second tenant.

Grant.—What a melancholy fate!

Serjeant.—Sad, indeed, sir.   But there are many stories of
the same kind connected with this wild path through these
desolate mountains.

Author.—Do you remember any more of them, Archy?

Serjeant.—Ou, yes, sir.   It was upon that terrible night of
drift, the 25th of November, 1826, no farther gone, when so
many poor people perished, that a man, three women, and two
horses, were buried in the snow upon yon hill, which is called
Cairn Elsach, as they were on their way back from the
Tomantoul market.   So deep was the snow in many places,
that one of the horses was found frozen stiff dead, and the
beast was so supported in it, as to be sticking upright upon his
legs, and a woman was discovered standing dead beside him.

Some little time afterwards, a shepherd, who happened to have occasion to cross the hill, had his attention attracted by some long hair which was seen above the icy surface, waving in the wintry blast. On scraping away the snow, he found that it was attached to a woman's head, who had unfortunately perished. He procured the assistance of some of his friends, who were afraid to dig out the body for fear it might have become offensive. I, who chanced to be there, had no such scruples, first, because I knew very well that the snow must have preserved it, and, secondly, because, if it had been otherwise, I knew that I had lost my sense of smelling in consequence of the desperate wound in my jaw, of which I told you. When the snow was removed, the poor young woman's body was found quite fresh and entire, but it was perfectly blue in colour.

Author.—These are melancholy details; yet, it must be confessed, they are quite in harmony with the wild and lonely scenery now before our eyes.

Grant.—They remind one of the horrors of the Alps.

Clifford.—The gaunt wolves are wanting, though, to make up the picture completely.

Serjeant.—We had the wolves also ourselves once upon a time, sir; and now the corby, and the hill-fox, and the eagle, do their best to make up for the want of them. But such a wilderness as this, covered deep with snow, and the howling wind carrying the drift across it, has quite terrors enough in it for my taste.

Author.—I am quite of your opinion, Archy.

Serjeant.—Yet it is wonderful how Providence will interfere to preserve people alive, amid such complicated horrors. I remember a story of a man of the name of Macintosh, who left Braemar, with his wife, to come over this way. A dreadful snow storm came upon them, and, being blinded by the snow-drift, and encumbered in the deep and heavy wreathes, the poor people were separated from each other. The man made his way, with great difficulty, to a whisky bothy, where he arrived much exhausted, and quite inconsolable for the loss of his wife. Being thus saved himself, he procured the assistance of people to help him to look for the corpse of his lost partner. For two whole days they sought in vain; when, just as they were about to abandon their search, till the surface of the ground should become less burdened with snow, they observed a figure coming slowly and wearily down the hill of Gart. This, as it drew nearer, appeared to be a woman; and, on her approaching nearer still, the overjoyed husband discovered that she was his living wife, for whom he had been weeping as dead. She had been wandering for nearly three days, without either food or shelter, amid the mountain snows, but, although she was dreadfully exhausted, she eventually recovered.

Grant.—That was indeed the support of Providence, Archy !

Author.—Most wonderful indeed ! Her preservation was little short of a miracle.

Serjeant.—Aye, truly, you may well say that, sir. Nothing but a miracle could have preserved the poor woman from so many perils as she must have encountered in her wanderings,—not to mention those of cold, hunger, and fatigue. It was the hand of Providence, assuredly, that supported her. By what means he worked, we have no opportunity of knowing. But surely it was strange that he could have enabled any human being, and especially a woman, to have come through so much fatigue and suffering alive.

Clifford.—Truly, most miraculous !

Serjeant.—And then, gentlemen, how very strangely—so far as we blind mortals can perceive—are others permitted to perish at the very door, as it were, of help. I think it is now about sixteen years ago—and, if I remember rightly, it was about the Christmas time—that James Stewart, son of the miller of the Delnabo, perished, on the very haugh there, just below the House of Inchrory. The poor fellow passed by this place, on his way over to Braemar, one morning that I happened to be here. He stopped a few minutes with me, and had some talk. " I'm likely to get a fine day for crossing the hill, Archy," said he. " Well," said I, " I hope you will, and wish you may. Yet I don't altogether like yon *mountaneous* heap of white tumbling-looking clouds, that are casting up afar off over the hill-top yonder." " They dinna look awthegither weel, to be sure," said Jemmy ; " but I houp I may be in weel kent land lang or they break." We parted. The snow came on in a dreadful storm, about mid-day ; and I had two or three anxious thoughts about Jemmy Stewart, as the recollection of him was ever and anon brought back to me, during the night, by the fearful whistling of the wind, and the rattling of the hail. Next morning, I, and some of the other men about the place, found a human track, running in a bewildered, irregular, and uncertain line, between the house of Inchrory and the burn yonder, which must be a width of not much more than forty yards. We had not followed this far, when we came to the poor man, whose worn-out feet had made these prints. His

walking-stick was standing erect among the snow beside him,
—and there lay poor Jemmy Stewart, on his face; his hands
were closed, and his head rested on them, just as if he had
lain quietly down to sleep. The lads who were with me,
stupid gomerills that they were, had a superstitious dread of
touching him; but, deeply as I grieved for the poor fellow, I
had seen too many dead men in my time to have any
such scruples. I accordingly turned him, and found, alas!
that he was quite gone. It appeared that he had been
suddenly surprised and bewildered by the snow-drift among
the hills, and that, having lost all knowledge of his way, he
had unconsciously wandered in the very opposite direction to
that in which he had intended to go. Becoming more and
more confused, as he wandered and wandered, he became at
last so entirely stupefied by the multiplied terrors of that awful
night, that he ultimately yielded to the last drowsiness of
death, and so laid himself down to court its fatal repose.
Alas! he was unhappily ignorant that he was within a few
yards of the friendly house which he had passed on his way
upwards on the previous morning, to the reviving shelter of
which, the least possible additional exertion might have easily
brought him, had he but known in what direction to have
made it.

Clifford.—What a sad and fearful story?

Serjeant.—Aye, sir, sad and fearful indeed! Is it not
dreadful to think how often the recollection of him crossed my
mind during that fatal night, and how little trouble, on my
part, would have saved him, had I only known that he was
wandering in the snow so near me? Aye, and to think that I
should have lain ignorantly all the while in my warm bed,
allowing him so cruelly to perish! Willing would I have been
to have travelled all night through the drift to have saved
poor Jemmy Stewart!

Author.—No one can doubt that, Archy.

Serjeant.—Well, but sir, you see these matters are in the
hand of God, and at his wise disposal; and although we, blind
moles of the yearth as we are, cannot easily descry why a worthy
well-doing young man like Jemmy Stewart should be permitted
thus wretchedly to die, without aid, either human or divine,
we cannot doubt the justice and wisdom of God's ways, which
are inscrutable, and past man's finding out. Well, I did all
I could for the poor fellow, for I had his corpse carried down
to his afflicted father at Delnabo, and I saw him buried at
Dounan, near the Bridge of Livat.

Clifford.—That, indeed, was all you could do for the poor man, Archy; and the manner in which you did that little, together with all the sentiments that you have uttered regarding him, are enough to convince anyone that you would not have scrupled to peril your life, if you could have thereby saved that of a fellow-creature, still more that of a friend.

Serjeant.—Thank you, sir, for your good opinion of me; but, as I said before, these matters are in the hand of God: and, whilst he allows the strong to perish, he can, if he so wills it, preserve the weakest. I remember an extraordinary circumstance that happened about eighteen or twenty years ago, which I may mention to you as an example of the truth of this observe of mine. Four women, who had been in the south country, at the harvest, were on their return home over these mountains, when they were caught in a storm. The snow came on so thickly upon them, and the wind raised so great a land-drift, that they became bewildered, lost their way, and, after much wandering, they at last got into the ruins of an old bothy, near the side of the river Gairden, which runs, as I may tell ye, beyond those farther hills there to the south. By this time their shoes were worn off. They were without food—without all means of making a fire—and the cold came on so intense during the night, that the poor things were all frozen to death. There they were found in the morning by a party of smugglers, who had been early astir after their trade. The whole of the four women were cold and stiff. But the most wonderful, as well as the most touching circumstance of all was, that a female child, of about sixteen months old, was found alive, vainly attempting to draw nourishment from its mother's breast. The poor woman's maternal anxiety had enabled her to use precautions to keep her babe warm and in life, which she had failed to exercise for her own preservation. The child was taken charge of by Donald Shaw of Lagganall, and brought up by him under the name of Kirstock; and she afterwards went to service in Glen Livat, where ——— But mark me now, gentlemen! Here we are at Caochan-Seirceag, of which you heard so much from me in my Legend of the Clan-Allan Stewarts.

Clifford.—I see there are no trees here now, as you say there were in the days of Sir Patrick Stewart of Clan-Allan.

Grant.—The cliffs are fine, though, and the ravine itself romantic. How comes it that some of these rocks are so brilliantly white? They absolutely shine like alabaster amid the dazzling radiance of that setting sun.

Author.—If I answer your question, it will draw me into a disquisition which may bring an attack upon us from Clifford, for prosing about geology to one another.

Grant.—Never mind him ; he may shut his ears, if he likes.

Author.—Those brilliant streaks of alabastrine white, are nothing more than incrustations of calcareous stalactites, formed on those rocks of gneiss, by the evaporation of these trickling rills, the water of which holds lime in solution, probably derived from the little aquatic marl snail in the moss above, from which they drain themselves.

Clifford.—I'd advise you to think less of your alabastrine incrustations of calcareous stalactites on gneiss, and more of your necks and limbs, during this steep and somewhat hazardous descent, else you may evaporate like some of those trickling rills you are speaking of. These fellows you told us of, Mr. Serjeant, must have had some little difficulty in carrying the Lady Catherine down and up here. But tell me, I pray you, what is the meaning of the name of Caochan-Seirceag? for I know that all your Gaelic names of places are highly poetical and descriptive.

Serjeant.—The meaning of Caochan-Scirceag, sir, so far as I can make it out, is *the rivulet of the beloved maiden.*

Clifford.—Poetical in the highest degree ! Why, what scope does it not afford to the poet's mind to fancy the ardour of the passion of the lovers who must have made the romantic bed of this rivulet their·trysting place, as well as the beauty of the maiden by whose beloved image the youth thus happily chose to distinguish it—to imagine all the obstacles which the pure stream of their love may have encountered in its course, and of which this vexed and tortured little brook may have formed but too lively a type, until at length it glided into a peaceful channel, as this does in its passage across the green meadow yonder below ! What a glorious poetical romance might be suggested by these rocks and rills ! Confound them ! I had nearly tumbled headlong over this slippery stone ! What a fall I should have had !

Grant.—You made a narrow escape there, indeed, Clifford. I would have you to remember, that it would have been quite as bad to have died the victim of romantic enthusiasm, as of dry geological speculation.

Clifford.—I beg your pardon, my good fellow, you are quite wrong there. I at least would have infinitely preferred to have died from thinking of the beloved maiden, than from a confusion of brain occasioned by a mixture of alabastrine incrustations of calcareous stalactites and gneiss and marl snails! But to return to my speculations as to the rivulet of the beloved maiden, why may it not have had its name from the Lady Catherine Forbes herself?

Serjeant.—As I shall answer, you have hit the very thing, sir. There cannot be a doubt that it was from her that the rill was so called.

Clifford.—See now how lucky it was for you, Mister Archy, that I was not killed by a fall, as I had so nearly been, else had you been deprived of my ingenious elucidation of this most difficult point. But now, thank heaven, we are all safe in the meadow, and I shall have one touch at the trouts yet ere the light goes away entirely.

Author.—I wish you great success, Clifford. Pray do your best, my good fellow, for I know not what commons we may have in this our hostel of Inchrory here.

Clifford.—Aha! you see that my rod and my piscatorial skill are not without their use. Depend upon it, you shan't go without a supper, if I can help it.

As I suspected, we found that our accommodations at Inchrory were rather of the simplest description. But the good people of the house showed every disposition to do the best for our comfort that lay in their power. A dozen and a half of large trouts, which Clifford soon brought in, added to some of those provisions which we carried with us, made up the best part of our repast, and we very speedily prepared ourselves for the intellectual enjoyment of the evening.

Clifford.—One would think that the worthy people here had been forewarned of our story-telling propensities, and that they had made especial provision accordingly for the serjeant's long yarns. Did you ever see a more magnificent pair of wax candles on any table? Why, these would see out all the narratives that ever were told by Sindbad the Sailor.

Grant.—Who could have expected to have met with wax candles, such as these, in an humble place like this, in the midst of these lonely mountains, and so far from the haunts of men? Nay, who could have expected to have met with any candles at all here?

Author.—How happens it, Archy, that they can give us candles so superb as these, in a place like this, where they have so little else to produce, and nothing at all that can in the least degree correspond with them? They are of enormous size— nearly three inches in diameter, I should say. I have seen no such candles as these, except in a Roman Catholic Church, or procession.

Serjeant.—Troth, sir, I imagine you have solved the mystery. The truth is, as I told you before, that the great mass of the population of this Highland country consists of Roman Catholics; and it is probable that these candles, which have been originally used for some religious rite, have, from necessity, been this night lighted for your use.

Clifford.—Come, then, serjeant, do you proceed to use the candles as fast as may be. Open your budget, my good man, and give us one of your many legends.

Grant.—You had better allow the serjeant to mix a tumbler of warm stuff in the first place, and whilst he is doing so, he can be considering as to what he had best give us.

Serjeant.—Thank you, sir. I'll just be doing that same. Would you have any objections to another legend of the Clan-Allan Stewarts, gentlemen?

Author.—Certainly not, Archy, if it be only as good as the last you gave us.

Serjeant.—It is not for me to speak in its praise, sir, though I must e'en say that I think it no worse than the last. But it is a hantel longer.

Grant.—The longer the better, if it be good. We have a long night, and great candles before us, so that you may give your tongue its fullest licence.

Serjeant.—Well, gentlemen, it's a good thing to be neither gagged in the mouth, nor stinted in the bicker.

Author.—Depend upon it, Archy, you shall be neither the one nor the other.

Clifford.—Come away, then, serjeant, begin as soon as you please.

Archy then took a long snuff out of the box which I handed to him, during which he seemed to be collecting his ideas, and then he began his narrative. Although I regret that I cannot always give the precise words used by him, I shall endeavour to preserve as faithful an outline of its particulars as I can, and that in language which I hope may be at least as intelligible.

THE LEGEND OF CHARLEY STEWART TAILLEAR-CRUBACH.

THERE is a long, low, flat-topped, and prettily wooded eminence, that rises out of the middle of the bonny haughs of Kilmaichly, at some distance below the junction of the rivers Aven and Livat. I don't remember that it has any particular name, but it looks, for all the world, like the fragment of some ancient plain, that must have been of much higher level than that from which it now rises, which fragment had been left, after the ground on each side of it had been worn down to its present level, by the changeful operations of the neighbouring streams.   But whatever you geology gentlemen might say, as to what its origin might have been, every lover of nature must agree that it is a very beautiful little hill, covered as its slopes are with graceful weeping birches, and other trees.   The bushes that still remain show that, in earlier times, it must have been thickly wooded with great oaks, which probably gave shelter to the ould auncient Druids, when engaged in their superstitious mysteries.   At the period to which the greater part of my story belongs—that is, in and about that of the reign of King James III.—the blue smoke that curled up from among the trees betrayed the existence of a cottage, that sat perched upon the brow of its western extremity, looking towards the Castle of Drummin.   This little dwelling was much better built, and, in every respect, much neater than any of those in the surrounding district; and its interior exhibited more comforts as to furniture and *plenishing* of all sorts, and those too of a description superior to anything of the kind which a mere cottager might have been reasonably expected to have possessed.

The inhabitants of this snug little dwelling were a very beautiful woman, of some four or five and twenty years of age, named Alice Asher, and her son, a handsome noble-looking boy, who, from certain circumstances affecting his birth, bore the name of Charles Stewart.

There was a well-doing and brave retainer of the house of Clan-Allan, called MacDermot, who had lived a little way up in Glen Livat, and who, for several years, had done good service to the Sir Walter Stewart, who was then chieftain of the Clan, as son and heir of that Sir Patrick whom my last Legend left so happily married to the Lady Catherine Forbes, and quietly settled at Drummin.   This man MacDermot died bravely in a skirmish, leaving a widow and an infant daughter.   It happened that some few months after the death of her husband, the good woman Bessy MacDermot went out to shear one of those small patches of wretched corn, which were then to be seen, almost as a wonder, scattered here and there, in these upland glens, and which belonged in *run-rig*, or in alternate ridges, to different owners, being so disposed, as you probably know, gentlemen, that all might have an equal interest, and consequently an equal inducement to assemble for its protection in the event of the sudden appearance of an enemy. Charley Stewart, then a fine, kind-hearted boy of some nine or ten years of age, had taken a great affection for the little Rosa, the child of Bessy MacDermot; and this circumstance had induced the mother to ask permission of Alice Asher to be allowed to take her son with her on this occasion to the harvest-field, that, whilst she went on with her work, he might watch the infant. Charley was delighted with his employment; and accordingly she laid the babe carefully down by him to leeward of one of the *stooks* of sheaves. Many an anxious glance did the fond mother throw behind her, as the onward progress of her work slowly but gradually increased her distance from Charley and his precious charge. The thoughts of her bereft and widowed state saddened her heart, and made it heavy, and rendered her eyes so moist from time to time, that ever and anon she was compelled to rest for an instant from her labour, in order to wipe away the tears with her sleeve. Her little Rosa was now all the world to her. The anxiety regarding the child which possessed her maternal bosom was always great; but, at the present moment, she had few fears about her safety, for, ever as she looked behind her, she beheld Charley Stewart staunchly fixed at his post, and busily employed in trying to catch the attention of the infant, and to amuse it by plucking from the sheaves those gaudy flowered weeds, of various kinds and hues, which Nature brought up everywhere so profusely among the grain, and which the rude and unlearned farmers of those early times took no pains to extirpate.

Whilst the parties were so occupied, the sun was shining brightly upon the new shorn stubble, that stretched away before the eyes of Charley Stewart, when its flat unbroken field of light was suddenly interrupted by a shadow that came sailing across it. He looked up into the air, and beheld a large bird hovering over him. Inexperienced as he was, and by no means aware that its apparent size was diminished by the height at which it was flying, he took it for a kite, or a buzzard, and it immediately ceased to occupy his attention. Round and round sailed the shadow upon the stubble, increasing in magnitude at every turn it made, but totally unheeded by the boy amid the interesting occupation in which he was engaged. At length a loud shriek reached him from the very farther end of the ridge. Charley started up from his sitting position, and beheld Bessy MacDermot rushing towards him, tossing her arms, and screaming as if she were distracted. She was yet too far off from him to enable him to gather her words, amidst the alarm that now seized him; and, accordingly, believing that she had been stung by some viper, or that she had cut herself desperately with the reaping-hook, he abandoned his charge, and ran off to meet her, that he might the sooner render her assistance; but by the time they had approached near enough to each other to enable him to catch up the import of her cries, he halted—for they made his little heart faint within him.

"The eagle! the eagle!" wildly screamed Bessy MacDermot. "Oh, my child! my child!"

Turning round hastily, Charley Stewart now saw that the very bird which he had so recently regarded with so little alarm, had now grown six times larger than he had believed it really to be. It was in the very act of swooping down upon the infant. Charley ran towards the spot, mingling his shrieks with those of the frantic mother; but ere their feet had carried them over half the distance towards it, they heard the cries of the babe, as the fell eagle was flapping his broad wings, in his exertions to lift it from the ground; and, ere they could reach it, the bird was already flying, heavily encumbered with his burden, over the surface of the standing corn, from which he gradually rose, as his pinions gained more air and greater way, till he finally soared upwards, and then held on his slow but strong course towards his nest in the neighbouring mountains.

"Oh, my babe! my babe!" cried the agonised Bessy MacDermot, her eyes starting from their very sockets, in her anxiety to keep sight of the object of her affections and her terrors.

But she did not follow it with her eyes alone. She paused not for a moment, but darted off through the standing corn and over moor and moss, hill and heugh, and through woods, and rills, and bogs, in the direction which the eagle was taking, without once thinking of poor little Charley Stewart, who kept after her as hard as his active little legs could carry him; and, great as the distance was which they had to run, the eagle, impeded as he was in his flight by the precious burden he carried, was still within reach of the eyes of the panting and agonised mother, when a thinner part of the wood enabled her to see, from a rising ground, the cliff where he finally rested, and where he deposited the child in his nest, that was well known to hang on a ledge in the face of the rock, a little way down from its bare summit. On ran the frantic mother with redoubled energy—for she remembered that an old man lived by himself in a little cot hard by the place, and she never rested till she sank down faint and exhausted at his door.

"Oh, Peter, Peter!—my baby, my baby!" was all she could utter as the old man came hobbling out to learn what was the matter.

"What has mischanced your baby, Mrs. MacDermot?" demanded Peter.

"Oh, the eagle! the eagle!" cried the distracted mother. "Oh, my child! my child!"

"Holy saints be about us! has the eagle carried off your child?" cried Peter, in horror.

"Och, yes, yes!" replied Bessy. "Oh, my baby, my baby!"

"St. Michael be here!" exclaimed Peter. "What can an old man like me do to help thee?"

"Ropes! ropes!" cried little Charley Stewart, who at this moment came up, so breathless and exhausted that he could hardly speak.

"Ropes!" said Peter; "not a rope have I. There's a bit old hair-line up on the baulks there, to be sure, that my son Donald used for stretching his hang-net; but it has been so much in the water that I have some doubt if it would stand the weight of a man, even if we could get a man to go down over the nose of the craig;—and there is not a man but myself, that I know of, within miles of us."

"You have forgotten me," cried Charley Stewart, who had now somewhat recovered his wind. "I will go down over the craig. Come, then, Peter!—get out your hair-line. It will not break with my weight."

"By the Rood but thou art a gallant little chield!" said Peter.

"Oh, the blessings of the Virgin on thee, my dearest Charley!" cried Bessy MacDermot, embracing him. "And yet," added she, with hesitation, "why should I put Alice Asher's boy to such peril, even to save mine own child? Oh, canst thou think of no other means? I cannot put Charley Stewart in peril."

"Nay," said Peter, "I know of no means; and, in truth, the poor bairn is like enough to have been already half devoured by the young eagles."

"Merciful Mother of God!" cried poor Bessy, half fainting at the horrible thought. "Oh, my baby, my baby!"

"Come, old man," cried Charley Stewart, with great determination, "we have no time to waste—we have lost too much

already. Where is the hair-line you spake of? Tut, I must
seek for it myself;" and rushing into the cot, he leaped upon a
table, made one spring at the rafters, and, catching hold of
them, he hoisted himself up, gained a footing on them, and ran
along them like·a cat, till he found the great bundle of hair-
line. "Now," said he, throwing it down and jumping after it;
"come away, good Peter, as fast as thy legs·can carry thee."

Having reached the summit of the craig by a circuitous path,
they could now descry the two eagles to whom the nest belonged
soaring aloft at a great distance. They looked over the brow
of the cliff as far as they could stretch with safety, but although
old Peter was so well acquainted with the place where the nest
was built as at once to be able to fix on the very spot whence
the descent ought to be made, the verge of the rock there
projected itself so far over the ledge where the nest rested as to
render it quite invisible from above. They could only perceive
the thick sea of pine foliage that arose up the slope below, and
clustered closely against the base of the precipice. A few
small stunted fir trees grew scattered upon the otherwise bare
summit where they stood. Old Peter sat himself down behind
one of these, and placed a leg on·each side of it so as to secure
himself from all chance of being pulled over the precipice by
any sudden jerk, while Charley's little fingers were actively
employed in undoing the great bundle of hair-line, and in tying
one end of it round his body, and under his armpits. The
unhappy mother was now busily assisting the boy, and now
moving restlessly about, in doubtful hesitation whether she
should yet allow him to go down. Now she was gazing at the
distant eagles, and wringing her hands in terror lest they
should return to their nest; and torn as she was between her
cruel apprehensions for her infant on the one hand, and her
doubts and fears about Charley Stewart on the other, she
ejaculated the wildest and most incoherent prayers to all the
saints for the protection and safety of both.

"Now," said Charley Stewart at length; "I'm ready. Keep
a firm hold, Peter, and lower me gently."

"Stay, stay, boy!" cried the old man. "Stick my skian
dhu into your hoe. If the owners of the nest should come
home, by the Rood, but thou wilt need some weapon to make
thee in some sort a match for them, in the welcome they will
assuredly give thee."

Charley Stewart slipped the skian dhu into his hoe, and went
boldly but cautiously over the edge of the cliff. He was no
sooner fairly swung in air than the hair rope stretched to a

degree so alarming that Bessy MacDermot stood upon the
giddy verge, gnawing her very fingers, from the horrible dread
that possessed her, that she was to see it give way and divide.
Peter sat astride against the root of the tree, carefully eyeing
every inch of the line ere he allowed it to pass through his
hands, and every now and then pausing—hesitatiug, and shaking his head most ominously, as certain portions of it, here and
there, appeared to him to be of doubtful strength. Meanwhile,
Charley felt himself gradually descending, and turning round
and round at the end of the rope, by his own weight, his brave
little heart beating, and his brain whirling, from the novelty
and danger of his daring attempt—the screams of the young
eagles sounding harshly in his ears, and growing louder and
louder as he slowly neared them. By degrees he began distinctly
to hear the faint cries of the child, and his courage and self-
possession were restored to him, by the conviction that she was
yet alive. In a few moments more he had the satisfaction to
touch the ledge of rock with his toes, and he was at last enabled
to relieve the rope from his weight, by planting himself upon
its ample, but fearfully inclined surface. He shouted aloud, to
make Peter aware that the line had so far done its duty, and
then he cautiously approached the nest, where, to his great joy,
he found the infant altogether uninjured, except by a cross cut
upon her left cheek, which she seemed to have received from
some accidental movement of the beak or talons of one of the
two eaglets, between which she had been deposited by the old
eagle. Had she not been placed between two so troublesome
mates, and in a position so dangerous, nothing could have been
more snug or easy than the bed in which the little Rosa was
laid. The nest was about two yards square. It was built on
the widest and most level part of the ledge, and it was composed
of great sticks, covered with a thick layer of heather, over which
rushes were laid to a considerable depth. Fortunately for the
infant, the eaglets had been already full gorged ere she had
been carried thither, and there yet lay beside them the greater
part of the carcass of a lamb, and also a mountain hare,
untouched, together with several moorfowl, and an immense
quantity of bones and broken fragments of various animals.

Charley Stewart did not consume much time in his examination of the nest. Being at once satisfied that it would be worse
than hazardous to trust the hair-line with the weight of the
child, in addition to his own, he undid it from his body.
Approaching the nest, he gently lifted the crying infant from
between its two screeching and somewhat pugnacious com-

panions. The moment he had done so, the little innocent
became quiet, and instantly recognising him, she held out her
hands, and smiled and chuckled to him, at once oblivious of all
her miseries. Charley kissed his little favourite over and over
again, and then he proceeded to tie the rope carefully around
and across her, so as to guard against all possibility of its
slipping. Having accomplished this, he shouted to Peter to
pull away—kissed the little Rosa once more, and then committed
her to the vacant air. Nothing could equal the anxiety he
endured whilst he beheld her slowly rising upwards. And
when he beheld the mother's hands appear over the edge of the
rock, and snatch her from his sight, nothing could match the
shout of delight which he gave. The maternal screams of joy
which followed, and which came faintly down to his ears, were
to him a full reward for all the terrors of his desperate enterprise. For that instant he forgot the perilous situation in which
he then stood, and the risk that he had yet to run ere he could
hope to be extricated from it.

But a few moments only elapsed ere all thoughts of anything
else but his own self-preservation were banished from his mind.
The angry screams of the two old eagles came fearfully through
the air, and he beheld them approaching the rock, cleaving the
air with furious flight. He cast one look upwards, and saw
the rope rapidly descending to him—but the eagles were coming
still faster, and he had only time to wrench out a large stick
from the nest, to aid him in defending himself, when they were
both upon him. He had nothing for it but to crouch as close
in under the angle of the rock as he could, and there he planted
himself, with the stick in his right hand, and the skian dhu in
his left, resolved to make the best fight he could of it. They
commenced their attack on him whilst still on the wing, by
flying at him, and striking fiercely at him with their talons,
each returning alternately to the assault after making a narrow
circuit in the air. Whilst thus engaged, Charley neither lost
courage nor presence of mind, but contrived to deal to each of
them a severe blow now and then with the rugged stick, as they
came at him in succession. Finding that they could make no
impression upon him in this way, sheltered as he was by his
position under the projecting rock, they seemed at once to
resolve, as if by mutual consent, to adopt a more resolute mode
of attack.

Alighting on the ledge of rock at the same moment, one on
each side of the place where he was crouching, both the eagles
now assailed him at once with inconceivable ferocity. Half

fronting that one which was to his right, he laid a severe blow on it, which somewhat staggered it in its onset. But whilst he was thus occupied with it, the other, which was to his left, tore open his cheek, with a blow of his talons, that had nearly stunned him. More from mechanical impulse, than from any actual design, he struck a back-handed blow with his skian dhu. Fortunately for him it proved most effectual, for it penetrated the eagle to the very heart, laid it fluttering on its back, and, in the violence of its struggles, it rolled over the inclined ledge, and fell dead to the bottom of the craig. But poor Charley had no leisure to rejoice over this piece of success. He looked anxiously to the hairline, which hung dangling within reach of his grasp; but, ere he could seize it, his other enemy was at him again. As if it had profited by the severe lessons it had gotten, the strokes of this second eagle were given with so much rapidity and caution, that close as Charley Stewart was obliged to keep into the angle of the rock, and stupified as he was, in some degree, by the wound he had received, he was able to do little more than to defend his own person from injury, whilst he was obliged slowly to give ground before his feathered assailant. Whilst retreating and fighting in this manner, one blow of his stick, better directed than the rest, struck the eagle on the side of the skull, close to its juncture with the neck, and it went fluttering down over the rock, in the pangs of death, after its fellow. But alas! poor Charley Stewart's victory cost him dear.

The two listeners above, who had seen the approach of the eagles, were dreadfully alarmed by the noise of the terrific conflict that was going on upon the ledge below. In vain did they shout to terrify the birds. In vain did old Peter frequently try the hair-line, by pulling gently at it, in the hope of finding that the weight of Charley's body was attached to it. They were tortured by anxious uncertainty regarding him, until a piercing shriek came upwards from him, and all was quiet. Winged by terror, Bessy MacDermot rushed, with her child in her arms, down the winding path, to a point whence she could command a view of the ledge. The boy was no longer there! She rubbed her dimmed eyes, gave one more intent gaze. From the very nature of the place, it was impossible that he could be there unseen by her, from the point she now occupied, and she was thus too certainly assured that he was gone. Uttering a despairing scream, she flew frantically down to look for him among the trees at the bottom of the cliff. There she sought all along the base of it, dreading every

10

moment to have her eyes shocked with the sight of his mangled remains, and uttering the most doleful lamentations that she had murdered her dear friend's gallant boy. She found both the dead eagles indeed, but she could see nothing of Charley Stewart. Old Peter then came hobbling after her, to join her in her search, and both of them went over the ground again and again in vain. A faint hope began at length to arise in the minds of both, that he might, after all, be still on the ledge above, though, perhaps, lying wounded, or in a swoon; and, although both felt it to be almost against all reason to indulge in it, they instantly prepared to return, to endeavour more perfectly to ascertain the fact; and, if it could be done no otherwise, Bessy MacDermot resolved to run and rouse the country, in order to procure strong ropes, and men to go down to examine the ledge itself.

Full of these intentions, they were in the act of quitting the bottom of the cliff, when a faint voice arrested their steps. They stopped to listen, and, after a little time, they were aware that it came down from over their heads. They looked up, but, seeing nothing, they became more than ever convinced, that it was Charley's voice calling to them from the ledge, and they again turned to hurry away to assure him of help. But the voice came again, and so much stronger, as to satisfy them that the speaker could be at no very great distance from them.

"Peter!—Bessy!—I am here in the tree," said Charley Stewart, "for the love of Saint Michael, stop and take me down!"

Some minutes elapsed before they could catch a glimpse of the poor boy. At length they discovered him, half way up a tall pine tree, hanging by his little coat to the knag of a broken branch. I may as well tell you at once how he came there. Whilst he was in the very act of dealing that last well directed blow of the stick, that proved so fatal to the second eagle, his foot slipped on the narrower and more inclined part of the ledge, to which he had been gradually driven back during the combat, and uttering that despairing scream which rang like his knell in the affrighted ears of Bessy MacDermot and Peter, he fell through the air, and crashed down among the dense foliage of the pine-tops below. One of his legs was broken across a bough, which it met with in his descent through the tree, but his head, and all his other vital parts, had luckily escaped injury; and the knag, which so fortunately caught his clothes, and kept him suspended, had been the providential means of saving him from that death, which he must have otherwise inevitably met with on coming to the ground.

But how were they to get poor Charley down from the tree? Old Peter could not climb it; but, seeing that it was furnished with branches nearly to its root, Bessy MacDermot gave her child into the hands of the old man, and, taking a double end of the hair-line with her, she clambered up the stem to the place where the boy was hanging. Tenderly relieving him from his distressing position, she quickly passed two or three double folds of the rope around him, and then lowered him gently down to Peter. So patient had Charley been under his sufferings, excruciating as they were, that it was not until they were about to move him from the ground, that they discovered the injury that his limb had received.

"Oh, what shall I do?" cried Bessy MacDermot, wringing her hands; "Oh, how can I face Alice Asher, after thus causing so sad a mischance to her darling, her beautiful boy?"

"Tut, Bessy, never mind me!" said Charley faintly, but with a gentle smile, that sorted but ill with his wounded and bloody countenance; "I shall soon get the better of all this; but if it had been twice as bad with me, Bessy, nay, if I had been killed outright, I should have well deserved it, for quitting my poor little Rosa there, as I did upon the harvest rig."

"Nay, nay, my dearest boy, Charley," said Mrs. MacDermot, kissing him, and weeping fondly over him; thou did'st thy part faithfully. Had it not been for my foolish fright, and my silly screams when I first saw the eagle, thou wouldst never have left my child, and nought of these sad mischances could have happened."

With some difficulty, and not without Bessy MacDermot's help, old Peter managed to carry Charley Stewart down to his hut, whence he was afterwards moved home when proper assistance could be procured. Alice Asher was overpowered with grief when the darling of her heart was brought to her in this melancholy and maimed condition. But she readily forgave Bessy MacDermot for the innocent share she had had in producing it; and after Charley's wounds were dressed, the bones of his fractured limb set, and that she was satisfied that his life was perfectly safe, she not only felt grateful to God that he had been so wonderfully preserved, but she began to regard him with honest pride for the gallant action he had performed.

"Well hast thou proved thyself, my boy, to be a true Clan-Allan Stewart!" said she to him, with a deep blush on her

countenance, as she sat fondly watching by the bed where
Charley was quietly sleeping, from the effects of the drugs that
had been given him, till the tears began to follow one another
fast from her eyelids. "Well might thy father now, methinks,
make thee his lawful son by extending to me those holy rites,
the false hope of obtaining which betrayed mine innocent and
simple youth! Thou at least ought not to suffer for thine
unhappy mother's fault, which now nearly nine years of sorrow,
of remorse, and of heartfelt penitence, and prayer, and penance,
have not yet expiated! But God's holy will be done!"

Poor afflicted Alice Asher had occasion to repeat these last
words of pious resignation to the will of God more than once
after the recovery of her son. She was deeply grateful to
Heaven indeed that his life had been spared to her, and that
his health and strength were completely restored to him, but
his handsome countenance had been greatly and permanently
disfigured by the deep cross-like scar that remained upon his
left cheek, and the grace of his person had been much destroyed
by the limping of his left leg, occasioned by the bad surgery of
the rude practitioner who had set the broken bones. She bore
this affliction, as she did all others, with meek submission, as a
divine chastisement which her sin had well merited, though
she wept to think that she had been visited through the suffering of her innocent boy. Some eight or nine long years passed
away, during which Sir Walter Stewart of Drummin was
liberal in providing richly for the wants of the mother, as well
as for the education of her son, though he strictly avoided seeing either of them. The story of Charley's brave achievement
and severe accident reached him not, for he was at that time
abroad upon his travels in foreign lands, and ere he returned
home the talk about it had died away, so that it had never been
permitted to exercise any influence upon him whatsoever.

Passing over these years, then, we find Alice Asher paler and
thinner than before, but still most beautiful, sitting one morning, at the window of her cottage, that looked towards the
tower of Drummin, which was partially seen from it through
between the thick stems of the trees. Her elbow rested on
the window-sill and supported her head, which was surrounded
by a broad fillet of black silk, from beneath which her hair
clustered in fair ringlets around her finely formed features, and
fell in long tresses over her neck and shoulders. Her close
fitting kirtle and her loose and flowing gown were of sad-
coloured silk, and the embroidered bosom of her snow-white
smock was fastened with a golden brooch that sparkled with

precious stones, and more than one of her fingers glittered with rings of considerable value. Alice was not always wont to be so adorned ; but, ornamented as she thus was beyond the simplicity of that attire which she usually wore, her countenance bore no corresponding expression of gladness upon it. She sat gazing silently towards the distant stronghold of the Clan-Allan Stewarts, sighing deeply from time to time, until the thoughts that filled her heart gradually dimmed her large blue eyes, and the tears swelled over her eyelids and ran down her cheeks, and she finally began to relieve the heaviness of her soul by thinking aloud in broken and unconscious soliloquy.

"Aye! he is going to-day!" said she, in a melancholy tone. "He is going to the court to mix with the great, the proud, the gay, and the beautiful, and I shall not see him ere he goes! Yet the vow of separation which we mutually took had a saving condition in it. He might have come—he may at any time approach me—aye, and honourably too—when the object of his visit may be to do me and my boy justice. But, after so many years have passed away in disappointment, why should my fond and foolish heart still cling to deceitful hope? a hope, too, that wars with those of a purer and holier nature, which may yet ally me, a penitent sinner, to Heaven. Then what have I to do with those glittering gauds that would better become a bride? Yet they are his pledges, if not of love at least of kindness and of friendship, sent to me from time to time to show me that I am not altogether forgotten, and surely there can be no harm in my wearing them? and then to-day—to-day, methought that he might have come. But if he had ever intended to come, would he have sent, as he has done, for Charley? Oh, my boy! would that he could but think of doing thee justice, and thy poor sinful mother would die contented! But, if he is pleased with the youth, may he not yet come hither along with him? How my silly heart beats at the very thought! What sound was that I heard? Can it be them? No, no, no, he will never come more to me! Alas, alas! my poor boy's face and person have suffered too much to win a father's eye, and he knows not the virtues that lie so modestly concealed within them. But what is that I see yonder! The bustle of the horsemen before the gate with their pampered steeds and their gay attire—their pennons fluttering, and the sun glancing from the broad blades of their Highland spears? What! was that a distant bugle blast I heard? Again! Then they are moving—aye, indeed! They are now

galloping off along the terrace!   Alas, alas, they are gone! and
my vain and foolish hopes have gone with them!"

These last words were uttered in the deepest tone of anguish,
and Alice drew hastily back into the darkest recess of the
apartment, where she seated herself, covered her face with the
palms of her hands, and wept aloud.   Having thus given full
vent to her feelings, she retired to the privacy of her closet,
where she endeavoured to divert her mind by holy exercise
from the sorrows that oppressed her.   At length a gentle tap
at the door informed her that her son had returned from his
visit to Drummin, and tremblingly anxious to know the result
of it, she immediately admitted him.

"Mother! my dearest mother!" said Charley Stewart,
tenderly embracing her, and with a manifest effort to subdue
certain emotions that were working within him; "Why hast
thou been weeping?"

"Alas! I weep often, my beloved, my darling boy!" replied
she, warmly responding to his caresses; "I weep, and I deserve
to weep!   But hast thou aught of tidings for me, that may
give me a gleam of joy?   Say—how wert thou received?"

"Why, well, mother!" replied Charley, endeavouring to
assume a lively air; "I was well and kindly received, though
neither, forsooth, with parade of arms, nor with flourish of
trumpets, nor of clarions; but Sir Walter received me kindly."

"Did he embrace thee, dear Charley?" demanded his mother
with great anxiety of expression.

"Um——Aye," replied her son, with some degree of hesitation; "he did embrace me, though hardly indeed with the
same fervour that thou art wont to do, dearest mother.   But
then thou knowest, mother, that Sir Walter is a courtly knight
of high degree, and they tell me that the fashion of such folks
allows them not to yield themselves altogether, as we humbler
people are wont to do, to the feelings that are within us."

"Alas! thou say'st that which is but too true!" replied
Alice, in a desponding tone; "but go on, boy."

"Sir Walter put his hand on my shoulder, and turned me
round," continued Charley.   "Then he made me walk a step
or two, and eyed me narrowly from top to toe, pretty much as
if he had been scanning the points and paces of a new horse.—
'How camest thou so lame and so disfigured?' demanded he.
—'By a fall I had in climbing an eagle's nest,' replied I.—'A
silly cause,' said Sir Walter; and yet, perhaps, the bold blood
that is in thee must bear the blame.   But know, boy, that fate
hath not given to all the power to climb into the eyry of the

eagle.' And having said this much he changed the subject of his talk."

"Would that thou could'st but have gathered couraged enow to have told him all the circumstances of that adventure!"

"Nay, mother, I had courage for anything but to speak aught that might have sounded like mine own praise," replied Charley.

"Would that he but knew thee as thou art!" said Alice, with a sigh. "Would that he but knew the soul that is within thee! With all his faults—and perhaps they are light, save that which concerns thee alone—he hath a generous spirit himself, and he could not but prize a generous spirit in one so kindred to him. But tell me all that passed. Did—did he—did he ask thee for tidings of me?"

"He did question me most particularly about thee," replied Charley. "He questioned me as if he would have fain gathered from me the appearance and condition of every, the minutest feature of thy face, and of every line of thy form. He questioned as if with the intent of limning thy very portrait on the tablet of his mind; and, as if he would have traced it beside some picture, which he still wore in fresh and lively colours there, for the purpose, as it seemed to me, of making close and accurate comparison between them. Thus he would pause at times during his questioning of me; and, after a few moments of deep abstraction, he would say, as if forgetful of my presence, and in converse with himself alone,—'Strange! aye, but she was then but fifteen, scarce ripened into woman—the change is nothing more than natural—the same loveliness, but more womanly;' and so he went on, now to question, and now to talk of thee, for a good half hour or so."

"And he!" cried Alice, with unwonted animation; "Say, boy, looked he well? I mean in health; for of his manly beauty, his tall and well knit form, his graceful air, his noble bearing, and his eagle eye! how could I have lived till now, without hearing from those who have seen and admired him? Alas!" added she, in a melancholy and subdued tone, "of such things I have perhaps inquired too much!"

"Sir Walter had all the ruddy hue, as well as the firmness of vigorous health, dear mother," replied the youth.

"Thanks be to all the saints!" exclaimed Alice fervently. "Then, come boy—tell me what passed between you?"

"After all his questions touching thee and thy health were done," said Charley, "and that we had talked of other matters of no import, he sat down, and thus gravely addressed me as I

stood before him : ' I have been thinking how best to provide
for thee, boy.   I can see that thou art but ill fitted for hardy
service, or the toils of war.   And, by the Rood, it is well for
thee that, in these times, there are other ways of winning to
high fortune, yea, and to royal favour even, besides that which
leads to either by doughty deeds of arms, where so many perish
ere they have half completed the toilsome and perilous journey.
Thou must content thee, then, with some peaceful trade.   Let
me see—let me see.   Ah! I have it.   Now-a-days, men have
more chance to push themselves forward by the point of the
needle, than by the point of the lance.   What thinkest thou
of Master Hommil, the king's tailor, who, as all men say, hath
a fair prospect of shaping such a garb for himself as may yet
serve him to wear for a peer's robes, if he doth but use his
shears with due discretion?   This is the very thing for thee,
and it is well that I have so luckily hit on it.   I'll have thee
apprenticed to a tailor, and, when thy time is out, I'll have
thee taught in all the more curious mysteries of thine art, by
its very highest professors, that none in the whole land shall be
found to equal thee.   Thou shalt travel to France for learning
in the nicer parts of thy trade, and then, I will set thee up,
close under the royal eye, with such a stock of rarest articles
in thy shop, as will make it a very Campvere, for the variety
and richness of its merchandize.   But thou must begin thy
schooling under Master Jonathan Junkins here, who, though
but a country cultivator of cabbage, hath an eye towards the
cut of a cloak or doublet, that might well beget the jealousy of
the mighty Hommil himself.   I once wore a rose-coloured suit
of Jonathan's make, that did excite the envy, yea, and the
anger, too, of that great master, by the commendations that
royalty himself was heard to pass upon it.   Though there were
some there, who, from malice, no doubt, did say, that the merit
lay more in the shape of the wearer, than in that of the garments.   But I am trifling.   I have some orders to give ere I
mount, and this, as to thy matter with Junkins, shall be one ;
and time wears, boy, and thou, too, hast some little way before
thee to limp home ; therefore, God keep thee.   Bear my love,
or, as she would herself have it to be, my *friendship*, to thy
mother.   And, see here ; give her this ring as a fresh remembrance of me.   Farewell—I shall see that all be well arranged
regarding thee ere I go ; and I trust that thou wilt not idly
baulk the prudent plans I have laid down for thee, or the good
intentions I have towards thee ; and so again, farewell, my
boy !'—And thus, my dearest mother, was I dismissed."

"Well, God's will be done!" said Alice, with a deep sigh, after a long pause, and after having betrayed a variety of emotions during her son's narrative. "I had hoped better things for thee, my boy, but God's will be done! Thou hast no choice but to submit, Charley. Forget not that Sir Walter Stewart is thy father, and that thou art bound by the law of nature to obey him."

"It is because I do not forget that Sir Walter Stewart is my father, that I find it so hard a thing to obey him in this," said Charley, with a degree of excitement, which all his earnestly exerted self-command was, for the moment, unable entirely to control. "But, as it happens, that it is just because he is bound to me by the law of nature, and by no other law, that he thus condemns me to be nailed down to the shop-board of a tailor, instead of giving me a courser to ride, and a lance to wield, so, as thou most truly sayest, dear mother, by the law of nature, but by that law alone, am I compelled to submit to this bitter mortification, and to obey him."

"Nay, nay, dearest Charley, talk not thus!" cried Alice, throwing her arms around her son's neck, and fondly kissing him; "talk not thus frowardly if thou lovest me!"

"Love thee, my dearest mother!" cried Charley, returning her embraces with intense fervour, and weeping from the overpowering strength of his feelings; "Nay, nay, thou canst not doubt my love to thee; thou canst not doubt that, on thy weal or thy woe, hangs the happiness or the misery of your poor boy. Be not vexed, dearest mother, for though I have spoken thus idly, trust me that a father's word shall ever be with me as the strictest law, which I, so far as my nature can support me, shall never wilfully contravene."

Charley Stewart again tenderly embraced his mother, and, scarcely aware that he was leaving her to weep, he hurried away to seek some consolation for himself, in a quarter where he never failed to find it. This was at the cottage of Bessy MacDermot, whither he was wont frequently to wander, for the purpose of listening to the innocent prattle of his young plaything Rosa, who, having now seen some eight or nine summers, was fast ripening into a very beautiful girl. As Charley approached the widow's premises on the present occasion, he found Rosa by the side of a clear spring, that bubbled and sparkled out from beneath a large mossy stone, that projected from the lower part of the slope of a flowery bank, under the pensile drapery of a grove of weeping birches. The moment she beheld him, she came tripping to meet him, with a rustic wreath of gay marsh marigolds and water-lilies in her hand.

"Where have you been all this long, long morning, dearest Charley?" cried Rosa; "I have been so dull without you; and see what a wreath I have made for your bonnet! But I have a great mind to wear it myself, for you don't deserve to have it, for being so long in coming to me."

"I have been over at the castle, Rosa," said Charley, stooping to embrace her, as she innocently held up her lips to be kissed by him. "I have been over at Drummin, looking at the grand array of steeds and horsemen. But what are these flowers? Water-lilies, as I hope to be saved! Holy Virgin! Rosa, how didst thou come by them?"

"I got them from the pool," replied Rosa, hesitating, and gently tapping his cheek with a few stray flowers which she held in her hand; "I got them in the same way that you pulled them for me the other day, that is with a long hazel rod, with a crook at the end of it."

"From the pool, Rosa?" cried Charley. "What could tempt thee to risk thy life for such trifles? If thou hadst slipt over the treacherous brink, where there was no one by to save thee—thou wert gone! irrecoverably gone! How couldst thou be so rash? my very flesh creeps to think on't!"

"Don't be angry with me, Charley!" said Rosa coaxingly— "What risk would I not run to give thee pleasure?"

"But you have given me anything but pleasure in this matter, Rosa," said Charley; "I tremble too much to think of the hazard thou hast run, to look with pleasure on anything that could have occasioned it."

"So thou wilt not let me put the wreath on thy bonnet, then?" said Rosa, with a tear half disclosing itself in her eyelid; "Come, come, Charley! sit down—sit down on this bank, and do let me put it upon thy bonnet."

"If it will pleasure thee to make a fool of me, Rosa," said Charley, smiling on her, and kissing her; "thou shalt do with me as thou mayest list."

"That is a dear kind Charley," cried Rosa, her moist eyes sparkling with delight, and throwing her arms around his neck; "I'll make no fool of thee: I'll make thee so handsome!"

"Handsome!" exclaimed Charley, laughing. "Why Rosa, it is making a fool of me, indeed, to say that thou can'st make me handsome, with this ugly deep cross-mark on my cheek."

"That cross-mark on your cheek, Charley!" cried the little

girl, with an intensity of feeling much beyond anything which her years might have warranted; "To me that cross-mark is beautiful! I love that noble brow of thine—those eyes, that whenever they look upon me, tell me that I am dear to thee—those lips, that so often kiss me, and instruct me, and say kind things to me—but that mark of the cross on thy cheek—oh, that hath to me a holy influence in't; it reminds me that, but for thy noble courage which earned it for thee, I should have been food for the young eagles of the craig. Charley! I could not fail to love thee, for thy kindness to me; but I never could have loved thee as I do love thee, but for these living marks which you bear of all that you suffered for thine own little Rosa. Kiss me my dear, dear Charley!"

"My little wifey!" cried Charley, clasping the innocent girl in his arms, and smothering her with kisses.

"Aye," said Rosa, artlessly, "I am thy little wifey. All the gossips say that I am fated to be so; for you know I have got my cross-mark as well as you, aye, and on my left cheek too. The eagles did that kind turn for me. They marked us both with the cross alike. See! you can see my cross here quite plain."

"I do see it," said Charley, kissing the place. "But thanks be to the Virgin thy beauty hath not suffered one whit by it. I can just discern that the mark is there, and that is all; and I trust that it will altogether disappear as you grow up to be a woman."

"The Virgin forbid!" cried Rosa energetically. "The gossips say that we have been so miraculously signed with the cross expressly for each other, and I would not lose so happy a mark, no, not to be made a queen! But do let me put on thy chaplet, dear Charley. I hope to see thee some day with a grand casque on thy head—a tilting spear in thy hand—bestriding a noble steed, and riding at the ring with the best of them."

"Alas, Rosa!" said Charley, with a deep sigh, "that will never be my fate!"

"Why not?" demanded Rosa; "surely Sir Walter Stewart may make thee his esquire?"

"Alas, no!" said Charley, despondingly. The casque he dooms me to is a tailor's cowl—the shield a thimble—the lance a needle—and the gallant steed I am to mount is a tailor's shop-board, and if ever I tilt with silk, velvet, or gold, it will be to convert them into cloaks and doublets for my betters!"

"A tailor!" exclaimed Rosa, with astonishment; "surely thou art jesting, Charley."

I'faith, it is too serious a matter to jest about," replie
Charley. "Truly I am doomed to handle the goosing iron c
Master Jonathan Junkins."

"Ha, ha, ha, ha!" shouted Rosa. "Ha, ha, ha, ha!—wha
an odd fancy of Sir Walter!"

"Nay, laugh not at my misery, Rosa," said Charley, gravely
and somewhat piteously. "I cannot bear the thought of sucl
a life! What think you, Rosa, of being a tailor's wife?"

"So that thou wilt always call me thine own dear littl
wifey, I care not what thou art," replied Rosa, tenderly, an
throwing her arms around his neck. "And why, after al
mayest thou not be quite happy as a tailor? Old Johnn
Junkins sings at his task from morning till night. Besides h
hath no risk of being killed in battle, as my poor father wa
He always sleeps in a whole skin, save when his wife Jane
beats him with the ell-wand, and surely thou wouldst have n
fears that I should do that for thee, dear Charley?"

It was now Charley's turn to laugh, which he did ver
heartily, and having thus gained a temporary victory over hi
chagrin, he improved upon it by immediately taking a sma
Missal from his sporran, and commencing his daily occupatio
of giving instructions to Rosa, who greedily learned from hi
all that he could impart.

I mean now to give you some little account of Sir Walte
Stewart, gentlemen. You must know that he was one of th
prettiest and most accomplished men of his time, and a gre
favourite at court. His perfection in all warlike exercises-
his fondness for horses—and his fearless riding, were qualific
tions which fitted him for being the companion of the king
brothers, the spirited Alexander Duke of Albany, and the ta
and graceful John Earl of Mar, whilst his skill in fencing—h
proficiency in music—and his taste in dress, secured for him
high place in the good graces of that elegant, but weak mo
arch, James the Third. With young Ramsay of Balmai
afterwards created Earl of Bothwell, he was in the best habi
of intimacy. But with the lower minions of the king, I mea
with such as Cochran the mason—Rogers the musician-
Leonard the Smith—Hommil the tailor—Torfelan the fencin
master, and Andrew the Flemish astrologer, he was mo
polite than familiar. With the ladies of the court Sir Walt
Stewart was an object of admiration, nay, he was the theme
the praise of every one of them, from the beautiful, fascinatin
and virtuous Queen Margaret herself, down to the humblest
her maids of honour. It is no wonder, then, that Sir Walt

was induced to spend more of his time at court than among the
wilds of his native mountains. On the occasion of which I am
now speaking, he was on his way to the castle of Stirling,
where James the Third was at that time residing, and after a
long and tiresome journey, he and his attendants entered the
city, and rode up to their hostel in the main street, at such an
hour of the evening as made it neither very seemly nor very
convenient for him to report himself to his majesty.

Sir Walter Stewart was too well known not to command
immediate attention from every one belonging to the inn. The
horse-boys, who were grooming the numerous steeds, that were
hooked up to various parts of the walls surrounding the yard,
made way respectfully, not only for himself, but also for his
people and their animals, and the cattle of some persons of less
note and consideration, were turned out of their stalls for the
accommodation of his horses. Meanwhile, the knight was
ushered up stairs into the common room, by mine host in person,
who, with his portly figure, stripped to his close yellow jacket
and galligaskins, and with a fair linen towel hanging from his
girdle, puffed and sweated up the steps before him, his large
rubicund visage vying in the brightness of its scarlet, with the
fiery coloured cap of coarse red cloth which he wore. Sir
Walter found the large apartment surrounded by oaken tables
and chairs, which were occupied by various guests, some eating,
and some drinking, whilst the rattling of trenchers, the clink-
ing of cans, the buzz of voices, and the hum of tongues, were
so loud and continuous, as to render it difficult for him to detect
a word of the conversation that was going on anywhere, except
the clamorous calls for fresh supplies of provender, ale, or wine,
which the bustling serving men and tapsters were hurrying to
and fro to satisfy.

As the host showed Sir Walter to an unoccupied table at the
upper end of the place, most of the guests arose and saluted
him as he passed by them. To some of these he gave a condescending bow of recognition, whilst to others he hardly deigned
to bestow more than a dignified acknowledgment of their
courtesy. But he was no sooner seated, than he was left to his
own reflections, for each man again turned his attention to his
own particular comforts, and the knight was not sorry to be
very soon enabled to do the same thing for himself, by paying
his own addresses to the smoking pasty that was placed on the
table before him. He had but just finished his meal, when the
host entered, ushering in a very elegant young man, the richness of whose attire, as well as the perfection of its make,

together with his noble air, at once showed him to be a gentleman of the court. His rose-coloured jacket, and amber trewse,
were of the richest silk, and made to fit tight, so as to show off,
to the greatest advantage, his very handsome person. His
girdle-belt of black velvet, together with the pouch of the same
material, sparkled with gems, as did also the sheaths and hilts
of his sword and dagger. Several rich chains of gold were hung
about his neck; his shoes had those long thin points, which
were worn at that period, though they were not, in his instance,
carried to any very absurd extravagance. His cloak was of
blue velvet richly bordered with silver, and his broad jewelled
hat, of scarlet stuff of the same material, was drawn over one
side of his head, as a necessary precaution of counterpoise to
the weight of the long feathers of green, blue, red, and yellow,
which stretched out from it so far as to threaten to overbalance
it on the other. From beneath this his brown hair hung down,
curling over his ample brow, and spread itself in wide profusion
over his shoulders.

"What, Ramsay!" exclaimed Sir Walter Stewart, rising to
meet him with a cordial salutation, which again silenced the
clatter of the trenchers and cans, and brought all eyes for some
moments upon the two gentlemen. "This is a lucky meeting
indeed."

"Lucky!" replied Ramsay, smiling jocularly; "what a
boorish phrase! It is indeed well worthy of one, who hath
been rusticating so long amidst northern moors and mountains."

"Cry your mercy, my lord of the court," said Sir Walter
Stewart, laughing.

"Nay," continued Ramsay; "I know not whether thy
clownish expression be most discourteous to me, or to thyself,
—to me, as it would deny me all credit for this mine expressly
purposed visit to thee,—or to thyself, for supposing that such a
preux-chevalier, as thou art, could be, for the smallest fraction
of time, within the atmosphere of the court, without being run
after by those who love thee."

"Thank thee! thank thee, my dear Ramsay," replied Sir
Walter, shaking him cordially by the hand, and laughing
heartily; "Then will I say, that it was most kind of thee to
find me out so soon, and to come thus purposely to take a stoup
of French claret with me, and to pour thine agreeable talk into
mine ear, so as to fill the empty vessel of mine ignorance, to a
level with that of thine own full knowledge of courtly affairs,
and of all the interesting occurrents which have chanced about
the court since I last left it. So, sit thee down, I pray thee.

We shall be private enow at this table, which is well out of ear-shot of all those noisy gormandizers and guzzlers."

"Nay," replied Ramsay, as he seated himself beside his friend; "thine emptiness is of too vast a profundity for me to be able to fill it at this time. On some other occasion I shall do my best to replenish thee, when we can have leisure for a longer talk together, than we can look to have to-night. I came hither only to carry thee away with me."

"Whither wouldst have me go?" demanded Sir Walter. "Trust me, I am more disposed, at this moment, to enjoy mine ease in mine inn, than to move anywhere else."

"But I must have thee," replied Ramsay, "rustic as thou art, thou must submit to be led by me for some little time, like a blind man who hath but newly recovered his eyesight, lest thou shouldst stumble amidst the blaze of courtly sunshine. I came to bring thee to a small supper, at the lodging of Sir William Rogers, that most cunning fingerer of the lute and harp, and whose practice thereupon," continued he, sinking his voice almost to a whisper, "seems to have taught him a most marvellous power, of bringing what music may be most profitable for himself, out of that strange and many-stringed instrument called a Royal Sovereign."

"Hush, hush, Ramsay!" replied Sir Walter. "Thy talk is dangerous in such a place as this. But say, does the King go to this party!"

"No," replied Ramsay; "he is to be employed to-night in the occult science, to which he hath of late so much addicted himself. He is to be occupied with that knave Andrew the astrologer, in regarding and reading the stars."

"Then, what boots it for us to go to the party of this empty piece of sounding brass?" demanded Sir Walter.

"Much, much, my dear Stewart," replied Ramsay. "In the first place, thou shalt be introduced to his niece, who hath lately arrived from England. Thou shalt see and hear that fair Philomela, yclept Juliet Manvers, who plays and sings to admiration. Though here it behoves me, as thy friend, to bid thee take care of thy heart, for the uncle seems to have imported her, with the wise intent, of marrying her to some one of the court, and mine own heart hath already been very sorely assailed."

"A dangerous siren, truly!" said Sir Walter, laughing; "yet methinks I may safely enough bid defiance to her enchantment."

"We shall see," replied Ramsay, with a doubtful nod of his head; "but be that as it may, my second reason for taking thee thither, is that, with exception of our host himself, we may at least spend one tolerably pleasant evening undrugged and unencumbered, with the base society of those vulgar fellows, whom the King, with so much mistaken judgment, hath chosen to associate in his favour, with two such well-born gentlemen as you and me. Cochran, that man whom nature hath built up of stone and mortar, and who would yet ape the graces of a finished lord of the court, as a bear would copy the gambols of a well educated Italian greyhound."

"Hommil!" cried Sir Walter, laughing, and following up his friend's humour. "Hommil! that thread-paper, whose sword and dagger would be better removed, to have their places supplied by his shears and his bodkin."

"Leonard!" cried Ramsay, "Leonard! that man of iron, whose very face is a perfect forge, his chin being the stithy, his mouth the great bellows, his eyes the ignited charcoal, his nose the fore-hammer, and his brows the broken and smoke begrimmed pent-house that hangs over all."

"Torfefan!" continued Stewart; "Torfefan! that bully of the backsword, rapier, and dagger, who, except when he is pot-valiant, is always so wise in his steel-devouring courage, as to spread it forth like the tail of a turkey-cock, always the wider, the weaker the adversary he may have to deal with."

"Bravo! bravo!" cried Ramsay, absolutely shouting in his mirth; "bravo! bravo!—and then, last of all, Andrew, that solemn and mysterious knave, who seems as if he would pluck the stars from the skies, as I would the daisies from a flower border, and who, if I mistake not, will yet contrive to weave a good rich garland of fate out of them for himself, whatever he may do for others. To be compelled to keep such company, Stewart, is to pay a severe penalty for the daily converse and favour of a king. But this night, the monarch being engaged, as I told thee, each of these precious fellows hath gone on his own private amusement, for, as thou knowest, there is no such great love among them, as to make any two of them much desire to company together, so, to get rid for one single night of the whole of them but Rogers, whom we must admit to be by far the least offensive and most tolerable individual among them, is certainly a matter upon which we may very well congratulate ourselves."

"True," replied Sir Walter; "but I see no reason why we should not rid ourselves of Rogers, as well as of the rest, by staying and spending the evening together over this excellent wine. I must confess that I am somewhat travel-worn, and but little inclined for any such entertainment as he may give us."

"Nay, that cannot be," said Ramsay; "I gave my promise to him, ere I knew of thy coming, and when I heard of thine arrival, I pledged my word to bring thee with me. So, now, thou must not abandon me. Besides, as I told thee, the fellow is the best of these minions, and his music, not to mention that of his niece, is always some recompense for the endurance of his company. So haste thee to doff thy travelling weeds, and pink thyself out in such attire, as may make thee pleasing in the eyes of the fair and philomela-voiced Juliet. Be quick! for I shall wait for thee here."

Sir Walter Stewart, rather unwillingly, summoned his servants—was lighted to his chamber, and soon returned, in a dress, which was in no wise put to shame by that of his friend, and they proceeded together to the lodgings of Sir William Rogers.

The apartments of this favourite minstrel of the king were not extensive, but, as the custom was, down to a very late period of our history, even the principal bed-room, which purposely contained a richly carved and highly ornamented bed, was thrown open, and all were lighted up with a blaze of lamps. The furniture was gorgeous and gaudy. The serving-men numerous, but not always expert, and the company was small, and chiefly composed of such persons as were likely to be willing to scrape their way up into favour at court, by grasping the skirt, and scrambling after the footsteps, of any one, however worthless, who might be rising there. The entrance of two gallants so distinguished as Ramsay and Sir Walter Stewart produced just such an effect as one might look for from the sudden arrival of two noble peacocks, in full glory of plumage, in the midst of a vulgar flock of turkeys. Each small individual present vainly endeavoured to hobble-gobble itself into notice, whilst the two greater and grander birds permitted their own agreeable admiration of themselves to be but little interrupted by the ruffling and noise of the creatures around them. To Sir William Rogers himself, however, court policy induced them to yield a full and respectful attention. He was a good looking, and rather stoutish man, with more of talent than of gentility in his face, for though his brows were heavy, his large eyes were always ready to respond, with powerful expression, to the varied feelings which music never failed to awaken within him. In music he was an enthusiast, but when not under the excitement which it invariably produced in him,

11

his whole features betrayed that dull, sordid, self-complacency, only to be disturbed when his own immediate interest moved him.

The musical knight came forward to receive the two friends, with manifest satisfaction, as persons who raised the tone of his little society and gave him additional consequence in the eyes of his other guests. He presented Sir Walter without delay to his fair niece, who arose gracefully from the harp, over which she had just begun to run her fingers in a prelude, and returned his salute with condescending smiles. She was very beautiful; but, although she appeared to be young, her beauty seemed somehow to want the freshness of youth. She looked like a gay garment which, though neither soiled nor worn, had lost somewhat of that glossy newness of surface with which it first came forth from the tailor's shop. Whilst her regards were turned towards Ramsay or Sir Walter Stewart her countenance was covered with the most winning smiles she could wear; but when they chanced to wander round among the meaner personages of the company it assumed a degree of haughtiness that was not unmingled with contempt. This proceeded from her very expressive eyes, which beamed forth warm rays, when half veiled by her long dark eyelashes, and were quite in harmony with the mildness of her oval face, her polished forehead, and her dark and finely arched eye-brows. But when their orbs were broadly displayed by the rise of her full eye lid, the fires that shot from them were too formidable to be altogether agreeable. As was the fashion with ladies of any distinction in those days, her hair was but little seen—the greater part of it being capped up under a very tall, steeple-looking head-dress, which was of a shape much resembling an overgrown pottle-basket. This was of crimson velvet, ornamented with gold embroidery, and from the taper top of it descended a number of streamers of different colours, which hung down behind and floated over three-fourths of her person. She wore a rich robe of the same material and colour as the cap. This was made to fit her tightly as low as the waist, where it was confined by a richly wrought girdle of gold, from which it flowed loosely down, and swept the ground in a wide train, that covered a large extent of the floor around her, but which was so looped up at the sides as to display a deep cherry-coloured silk petticoat flowered with gold.

"Better had it been for thee, Juliet, to have sung when I first asked thee," said Sir William Rogers to her; "thy minstrelsy might have passed well enough with our good friends here : but now thou must undergo the severe ordeal of the nicely critical ears of these our honoured and highly accomplished guests of the court. Sir Walter Stewart here, especially, is well known to be a master of the divine art of music—as, with his gracious favour, you may perchance by and by hear."

" Alas ! uncle, I know too well how silly I have been in allowing myself to be thus caught, and I feel too surely I am about to be punished for it !" replied the lady with a sigh, accompanied by a languishing glance at Sir Walter ; " for who hath not heard of the exquisite science of Sir Walter Stewart ? The fame of his accomplishments have made the proudest gallants of England envious. But his eye hath too much benevolence in it to leave me to doubt that he will pity and pardon the faults that may spring from this trembling weakness of hand and fluttering of heart which his presence hath so suddenly brought upon me."

The lady, quite accidentally no doubt, then assumed that attitude which was best calculated to display her person to advantage, and began to run her fingers over the chords with a boldness and strength of touch that proved her to be a very perfect mistress indeed of the instrument she handled, since she could thus make it discourse such music under circumstances which she had herself declared to be so unfavourable. Notwithstanding the overawing presence of Sir Walter Stewart, whose critical powers she had declared she so much dreaded, she commenced a beautiful love-ballad, in a full, firm, and clear voice, with which she very speedily whirled away the musical soul of the Knight of the Aven, who, in spite of his boast to the contrary, was immediately drawn towards her chair, over which he continued to hang during all the time of her performance. Song after song was sung by this siren in a style so superior to anything which he had ever heard before that he was perfectly enraptured. He was called upon to play and to sing in his turn, and the praises which he received, in terms of no very limited measure, from both uncle and niece, and which, if fame does not belie him, were not altogether unmerited, were re-echoed by the whole flock of gobbling turkeys who pressed around them. The lady then joined her voice to his in a tender and melting lay—and thus the evening passed away, till Sir Walter was called upon to hand her to the table, where an ample feast was spread, and where her very agreeable talk was rendered even yet more spirited by the rich wines which enlivened the imagination of both speaker and listener. The hours fled most agreeably ; and before Sir Walter took his leave he readily entered into certain arrangements with the lovely Juliet, by which it was settled that next day was to be the first of a series of meetings for mutual practice in the art in which both so much delighted, their studies being of course to be carried on under the direction of Sir William Rogers himself.

" Well, Julietta," said the uncle to the niece, after they were left alone, " how likest thou this new instrument, now that thou hast run the fingers of thy fancy over his stops ?"

" The instrument is a handsome instrument enough," replied Juliet. " The strings sound melodiously too. But much of mine affection must rest on the gold with which it may be enriched, and the value of the case which may contain it. Is this Stewart wealthy, I pray thee; and are his possessions ample enough for my desires ?"

" I know that thy desires are ample enough," replied Rogers; " but report speaks well of the wealth and possessions of this Sir Walter."

" Somewhere in the bleak north, are they not?" said Juliet. " By all the saints, the cold and barren sod of this northern clime had hardly ever been pressed by my foot at all, had I not hoped to have mated me with some of its most wealthy nobles !"

" Thou hadst little chance of any such noble match where thou wert, Julietta," replied Rogers; " and, let me tell thee, the fates are quite as much against any such chance for thee here. These proud and dogged Scottish nobles scorn to grace a court, where the King makes so little account of them. And truly there is little wonder that they should thus take offence, seeing that the places in the royal favour, which by inheritance belong to them, should be filled by such beasts as Leonard— Torfefan—Hommil—Andrew—aye, and that prince of brutes, Cochran, too."

" They are all beasts, as thou sayest, uncle," replied Juliet; " though, if I were obliged to choose among them, I should rather tie myself to that coarse, clumsy elephant whom thou hast last named as king of these brutes, than to any of the others. He is the man, depend on't, who hath the true and proper art to raise the edifice of his own fortunes; and, by using his broad shoulders as a scaffold, a bold woman might thereby mount, methinks, to wealth and honours."

" He is a pestilent, pushing, proud, overbearing, ignorant, vulgar beast, I tell thee," replied her uncle, much excited. " The brute despises music! Depend upon it, he will never rise to anything but to the garret story of one of his own buildings, from which, if some kind devil would but throw him down, to the dislocation of that accursed bull neck of his, I should cheerfully compose an especial jubilate. Oh, Apollo and Terpsichore! that a man of my musical science and learning, should be compelled to associate with so vile a piler of stones, and compounder of mortar !"

"I have a shrewd suspicion, that the measure of thy rage against Cochran, is but that of thy fears for his outstripping thee in thine ascent of the lofty tower of ambition," replied Juliet. "But spurn him not, good uncle, if thou art wise; for his ladder is long, and strong; and might, with proper management, be useful to thee."

"I should be right glad to see it so, July, could I but kick down both the ladder and its owner, after I should have so used them," said Rogers. "But methinks thou wouldst fain carry ladder, hod and mortar and all, to the very top of the tower, on thine own shoulders, rather than lose the man they belong to."

"Thou art grievously mistaken, uncle," replied Juliet, keenly. "To rise into a high and wealthy station, and the higher and wealthier the better, would certainly be my desire; but I should much prefer youth, and beauty, and accomplishment, in the instrument which I might use for the gratification of mine ambition. If fate denies me all these indeed, then would I embrace age and deformity itself, rather than fail of mine object. Nay, thou canst hardly as yet guess to what means I should resort to secure its completion. As for Cochran, I know he loves me; for, in his great condescension, he hath vouchsafed to tell me so. Nor have I altogether kept the bear aloof. To wed myself to him would be to speculate, and that too with but an ungainly and unloveable subject. But if I could read the book of his fate, and find fortune and honours therein, it would not be the coarse edifice of his body, supported as it is upon such rustic pillars, and crowned by so vulgar and heavy a capital, that would deter me from embracing it. Yet 'tis but a speculation ; and, being so, I must confess that I am disposed rather to grasp at this handsome Corinthian column of the Stewart, than to tie myself to that clumsy Cochran, whose clay image might, after all, crumble to pieces, and suffocate me in its dirty dust."

"I am right glad that thou hast so determined, Juliet," said Rogers. "I have no jealousy of this well-born knight, who hath, moreover, a greater feeling for the divine art of music than any of his cold countrymen with whom I have yet met, without even excepting Royalty itself. But I might as well see thee built up into a stone wall, as see thee the wife of Cochran! To see thy great musical genius tied to this most unmelodious and croaking chisseler of stones, and compounder of lime, sand, and cow's-hair! I quaver at the very thought! But get thee to bed, my girl. Now that I know my ground-notes, I shall wonder if I work thee not out a piece that shall not only win thee this instrument of thy more recent desires, but enable thee to play upon it too, according as thou wilt, with thine own variations."

Whilst this precious conversation was going on between the uncle and niece, Sir Walter Stewart gave the convoy to Ramsay as far the Royal Castle-gate, after which he returned towards his hostel. As he was pursuing his solitary way thither, he heard the clashing of swords; and, on moving quickly down the deserted street, he discovered, by the faint light that came from a new moon, two men pressing hard in fence against one, who was defending himself with great courage, with his back to a wall. Though he had no knowledge of the combatants, he could not stand by and see such foul play.

"For shame! for shame, gentlemen!" cried he. "What! two upon one!"

"Gentlemen, indeed!" cried he that was assailed, in a contemptuous tone, during the moment of breathing afforded him by Sir Walter's interference; "Gentlemen indeed!—Tailors and scaramouches, else am I not the Earl of Huntly!"

"Again dost thou dare so to miscal the gentlemen of the court of his most Royal Majesty of Scotland?" cried one of the individuals, whom Sir Walter immediately discovered to be the pot-valiant Torfefan. "By all the gods of fire, thunder, and battle, thou shalt eat this good bilboa of mine. Have at thee, then, earl, or carl, or devil, if thou likest it!"

"Nay, then, my Lord of Huntly, I will myself relieve thee of this bold bird," cried the knight; "do thou deal with the other."

"Thanks for thy rescue, Sir Walter Stewart," replied Huntly, now recognising his friend. "But thou hast left naught to me but the very shred of the skirt of the garment of this broil—the vile cabbage—the very tailor himself."

"Trust me, thy man, though but the ninth-part of one, is as good as mine," replied Sir Walter.

The combat was now renewed upon fairer terms, and, in a few moments, Torfefan's sword was sent spinning into the air, and, falling from its flight, it rang upon the stones of the cause-

The weapon of his noble ally had pierced a fleshy part of his
opponent as he turned to run away.—Page 151

way, and was shivered into pieces, whilst its owner was prostrated on his back by his over-anxiety to withdraw from the fury of his adversary's onset.   Sir Walter's sword-point was immediately at his throat; and, at that very moment the weapon of his noble ally had pierced a fleshy part of his opponent, as he had turned to run away, which act of discretion, however, it did not prevent, for it rather pricked him on to a more active exertion of speed.

"Spare my life, good Sir Walter Stewart!" cried Torfefan, in an agony of fear.   "Most noble Knight, spare the life of a fellow-courtier!"

"Get up, sir; I have no intention of taking it," replied Sir Walter.   "'Tis enow for me that I have thus exorcised the spirit of the pottle-pot out of thee.   'Twas that which made thine otherwise peaceful sword leap from its scabbard against thy betters.   Get thee up, I say, and go home."

"Thou art right, Sir Knight," replied Torfefan, rising humbly upon his knees, and gradually gaining his legs.   "I am at all times mild and peaceful, as so brave a man, and so perfect a master of fence ought to be, save when the flask hath somewhat inflamed my brain, and then, indeed, I am as dangerous as a devil.   'Twas well that thou camest, else my Lord of Huntly, whom otherwise I so highly respect, had certainly died by my murderous hand."

"'Twas well, indeed, that thy bloody Bacchanalian rage was stayed in time," said Sir Walter Stewart, ironically.   "In this bout, thou hast so well proved thy title to bravery, as well as to science in fence, that who shall dare henceforth to deny these thy perfections?   So take the advice of a friend, Signor Torfefan, and get thee straightway to bed, lest the dregs of that same pottle-pot, working in thee still, should draw down upon thee some more serious fracture than that of thy bilboa-blade."

"Ha! true," said Torfefan; "that was a loss indeed!   But murderers will suffer at last; and if thou didst but know the blood which that same lethal weapon hath shed in my hands, and the lives which it hath sacrificed, thou would'st say, Sir Knight ———"

"I would say that thou should'st forthwith hasten to thy bed," interrupted Sir Walter.   "If the King should hear of this brawl ———"

"Gad so, that's true, Sir Walter!" cried Torfefan; "thank thee for the hint.   Were these reptiles, Cochran, Rogers, and the rest, to hear of this, they might work mine absolute destruction.   Ah, that's the worst feature of our King's court,

Sir Walter ! The worst misfortune that has happened, I say,
to us gentlemen of the court, is the admission to it of such vile
scum as these Cochrans, and Rogers, and Leonards, and such
like base mechanics. My very broil this blessed night, may be
said to be owing to my permitting that lily-livered hog in
armour, Hommil, to company with me. But while I am
prating, these villains may get sight of me, and make their own
story out of me. So I'll tarry here no longer. Good night,
Sir Walter Stewart ; you are a brave gentlemen, well fitted to
company with the King."

"What a cowardly boasting knave !" said Sir Walter, after
he was gone.

"Yet, to such vermin are all the crumbs of royal favour
thrown, to the utter starvation of those who are of noble breed !"
cried Huntly, with bitterness. "I would fain drink one flask
of wine with thee, Stewart, at thy hostel, ere I go home, to
wash down the indignation and loathing, which the very sight
of these scoundrel caitiffs hath brought into my throat. Let
me go thither with thee straightway."

"Willingly, my lord," replied Sir Walter, and, arm and arm
together, they proceeded to the hostel.

"Stewart," said the Earl of Huntly, after they were seated
at their wine, and leaning across the table to address his friend
in a half whisper, though they were the only guests in the room
at that late hour, "thou hast so much of the good will of great
and small, that no one grudges thee the favour the king shows
to thee ; and there are few who have much jealousy of Ramsay
either, seeing that he was whipping-boy to James, and, moreover, that he is a gentleman of good descent. But neither
lords nor commons, knights nor burgesses, can long tolerate the
undue elevation and preferment of wretches, so worthless, as
those who block up the royal presence from the approach of
better men."

" 'Tis unfortunate that it should be so," said Sir Walter ;
"but has it never occurred to your Lordship, that the nobles
of Scotland may have some small share of the blame, by absent-
ing themselves from court as they do, so that the King lacks
all opportunity of having their several merits brought under
his eye."

"You would not have the high-blooded war-steed to throw
himself down in the same stye with obscene swine ?" replied
the Earl. "I would as soon thrust myself into a den of bad-
gers, as sit down to partake of a king's feast, with such
company as that arrogant mason Cochran, and the other dung-

hill companions whom James so much delights to honour. The court must be cleared of all such, aye, and swept, and garnished, and perfumed too, before I shall dare to trust my nostrils within its precints."

"No one can say that such feelings are not quite natural, my lord," replied Sir Walter Stewart; "but yet, I fear that the indulgence of them, can do nothing else but increase the disease which you would so fain cure. 'Tis pity that some few of the nobles do not so far overcome them, as to appear now and then at court. As a soft answer turneth away wrath, so gentle conduct will often effect that which may defy the sternest boldness."

"Nay, but how are we used when we do appear!" demanded the Earl. "Even Albany and Mar are treated as aliens; and if the very royal brothers of the monarch are scarcely noticed, in comparison with those nauseous toads who crawl about the king's footstool, what can we of the humbler peerage expect?"

"There is great reason in what you say, my lord," observed Sir Walter; "but hush! who comes here?"

A tall thin figure in black trewse, with a doublet of black slashed with flame-coloured silk, the body strangely covered with silver stars and having the signs of the zodiac on the broad belt that confined it, with a black cloak hanging from his shoulders, which had on it the sun and moon and seven stars, and his head shaded by a broad hat that bore a large plume of feathers, all of the same gloomy hue, stalked into the common room. From the small quantity of illumination which the single lamp that burned on their table threw around it, the person that came was but indistinctly visible in the obscurity that especially prevailed at the lower end of the apartment; but when he came slowly forward within the influence of the light, Sir Walter Stewart and his friend the Earl of Huntly recognised the pale, thin, sharp, and prominent features, the cadaverous hue, the dark eyebrows, the piercing eyes, and the long black locks and beard of Andrew the Flemish Astrologer. He came as if in a walking dream; he stopped within a few feet of the table where they sat—started, as if suddenly returning to the consciousness of the realities around him—darted an inquiring look, first at Lord Huntly and then at Sir Walter Stewart, and then slowly inclining his head in silent and sombre salutation he turned from them and stalked away, without uttering a syllable.

The Earl and the Knight could not for some time shake off

the superstitious dread that involuntarily crept over both of them at the sight of this man, who had thus so strangely and mysteriously visited them. His deep knowledge of the science to which he pretended was admitted by all, and his powers were supposed to extend over other regions besides those of the heavens. Their hearts were so chilled by his very aspect that both felt quite unfitted for renewing their conversation; and, without making one single remark on this strange intrusion, each drained the full cup that stood before him, and bidding one another good night, the serving men of the hostel were called, and they separated to seek their respective places of repose.

A TEMPEST.

Clifford.—What a dreadful tempest out of doors? Forgive my interruption, Serjeant; but ere you go farther with your interesting story, I think we had better get in some more wood and peats lest the fire should get hopelessly low, a thing that is very likely to happen where people are so engaged as we are.

Grant.—The Serjeant's stories might well make one forget everything else.

Clifford.—Come, Mister Serjeant, whilst the fire is mending and the Earl and the Knight are retiring to their repose, you may have leisure to wet your whistle a little.

Serjeant.—I shall not be sorry to do that, sir; my mouth is a little dry to be sure. Keep us all, such a night of wind and rain! How the blast thuds against the windows! That is awful indeed! God help the poor man that may be out in such a night! 'Tis well for us to be in bigged land.

Grant.—As you say, it is well for us to be under a roof Archy; and yet I wish that the roof of this old house may not be blown away. How furiously the tempest howls along!

Author.—'Tis fearful to listen to it; yet I suspect that this is nothing to the blasts which its walls must sometimes endure.

Serjeant.—Ou! bless you, sir! The wind comes down the trough of this glen at times enough, one would think, to blow every house and living thing out of it, stones and rocks and all, like peas out of a pop-gun. But this house has stood many a blast, and I hope it will weather out this one yet.

Author.—It came on very suddenly. It is not half an hour ago since all was quiet, and hear how the wind rages and the rain rattles now.

Clifford.—Our friend Willox must be abroad with his kelpie's bridle.

Author.—Aye, or Andrew the Flemish Astrologer may have done it.

Clifford.—Andrew the Astrologer! yes, I daresay he was quite equal to kicking up such a rumpus among the elements. I would fain know more of that fellow.

Serjeant.—Be assured, sir, I shall tell you all I know about him in due course of time. Meanwhile I am ready to take up the clue of my discourse whenever you please.

Clifford.—You may do so when you like, Serjeant; for, as I suppose that this terrible night puts all hope of an early start in the morning out of the question, we may e'en sit up as late as we like.

Serjeant.—If the rain holds on at this rate the rivers will all be up, and the mosses swimming, so that our travelling further to-morrow will be impossible.

Clifford.—Come away, then, Serjeant, proceed with your legend, and let the storm roar and rattle as it will.

THE LEGEND OF CHARLEY STEWART TAILLEAR-CRUBACH CONTINUED.

Sir Walter Stewart was received next day by King James with all that kindness which he was used to lavish upon his favourites, among whom the accomplished knight held by no means the lowest place in his estimation. Apartments were immediately allotted to him near the royal person, and his time became almost entirely occupied by his duties as a courtier. He failed not, however, to take all opportunities that occurred of cultivating his talent for music under the auspices of Sir William Rogers and his fascinating niece. Notwithstanding the knight's bold confidence to the contrary, the lady's designs against his heart might have been very rapidly successful had not the baseness of her motives inclined her to waver from time to time between the balance of rival advantages, which were offered to her by an encouragement of Cochran, who had declared himself to be her lover. Thus it was that she often scared Sir Walter Stewart at the very moment when, to all appearance, he seemed most likely unconsciously to gorge the bait, and thus it was that several years glided imperceptibly away without the lady finding herself one bit nearer to the attainment of either of her objects. Still, however, Sir Walter would ever and anon return within the sphere of her attraction, and the fair Juliet always the more easily managed to conjure him back thither, that they were frequently brought together to sing and to play in presence of the royal pair in those little private meetings which were held almost nightly in the Queen's apartment. As for Sir William Rogers, he did all he could to fix his niece's determination towards securing an alliance with Sir Walter Stewart, not only from his unconquerable abhorrence of the unrefined· mason on the one hand, but also from his conviction that his own ambitious views were fully as likely to be helped forward by the lady's union with the gallant knight, for whom moreover he had an especial respect, because of his genius and accomplishment in that divine art to which he was himself so enthusiastically attached.

The royal party was one night assembled, as usual, in the apartment of Queen Margaret, who, seated in a gorgeous chair, richly attired, as became her station, and attended by Ramsay, and some of her maids of honour, and with her angelic countenance lighted up with unfeigned rapture, listened to the mingled voices and minstrelsy of Sir William Rogers, Sir Walter Stewart, and the lovely Juliet Manvers. The King was engaged with Cochran, at a table at one end of the room, in looking over some plans, which had reference to the buildings then going on within the castle. Anyone who had witnessed them, whilst so employed, would have said that neither his Majesty, nor his architect, were much occupied in the subject which was the ostensible object of their consideration, for whilst the ears of the monarch seemed ever and anon to draw off his attention to the music, the heavy eyes of Cochran were perpetually wandering towards the person of the songstress. Ere the music had been long continued, each of them yielded to the irresistible impulse which had moved him, and, whilst the King drew a chair, and seated himself opposite to the performers, Cochran placed himself behind it, and, with that vulgar and unpolished air, which the magnificence of his dress rendered only the more apparent, leaned awkwardly over the back of it, and riveted his gloating gaze upon the lady's charms. The piece had come to its close, and the royal pair were bestowing their commendations liberally upon those who had executed it, when three loud and solemn taps were heard at the door of the chamber. King James started, and at once assumed an air of intense and serious anxiety, and the Queen, and all present, were more or less disturbed at this interruption.

"I had forgotten!" exclaimed the King, as if speaking to himself alone,—"Enter! thou art at all times welcome!"

The door slowly opened at his word, and the tall thin figure of Andrew the Flemish Astrologer stood in the doorway, habited as he has been already described, and with a long white rod in his right hand. With his left hand upon his breast, he made a low and solemn reverence to the King, and then pointing his rod over his shoulder, he seemed silently to indicate his desire that his Majesty should follow him.

"Lead on!" cried the King, with an awe-stricken voice and air, whilst he arose from his chair, and hastily put on his hat and cloak. "If we are called by the stars, we are at all times ready to give due obedience to them," and, with these words, he immediately retired with the Astrologer.

Ramsay, Stewart, Rogers, and Juliet Manvers, made their several reverences to the Queen, in which they were clumsily joined by Cochran, and all took their leave. They were no sooner out of the Royal presence, than Cochran, rudely thrusting himself before Ramsay and Sir Walter Stewart, bustled busily up to the lady, as she hung on her uncle's arm, so as to engage the unoccupied place next her, to the exclusion of everyone else. Sir Walter was somewhat chafed at this rudeness, and might have forgotten himself, had not his rising anger been checked by the voice of one of the Queen's ladies, who called him by his name. The Knight stopped to ascertain what she wanted.

"Sir Walter Stewart," said the lady, "the Queen commands thee to return, for a brief space, to her apartment, that she may again hear thee sing that French ballad of thine own composition, which so much pleased her Majesty two nights ago. Her Majesty would fain have the words, and catch the notes of it."

"I humbly obey her Majesty's command," replied the Knight, returning with the lady immediately.

On entering the Queen's apartment, he made his reverence to her Majesty; and she, having again signified her wishes to him in a very gracious manner, she motioned him to take up a lute, and seat himself on a stool near her chair; and after having done as she desired, he began to sing the ballad she had named, and to accompany himself on the instrument.

In the meanwhile the King followed the solemn step and apparition-like figure of the Astrologer till he brought his Majesty to an angular part of the castle-wall that, skirting the giddy precipice of lofty rock on which the fortress stands,

looked out over the country to the south and west. But that
which was an extensive and magnificent prospect by day, was
at this moment shrouded in the shades of night. There he
took his stand, and pointed upwards with his rod. The moon
was in its second quarter, and shed a pale and partial light.
A strange and portentous arch of black and very opaque
clouds, rested its extremities on the verges of the northern and
southern horizon, and spanned the heavens through the zenith.
Behind this, all to the eastward, was one dark vault, impenetrable to the eye, whilst the western edge of the arch was
tinged with bright rainbow hues, and the whole sky below it,
upon that side, was serene and cloudless. As the king gazed
upwards in wonder, not unmingled with dread, a bright flash
of lightning suddenly illumined the whole of the black and
solid concave of clouds behind them, and the walls of the castle
were shaken by a tremendous peal of thunder. The heart of
the royal James quailed within him. The peal was rever-
berated from the bold front of Dumyot, with a harsh and
crashing sound, and then, after visiting and rousing up every
echo among the Ochills, it rolled away fearfully up the valley
of the Forth, until it died amid the distant western mountains.
Filled with superstitious dread, the King grasped the left arm
of the Astrologer, who stood unmoved, with his rod extended
in his right hand.

"Holy Virgin Mother, Messire Andrew! what do these
dread signs portend?" cried James, with deep anxiety of voice
and manner.

"These!" exclaimed Andrew, in French, and in a wild and
enthusiastic tone, that would have sounded as contemptuous
in the King's ear, but for the intensity of his desire to have his
fears and doubts put to rest; "these are but the mere
auxiliaries of Heaven's appalling oratory. See!—know ye
not yonder stars which now approach each other to a conjunction so threatening!"

"Mars and Venus approaching to strange and fearful conjunction indeed," replied the King, shuddering. What can it
bode?"

"And see ye not that they are in the ascendant, whilst
Jupiter is sinking fast? Now, they are almost in contact—
and now!"

"Heaven in its mercy defend us, what a dreadful peal!"
cried the King, as the thunder again burst terribly over
his head. "And see, the thick and inky veil begins to rend
asunder into separate clouds, like some vast army breaking its

general mass into its several legions. And behold now, how they divide and subdivide, careering swiftly like squadrons of horsemen over the vault of the heavens. And now, look how strangely and capriciously the broken-up clouds have here veiled, and there revealed, the different portions of the sky!"

"Aye," said the Astrologer, solemnly, "and now the mystic dance is done. Each several fragment of vapour hath taken his place. The characters are fixed; and now 'tis man's fault if he read not enough of Heaven's will in so wide-spread and so plainly written a book. There we can see the Hydra, and there the Greyhounds—there the greater, and there the lesser Dog. But where is the Lion? And where the Northern Crown?"

"Alas, Messire Andrew! thou lookest as if thou wert dismayed by these fearful prodigies," exclaimed the King again, with an anxiously inquiring eye. "What is it that you dread they may portend?"

"It is grievous for me to translate to your Majesty the meaning of these direfully ominous portents," replied Andrew, gravely, after a long pause, during which he seemed gradually to call down his spirit from the heavens, where it had been soaring for sometime amid all the wonders they displayed. "Yet is it better for you to know their fearful warnings, so far as mortals may interpret them," continued he, rising into a wild kind of inspiration. "Danger is threatened to the King!—to the King of Scotland! Beware of the princes and lords of the land! Those in whom thou takest the most pleasure may prove thy greatest bane! Commotions and wars are to be looked for and dreaded! Beware! beware! Oh, King! lest the Scottish Lion be devoured by its whelps!"

"The Scottish Lion devoured by its whelps!" re-echoed the King, in the muttered voice of dismay. "Danger from the princes and nobles of the land! Danger from those in whom we take most pleasure! What doth all this import? And in especial, what meaneth this last strange enigma? What!—the Queen! speak Messire Andrew? Or would it point at those who most enjoy my favour? Why dost thou not answer me? Wars and commotions—the powerful influence of Mars is plain—but that of Venus!—say!—speak! Surely, surely that doth not touch the loyalty of our Queen?"

"The moment of divination has passed away for this night," said the cunning Astrologer, in a low hollow voice, like that produced from an over-exhausted spirit. "I am now weak and blind as other men. Yet said I nothing of her most gracious

Majesty Queen Margaret, whom God long preserve! The planet your Majesty speaks of hath two several and distinct influences—one, the which may operate as touching things more immediately under the dominion of woman's passion, and the other, as denoting a mere point of time. This latter interpretation would seem to me, at this moment, to be by far the more likely, for, as Mars would predict battles, his conjunction with the Star of Evening would rather appear to me to mark that they will arise in the evening of your Majesty's reign, which may God and St. Andrew render long and prosperous!"

"Nay, but cans't thou not yet inquire more closely, Messire Andrew?" demanded the King, impatiently. "These doubts are worse than ignorance."

"Another time we may find fit opportunity to solve them, good my liege," replied the Astrologer, with a low reverence. "The spirit of divination hath passed from me, and I am now no more than a weak and blind mortal. And see! even the heavens have refused to yield up farther knowledge of future events to the sons of earth, for they have wrapped themselves up in one dark and impenetrable veil of cloud. To-night the book of fate is shut!—Saw ye that! The elements themselves forbid all farther question."

As he spoke, a terrible glare of lightning blazed around them, momentarily illuminating every feature of the grand scenery by which they were surrounded. A fearful clap of thunder again burst over their heads with awful magnificence, and rolled terribly away. A furious wind began to blow, and large drops of rain descended, a tempest was approaching, and the King, sunk, disheartened, and unsatisfied, was driven in by the natural results of those threatenings in the sky, which he had been so attentively watching, to brood upon those fanciful horrors and dangers with which they, in reality, had no connection. He returned towards the Queen's apartment in deep thought, and he had entered it fully, before the notes of the music that still sounded in it had power to rouse him from his abstraction. Sir Walter Stewart still sat near the Queen's footstool, singing to the accompaniment of his lute, and her Majesty and her maids of honour were still eagerly occupied in listening.

"Ha!" cried King James, as he recovered perfect consciousness of the scene before him, and speaking with a highly disturbed air and tone; "methought our privacy had been relieved from all further interruption for this night?"

"Pardon, my liege!—my love!" cried the Queen, rising from

her chair, and affectionately taking his arm. "Pardon, if we have done aught to displeasure thee! I and my maidens had a mind to hear again that sweet ballad of Sir Walter Stewart's making, which he sang so pleasantly to us the other night, as you may remember. He was brought back, therefore, in obedience to my command, and if there be aught of blame in this, it is all mine own. That he hath stayed so long after he did return, if fault in that there be, it must be charged against his own pleasing minstrelsy, which did so enchain the ears of his hearers, that time passed by unheeded."

"Permit me, your Majesty, to take my leave," said Sir Walter, making his wonted obeisance to the King as he retired.

"Good night," said the King, with more of condescension, but with less of warmth than he was accustomed to use towards one whom he so much favoured.

All that night the royal mind was vexed by frightful waking visions, that haunted it to the exclusion of sleep. In vain did his Majesty try to embody them into anything like a clear and connected picture of coming events. But dark though the ground was upon which he worked, certain prominent lights continually started from it, and remained stationary before him, so as ultimately to fix themselves in some degree upon him as probable truths. The most stimulating of these might be guessed at, from the royal orders which were issued on the following morning. The court was hastily and unexpectedly removed to Edinburgh Castle; and soon afterwards, the two Princes of the blood-royal, the Duke of Albany, and the Earl of Mar, were, to the astonishment of all men, seized and made prisoners. Mar was confined in Craigmillar Castle. But of Albany, the King seemed anxious to take especial care, for he was committed to custody in Edinburgh Castle itself, where he might be more particularly guarded under the royal eye.

Yet all this did not seem to have relieved James' mind from the terrors which had taken possession of it. The approach of the nobles to the royal person was less encouraged than it had ever been. The King's favourites, though still permitted to have their usual intercourse him, were all in their turns looked upon at times with an eye of doubt. Sir Walter Stewart sensibly felt, that he was subjected to a greater portion of the effects of this suspicious temper than any of the others. An excuse had been found for his being deprived of such apartments in the Castle of Edinburgh, as he had had in that of Stirling, and he was obliged to hire lodgings within the walls of the city. His presence at the private parties in the Queen's

apartment was rarely, if ever, required.   The musical meetings
there were of themselves less frequent, and when they did take
place, he was not among the number of the performers.   To
make amends for this, he spent more of his time in the pursuit
of his favourite science, with the fair Juliet Manvers, in the
apartments of Sir William Rogers, and as the lady seemed to
be making, day after day, greater inroads upon his heart, so
did Sir Walter Stewart himself rise every day more and more
in the estimation of the musical knight.   With such a source
of amusement, Sir Walter was less affected by the coldness
which he experienced at court, than might have been naturally
supposed.   But he felt deeply for the confinement of the
Princes, with whom he had been admitted into habits of intimacy that bordered upon the warmth of friendship.   Yet,
much as he was personally attached to them, and anxiously as
he would have wished to have befriended them, he knew enough
to convince him that he could make no effort in their behalf,
that would not have a certain tendency to lead to some fatal
issue, both as regarded them and himself.   But the death of
the Earl of Mar, which happened soon afterwards, and which
was most suspiciously given out as having taken place
suddenly, by apoplexy, in a warm bath, so roused his feelings,
that he resolved to take the first opportunity of making some
attempt to save Albany, and to this he was more immediately
stimulated by something that occurred to him one night, as he
was walking and ruminating on the Castle-hill.

"Sir Walter Stewart," said a man, who stood muffled up in
a cloak, to him, as he was striding slowly past, unconscious
that there was anyone near him, "wilt thou not halt for a
moment to speak to an old friend?"

"My Lord Huntly!" cried Sir Walter, in astonishment,
after approaching the figure, and ascertaining who it was that
spoke.

"Hush!—name me not so loudly!" replied Huntly. "The
very air hath ears, yea, and eyes too.   I am here in secret and
in disguise.   Were I discovered, my life might pay for it.
Come farther this way into the shadow.   I would speak with
thee about matters which no one else must hear, and my time
is short.   We must save Albany!"

"Most willingly would I aid in doing so," replied Sir Walter.
" But how is his safety to be secured?"

"Thou canst be eminently useful," replied Huntly.

"I know thy zeal in a friend's behalf, and although thou
mightest have shown some unwillingness to take part with us,

when our grievances amounted to nothing more than royal neglect, yet perhaps thou mayest now be more sharpened to our purpose, when thou seest that the murderous knife hath already been drawn upon us, that the first victim hath been already sacrificed, and that victim too a high and noble prince of the blood royal, who was, moreover, thy friend."

"Nay, surely thou dost not believe that my Lord Mar died other than a natural death?" said Sir Walter.

"A natural death!" exclaimed Huntly. "Aye, a death naturally occurring from a weak and cruel brother's jealousy. That species of natural death, to wit, which the sheep may very naturally receive from the hand of the butcher!"

"Why, they say he died in a bath," said Sir Walter.

"And in so saying they say truly," replied Huntly. "Of a truth he died in a bath—a hot bath, into which he was kindly put to recover him from a deep cut in the main artery of his arm, given him by one of the royal executioners."

"'Tis horrible, if true!" said Sir Walter, shuddering.

"'Tis as true as it is horrible," continued Huntly. "And now methinks I may trust to your being less scrupulous in listening to the grievances of the lords, than thou wert when I last touched the topic with thee at Stirling."

"My Lord," replied Sir Walter, "I will honestly tell thee, that to save Albany, a man whom I honour as a royal prince and a highly accomplished knight, and whom, moreover, I hold in deep affection as a friend, I am willing to put mine own life to utmost peril, and this the more too, that if I can save him I shall think that my so doing will be the preserving of the right arm of Scotland. But in anything that may touch my fealty directly to the person of King James, I must be held excused, seeing that I have already received too much kindness from his Majesty, to permit me to prove in anywise a rebel to him,—but in this matter of the Duke of Albany, my judgment tells me that I shall, by saving him, be doing good service to my king as well as to my country."

"Then let us leave all else at present, and talk of this matter in hand," said Huntly. "Thou art well versed in the customs and affairs of France, and canst speak its tongue. Couldst thou not contrive to discover, whether some barque may not be soon looked for from thence with merchandise?"

"So far, my Lord, I can answer thee here upon the spot," replied Sir Walter. "It so chances that I look daily for the arrival of a captain, well known to me, who trades in wine. He is the bearer of certain casks for me, and I can therefore go to inquire regarding him without much suspicion. It shall be done to-morrow."

"This is most lucky," said Huntly. "So now let us consider well as to our plans. Knowest thou how the Duke is guarded?"

"I do not lodge within the castle," replied Sir Walter. "Nor am I so often within its walls as I wont to be. But this I know, that the Duke is guarded most strictly. The captain of the guard himself keeps the key of the apartment where he is imprisoned, and where, to make all things secure, his chamberlain is locked up with him, and no one is allowed to go in or out who is not in the first place most narrowly examined. But yet will I scrupulously observe, and make myself master of the whole circumstances, and of the exact position of things, and it will go hard with me if I cannot find some way of baffling their vigilance."

"Then let us part to-night, lest we be observed," said Huntly. " That accursed astrologer, Flemish Andrew, may again start up before us, like the devil in our path."

" Um," replied Sir Walter, doubtingly; "thou mayest not be very far from the truth in thy evil suspicions of him, my Lord. I liked not his last visit."

" Well, no matter," said the Earl; "to-morrow night we may meet again."

" Aye, to-morrow night—here, and at the same hour," replied Sir Walter. " But if I come not, my Lord, I would have thee believe, that if not unwillingly detained by the King, I may perhaps be employing myself more usefully elsewhere."

"I shall so believe," replied Huntly; "then farewell till our next meeting, be that when it may."

The friends then parted, and took different ways, to avoid all chance of been seen together, and Sir Walter Stewart was about to enter the head of the close where his lodging was situated, when he was accosted by a person who came limping up to him, with all the appearance of a jaded foot traveller, and who addressed him in humble, but by no means clownish, salutation.

"Sir Knight," said he, "wilt thou vouchsafe to pardon me, a stranger, and deign to tell me whether thou canst direct me to the lodging of Sir Walter Stewart of Stradawn?"

"Surely I have heard that voice before," said the knight, without replying to the question.

"Sir Walter!—my father!" exclaimed the other in great surprise.

" What!" exclaimed Sir Walter, in no less astonishment, and in anything but a gracious tone, "Charley Stewart! In the name of all that is wonderful what hath brought thee to Edinburgh? This is not well. Methought I had arranged all things to thy heart's content, for thy proper employment in thine own native district. But I forget how time flies. Doubtless ere this thou art as learned in thine art, and in the use of the goose, needles, shears, and bodkin, as the great and accomplished Mr. Jonathan Junkins himself."

"I crave your pardon, Sir Knight," replied Charley. "Ill as the spirit of the Stewart that is within me might brook such mean drudgery, I struggled hard to break it into the destiny which thou hadst been pleased to assign me. But the rude caitiff churls that worked in Junkins' shop, and some of the boorish neighbours too, presuming on my youth, fastened on me the offensive nickname of *Tàillear-crubach*, or the lame tailor. This I could not bear; and after having well pummelled some dozen or so of them, one after the other, I deemed it as well to secure peace for the future, by giving up all just claim to so ignominious a title."

"By saint Michael, my boy," cried Sir Walter, cordially taking Charley's hand; "I cannot say but thou didst well. What a strapping burly chield thou hast grown! But what hast thou been doing with thyself then, since thou gavest up tailoring?"

"I have learned to ride, and to use a sword and a lance indifferent well," said Charley.

"Bravo!" cried Sir Walter. "By the Rood, thou art mine own very flesh and blood! Trust me, had I guessed that thou wert made of such metal, I should never have thought of tying thee to a tailor's board, I promise thee. Would I had known this sooner! But now!—How fares it with thy mother,.boy?"

"Well, Sir Walter," replied Charley with a deep sigh. "She was well when I last saw her."

"Would that I had sooner known thy merits, Charley!" said Sir Walter, with a depth of feeling which he had not yet displayed. "I might then have——But now I fear I am too far involved with another——The fates have been cruelly against thee, boy."

"They have indeed!" said Charley, with an emotion which almost choked him.

"Well! well!" said Sir Walter, affectionately squeezing his hand. "Come—cheer up, Charley! I may yet have it in my power to do something for thee. And by Saint Andrew," continued the knight, after a short pause, "now I think on't, thou hast come to me in the very nick of time. Thine aid will be most useful to me. But this is neither the time nor the place to talk about such matters. Come, let us to my lodging, that I may procure you refreshment and rest; for your pale face, hollow eyes, and clinging cheeks, would seem to say that thou greatly lackest both; and as thou mayest require to be up betimes, I shall delay farther questioning of thee till a fitter opportunity."

But as you will hardly wish to wait, gentlemen, until Charley Stewart has had such necessary restoration of exhausted nature, as shall enable him to tell his own story, I shall hastily sketch, at somewhat greater length than he had time to do, what took place with him during those years that have elapsed since we last heard of him. A few months had sufficed to sicken him, as we have seen, of the shopboard of Mister Jonathan Junkins. For a time he lived quietly with his mother, soothing her sorrow with all the tenderness of the kindest of hearts, following out his learning under the kind instruction of the then priest of Dounan, who had taken an especial favour for him; and, lastly, occupying himself in the delightful task of communicating to Rosa MacDermot, that knowledge which he thus gained. Now and then, to be sure, spite of his lameness, he took pleasure in exercising himself in athletic feats; and in this practice, he was much aided by an accidental acquaintance, which he chanced to make with a certain Sir Piers Gordon, a small land-holder in a neighbouring glen, who, himself a dependant of the Earl of Huntly, was glad to collect a few retainers about him, in any way, to help him to uphold his dignity. Under the auspices of this well-trained soldier, Charley became an expert handler of the claymore, a fearless horseman, and no very contemptible wielder of a lance; and he had more than once had the satisfaction, of making one of the party who accompanied his patron, in some of those skirmishes or minor movements of warfare between clans, which the wild and unsettled state of the country rendered much too common in those days to be always particularised, far less to be chronicled.

Charley was one day seated, with Rosa MacDermot, on their favourite flowery bank, by the side of the same spring I formerly described as gushing from below a mossy stone, under the grove of weeping birches, where we last heard of them together. But Rosa was now grown almost a woman, being tall of her age, and of very handsome person; and the scar of the cross-mark on her cheek had now become so slight, that so far from being a deformity, it rather gave an interesting expression to her otherwise blooming and richly beautiful countenance. Her love for Charley, and his for her, had grown with every day they had lived. But maiden modesty on her part, and delicacy on his, had made both of them somewhat more reserved, and more guarded in giving way to the expression of it. She no longer talked of being his wifey ; and when he, hurried on by the feelings of the moment, was led to allude to their future union, when future prospects should smile more kindly upon them, her words, though tender, were few, whilst her eyes and her blushes spoke volumes.

They were intently engaged in converse together, when they were interrupted by a most unseemly looking object that appeared before them. If they had never beheld it until that moment, they might have had doubts as to which of the sexes it belonged to. The face was hideous, the nose being very prominent and hooked, so as to project over the mouth, which was hardly perceptible. The eyes, when open, were great, round, and fiery, and they were covered by eyelids of an unnatural largeness, so that the strange and regular alternation of the muscular motion, which was exerted in the dropping and raising of them, produced the most fearful effect. Enveloped as the head was in an old soiled red tartan plaid, which was twisted around it, and fell in large folds over half the person, after being knotted behind over the back, the whole body had a bunchy bird-like appearance, which was rendered still more uncouth, by its being supported on the bare, wiry, dirt-begrimmed shanks, and claw-like talons, which sprawled out beneath a short grey petticoat. The real name of this strange, unearthly looking monster, was lost in her antiquity. She had appeared in that district many years before, no one knew from whence ; and as all her marks were then the same as I have described them now, it is not wonderful that she should have acquired, from the rude people, the name of *the Howlet*, from her extreme likeness to that ill-omened bird. And tired as she had long been of kicking against the scorn of the world, and callous as she had been rendered under all the miseries it had heaped upon her, she now answered to that appellation, with the same readiness which she might probably have shown in the more sunny days of her youth, when she cheerfully replied to her own proper name, and to the fond endearments of a father and a mother. Yet, let it not be imagined that she, miserably abandoned as she had so long been to all that was wretched in human existence, had not her moments of reflection on happier days, long since gone by, the recollection of which only the more embittered the present. Nor is it to be supposed that, much as she had suffered, she herself had been bereft of all the better feelings of humanity. Her external appearance was enough to endow her, in the estimation of the vulgar, with all the attributes of malignity, as well as with the dread powers of sorcery. But although her approach never failed to produce a certain sensation of awe in the gentle mind of Rosa MacDermot, it was always mingled with a very large share of pity for the poor creature's penury and distress ; and this was fully participated by the good hearted Charley Stewart.

"Poor Howley !" cried Rosa, the moment she beheld her ; "it is long since I have seen thee. Where hast thou been wandering during this many a day ?"

"Some food for charity's sake !" said the Howlet, in that half shooting, half whistling tone of voice, which strangely carried out her otherwise remarkable similarity to the bird she was called after. "I am starving ! I am famished ! Some food for charity's sake !"

"Poor Howley, thou shalt never want it whilst I can help thee to it !" said the compassionate girl.

"Though hard-heartedness and scorn may meet me at every other door in this weary and wicked world," said the Howlet, "I still find charity here."

"Sit down then on the bank there," said Rosa, "and I will run and bring thee food in a moment."

"God's blessing be upon thee, fair maiden !" said the Howlet, with deep feeling.

"Thou canst bless, then !" said Charley Stewart gravely, after Rosa was gone.

"I can pray to God to bless !" replied the Howlet ; "and, unlike the men of this world, a God of all goodness will not refuse to listen to such a prayer, because it comes from the heart of a poor outcast, the scorn of this heartless world, clothed in rags, and starving for food. And who should I pray for, if I did not pray for blessings on that angel ?"

"She is an angel, Howley !" cried Charley, with ecstacy— "an angel in soul as well as in form. See how she comes tripping with her basket and pitcher, as if she hardly trod the earth !"

The old woman fastened her long hands greedily on the viands, the moment they came within her reach, her eyes glaring wide, and shutting alternately, and her ravenous hunger urged her to devour her food so fast, that it was fearful to behold her ; and then, as she did so, she went on muttering in her whistling voice, "The holy Virgin bless thee, my fair maiden! Och! och! what pain it is to swallow. Three days have I been denied food by my flinty-hearted fellow creatures! yet may God, in his mercy, forgive them! Three days! three whole days! The blessing of Heaven, its best blessings on thee, thou angel! Och, such pain! Thou shalt be a landed lady yet! Och, och! Thou shalt marry a man with a knight's spur at his heel! Och! such a pang at my heart! Och! oh!"—

Rosa and Charley Stewart, who had both been swallowing her words, with as much avidity as she had been devouring the food that had been given her, now both started up in dire alarm, and ran towards the old woman. Her eyes rolled dreadfully for a moment, and then they became fixed; the basket she held dropped from her hands; her arms and limbs stretched themselves out in rigid convulsion; her head fell stiffly back on the bank, and when they essayed to raise it up, they found that she was dead.

It was many a long day before Rosa MacDermot could shake off the horrible impression which this scene had made upon her young mind, so far as to be able to recal it with anything approaching tranquillity. Charley, however, had often pondered deeply on the words which had fallen from the old woman, and he was impatient till the time did come, when he felt that he might venture to allude to them.

"Charley," said Rosa anxiously, and tenderly taking his hand, as they were one day sitting together on their favourite spot; "something grieves thee in secret. Thou wert not wont to conceal a thought from me; why shouldst thou do so now? Why shouldst thou deny me my share of that sadness, which, being thine, ought to belong to both of us!"

"Rosa," replied Charley, fervently returning her gentle pressure; "I will honestly confess my folly. Those idle words of the poor Howlet have clung to my soul with a heaviness which I cannot shake off."

"Idle words they were indeed," replied Rosa; "words idly uttered by the poor crazy creature in the delirium of starvation. But, idle or not, they boded no evil to me; and is it by Charley Stewart that they are to be grudged to me?"

"Think of their import, Rosa," replied Charley, gravely; "and then you will see that I can scarcely be expected calmly to contemplate them."

"What!" exclaimed Rosa, smiling—"that I am to be a landed lady! Is that a matter that should give thee pain to think of?"

" Reflect, Rosa, by what means it was said that thou art to become so," replied Charley, with a sigh. " By marrying a man with a knight's spurs at his heels! Ran not the old woman's words so? And canst thou believe that I can coolly contemplate the probable accomplishment of any such prophecy?"

"Charley!" cried Rosa, with great feeling, whilst tears swelled from under her beautiful eyelids, "canst thou believe it possible that I should ever forget all I owe to thee? Canst thou believe that I can forget my often repeated vows? Canst thou believe that those infant affections which have grown up with me, strengthening as they grew, until they have now ripened with me in womanhood, can ever perish but with my life? My life is thine, for to thee I owe it. My soul is thine, for to thee I am indebted for that culture and expansion which may best fit it for heaven. My heart is thine, for it is to thee that I have been indebted for stocking it with its best and purest sympathies. Canst thou then doubt that I ever could be any other's than thine?"

" May the Virgin ever bless thee for thy words, my love!" cried Charley, with ecstacy. " I am satisfied of the truth of thine affection. Yet had I been better pleased if that old woman had never given utterance to those idle dreams of hers. At such a time too!—so awful! Just before her vexed and worn out spirit took its flight from its wretched earthly tenement!"

"It was awful indeed!" said Rosa, solemnly. "But methinks," added she, after a pause, and in a more cheerful tone—"Methinks the poor Howlet's words might bear a more pleasing interpretation than thou wouldst seem inclined to put upon them; yea, and to my fancy, much more natural withal."

" As how?" demanded Charley, eagerly.

" Marry, that thou mayst be the man with the knight's spurs at his heels," said Rosa, drooping her voice and her eyes, and blushing deeply.

" What!" exclaimed Charley, energetically. " By all the saints in the kalendar, but that were an interpretation indeed! I thank thee, Rosa, for thy augury. Trust me, if it lacks accomplishment, in due time, it shall not be my fault. Though I have been turned over into the dirt, by him to whom I should have looked for countenance and support, to encourage me in a nobler career—by him to whom I reasonably looked for the education befitting a soldier,—thanks to mine honest patron, Sir Piers, I am not now altogether in want of it. Thanks, moreover, be to God, that I have never done anything which may, with reason, make my father ashamed of me. And, with the blessing of Saint Andrew on this arm of mine, I may yet live to earn those honours, which his indifference towards me would have denied me."

Rosa did not altogether enjoy perfect ease of mind after Charley Stewart had left her. She thought, with some pride to be sure, of the nobleness of that spirit which she had thus seen blaze up within him. But she felt that she had now the dread responsibility of having thus roused it; and all a woman's fears for the consequences were awakened in her bosom. Nor was the happiness of the days that followed increased by this accidental conversation. For now, she rarely or ever saw him, in whose society her whole life had hitherto glided on with so much felicity. Alice Asher too, had her complaints to make. of her son's frequent and long absence from her; and the only consolation the maiden had, was in frequently visiting the mother of Charley Stewart—to talk over his merits—a theme of which neither of them were very likely to tire—and to sigh for his presence.

Meanwhile Charley was almost constant in his attendance upon Sir Piers Gordon; and he very soon distinguished himself so much in all the accomplishments of a soldier, that he became the most cherished and favoured of the old soldier's followers. But this was not all; for, unknown to himself, and altogether without any effort on his part, he found especial favour in the sight of Marcella Gordon, niece, and acknowledged heiress of his patron, Sir Piers. This was a lady, by no means uncomely, though of most uncommonly masculine manners and mind, who, at any time, would have much preferred to witness a fray, or even to take her share in it, than to sit down to a feast, or to mix in a dance or a masking party. She became smitten with Charley Stewart for his martial acquirements, bold bearing in the saddle, and hardihood at all times ; and for all these he well merited her admiration.

Sir Piers Gordon and his party were one day returning from an expedition, which had been suddenly undertaken in pursuit of some Catteranes, whom, as being public marauders, and general enemies to all, he had, without scruple, followed across the territories of the Stewart of Stradawn. He passed at no great distance from the humble dwelling of Mrs. MacDermot.

"So please thee, Sir Knight," said Charley Stewart to Sir Piers, "I will turn aside a brief space to yonder cottage, to say a few words to an old friend, whom I have not seen for many a day; and I will join thee again ere thou hast ridden a long mile."

"I care not if I go with thee, Charley," said Sir Piers; "that is, if thy friend's house can furnish me with a draught of anything better than water, for my throat is parched like a mountain corry in the dog-days."

"Such as that humble roof may afford, I think I may venture to promise thee," replied Charley, somewhat disappointed at being so attended.

"I shall go with thee to," said Marcella Gordon, who, on this occasion, had followed her uncle in his expedition.

The men-at-arms having been halted by the road-side, Charley led the way to the widow's cottage. As he rode forth from among the trees of the birch-grove, that flanked one side of the house, and partly shaded half its front, Rosa's quick eyes caught his figure—her heart bounded with joy, and in a moment she was at the door, and, from the first irresistible impulse of her heart, she almost sprang into his arms; but immediately perceiving that her lover was not alone, she blushed, and hastily retreated within doors.

"Is that your sister, young man?" demanded the Lady Marcella.

"No, lady," replied Charley, in some confusion; "but she is a very old friend of mine."

"A very young friend of thine, methinks!" said Sir Piers. "She is very beautiful."

Mrs. MacDermot now appeared, and ushered the strangers into the house with well-blended humility and kindness, and proceeded to do the little hospitalities of her unpretending roof. Charley was himself abashed and baulked; but yet he conversed with Rosa, though in that chastened manner that more than anything else betrays the consciousness of lovers, in the eyes of those who may be observing them. No eyes were more penetrating than those of Marcella Gordon. They shot basilisks at the pair. The visit was necessarily short, and the parting between Rosa and Charley was doubly severe to both, since they were thus compelled by the presence of others, to conceal their emotions.

"By all the saints, but thou art a happy fellow, Stewart!" said Sir Piers Gordon to Charley, as they turned away to join the party. "That is the prettiest young creature I have seen for many a long day."

"I see little to admire about her," said the Lady Marcella, with a scornful air; "a waxen child! a smock-faced red and white pippin!"

"Nay, Marcella, women are no judges of beauty in their own sex," replied Sir Piers. "I say she is very lovely; and I say again thou art a happy fellow, Stewart; for, judging from appearances, thou seem'st to be right well established in her affections."

"We have known one another since her childhood," said Charley Stewart, hurriedly.

"And so now thou wouldst fain convert her from thy play-mate into thy wife," said Sir Piers, laughing.

"My wife, Sir Piers!" said Charley, in great confusion. "What could I do with a wife, who am so poor and unknown? I must e'en follow Fortune for some time as my mistress, and court her till she smiles upon me."

"Fear not that she will refuse to smile upon one of thy merit," said the Lady Marcella. "One who can ride, and wield his weapons as thou canst, may well look to Fortune providing something better for him than the obscure and low-bred orphan of a common man-at-arms."

Charley Stewart was silent, but Sir Piers was not altogether so blind as not to perceive how matters stood with his niece. He had observed the Lady Marcella's manner,—was struck with her words,—and a strong conviction entered his mind that she had allowed herself to fall in love with Charley Stewart. Now his affection for Charley had waxed so strong, that, knowing the good blood that was in him, he would have rejoiced to have seen him the husband of Marcella. But feeling that it would be prudent, before giving encouragement to any such scheme, that he should privately satisfy himself as to the suspicions he entertained of an existing attachment between Charley and Rosa MacDermot, and, having failed in one attempt to lead Charley to be explicit, he privately resolved in his own mind, secretly to visit Mrs. MacDermot herself, from whom he looked to receive clearer and more ready information.

Having accordingly ridden over to her house alone, the very next morning, he soon learned from the worthy woman the whole history of the lovers. He was not a little disappointed to find that he had made no shrewd a guess, and that, to so honest and honourable a mind as his, there thus remained no fair hope of the completion of that alliance, which would have been so agreeable to him, as well as to his niece. All that he had learned from the widow regarding Charley, had only served to increase his admiration of him, and to make his regret the greater. But being now in possession of the fact, he thought it his duty to deal plainly with the Lady Marcella, and he accordingly embraced the very first opportunity he could command of speaking with her in private.

"Marcella," said he to her abruptly, "what think ye of Charley Stewart?"

"A proper young man, I promise thee," replied the lady, with the same want of ceremony.

"His lameness is unfortunate,—it mars his appearance much," said Sir Piers. "And that cross scar on his cheek is anything but ornamental."

"Pshaw!" cried the lady; "a fico for his scar! I hope, ere he dies, to see his manly face seamed by many a deeper ornament of the same sort, gained in tough fight, man to man. And as to his lameness! show me one that will vault into his saddle with him, or ride with him, or hold a lance with him after he is in it! Charley Stewart is a prince of a fellow!"

"All that is very true, niece," said Sir Piers; "but me-thinks thou speakest of him with unusual warmth. Pray Heaven thou be'st not in love with the young man!"

"Nay, uncle, since I must needs say so, that is already past praying for," replied Marcella, with a sigh; which, as it was the first that ever in her life escaped her, was a precious deep one.

"I am sorry to hear thee say so, niece," said Sir Piers; "for thy case is hopeless, seeing that thou hast already a rival, to whom he is not only attached, but affianced."

"What, uncle!" exclaimed the lady, in a supercilious tone; "dost thou think so very meanly of thy niece, as to suppose that the whey-faced orphan of a miserable man-at-arms, can have any chance with me, when I, the heiress of thy lands, choose to enter the lists?"

"I think and hope too well of my niece and heiress," said Sir Piers gravely, "to believe, that, for her own gratification, she will try to divide two hearts already united by the tenderest vows that affection can form."

"Affection!" exclaimed the lady; "tush, nonsense, uncle! the affection of children! the brotherly and sisterly affection of babes, for such was the sort of affection of which Stewart himself spoke, and his words are all we have yet to go upon."

"Pardon me," said her uncle calmly; "I have yet better information than anything we have gathered from him. Suspecting that Charley Stewart's merits were beginning to render him not altogether without interest in your eyes, I deemed it to be my duty to know the truth regarding this attachment between him and Rosa MacDermot. With this view I visited the Widow MacDermot herself, and from her I learned, that the bond between the pair, lacks nothing to complete it, but the holy sacrament that may fasten the tie for ever."

"And until that tie be fixed, it is nothing," said the lady. "Yet what sort of evidence would you bring me, truly, of this same attachment? That of an old woman, who, in her folly, sees everything just according to the way her wishes may lead her fancy. I will believe Stewart himself before a dozen such crones, especially where self-interest, and the interest of her girl, must so evidently sway her. Let me but try my influence on him, and thou shalt see how soon he will forget this peasant maid. Thou shalt see "———

"I grieve to find that thou art so resolved to blind thyself, niece!" interrupted Sir Piers, very seriously; "but it is alike my duty to see that you neither run into hopeless misery, nor try to convert that misery into happiness, by unjustly and cruelly ruining the peace of another. I shall again visit the Widow's cottage, this very afternoon. I shall see and converse with the daughter herself, after which I shall hold plainer converse than I have ever yet done with Stewart. If I find that you have judged correctly, and that there is nothing more in this matter than that the mother hath allowed her judgment to be warped by her wishes, my best endeavours shall not be wanting to accomplish those desires which thou hast so clearly exposed to me. But I tell thee honestly, that if, on the other hand, I find that the Widow has judged and reported truly, I shall, for your sake, as well as for that of Stewart, do all I can to promote his union with Rosa MacDermot."

"Say'st thou so, old man?" muttered the Lady Marcella to herself, after her uncle had left; "then must I act—aye, and act quickly, and boldly too."

After a moment's thought, she clapped her hands for her page, and sent him directly to entreat that Stewart would favour her with a private interview immediately. He came at her summons; and, after the usual salutations were over, she, with a face that, spite of her determined and dauntless character, absolutely burned, from the very nature of the communication she had resolved to make, entered upon it in a low yet steady and unbroken tone.

"I take it for granted, Stewart," said she "that the few words I let fall, the other day, when we were returning from our pursuit after the caitiff Catteranes, were not thrown away upon one of your quick wit. They were not uttered without intention; and they have, I trust, proved to thee that thy rare merits have not escaped my notice, and that I take no common interest in thee."

The Lady Marcella paused for an answer; and the astonished Charley Stewart, having mumbled some confused and ill-connected expressions of gratitude for her good opinion, she continued in a yet calmer and more collected tone.

"I have thus sent for thee, honestly to confess to thee, that the interest I take in thee is of a nature, which could not permit me to see unmoved, one, who is so manifestly born for better fortunes, ignorantly to mar them from too humble an estimation of his own merits, and, without looking higher, blindly to tie himself down from all chance of rising, by rashly binding himself to baseness and poverty. If ever a desire of turning the issues of fate into their proper course, might be an excuse for a woman speaking out more openly and plainly than tyrant custom has permitted her sex to to do, certain I am it might be reasonably held to be in the present case. But, were it otherwise, thou hast already seen enough of me to know, that I am no ordinary woman; and I, who have dared much, would dare this too—yea, and ten times more, to secure mine own peace, and thy happiness. Reflect, then, on the words I uttered as we returned from our expedition. Know, that Fortune hath not refused to shine on thy deserts, for she now offers thee the hand and fortune of her who addresses thee."

"Lady!" exclaimed Charley Stewart, staggering back with absolute amazement, and altogether unable to answer coherently, from the confusion he was thrown into—"I have been foolishly reserved, lady. I have been strangely and grievously misconceived. Yet I thought I had spoken plainly enough. I—I—I am altogether unworthy of any one of thy station. I am already pledged to another."

"I was not altogether unprepared for some such confession," said the lady, with a self-possession, arising from the circumstance that she spoke truly. "I had heard, and I did see enough to make me aware that something had passed between thee and the silly girl MacDermot. But these were childish ties, entered into when thou couldst have no foreknowledge of thine own fortunes; and they must of stern necessity, yield to that expediency which now demands thine exaltation."

"Lady," replied Stewart, who by this time began to be somewhat more master of his faculties, "I have learned enough to know that true exaltation can never be purchased by treachery, perfidy, and cruelty. Rosa MacDermot and I loved one another whilst she was yet a child, it is true, but we have loved one another ever since with a growing affection, which has produced vows of the most solemn nature between us. I love her more than I do life itself; and not for all the wealth or honours that this world could bestow, would I cease to love her."

"So great a constancy, and so true a heart, proves but the more how much thou wert born for knighthood," said the lady, calmly. "And perhaps, entangled as thou seemest to have been, it might have been due to such honour as might befit a knight, to have clung to engagements so made. But to render such a case of so great self-devotion rational, it would at least be requisite that it should be mutual. Hast thou proof that it is really so? Hast thou never had doubts on that score? No suspicions?"

"Proof of the love of Rosa MacDermot, lady!" exclaimed Charley, with astonishment. "Doubts of Rosa! I should as soon ask for proof that the blessed sun gives light, or have doubts that the glorious orb might drop from the firmament."

"Other men before thee have been as honestly confiding, and yet have been deceived," said the lady. "The humble soil where thou hast rooted thine affections, is not always that which produces the most virtuous fruits."

"What wouldst thou hint, lady?" demanded Charley, in a disturbed and agitated tone.

"I grieve to tell thee," replied the lady. "It pains me to be compelled to underceive thee, by withdrawing thee from thy pleasing dreams, to look boldly on the afflicting truth. Yet I must tell thee, that thy heroic constancy hath not been met by a like unshaken return of it."

Say—what? Holy saints protect me!" cried Charley Stewart, in a greatly agitated and excited manner. "What wouldst thou insinuate, lady? Rosa unfaithful?—oh! impossible! Where is the liar who hath thus abused thine ear regarding her who is purity and truth itself? Tell me his name, that I may make my sword drink his base black heart's blood!"

"Be calm, Stewart," replied the lady, with imperturbable placidity of manner. "Thou wilt gain nothing by yielding thyself up to blind rage. I trust thou wilt see that it is no ordinary affection in me that can prompt me to the disclosure that I am now about to make to thee."

"Speak on, lady. Oh keep me not in suspense!" cried Charley Stewart, wildly breaking in on her mysterious pause.

13

"Stewart," said the lady, solemnly, "thou wert prepared to withstand all temptation that might be calculated to break the rash vows of youthful ignorance. But she for whom you made them—she for whose sake thou wouldst have so honourably maintained them to the sacrifice of wealth and advancement—she, I fear, has had less resolution to resist their allurements. Be not too much astonished or shocked, for I must tell thee, that mine uncle, Sir Piers Gordon, is the favoured lover of Rosa MacDermot."

"Thine uncle Sir Piers, Lady?" cried Charley, petrified with surprise. "Impossible! it cannot be!"

"Strange as it may seem to thee, and strange as it unquestionably is," replied the Lady Marcella, "it is in reality but too true that she favours his visits for her own purposes. He has already found his way to the widow's cottage more than once, and he has even ventured to hint to myself that he has not been coldly received—and then, Stewart——"

"Lady," interrupted Charley, impatiently and violently, "I would not believe even Sir Piers himself if he were to tell me this!——and yet," added he, after a pause, during which he struck his forehead with the palm of his hand, and seemed to be immersed in deep thought, "and yet, he was strangely struck with her when first they met! But the time is so short—so very short since then—she!—Rosa! Oh, Rosa never could have been brought, in so short a time, to forget the days of her childhood, and her oft repeated vows to me!"

"Reflect, Stewart," said the lady, "that mine uncle is a landed laird, and a belted knight, with spurs at his heels!"

"What!" exclaimed Charley Stewart, in an intense agony of excited feeling, and with a half choked voice, "landed laird, saidst thou! a belted knight, with spurs at his heels! Can it be? Oh! that accursed prophecy of that most accursed hag! But art thou sure of what thou sayest, lady? How canst thou satisfy me? By all the holy saints I must be satisfied!"

"Nay," replied Marcella, coolly, "I can satisfy thee no otherwise than by saying that I have his own word for it, and—"

"His own word!" cried Charley; "oh, wicked, wicked, and most deceitful man, thus wilfully to undermine me! Though I was less open in thy presence, lady, yet I said enough to him afterwards, to have enabled even a fool and a dotard, to have read my meaning."

"So indeed he hinted," replied Marcella; "but then his apology for the interpretation which he hath found it convenient to put upon thy words is, that he has been encouraged by the

girl herself. And as he was with her but yesterday, if he had
not spoken truly as to this, he would have hardly hurried back
again thither as soon as he has now done."

"Back, didst thou say, lady?" exclaimed Stewart, growing
black with rage and jealousy. "Back!—whither?—when?—
how?—Oh, my brain is burning! Back, didst thou say?"

"Yea," replied the Lady Marcella, with perfect calmness,
"mine uncle, Sir Piers, hath gone to visit Rosa MacDermot
this very afternoon. He parted from me for that purpose but
a few minutes before thou camest in hither. He is on his way
thither now. Go!—convince thyself! But be prudent. Act
not rashly. Forget not that a knight, such as he is, hath a
natural belief in him that he is entitled to some little license,
where the matter concerns those only of such low degree as
the girl Rosa MacDermot can boast of."

Charley Stewart listened to those words of the Lady Marcella
with a fixedness of eye, and of aspect that was almost too
fearful for her, bold as she was, to look upon. He seemed
intent upon devouring every syllable she uttered. And yet,
his intentness of gaze was more like that of a maniac than of a
rational man. She had no sooner finished than he ground his
teeth, clenched his hands, struck them both with violence upon
his bosom, and then rushed from the chamber, without giving
utterance to a word.

"I have stung him to the quick," muttered the Lady
Marcella, in soliloquy, after he was gone. "And now," added
she, bitterly, "my prudent uncle has some chance of learning,
to his cost, that it were better to face the lean and starving
lioness when preying for food for her famished whelps than to
step between a woman and her love. I never meant to have
brought this upon him. He hath brought it altogether upon
himself; and now let him look to it, that his heritage be not
mine some few good years before he would have had it descend
upon me. Should the plot chance to work so, my triumph
over this youth will be easy and certain."

The honest old knight, Sir Piers Gordon, had ridden quietly
over the hill, attended only by two of his people, and having
left them to take charge of his horse in the wood at no great
distance from the widow's cottage, he had walked up thither
alone. Mrs. MacDermot had been too much gratified by his
friendly talk during his former visit to her not to have made
her daughter acquainted with all that passed. Though his
present call was unlooked for, Rosa was already so far prepared
to expect that his visit was a visit of kindness that she readily

obeyed the request, which he conveyed to her through her mother, to favour him with her presence. He spoke to her with all the kindness of a father, and, in answer to his inquiries, she blushingly unbosomed herself to him as if he had stood to her in that degree of relationship. She felt, indeed, that he was the patron and the benefactor of him who was all in this world to her, and she was from this cause already prepared to love and reverence him. He was full of benevolent plans for the accomplishment of their union, and the furtherance of their happiness, and he sat with her on the turf-seat at the cottage door, expounding them to her, with her hand affectionately in his, and with his face eagerly turned towards her, in the earnestness of his conversation, till the sun, which shed his parting radiance upon them, was just about to sink behind the opposite mountain. Even the sound of a furiously galloping horse, which came thundering towards them, failed to arouse them from their interesting talk. Suddenly it burst out from the woodland, foaming and panting upon the green, within a few yards of the spot where they were sitting, and a man, more like a maniac than a rational being, threw himself from the saddle. His naked sword was gleaming in his hand ere his feet had well touched the ground. It was Charley Stewart.

"Traitor!" cried he in a hoarse choking voice, "up and defend thy vile life!"

"Charley! Charley!" cried Rosa, springing towards him, "harm not a hair of his head!"

"What! perjured girl!" cried Charley, pushing her from him so rudely as to extend her at some distance from him nearly senseless on the green; "wouldst thou whet the very edge of my sword against him by thy base entreaties for him? Come on, traitor!"

"Stewart, are ye mad?" cried the Knight; "listen to reason."

"Cowardly traitor that thou art, I will listen to nothing from thee," cried Charley Stewart, gnashing his teeth and foaming at the mouth with fury. "Draw and defend thyself, or by Heaven I will forthwith rid thee of thy vile dastard life! draw, I say!"

"Nay, he must be mad!" cried Sir Piers; "yet I must defend my life, though it should be to the peril of his."

But Sir Piers, who sought only to protect himself from Charley's furious assault, accidentally failed in his very first guard. The weight of his assailant's blow broke through it, and falling upon the knight's head, which had then nothing on it but a bonnet, it stretched him motionless on the sward. Charley Stewart stood for a moment to look with horror upon his work—the blood was gushing forth from the wound, and dyeing the white hair of him who had been his patron and friend. From that he turned and gazed upon the prostrate figure of Rosa MacDermot, who still lay in a kind of half-swoon from the effects of his violence. He felt as if his bursting heart would have forced its way through his side. Roused from his trance by the screams of the Widow MacDermot, he heard the galloping of horses approaching, and rushing mechanically into the thickest part of the wood, he made his way towards the mountains, where night soon overtook him. Still he continued to wander on, however, without fixed intention or direction; and it was only on finding at daybreak that he had already fled far towards the south that, after having given due way to his affliction, he resolved to travel towards Edinburgh to seek his father, where, as we have already seen, he ultimately arrived weary and woe-begone.

The next morning after Charley Stewart's appearance in Edinburgh his father, Sir Walter Stewart, aroused him from the deep sleep into which his fatigue of body had thrown him, and which, as it was nearly the first he had had since the sad events which had driven him from the north, even their cruel influence upon his mind could not disturb. In reply to Sir Walter's inquiries, he gave him a brief statement of his history and his misfortunes, and his wounded spirit was soothed by the kind sympathy which Sir Walter manifested towards him.

"Charley," said he, "thy fate hath been a cruel one, truly; but thou must bestir thee to shake off thy sorrows. Nothing better as a cure for melancholy than action. I have an emprise on hand that is for thee the very medicine that thou lackest, and as it may speedily end with thee in a journey to France as the esquire of a knight whom it will do thee much honour to serve, it is, of all others, the very best chance that could befal thee under present circumstances. But the morning wears, and we must go to work without farther loss of time."

Sir Walter Stewart having disguised himself and his son Charley in broad slouched hats and cloaks, they sallied forth together. At the head of the close, they found two hacknies in the High Street, held by a single groom. They leaped into their saddles, and, without any inquiry or explanation as to whither they were bound, they rode forth together, at a gentle pace, from the southern part of the city, as if they had been bent more on pleasure than business. They had not gone farther in that direction than just beyond the Burgh Loch, a piece of water which then occupied that extent of flat low ground now known by the name of *The Meadows*, when Sir Walter turned his horse's head to the westward, and, spurring forward, he and Charley galloped together through the woodland, the groves, and the thickets, which partially covered the Burgh Muir, and gradually sweeping round at a point considerably to the westward of the Castle rock, they then pushed forward at a furious pace in a northerly direction, making straight for that part of the shore of the Firth of Forth, lying immediately to the westward of the citadel of Leith. That which is now a continuous town, was then almost a wilderness of sandy hillocks, which stretched considerably farther into the sea than the land now does, its waters having since much encroached on that part of the coast during the lapse of ages. Taking up a position on a bare elevated spot, Sir Walter looked with anxious eyes towards the roadstead. There were but a few vessels there; but one seemed to be slowly coming up to her anchorage, with a fair breeze from the east, but with her sails so curtailed as betokened caution in those on board. Sir Walter seemed to eye her with peculiar interest for some time, and then he addressed a rough red-faced pilot, who was standing below on the beach, beside his boat, watching the vessel steadfastly, as if he wished to make out what sort of craft she might be.

" Is not that a foreign barque, friend ?" demanded Sir Walter.

" Aye, aye, sir," replied the pilot ; " she is a furrener. If I'm not far mista'en it's the Garron of Burdy, Captain Davy Trummel, with wine aboard. I think I ken her rig —and a clever rig it is, let me tell ye."

" She seems a goodly sea-boat, well fitted to fly quickly over so long a voyage," replied Sir Walter, carelessly.

That she is, I'll be sworn sir," answered the pilot. " Few in the trade can match her, I promise ye. But what strange mortals them French Munseers are after all : why they should call a vessel a Garron, the which is the swiftest bit of a craft my eyes ever came across, I can't nowise reasonably comprehend, unless it be out of a mere spirit of contradiction. But I must call out the lads, and be off to her, for there's the signal flying for me."

" Thou shalt take me aboard with thee, and have something for thy guerdon," said Sir Walter. " I would taste this Frenchman's wines, ere the palates of the good Burghers become acquainted with them."

" Willingly will I do thy pleasure, sir," replied the man; and, running towards a solitary cottage which stood upon a bank hard by, he began shouting out "Jemmy!" and "Harry!" till two lads, who were his sons and assistants, appeared.

"Thou must tarry here with the horses, till I return from on board, Charles," said Sir Walter. "This is the very vessel I looked for—the Garonne of Bordeaux, Captain De Tremouille. He is an old friend of mine, and I would fain have some talk with him."

Sir Walter was speedily rowed on board by the pilot and his two sons. The barque took up her proper ground, under the directions which the helmsman received from the experienced old sailor. The anchor was let go, and she swung round to her moorings. Charley Stewart passed a considerable time in walking the horses about ere he saw the boat leave the barque. At length he beheld it pulling towards the shore, and Sir Walter again joined him, bearing two large bundles, which were stowed away behind their saddles, in such a manner as to be covered by their cloaks as they rode, and following the same circuitous route which they had taken in their way out, they returned to the city, and regained the Knight's lodgings without observation.

AN UNWELCOME VISITOR.

Clifford.—Stop one moment, Serjeant. See how the rain has made its way through the chinks of the window, and deluged the floor.

Serjeant.—Mercy on me, so it has, sir! Well, I'm sure it's no wonder. Such a blast as that which is rairding without, would drive it through a stone wall.

Grant.—Call the girl from the kitchen, like a good man.

Serjeant.—Here, lassie! we're like to be all drowned at this end of the house. Bring some cloths, will ye, and dish-clouts, and dry up this deluge here.

Lassie.—Keep us a', siccan a sight! But we're no one hair better in the other end o' the house.

Clifford.—Aye, that's a good girl. Now lay some of these cloths along the window here. Aye, that will do. I think that ought to make us water-tight. Now, heap some more wood and peats on the fire before you go. Thank ye—that's glorious. Now, let the storm howl as it likes.

Grant.—Do go on with your story, Serjeant.   You were interrupted in a most interesting part of it.

Clifford.—" Blow, winds, and crack your cheeks !"   I beg your pardon, Serjeant ; pray proceed.

Author.—Aye, pray do proceed.   I am anxious to know what Sir Walter Stewart's plans are, and how he succeeded in carrying them into effect.   This part of the history is well known ; but the minuter details are nowhere told in any book I am acquainted with, and I am curious to hear them.

Serjeant (taking a long draught from his punch-jug).—You shall be satisfied immediately, sir.

THE LEGEND OF CHARLEY STEWART TAILLEAR-CRUBACH CONTINUED.

Soon after his return home, from his visit to the barque Garonne, Sir Walter Stewart got rid of his disguise, put on a courtier's attire, and hastened to the Castle, to pay his usual attendance of ceremony on the King.   This he made a point of never neglecting, notwithstanding the marked curtailment which his private, and more familiar intercourse with his Majesty had received.   Whilst within the walls of the fortress, he contrived, quietly and without suspicion, to make himself master of the state of the roster of the officers of the royal guard.   To his no small satisfaction, he discovered that the captain of the guard, for the next day, was to be a certain individual of the name of Strang, whom he knew to be a worthless, reckless, hard-drinking, gaming fellow.   He then made all the observations that circumstances permitted, and, pleased with the information he had acquired, he returned to his lodging, in order fully to acquaint Charley with it, as well as with the whole of his plans, and with the manner in which he proposed to carry them into execution, so as to make him perfectly comprehend the part which he intended that he should play in them.   To lull all after surmise regarding himself, as much as possible, he that evening appeared in the apartments of Sir William Rogers, and bore his share in the performance of the music that was given there.   He then kept his appointment with the Earl of Huntly, in order to tell him that all was prepared, and, after a hasty interview, shortened by their apprehensions of being detected together, a circum-

stance which might have been ruinous to their projects, Sir
Walter retired to his lodging for the night.

Some little time after guard-mounting, next morning, the
bundles which they had brought from the French vessel were
opened, and the Knight, and his son, proceeded to disguise
themselves, by putting on the attire of French sailors, which
they contained ; and so perfectly did Sir Walter succeed in this
operation, that his most intimate friend could not have known
him. Wrapped up in cloaks, they then took their stand
within the dark threshold of a deep doorway, that opened from
the obscure entrance of the close where Sir Walter lodged.
This was a position from which they could see every one who
passed up or down the High Street, without a chance of their
being themselves seen.

They had not stood long there, until their ears caught the
distant, but unceasing jabber of the French tongue, coming up
the High Street. It came from half-a dozen or more voices at
once, all being talkers and none listeners. The noise grew
louder and louder, until Sir Walter, by stretching out his neck
from his lurking-place, espied the captain or skipper of the
French barque, approaching with some eight or ten of his crew.
They came walking along close to the houses on his side of the
way. They carried two small casks of wine, each of them
slung on a pole between two men, who were changed from
time to time as they required relief, whilst another man
carried a little runlet on his shoulders. Sir Walter gave a
particular whistle, and in a moment the whole party turned in
under the covered entrance of the close, and laid down their
burdens as if to rest themselves. In an instant, Sir Walter
and Charley Stewart threw off their cloaks, and transferred
them to two of the French sailors, who immediately retired
into the Knight's lodgings, whilst he and his son succeeded to
the burdens they had carried. Having effected this change,
Sir Walter held some private talk with Captain De Tremouille,
after which the party moved on up the street, and so up the
Castle-Hill, until they came to the castle gate. There the
French skipper, in broken English, told the sentinel that he
would fain speak a word to the captain of the guard, for whom
he was the bearer of a small present of wine, and he and his
whole party were speedily admitted.

" I do ave von leetil praisaint of vine for you, sare," said the
skipper, boldly addressing the scarlet-visaged captain of the
guard. " Dis leetil cask for your own taste. De richest vine
in de varld."

" Thou art an especial good fellow, sir," replied the captain, clumsily returning the exquisite bow which the Frenchmen had made him, whilst, at the same time, he eyed the runlet, and immediately consigned it to the particular care of one of his own people. " Nothing could possibly come more opportunely, and I am most grateful for thy courtesy. It must be confessed that you Frenchmen are the most perfect gentlemen in the world, and know how to do a thing genteelly."

" Ah, sare, dat is too mosh compliment for me as van Frainchman," replied the skipper, with a smile and a bow yet lower than his former one. " And de compliment is more bettaire dat she come from van so grait hero as de Capitaine Strang ! Admirasion for de fame of him, did make me ave de grait desire to honnaire myself wid praisant him vid dis leetil gift, for vitch liberty I do hope he is not offend."

" Offended, my dear fellow !" cried Captain Strang ; " thy runlet comes to me as welcome as the very flowers in May ! But how the pest dost thou chance to know my name, Sir Skipper ?"

" De name and de fame of de grat hero, is alvaise know by all men all ovir de varld," replied the skipper, with another most obsequious reverence.

" By St. Andrew, but this is a curious marvel though," said the captain. " Who would have thought that my name could have been known in France as a hero ! Yet certain it is that I have done some small deeds in my time, that these French mooshies may have heard of."

" Deeds, Monsieur le Capitaine !" cried De Tremouille, with feigned astonishment ; " Vondaires in battaile ! meeracailes in de feelde ! van Achille of Scotlande ! But all dat is nossing at all compare to de fame of Monsieur le Capitaine for his vonderful taste for de good vine ! Ven dey do talk of good vine in France, dey do alvaise say—Aha ! dis is vine fit for de pallait of van Empereur ; bot dis 'ere is more bettaire, dis is fit for de pallait of de famous Scottish hero, de Capitaine Strang, dat do know good vine more bettaire dan any oder man in de varld."

" By all the saints, that is wonderful !" said the captain ; " and yet that I can more easily understand. Yes, yes ; few people can match me there. And then, to be sure, these wine-dealers in France must know some little of those who are judges of the good stuff, and who, moreover, like myself, do so much to encourage their trade. But hark ye, Mr. Skipper ! what do ye with those other two casks which those fellows of thine are carrying ?"

"Ah hah! dat is von praisant pour de Duc d'Albanie," replied the skipper.

"Ha!" cried the captain of the guard, with a certain air of suspicion; "the Duke of Albany, saidst thou? How comest thou to have a present for the Duke of Albany?"

"Oh yaes, sare!" replied the imperturbable skipper, with great apparent innocence, "de vine is von cadeau, vat you do call praisant from de marchand at Bordeaux, vid de expectation dat de squisite taste of him may make mi Lor Duc to ave more of him pour de l'argent, and prevail on de Royal King, his broder, to ave some too also.

"Um—aye," said the captain of the guard, with hesitation; "likely story enough—though there be but little chance of the King drinking ought of the Duke's providing, whatever liquor the Duke may by and bye drink of his Majesty's brewing. But 'twas natural enow in the merchant to think so, Mooshie. As for the Duke, he is no bad customer to his own fist, when he is well set with a jolly boon companion, such as myself for instance. So thou mayest as well leave thy twin-casks in my charge, friend; and I shall see that they are properly delivered. —At least," added he, in an under voice, aside, "I shall take care most conscientiously to deliver them in due time of their contents."

"Tank you—very mosh tank you, sare," replied the skipper. "Mais I not trobil you. De marchand did ordaire me to see dem in de royal hand of de Duc heemself. If I not do dat, I most take heem back again. Jean! Francois! il faut——"

"Um!—don't be so hasty, man," interrupted the captain of the guard, by no means willing to lose sight of the casks, and hesitating, and cogitating within himself, that if the wine was taken back, he would lose all chance of tasting it; whereas, if it was once lodged with the Duke, he had a fair prospect of being invited to share in it. "You Mooshies are as pestilent hasty as a bit of touch paper. Thou shalt deliver the wine thyself to the Duke. Here, Laurence—the keys of the Duke's apartments! Now, Mooshie, do thou and three of thy fellows quickly shoulder the casks and follow me."

The skipper immediately took up one end of the pole that swung one of the casks, and addressing Sir Walter Stewart by the name of Jean, he called to him roughly, in French, to take up the other end. Charley Stewart and a sailor hoisted up the second cask; and so they followed the captain of the guard up to the Duke's apartments.

When the doors were opened, which gave access to the royal prisoner, they found the Duke of Albany sitting at a table in conversation with his chamberlain, his manly and somewhat stern countenance deprived of much of its wonted bloom and sunshine, from the confinement to which he had been subjected, and the melancholy anticipations which possessed his mind, though nothing had as yet been able to overpower his indomitable resolution. It was only when he arose from his chair, to ascertain what his visitors came about, that his powerful and well-proportioned person, and his broad chest, were fully exhibited.

"What is all this?" cried the Duke, somewhat impatiently.

"So please your Highness's Grace, this French Mooshie skipper is the bearer of a present of that which he states to be very choice wine of his country's growth," said Captain Strang, with a low obeisance.

"Who can have thus remembered me in my misfortunes?" demanded the Duke.

"Nay," replied Strang, "I question if either the giver of the gift, or he that hath it in charge, know ought of the position in which your Royal Highness is now placed. But stand forth, Sir Mooshie, and tell thine own tale."

"Eh bien," cried the skipper, advancing, and bowing three or four times to the ground; "Je le——"

"Hold! hold! Mooshie!" interrupted Captain Strang; "none of thine own outlandish language, dost thou hear? Thou canst speak our tongue well enow for all purposes, so keep to that, if it so please thee."

"Very vell, Monsieur le Capitaine String," replied the skipper, with a shrug, and a grimace, that showed his disappointment in being thus prevented from speaking to the Duke, in a language which would have veiled all he said from the apprehension of the captain of the guard—"Very vell, Monsieur le Capitaine; I vill make van attente to make onderstand de bad Englis of me to his Royal Highness de Duc d'Albanie.—I ave been send vid dis two cask of vine, as van cadeau from de marchand Beauvilliers at Bordeaux, to his Highness Royal de Duc d'Albanie, vid de ope dat de magnifiqne flaveur of de vine may please heem, and procure for de marchand van large ordaire from his Highness Royal, and from his royal broder, his Majesty de King."

"I can promise nothing for his Majesty, friend," replied the Duke; but for myself, I would have ye thank Monsieur Beauvilliers from me, and say to him, that if the wine liketh me well, I shall send him an order; that is to say, if there be aught of likelihood of my being alive to drink of it when it comes to hand. But what sort of wine is it that thou hast brought me?"

"In dat cask dere is shoice vine of Gascony," said the skipper, pointing to that which Charley Stewart had helped to bear; "bot, goot as it is, I am force to tink dat de oder vine, in dis cask, vill give more plaisir to son Altesse Royale."

"Sir," said Sir Walter, bringing forward the cask, and speaking to the skipper in French, as if he were merely applying to him for orders, but in a tone so loud and distinct as to insure that the Duke should catch every word that fell from him—"do not show surprise at what I say, or recognise me, if you discover me. We are all friends. This cask contains the means of escape, with instructions how you are to effect it. Let not the captain of the guard depart without an invitation to supper; the contents of this cask will tell you why."

"Sacre cochon!" cried the skipper, with an angry air, and at the same time bestowing a smart blow of a rattan on the shoulders of Sir Walter. "Sacre cochon que vous estes!"

"What did the fellow say to thee, friend skipper?" demanded the captain of the guard; "and what didst thou say to him?"

"Mine Got! Monsieur le Capitaine String," replied the skipper, "dis crew of mine is so great idil vans, dat dey vear out de patience of van Job heemself. I not be come to dis place ardly van moment, and bifore I decharge my cargo, ven dey must vant to leif me alone, and to go to run all over de cite, after de dance, and de Scottish preetee lasses. Be gar, Monsieur Jean, you sall vork pour dis, dat I do tell you, mon garçon."

"Fear nothing, sir," said Sir Walter, again in French, and humbly bowing to the skipper, as if making an earnest and contrite apology to his master; "act boldly; remember the south-western side—there thou shalt find friends beyond the walls."

"Aha, Cocquin!" cried the skipper; "mais vous avez joué votre role à merveille ——"

"What said the fellow? and what was thine answer to him?" demanded the captain of the guard again.

"Par bleu, Monsieur le Capitaine String, I ave make heem bon garçon at last," replied the skipper: "I do ave make heem cry peccavée."

"Was that all?" said the captain, gruffly. "Then come away, Mooshie, let us clear out of this. Thou and thy fellows have been long enough here."

"Before thou goest, I would speak with thee, Captain Strang," said the Duke. "If fame and mine own experience belie thee not, thou art great in thy judgment of wines. Wilt thou lend me thy company to-night at supper, that we may taste the stuff which this fellow hath brought me, of the rare quality of which he makes so great a boast ?"

"Your Royal Highness's Grace does me too much honour," replied Strang, with a most obsequious bow. "My taste is but a poor and uncultivated taste ; but I shall be proud to perfect it under your Royal Highness's superior judgment and instruction."

"Then let us have supper at four, good captain," said the Duke ; "and as my chamberlain here would fain invite those three poor knaves who guard the door, to watch for once within side of it, and to partake of his table, I would have thee see that, at my expense, enough of the best viands be provided for all."

"Your Highness is too considerate," replied Strang. "Yet, since your royal will runs so, it shall be obeyed to the letter. The supper shall be such as shall content you." And then retiring, and shutting and locking the door upon his prisoners, he descended the outer steps, muttering to himself,—"The supper may well be a good one indeed, and thou mayest well eat and drink thy fill ; for, if I be not far mistaken, it may be the last supper thou mayest eat, and the last wine thou mayest swallow."

The skipper and his party now left the Castle, without farther question ; and as they passed by the mouth of the close where Sir Walter Stewart lived, on their way down the High Street, the knight and his son were replaced by the two French sailors in the same adroit manner in which the change had been formerly effected ; and they gained their lodgings, and got rid of their disguise, without having subjected themselves to the least suspicion, whilst the skipper continued his way out of the city, with the same number of followers as he had always had with him.

No sooner was the Duke of Albany free from the chance of interruption, than he and his chamberlain proceeded to wrench up the end of that cask which Sir Walter Stewart had so ingeniously and so particularly indicated, as the important one to the royal captive. They found it altogether devoid of wine, but, to their no small joy, they found within it a long coil of rope, and a large roll of wax. Their first care was to replace the rope, and to shut up the cask again, and then to roll it into the corner, where they set it on end immediately in rear of that which contained the wine. They then hastily opened

the roll of wax, and discovered that it contained a letter from
Sir Walter, explaining the whole plan for their escape. Having
studied this again and again, so as fully to possess themselves
of its contents, they committed it to the ample fire-place, where
it was immediately consumed, and then they sat down together
to resolve and arrange all the minor parts and details of their
plot. Whilst they were so employed, Captain Strang was
unable to resist the devil that tempted him to taste his little
runlet. It was excellent wine. He boldly, and with great
determination, put in the spigot again, and gallantly retreated
from it. But again and again was he drawn to it by an
attraction as strong as that which the loadstone exerts over
the needle. Again and again he drew the spigot, and sipped
moderately. He would have drank deeply, had not economy
whispered him that he had better preserve it for a future opportunity, seeing that he had the prospect of that night drinking
so largely at another's expense. But still he sipped and sipped
from time to time, so that, although far from drunk when he
appeared in the Duke of Albany's apartment—nay, I may say,
far from being even what is usually called half seas over—he
had so whetted his thirst as to be ready to drink oceans ; and
the foundation he had laid was quite enough for a superstructure
of perfect intoxication.

As the supper was to be partaken of by him and his people
at the Duke's expense, the captain of the guard had taken
especial care to see that it was a good one. His Royal Highness sat at a small table near the huge fire-place, with Captain
Strang upon his left hand. There they were first served by
the chamberlain, and the three men of the guard, with all the
delicacies they chose to call for ; and large beakers of the new
wine being placed before them, the captain gave full way to his
Bacchanalian inclinations. By and bye they began to play at
dice and tables, whilst the chamberlain and his three guests
were supping. Though already not a little affected by the wine
he had swallowed, the captain preserved enough of his cunning
and knavish brains, to enable him to cheat most villanously.
This did not escape the Duke, but he took care not to appear
to perceive it—cursed his ill luck—and went on to lose,
much to the satisfaction of his opponent, whilst the knavish
Strang was secretly congratulating himself upon his own wonderful strength of head, which had so far prevailed over the
comparative weakness of his royal adversary. Meanwhile the
chamberlain was busily employed in supplying the captain, as
well as his own peculiar guests, with wine, in the greatest

abundance. By degrees, Strang became so much elevated, as to lose much of that obsequious respect with which he had at first treated his royal host.

" Delicious wine !" cried he, smacking his lips, after a long draught of it, which left his cup empty. " By the holy Virgin, delicious wine indeed ! But—aw—aw—its goodness inflames me—aw—aw—with a furious desire to taste—aw—aw—to taste, I say, that other cask the French knave spoke of—aw— aw—that I mean, which stands yonder, behind—aw—aw— behind the barrel from which we have—aw—aw—been tasting ; that, I mean—aw—aw—of which the French Mooshie spake so largely."

The chamberlain darted a look of agony at his master ; but the Duke preserved a perfect composure.

" Thou shalt taste it forthwith, Sir Captain," said the Duke, giving, at the same time, a private signal to the chamberlain. " Go, use thy wimble, and bring us a flask of that other wine."

The chamberlain, understanding his master, went to the barrels, and concealing them as much as he could by stooping over both of them, he fumbled with the wimble at the second cask ; and, whilst he pretended to fill the can from it, he slyly drew its contents from the same which had been running all night, and then he poured out two sparkling goblets, and set them down on the table.

" Well, Sir Captain," said the Duke, after Strang had taken a long draught of the wine, " what sayest thou to it ? Is it as good as that which thou hast been all night drinking ?"

" That which we have been drinking all night—aw—aw—is but as hog's wash compared to it," cried the Captain, his eyes beginning to goggle in his head, and emphatically dashing his empty cup down on the table. " No, no—aw—aw—my palate—aw—aw—is—aw—too true to be deceived that way. This, look ye, is a wine of—aw—aw—of superior growth, flavour, and body, not to be matched—not to be—aw—aw— matched, I tell ye—not to be matched."

" It is, indeed, excellent, as thou sayest," replied the Duke— " absolute nectar ! Come, fill our goblets again."

" By the Rood, but this is—aw—aw—wine indeed !" cried the captain of the guard again, after emptying his goblet for the second time. " It grows—aw—aw—better and better— aw—aw."

" I feel it whizzing in my very brain," said the Duke. " I doubt that thou wilt have but an easy conquest of me now, Sir

Captain. But come, nevertheless, play away, for I will have my revenge."

"What, ho, Sir Chamberlain," cried the captain, getting more and more inebriated, and becoming, at the same time, still more and more convinced of his own strength of brain and sobriety, and his superiority, in these respects, over the Duke, exemplified, as it was, by his still farther gains. " What ho ! —aw—aw—more wine—more wine and—aw—aw—from the same cask, dost thou hear, Sir Chamberlain—aw—aw—from the self-same virtuous cask. Why the fiend did'st thou not draw from that cask—aw—aw—at first ? Come, wine, I tell thee !—aw—aw—aw—pour us out more of that nectar ; my throat—aw—aw—is parched, and—aw—aw—the more I drink—aw—aw—the more I would drink. Wine !—aw—aw —wine, I say, Sir Chamberlain !"

The chamberlain spared not to fill and refill his goblet, nor was he less assiduous in filling those of the three men of the guard, until overcome by the soporific effects of the oceans of wine which they poured down, combined with those arising from the overwhelming heat of the rousing fire that had been purposely kept up, an irresistible drowsiness fell upon the captain and his men, and they, one after another, dropped into a deep sleep. The Duke, and his chamberlain, now armed themselves with knives from the table, and self-preservation having steeled up their minds to this bloody alternative, they sprang upon their defenceless victims. The work of death was speedy ; all were despatched in a few moments. The keys were taken from the captain's girdle-belt. The corpses were piled one over the other in the huge fire-place, and more fuel was heaped upon them, in order to consume them. The coil of rope was secured. The doors were opened with the greatest caution, and, having slipped silently down the outer stair, they stole away to a lonely corner of the rampart, on the south-western side of the fortress, where the height and precipitous nature of the rock had been supposed to have rendered sentinels unnecessary ; and where, though the descent might be more dangerous in itself than at many other points in the vicinity, there was less risk of their being surprised and frustrated in their attempt.

At the foot of the Castle rock, under that part of the walls which I have now indicated, Sir Walter Stewart, and his son Charles, had been waiting impatiently ever since the day-light had disappeared. The night was starry, but there was little moon. That they might the better observe the walls, they

14

climbed up the steep rock, immediately below the point where they knew that the attempt was likely to be made, till they came to the perpendicular part of the cliff, under the base of which they silently lay down to watch the event. After long and tedious expectation, during which they were often deceived by their fancy, they at length perceived a dark looking object getting over the top of the wall of the rampart, directly above them. They watched it with intense anxiety, as it began slowly to descend on them, till, as it neared them, they could distinguish it to be a human being, and the figure slowly grew upon their sight. The head and shoulders of another man thrust over the wall above, seemed anxiously to watch the success of him who was lowering himself. For a moment the descending figure rested on the narrow ledge of the rock at the foundation of the wall, and then it again began to come down gently over the perpendicular face of the cliff, until it was within some ten or fifteen feet of them. Their hope was now high, when all at once the figure seemed to be arrested in its progress downward, and swung to and fro for a time.

"What stops you?" demanded Sir Walter Stewart, in a distinct but subdued voice.

"If this be all the rope, it is too short," said the person above them, in the same tone; "I have nothing now for it, but to take my chance and drop."

"Fear not!" said Sir Walter; "we shall try to catch thee in our cloaks. Now! drop boldly!"

"Now then!" said the man in the air.

But although the united strength of Sir Walter Stewart and his son enabled them so to receive him, as to save him from utter destruction, the shock of his fall was so great, as to crush both of them down, and it was with difficulty that they prevented him and themselves from rolling down the rocky slope below them.

"How fares it with thee?" demanded Sir Walter.

"But indifferent well," replied the other, unable to rise, and manifestly in great pain. "I fear I have broken my thighbone."

"Holy Saint Andrew, what a misfortune!" exclaimed Sir Walter Stewart.

"Call it not a misfortune," said the attached and devoted chamberlain. "It was good that I tried it before the Duke, else might this accident have happened to him, and that indeed would have been a misfortune."

"What hath happened?" demanded a faint voice, that came from the Duke, whose head and shoulders still appeared over the wall above.

"A small accident, but not a fatal one," replied the chamberlain. "I am down; but beware, my gracious master, the rope is too short."

"How much may it want?" demanded the Duke.

"About four or five ells, or so;" replied Sir Walter.

"Tarry till I return then," said the Duke again. "But, hush! I must hide. Here come the rounds."

The tramp of feet, and the clink of arms, now came faintly on their ears, as they lay, drawn in as much as possible, under the rock. Voices, too, were heard, but at such a distance above them, that they could not tell whether they uttered sounds of jocularity, or of strife and contention. At last they passed away—but whether the royal duke had been detected or not, they had no means of knowing. A very considerable time elapsed, during which their eyes were fixed intently, and most anxiously, on that part of the top of the wall whence the head of the royal captive had last been seen to disappear. The pain of the chamberlain's fractured limb was excruciating, yet to him it was as nothing, compared to the agony of that suspense which was suffered by the whole three who waited for the result. At length, to their inexpressible relief, they beheld the Duke's figure getting over the wall above them,—and down he came, slowly and gradually, till his toes touched the rocky ground on which they stood. Warm, though not loud, were the congratulations he received, and heartfelt were the thanks which he poured out upon his preservers—and deep was the grief which he uttered for the painful accident which had befallen his faithful servant. They learned from his Highness, that ere the rounds had approached near enough to observe him, he had laid himself down at length on the ground, within the deep shadow that prevailed under the wall; that they had passed within a few yards of him, talking and joking with each other, and most fortunately without observing him. They were no sooner fairly gone to the other parts of the walls, than he had stolen back to his prison, cut his blankets into ropes, and by this means supplied what was wanting of the length of that which had been furnished to him.

Altogether unmindful of his own safety, the Duke of Albany's first desire was to provide for the proper care of his maimed chamberlain. It was with no small difficulty that they got him conveyed down the craggy slope, and when they reached the valley below, they halted, and held a consultation as to what was best to be done with him. The chamberlain himself proposed that they should carry him to the house of a friend of his own, near at hand, where he knew he would be concealed, and well cared for, and where he thought he could remain in safety until his broken limb should be so effectually cured as to enable him to make his escape.

"I will carry thee hither myself," said the Duke of Albany. "I can by no means flee hence, until I am assured of the safety of a servant, who hath ever been so devotedly faithful to me, and who is now, by the perversity of my fate, to be so painfully separated from me, when I most need his friendship."

"Nay, I do entreat your Royal Highness to flee without a moment's delay," said Sir Walter Stewart; "every moment is precious to you. Leave him to me, and trust me, I will take every care of him."

"Nay, I cannot consent to that," said the Duke. "Thou must not be seen nor suspected to have had aught to do in this matter. Thou hast already perilled thyself enough. The house he speaks of is but a little farther along this hollow way, I will carry him thither myself."

Sir Walter yielded to reason. They assisted the Duke to carry the chamberlain to a conveniently short distance from the house in question, the sufferer was then hoisted on his royal master's back, who speedily bore him safely into his place of concealment.

"Now," said Sir Walter to the Duke, when he had again joined them, a little way on beyond the house, "your Royal Highness must fly with all haste to the sea-side. This young man, who is a son of mine, will guide you to the spot where you will find a boat, which is ready waiting to convey you to the vessel that is prepared to carry you to France. He must supply the loss of your faithful chamberlain. Take him with you, my lord, and let him return to me when it may suit your convenience to part with him."

"He shall be mine especial esquire," said the Duke.— "Would I had a station to put him into, worthier of son of thine, and of one of his own apparent merits."

"Your Royal Highness is too kind," said Sir Walter. "Yet is the lad no disgrace to me, as I trust that you may find that he will prove none to you. May Saint Andrew give you safety and a prosperous breeze!—And here, Charley, take this ring as a pledge of a father's affection, and let the sight of it be ever to thee as a monitor to make thee do thy duty like a man."

Their parting was now warm, but brief. The Duke and his new attendant reached the seaside in safety. Sir Walter, who had hastened around the shores of the North Loch, and climbed the Calton Hill, waited impatiently upon its summit till the first dawn of daybreak. Then it was that he rejoiced to descry the white sail of the French barque, swoln by a merry and favourable breeze, pressing gallantly down the Firth, and he continued to watch it, until it was lost amidst the ruddy haze of the sunrise. He then walked slowly down the eastern slope of the hill, towards Holyrood, and making a wide circuit, he passed between Arthur Seat and Salisbury Craigs, through the hollow wooded valley, which, though now devoid of trees, is still well known by the name of the Hunter's Bog, and then, turning his steps towards the southern gates of the city, he muffled himself well up in his cloak, and entered it, unnoticed, amid the crowds of market people who were passing inwards at the Port of the Kirk of Field ; and so he gained his lodging without observation. There he soon afterwards heard of the astonishment, mortification, and dismay, which had possessed the King on learning this strange event, which he could not bring himself to believe until he went to see, with his own eyes, the half-consumed corpses of the captain of the guard and his men, and the rope which still hung dangling over the wall of the castle.

Sir Walter Stewart seemed to remain altogether unsuspected of any share in the escape of the Duke of Albany, though everyone was agreed in believing that his Royal Highness must have been aided from without the walls. But whether it was that ideal suspicion that conscience of itself begets, or whether there really were some grounds for it, the Knight could not help feeling persuaded that the King looked colder than ever upon him. He failed not, however, on that account, to pay his duties at court most unremittingly, though, frequent as were his visits there, they were comparatively small in number to those which he paid to the house of Sir William Rogers, where he now worshipped, more fervently than ever, at the shrine of that enchantress, the fair Juliet Manvers. He now found himself so irretrievably the captive of her charms, that he had for some time ceased to struggle in her net, and it was not long after the escape of Albany, that he sought an audience of King James, that he might humbly communicate his contemplated nuptials to him, and crave his royal leave for their consummation, as well as for his retirement for a time from court, that he might carry his lady to visit his own territories in Stradawn, of which he was to make her the mistress. From all that had lately passed, he was not much surprised that the King received his communication with apparent satisfaction, but he was very much astonished to find, that it procured for him the sudden and unexpected restoration of all that familiar cordiality of manner, which he had formerly, for so long a period, been in the constant habit of receiving from his Majesty.

"What!—marry!" cried the King. "And is this really so? —and a long attachment saidst thou?"

"An attachment that has grown since first we met, so please your gracious Majesty," replied Sir Walter.

"Strange!" said the King, as if pondering within himself— "strange that all this should have escaped me. And yet, now I think on't, I might have seen it.—We have done thee but scrimp justice, Sir Walter Stewart, but now, be assured, that we wish thee joy with all our heart. Thou hast indeed chosen a lovely bride. We—yea, and our Queen too—shall honour the wedding with our presence ; and thy fair and accomplished lady shall not lack such royal gifts, as may befit us to bestow, and thy wife to receive. Trust me, that this wise step of thine hath much relieved—nay, we would say that it hath given us unfeigned joy."

Thus reassured of the King's favour, though from what cause he could not by any means divine, Sir Walter Stewart was happy. His marriage took place with great pomp of circumstances, in presence of King James and his Queen. Some months passed quickly and pleasantly away over the heads of the newly-married couple, who were especially detained at court, from one week to another, by the royal mandate,—and I need not tell you, that the lady basked with peculiar delight under the sunshiny smiles that fell upon her from the royal pair. Cochran was the only one about court who had reason to be dissatisfied with the match, seeing that he had himself shewn pretensions to Juliet Manvers, and had been in no little degree encouraged by her. But whether real or feigned, he manifested an especial cordiality towards Sir Walter, and he availed himself of every possible opportunity of frequenting his society, and that of his lady. To the lady, indeed, he was at all times most particularly attentive, so much so, in fact, that Sir Walter hardly relished his uncalled for complaisance. Moreover, he thought he began to detect a certain relaxation of that earnest desire to please him, which, for her own purposes, Juliet had so long displayed towards him before their union. She had now less occasion for dissimulation, since her object was gained, and so it happened that on more occasions than one, when impelled by the humour of the moment beyond the full restraint of her dissimulative powers, she had unveiled enough of her real character to make him doubt, whether her acceptance of him as her husband had been altogether the result of a disinterested affection for him. The seeds of unhappiness were thus thickly sown within his breast, and they began to vegetate so fast, that he at length came to the sudden resolution of carrying off his wife to his castle of Drummin.

"If thou art resolved to quit our court for a season," said King James, when Sir Walter made his intentions known to his Majesty, "thou hast our royal permission, most unwillingly granted to thee, so to do. But say, what sort of habitation hast thou in the north?"

"'Tis but a rude dwelling, so please your Majesty," replied Sir Walter; "and somewhat the worse perhaps for the warfare which hath been waged against it by time and weather."

"Then shalt thou take Cochran, our architect, thither with thee, to plan and order its amendment," replied the King. "'Twas but the other day we were talking of thy concerns together, when he voluntarily offered to yield thee his best services."

"'Twas kind of him," said Sir Walter, biting his lips, "but I can in nowise think of so troubling him. Indeed, for the present, I cannot well brook the expense of building, and I must e'en remain as I am for a time."

"That shall be no hindrance to thee, Stewart," said the King. "The stream of our royal bounty hath been untowardly diverted from thee for a time; it behoves us now to refresh thy parched roots, so that thou mayest again raise thy drooping head. The means shall be found from our royal treasury for thy building, and Cochran shall go with thee to Drummin—so let us think no more of this matter, seeing I have so settled it."

Willingly would Sir Walter Stewart have dispensed with this most prominent mark of royal favour, but it was now impossible to decline it. Cochran received his Majesty's command to hold himself in readiness to accompany Sir Walter Stewart and his lady to Stradawn, with secret delight, though he appeared to do so with that servile submission merely, with which he always bowed to the royal will, and for which he made himself ample amends by the arrogance with which he domineered over others. To Sir Walter Stewart he took especial care to be always smiling, pleasant, and accommodating;

and although he complained, upon this occasion, that this
northern journey was a severe obstruction to the prosecution
of those architectural plans on which he pretended to rest his
fame, he went down to Drummin with the intention of spinning
out his visit to as great a length as he could decently make it
extend.

Sir Walter Stewart, for his part, had no sooner fairly set
his foot on his own threshold, than a thousand recollections
connected with the tower of Drummin, and its neighbouring
scenery, crowded upon his mind. This return to the abode of
his early days, recalled the remembrance of his young affections,
and the contrast which thus arose, in spite of him, between
those which he felt persuaded were bestowed upon a creature
who was innocent, natural, and true, and those which the
sacrament of the holy church now demanded of him, as due to
her whom he had so much reason to fear might turn out to be
artful, artificial, and false, awakened certain unpleasant qualms
within him, that he had failed to make that reparation to
Alice Asher, which he once had it in his power to have made;
and that now, by some strange witchery and infatuation, he
had been led to shut the door against that, and his own peace
of mind, by one rash and irrevocable act. A direful dread
now fell upon him, that he was about to be severely punished
for his neglect of one, whose only sin might, with more justice,
have been said to have been his—as it was incurred for him,
and whose devotion to him, and whose whole conduct since
her first and only error, had so well merited a different treatment
at his hands. He could not trust his mind to think how much
happier he might have now been with her. Nor did the image
of his gallant Charley fail to haunt his imagination and to fill
him with self-reproaches. Now it was that his soul winced under
the wholesome, though sharp stings of conscience, and the fair
visions of ambition, which had so continually flitted through
his brain, lost their sunshine, and disappeared for a time, amid
the dull and damp mists of self-dissatisfaction that settled
down upon it. He felt that though the trial must necessarily
be a painful one, it might probably be productive of a certain
degree of after-relief to him, if he could procure an interview
with Alice Asher. A vow existed between them—a vow that
she had extracted from him, immediately previous to the birth
of Charley Stewart, that they should never again meet, except
in the event of an approach to her on the part of Sir Walter,
for the purpose of offering her his hand in marriage. That,
alas, was a reason which he could not urge now! But, on the

ground of having to speak to her on the subject of her son, he sent for the good priest who was her confessor, and procured a dispensation from their mutual vow, so far as to admit of one short meeting between them. It took place ; and, as you may easily imagine, their conference was of the tenderest, though purest description. It had more in it of tears than of smiles. Reproaches were there, it is true; but they came not from the meek, penitent, and forgiving Alice Asher ; they were numerously and largely heaped by Sir Walter Stewart on his own devoted head. The parting was a scene which I could not venture to describe ; and far less could I convey to you the slightest notion of that accumulation of anguish which choked up the heart of Sir Walter, after having had this opportunity of more truly and perfectly knowing the full value of that gentle and devoted spirit, the innocent confidence of whose youth he had so abused, and whom he had so recklessly excluded from his bosom, in order to take home thither that cold and selfish heart which now legally possessed it. Full of such agonising thoughts as these, he had as yet got but a short way on his return from the dwelling of Alice, when his musing walk was suddenly broken in upon by Cochran, who came unexpectedly out upon him from a side-path that emerged from the wood, into that along which he was then going.

"That cottage, so prettily perched up yonder among the wood, on the brow of the hill you have this moment descended, belongs doubtless to some favourite forester of thine, Sir Walter," said Cochran ; "marry, the fellow is lodged in a palace, compared to those dens, scarcely fit for swine, in which the rude and savage inhabitants of this northern wilderness are seen to burrow themselves, like urchins, and which are hardly to be distinguished from the sterile and heath-covered soil on which they stand."

"It is a neat cottage," replied Sir Walter, hastily ; and, immediately changing the subject, he went on talking rapidly, and at random, until he got rid of Cochran, on their arrival at Drummin ; and, from the very dread of all farther impertinent questioning, he threw himself upon a horse, and rode away up the valley, under the pretence of some urgent business, and with the vain hope of shaking off his griefs.

"Now," said Cochran, as he freely entered the Lady Stra-dawn's private apartment ; "now, I can tell thee, that my suspicions are this very day verified. Now thou mayst have no grudge that thou hast at last restored to me some of that love, which was mine of right, and which should have always

been mine, had not the scrannel pipe of this Sir Walter so unfairly whistled it from me."

"What wouldst thou insinuate?" demanded the lady, in
some degree of surprise.

"I would only delicately hint, that thy husband Sir Walter
is more in tune with another, than with thee," replied
Cochran, with a coarse laugh. "I have told thee so before,
and now I have proof of the truth of what I told thee."

"Proof, saidst thou?" cried the lady keenly. "What proof,
I pray thee?"

"Did I not tell thee I had found him out?" said Cochran.
"Did I not tell thee that he visits the cottage that stands on
the brow of the wooded hill yonder? I have this day proved
that I was right, for I dogged his steps thither, saw him enter
it, and watched him patiently, for two good hours, till he again
issued forth. Nay, I know more. I know that she who
inhabits it is an ancient sweetheart of his; but though an
ancient lover, she is young,—aye! and moreover she is beautiful; for as I hovered about the place some two or three days
ago, I chanced to get such a glimpse of her, as satisfied me of
all that."

"Base villain!" cried the lady, in a rage; "I will be
revenged of him, and of her too. But," added she, again
assuming the command of her feelings, "I shall take mine own
time."

"Thou canst not be too speedy with thy vengeance as
regards thy husband, if thou wouldst have me to help
thee," said Cochran, with a vulgar leer—"for, hark ye!—a
secret in thine ear—I must go to-morrow—my time hath been
long enough uselessly wasted here,—thanks to thine obduracy;
and then this building is so far advanced towards completion,
as hardly longer to require my master eye, so that little
apology now remains for me for longer stay. Nor do I now
will it much, seeing that it is of none effect; so I shall e'en
hasten back to the court, to look after this earldom of Mar,
which the King hath been talking of bestowing upon me, as a
successor, much more worthy of it, than his traitorous brother
who held it. 'Tis well for me to be on the spot; yet couldst
thou but think of giving me back that love, of which this false
Sir Walter so wickedly robbed me, I might still contrive to
stay awhile to help thee to thy revenge."

"My vengeance must be deeply satiated ere any such
passion as love can find room in this heart of mine," said the
lady, with eyes that darted lightnings. "At this moment it is

over-charged with hate, which nothing can diminish till it is poured out in one vast flood of vengeance on those who have produced it. Go then, my good lord, for to that title thy fortune doth now most securely lead ; go—and push it boldly on to the pinnacle of that glory to which it so clearly points. When we meet again, we may have better will, as well as better leisure, to unfold our mutual thoughts and wishes. Meanwhile, believe that mine are ever for thy welfare, and for that honourable advancement to thee, to which the elegance of thy person, as well as thy superiority in mind and manners, doth so well and amply entitle thee."

"Thanks, lady ! thy discernment is great and penetrating !" cried Cochran, whose vanity was so blown up by her extravagant praises of him, that, ere she wist, he, by way of an act of gallantry, and in a manner quite suited to the vulgarity of his character, threw his great coarse arms around her delicate neck, and snatched a rude embrace. But though it brought the colour indignantly into her face, she had too much cunning to resent it.

When Sir Walter Stewart returned home that evening, Cochran told him that he could be his guest no longer, seeing that he had received certain communications from his Majesty, which demanded his immediate departure from Drummin for the court. Sir Walter was by no means much afflicted at this intelligence. He exerted himself, however, to do Cochran all manner of hospitality, and to show him every kindness, and every mark of respect in his power, ere he went. He arose early next morning, therefore, to perform the last duties of a host to a parting guest, and, after Cochran and his escort were mounted, he walked by the side of the architect's horse, talking with him by way of civil convoy, for more than a mile of the road, as in those days it was the usual custom of all hosts to do. As they were going up a little hill above Drummin, called the Calton, they espied a hawk perched upon the very top of a tall tree. Sir Walter had a birding piece in his hand, with which he had been for some time wont to practise.

"There is a fine fair shot for thee to try thy new-fangled weapon against, Sir Walter," said Cochran, pointing to the hawk ; "I wager thee five gold pieces that thou canst not bring him down."

"The distance is great," said Sir Walter, pointing his piece at the bird ; "but I accept your wager."

"He is safe," said Cochran.

"No !" cried Sir Walter exultingly, after discharging his

piece, the bullet from which brought the bird fluttering to the ground. "He's gone, an' he were a king!"

"A good shot, truly!" said Cochran, treasuring up Sir Walter's careless expression for his own future use and purpose. "Marry, but that is a dangerous piece of thine, Sir Knight. Take good care how you handle it, else may it perchance do thee a mischief. But I will keep thee no longer trudging thus by my horse's side; so again I bid thee commend me to thy lady." And so saying, he rode away more abruptly than might have very well beseemed any man of better breeding.

Cochran finished his journey to Stirling, where the King · then was, and immediately presented himself at court. He was gratified by the reception he met with from James, who manifested no little joy at the return of his creature. But all mankind are misers, when taking account of the favours of the great, on whom they depend. Unmindful of the large ones they receive themselves, they look only with envious eyes on those, however small, that may be bestowed upon others. Thus it was with the unrighteous Haman, and thus it was with Cochran; for all the kindness which the King showed to him, in this his first interview, became as nothing, when weighed against the eagerness which his Majesty manifested in his inquiries after Sir Walter Stewart. These were as gall and verjuice to Cochran. In vain did he try to make trifling and oblique insinuations against the Knight of Stradawn, his royal master was in no humour to listen to them at the time, and they were each of them in succession lost to his ear, in the eagerness with which he put his next question. James put question after question as to all the particulars of his occupation at Drummin, as well as regarding the progress of the work, and it was only when he had come down to the day of his departure, that the insidious favourite contrived to catch the royal attention, by relating the story of the birding-piece.

"Sir Walter Stewart is undoubtedly a pretty gentleman, and of very various accomplishments," said Cochran; "aye, and few know his qulifications better than he does himself."

"He knows not his own accomplishments better than we do," replied the King, in rather a dissatisfied tone.

"Pardon me," replied Cochran, obsequiously, "I never ventured to say that he was vain of them. But your Majesty's perception and judgment are unrivalled. Yet much as you have seen and observed of Sir Walter Stewart, I may venture to question, whether you have chanced to witness ought of his great skill and marvellous accuracy of eye in shooting with a birding-piece ?"

"A birding-piece !" exclaimed the King, "we knew not that he ever used any such new-fashioned tool."

"He hath not used it till of late," said Cochran; "but it would seem that he hath lost no time in perfecting himself in the use of it, now that he hath taken it in hand. Your Majesty would be surprised to behold how expertly he can employ it. The last shot I saw him make with it was just as we were about to part, and it astonished me and all those who were in my company."

"We shall ourselves see him use this strange weapon, the very first visit he may make to court," said the King. "But what of this famous shot of his ?"

"So please your Majesty, a sparrow-hawk sat on the very top of a straight upright pine tree of immense height. He was perched there so proudly and confidently in his lofty position, and, as he thought, so safely too, that he looked down as carelessly on our cavalcade below as if he had been the weathercock on the needle point of some lofty church-spire. 'There's a shot for you, Sir Walter,' said I, and I straightway offered to gage five gold unicorns that he could do nought against it. 'I take thy wager,' said he ; and with that he raised his piece, and without saying a word more, he presented it at the overconfident bird, and, to the astonishment of all present, down it came tumbling. 'He's gone !' cried he."

"Aye, and your gold was gone too," interrupted James, laughing heartily.

"Nay, your Majesty, I minded not my gold," replied the wily Cochran ; "and had but these words of his been all the speech he uttered, I had been well contented to have lost a wager."

"What said he else ?" demanded James.

"So please your most gracious Majesty, I had rather leave the rest unsaid," replied Cochran, with great affectation of discretion.

"Nay, but we would hear it all from thee," cried the King, impatiently.

"If your most gracious Majesty commands, your faithful servant must obey," replied Cochran. "Yet true as mine ears are wont to be to their office, I could hardly believe that I heard the words which they then conveyed to me."

"We would have thee keep us no longer in suspense," cried the King. "What words did Sir Walter Stewart utter ?"

"As the bird fell," replied Cochran, with a gravity and a seriousness of aspect that would have seemed to imply a heavy charge against the Knight of Stradawn—"As the bird fell, Sir Walter, as I have already signified to your Majesty, exclaimed, 'He's gone;' and then turning aside, he added, in a somewhat lower voice, '*He's gone! Would he were the King!*' So, and please your Majesty, did mine ears report his words."

"Ha!" exclaimed James, with an air of great dissatisfaction, "Ar't sure that he so spake? From all that thou hast seen, as well as heard at Drummin, it would seem to us that both thine eyes and thine ears have been wonderfully sharp to pick up evil against Sir Walter Stewart. Was it likely that he should have thus wantonly spouted forth foul treason in the ears of so many witnesses, some of whom it would appear were sufficiently willing to report to us whatever might be turned to his prejudice! Go to, sir! I like not this! Those accurate ears of thine must have failed of their honest duty for once. Or if, for some object of thine own, thou hadst wilfully misinterpreted that which they did truly hear, we can tell thee that thou hast not hit thy mark with the same skill or success that Sir Walter Stewart did his. But we shall judge of him in person, and that right speedily, for already hath he received our royal command, borne to him by an especial messenger, to present himself at court by a certain day, in order to be present at the grand tournament which it is our royal will to hold, that we may for once essay to bring our sullen and iron-sinewed nobles around us."

"I humbly crave your Majesty's most gracious pardon," said Cochran, much abashed, and with a cringing reverence. "Your Majesty's matchless wisdom hath put this matter into so clear a light, that I begin to believe that my doubts—I mean the strong doubts I entertained of it at the time—were correct, and that the words must have somehow or other come to mine ear awry. I appeal to all the Saints, and to the blessed Virgin to boot, that I would rather hide than publish aught against anyone so much in your Majesty's favour as Sir Walter Stewart would seem to be, especially one for whom I have, as I may say, so high a respect, and regard, and admiration."

"We are satisfied," replied the King. "'Tis clear, that in this instance thine ears have deceived thee. None but one demented could have so spoken in such hearing; and Sir Walter Stewart is no madman. But we would talk no more of this. We would now confer with thee as to those plans at which we last looked ere thou wentest——"

"I will go seek them straightway, your most gracious Majesty," replied Cochran, and making more than ordinarily low and fawning obeisances, he gladly retired to breathe more freely, and to recover from the alarm of that danger which his very unwonted imprudence had brought upon him, and which had so nearly hurled him into the very pit which he had digged for another.

But we must now return to Drummin.——Though the——

———

AN OLD FRIEND WITH A NEW FACE.

Grant.—Who, in the name of wonder, can that be, who knocks so loudly at the outer door, in this place, at such an hour ?

Serjeant.—Some belated drover, I'll warrant. What an awful night the poor man has had to travel in !

Clifford.—If there be, as philosophers say, no happiness equal to that of being relieved from misery, I think that he who knocks, whoever he may be, is to be envied for the sudden transition he is about to make from all the horrors of night, rain, tempest, and bogs, and swollen burns, to the comforts of this room, such as they are, and especially to this glorious fire.

Author.—What a time they are losing in letting him in !

Serjeant.—I suspect they will have enough ado to get the door opened, without being knocked down by the blast.

Author.—They have let him in at last. Whoever he may be, we must make room for the poor fellow at our fireside.

Grant.—Certainly; I'll go and bring him in here: nay, I see I need not, for here he comes.

Clifford.—What a figure the poor man is ! He looks like a newly landed river-god, or like Behemoth himself, come forth from the mighty deeps.

Serjeant.—Whoever he may be, his own father could not know him, were he to see him at this moment, with his whole clothes so bedraggled, and that face of his so clatched up with moss-dirt, that not a feature of it can be seen.

Clifford.—He is like a moving peat-bog, I declare.

Author.—Bless me, how the poor wretch shivers !

Serjeant.—He shakes as if he had an ague fit.

Clifford.—'Tis absolutely like an earthquake shaking the globe.—Here, sir ; pray swallow some of this warm punch—it will bring life into you.

Stranger (in a perfect palsy of cold).—Och? it's most reveeving indeed, though the taste of it is just altogether poisoned with the moss that's in my mouth.

Clifford (with astonishment).—Mr. Macpherson!

Author.—Is it possible?

Grant.—Where, in the name of all goodness, can you have dropped from, my worthy sir?

Clifford.—Though we know not where he has dropped from, we may see plainly enough, from the foul streams that drop from him, that he has dropped himself, head over heels, into some black peat-hag. Here—get towels, that we may rub the dirt out of his eyes.

Dominie.—Ech, sirs! give me another drop of yon comfortable stuff, and let me see a bit glisk of the fire.—Aye—hech me! I'm much the better of that.

Clifford.—Sit down here, sir. Sit down in this chair close to the fire; but first take off that streaming coat of thine. It reminds me of some of those vast black Highland mosses, the very drainings of which give origin to some dozen of rivers. Now, take another pull at this hot stuff, and then tell us your adventures if you can.

Dominie.—Oh, dear me, that is good! Why, gentlemen, my story is short, though my way has been long and weary enough. The fack is, that when I got to my brother Ewan's house, I found that he was away to the low country to make some bargain about the buying of a stock of iron, and that he was not to be home again for a fortnight. You may believe I was much disappointed at this intelligence, after the long tramp I had all the way from Caithness, to come and see him. But it would appear, that my letter to him must have somehow miscarried. Be that as it may, I had no sooner been satisfied that I had no chance of seeing Ewan for a time, than my heart began to yearn after those with whom I had so lately and so sorrowfully parted. So, thinks I to myself, I'll just take my foot in my hand, and after the gentlemen. I'll catch them at Inchrory. If the night had been good and clear, I should have been here good two hours ago. But on came the tempest; and the wind, and the rain, and the darkness together, so bamboozled and dumfounded me, that, as I was fighting along with might and main, I fell souse over head and ears into a deep peatpot,

Instabilis, tellus, innabilis unda,

out of which it is the mercy of Providence that I was at length able to swatter, after dooking and diving in it like a wild duck for the better part of a quarter of an hour, till I was nearly drowned in clean mud.

Clifford.—Clean mud, Mr. Macpherson! The mud you have been in would seem to me to have been anything but clean.

Dominie.—True, Mr. Clifford; but I used a phrase of our vernacular, meaning that there was nothing else there but mud—a truth I can speak to by having gone faithfully throughout every corner of the big hole into which I fell without finding any. Clean, truly!—such a fearsome sight I am! I declare I am worse than Serjeant John Smith must have been when he fell into the moss-hole about the time of the battle of Culloden. Would you like to hear that story, gentlemen?

Clifford.—Much, Mr. Macpherson, but not now, for several reasons. First, we must contrive to get you into dry clothes of some sort to prevent your dying of cold or fever; secondly, you must have something to eat before you are permitted to talk; and, thirdly, there is another Serjeant, one Serjeant Archy Stewart, who is at this moment on duty, and who was in the middle of a long story when your appearance interrupted him. We must have that out first; but, in my capacity of secretary, I shall take care to book you for producing your Serjeant John Smith when his time comes in the roster.

Dominie.—Eh, I'm sorry that I should have stopped the flow of my friend Serjeant Archy's narration.

Clifford.—How could it have been otherwise, my good man? Why, what flow could have possibly stood against such a flow as that which now streams from your wet garments, Mr. Macpherson? You have already made a lake in the room.

Dominie.—Keep me, so I have!

Serjeant.—Here lassie! Bring cloths and swab up the floor.

Clifford.—You had better not sit longer in that condition, Mr. Macpherson; come away with me up to the garret, where we are to sleep, and then I shall go and see what I can prevail on Mrs. Shaw to do for you to rig you out.

There was a waggish twinkle in Clifford's eye as he left the room with Mr. Macpherson. They were not long gone, and when they did return our young friend appeared leading in the Dominie clad in a shortgown and a blue flannel petticoat, both belonging to our hostess. The Scottish garment called the shortgown is a sort of loose jacket covering one half the person only, and when tied tight round the waist it is admirably calculated to show off the mould of a handsome woman to the best advantage. On the present occasion it was with some difficulty confined round the bulky Dominie by a red cotton handkerchief,

15

so as fully to display his shape; and as the petticoat reached but a little way below his knees, it exhibited the full proportions of his Herculean legs, enlarged as they were by a pair of the thickest grey worsted hose, and brogues of enormous size, accidentally left there by a Highland drover. Over his head was placed one of Mrs. Shaw's tartan shawls, which Clifford had recommended to be tied under his chin as a precaution against toothache, to which he declared himself to be frequently a martyr. Such a woman as the Dominie appeared to make is never to be seen on the face of this earth, except in some exaggerated specimen of those marine, or rather amphibious animals, to be found on the sea-coasts of Britain, and which are called bathing women. We were all so much taken by surprise with his appearance that to control our laughter was a matter of utter impossibility.

Clifford.—Gentlemen, allow me to introduce to you the great Princess Rustifusti.

Dominie (striding in like a Grenadier).—Truly, gentlemen, I am ashamed to appear among you in this unbecoming disguise. But my worthy and kind friend Mr. Clifford is so careful of me—mercy on me, what would my boys say if they beheld me?

Grant.—They would be astonished, no doubt, Mr. Macpherson. But come, sit down—here is something comfortable for you to eat. I am sure you must require food by this time.

Dominie.—I must honestly confess to you that I am downright ravenous.

Clifford.—Nay, now, do not disgrace the delicate feminine character which you are at present supporting, by eating like a masculine creature.

Dominie.—Masculine, feminine, or neuter, I am so famished, that I must eat liker, I fear, unto a male wolf, than a delicate leddy, such as fortune has this night forced me to represent.

Clifford.—Nay, then, if that be your way, I must cease to be your chaperon. So do you take charge of your own delicate self, and go on, if you must do so, to disgrace the lovely sex to which you now belong, by your immoderate eating and drinking, whilst I call upon Serjeant Archy Stewart to proceed with his narrative.

THE LEGEND OF CHARLEY STEWART TAILLEAR-CRUBACH CONTINUED.

Although the jealous dreamings of King James had lead him rather to desire the absence of Sir Walter Stewart from his court, whilst the Knight was yet a bachelor, he was no sooner fairly married, than all such fancies were dissipated from the royal mind. The renewed enjoyment in Sir Walter's society, which the monarch had experienced, previous to the departure of the newly married pair for Stradawn, only served to render the after absence of his favourite the more insufferable, and he soon began to weary for the return of so accomplished a companion. Sir Walter had sufficient opportunity of being rendered sensible of the satisfactory alteration in the King's manner towards him, before he left the court; but, notwithstanding all this, he was in no small degree surprised, as well as delighted, with the arrival of the special messenger, who was the bearer of the royal command for him, to attend his Majesty at the tournament, which reached him the very day after Cochran had left him. Sir Walter being one of the best equestrians of his time, he was naturally extremely fond of horses. His great passion was to possess himself of the most beautiful steeds that could possibly be procured, and he spared neither pains nor expense in the gratification of this knight-like fancy. Some time before the period we are now speaking of, he chanced to have acquired some piebald horses, which were of a white colour, marked in a very extraordinary manner with large patches of a sort of bluish tinge. This circumstance led him to indulge the whim of collecting more of the same description, and having, from time to time, procured individual animals, from all quarters, and a considerable addition to their numbers having recently arrived, he now at length found himself enabled to mount a large troop of his attendants on creatures of a similar description, and of the most exquisite symmetry of form. Prepared as he thus happened to be, the news of the tournament gave him particular gratification. His heart exulted, and his mind was all agog, at the prospect of such an opportunity of making so marvellous a display, before a more numerous, as well as a more experienced, collection of eyes, than his own glens could afford him. Accordingly, he began to busy himself, without loss of time, in making those arrangements which were necessary to enable him to appear with that degree of splendour which he

always wished to exhibit on such occasions. Mr. Jonathan
Junkins, and all the tailors for many miles round, were put in
requisition to make rich housings, and footmantles of scarlet
cloth for the saddles, and everything else was got up in a
proportionable style of splendour. But let us not imagine that
this, his so minute attention to such fopperies, should lower
Sir Walter Stewart in our opinion, for we must remember
that all such trifles, being integral parts of chivalry, assumed
the greatest importance in the eyes of every knight. For many
reasons, Sir Walter Stewart felt no great desire to take his
wife with him to court, but he could find no good plea for
leaving her behind. Amongst other preparations, therefore,
the lady's horse litter required to be new furbished up, seeing
that she was now in a condition that made riding somewhat
dangerous; but so great was the expedition used by all hands,
that by the day previous to that fixed for departure, all the
horses were duly trained, and all their equipments, as well as
those for the men-at-arms, and all other things necessary for
his expedition, were in the highest order.

Sir Walter Stewart retired to rest that night with the
intention of being up with the earliest dawn, that he might
himself see that nothing had been forgotten. Upon reaching
his lady's apartment, he found no one with her but her page,
English Tomkins, as he was familiarly called. This was a boy
of great beauty of countenance, and of an intelligence of eye
very superior to that which his years might have promised.
He had followed the lady from England, and he was so strongly
attached to his mistress, that if he was at all deep in her confidence, he had prudence enough to keep all that he knew strictly
secret from every one with whom his situation brought him into
contact. To all, except to her, he was reserved and distant, to
an extent much beyond that which might have been looked for
from the natural carelessness and ingenuousness of youth, and
even the good-humoured freedom which Sir Walter used with
him, was never successful in breaking through the parchment
case in which he seemed to wrap himself up. He was a most
impenetrable youth, and no long time elapsed after the Knight's
marriage, before Sir Walter began to look upon the boy with a
certain jealousy and dislike, which he could neither account
for nor overcome.

"Do it thine own way," said the lady to him with so great
earnestness in her communication with him, that she perceived
not Sir Walter's entrance. "Do it thine own way, I tell thee,
boy; but see that it be done, and that surely, and secretly

too—for I could have no will to leave Drummin, and no heart to enjoy the pleasures of the Court, unless I knew that this was done ere I went."

"What may this be, upon which so much of thy happiness depends?" demanded Sir Walter Stewart advancing.

"Holy Virgin, what a start you gave me!" cried the lady; "such puerile tricks are hardly worthy of thee."

"What tricks?" asked the Knight, with utter simplicity.

"Such boyish tricks, I tell thee," said the lady, smoothing her angry countenance, and throwing over it a playful smile, and at the same time gently tapping his cheek, as if in the most perfect good humour. "I mean such boyish tricks as that which thou hast now used, by stealing thus to my chamber, and secreting thyself, that thou mightest startle me for thine idle amusement."

"Credit me, I am no such idle boy, as thou wouldst suppose," said Sir Walter, gravely; "I have been guilty of no such silly conduct. I came, as I am ever wont to do, without either the intent or the thought of surprising thee. Nay, I knew not that I had done so, until thou didst utter that scream of surprise."

"Well, well, I believe thee," said the lady; "and if thou hadst stolen upon my privacy, thou couldst have gained nothing that would have amounted to treason, seeing that I was but cautioning Tomkins here, as to how he should execute a small deed of charity for me, ere we go to-morrow, which I could ill brook the neglect of. Now, boy, thou may'st go," continued the lady; "and see that thou doest my bidding to the very letter."

"Your commands shall be strictly obeyed, lady," said the boy, bowing as he retired.

The apartment in which the Knight and his lady slept had a window in it which looked down the vale, formed by the combined waters of the Aven and the Livat. A faint but glowing red light shot through this window towards morning, and falling upon Sir Walter Stewart's eyes, gradually unsealed their lids from the deep sleep in which they were closed. He started up at this appearance of approaching sunrise—hurried on his clothes, and hastened down stairs to the court-yard. There he found the men-at-arms, who had the watch, all at their posts; but none of the grooms, or the others whom he had expected to have found already busied with their preparations, were as yet astir. Having expressed his surprise at their laziness, he learned from those on guard, that it yet wanted two good hours of day. Being unwilling to retire again to his chamber, he walked forth beyond the walls, to the terrace on which the castle stands; and he had no sooner got there, than the cause of this his premature disturbance was made sufficiently manifest to him, for his eyes were immediately caught, and his attention fearfully arrested, by a column of fire that shot up from the cottage of Alice Asher, and inflamed the very clouds above.

Giving one loud shout of alarm to the people within the castle walls, he stayed not for them, but rushed frantically down the green slope, and crossing a rustic foot-bridge that spanned the river Livat, immediately under the fortalice, he flew towards the wooded hill, too accurately guided through the obscurity of the night, by the conflagration, the light from which blazed in his eyes. But whilst it thus served to direct him towards its object, it had also the effect of dazzling his vision; so that, in the furious precipitation of his speed, he ran against some living being that was coming hurriedly in the opposite direction. Whatever it might be, his force was so tremendous, that he drove it aside from the path, like a ball from a bat, and then rolling forwards on the ground himself, and over and over, he lay for some moments senseless upon the grass. But, having soon afterwards recovered himself, he sprang again to his legs, and, his whole thoughts being absorbed at the moment by his agonising anxiety for Alice Asher's safety, he stopped not to enquire what had become of the individual who had produced his accident, but rushed on again towards the burning house, on which he still kept his eyes fixed. Long ere he gained the foot of the hill on which it stood, a momentary depression of the flame, followed by an equally sudden and very great increase of it, told him that the roof had fallen in, and that, if the inmates had not already fled for safety, they must now be beyond all reach of assistance. Yet still he paused not; but, doubling his speed, he rushed breathless up through the wood on the side of the hill, and at length arrived at the cottage.

What a sad spectacle did it now present! The walls alone were standing, like a huge grate, in which the inflammable materials of the heather-thatched roof, and the furniture, and interior wood-work, were rapidly consuming. The roses and woodbines that crept over the walls, or trailed in rude luxuriance over the porch, were now shrivelled up and scorched by the intense heat within, nay, even the shrubs and flowers that grew around, were dried up and killed by it.

"Oh, Holy Virgin Mother, she is gone! she is gone!" cried Sir Walter, giving way to a paroxysm of grief.

And now people came running together from the nearest cottages. Eagerly did he enquire of all he met for some information, regarding Alice Asher; but no one could tell him aught of her. The men from the Castle came crowding up the hill, bearing buckets of water. These were now useless. But still Sir Walter called on those who carried them to exert themselves, and, urged by his commands, they ran to and from a neighbouring pool, bearing water, and pouring it over the sinking flames, till they were finally extinguished, at least so far, that they were enabled to rake amid the red-hot embers with long poles, without danger to themselves. With what torturing anxiety did Sir Walter Stewart stand, in the hope that no human remains would be found, by which circumstance he expected to satisfy himself that Alice Asher had escaped. But, alas! they had not searched far, when they found a body, or rather a half-consumed skeleton, in so fearful a state of mutilation, that although its size left no doubt that it was that of a woman, it was quite impossible to guess at the person. Sir Walter was frantic. But still hope lingered within his bosom. Alice had a servant maid in the house. This skeleton was nearer, as he thought, to the size of the woman, than to that of the mistress. Besides, these remains were found in a part of the house which this attendant inhabited. No doubt was left that they were hers; and Sir Walter's heart expanded with the temporary relief which it experienced.

But the search went on. And now Sir Walter Stewart's heart again fluttered betwixt torturing hope and fear,—till,—oh, wretched and bitterly afflicting sight; in that part of the cottage which Alice Asher more particularly occupied, another half-consumed body was found. This was also that of a woman; and, as it corresponded accurately to the size of her about whose fate he was so unhappily interested, every spark of hope was at once extinguished within him. His brain whirled in strange and bewildering confusion. He gasped for breath, and seemed to swallow down liquid fire; all consciousness left him for a time; and he sank down on an adjacent bank in a temporary fainting fit.

I shall not attempt to describe the flood of strong and resistless feeling to which Sir Walter Stewart, resolute as he might be, was compelled to give way, when his senses fully returned to him. Those who were around him respected them in silence. The sun soon afterwards arose upon the melancholy scene; and then it was that the brave Knight's countenance was observed by all, to bear powerfully-written testimony of the deep grief that had been at work upon it.   Making a strong and manly effort to subdue his affliction, he gave orders to his people to see that the remains, now so revolting to look upon, should be properly attended to ; and, despatching a confidential person to the priest who had acted as father-confessor to Alice Asher, he besought him to do all that might be requisite to ensure that the last sad duties should be decently and reverentially paid, and every religious rite duly performed to her, whose life of contrition and penitence, for a sin which he felt to have been his alone, had so fair a prospect of reconciling her to her Maker. And, having made these arrangements, he slowly and silently, and with a sorrowful, heavy, and lacerated heart, bent his steps back to Drummin.

When Sir Walter Stewart, and those who were with him, had reached the place where he had been so unaccountably thrown down, he was surprised to see a human figure lying a few yards off the footpath, with the head and shoulders crammed into a thicket.   On approaching it, the dress at once informed him that it was his lady's page, English Tomkins. Having ordered some of his people to pull him forth from the bushes in which he was half hid, and to raise him up, he was discovered to be quite dead ;—and his death was at once seen to have been occasioned by his head having come against the thick and knotty trunk of an oak, which grew up from amidst the black thorns and honeysuckles, so that his skull had been dreadfully fractured, and instant extermination of life had ensued.

"Jesus have mercy on me !" cried Sir Walter, with great feeling.   " I have been the innocent cause of this poor boy's death, by running against him in the dark ;" and having said so, he proceeded to explain to his people the circumstances which had produced and attended the accident.

" Methinks he hardly merits to be much wailed for, Sir Knight, unless thou canst say that these strange articles can have been innocently carried by him," said one of the attendants, pulling at the same time, from the bosom of the corpse, a small bundle of matches and a tinder-box, with a flint and steel. Marry, these would seem to say, that he had been better employed had he been in his bed."

" What do I see ?" cried Sir Walter Stewart, filled with horror, and greatly agitated.   " What! was it murder then ?— murder of the most horrible description ?   Oh, holy Mother of God, can there be such villainy upon earth ?"

" What shall we do with this wretched carcase," demanded one of the people.

"Oh, most unlucky accident!" cried Sir Walter, without heeding him. "Would that I had but caught him in life! But, alas! strong as suspicion is against him, his secret has died with him! We cannot now wrench forth the truth from him either by spring or by screw. He is gone to his account before that Judge at whose tribunal all secrets must appear. Yet, bear him along with you, and see that you take especial care to preserve those dumb instances of his hellish art, till I may require thee to produce them."

Sir Walter Stewart now left his people to carry the body at their own leisure, and shot away ahead of them, at a pace so furious, as to correspond with the violence of those various stormy feelings which then agitated him. On reaching Drummin, he hurried directly to his lady's chamber, where he found her putting the last finish to her travelling dress.

"Madam!" said he to her bower-woman, in a voice which sufficiently betrayed the disturbed state of his mind; "my lady will dispense with thine attendance for a brief space—we would be private."

"What strange conduct is this, Sir Walter?" demanded the lady after her attendant was gone, whilst her voice and manner might have led anyone to believe that she too was not altogether well at ease. "Why shouldst thou have thus sent Jane so rudely forth, when she hath yet so much to pack and to prepare?"

"Because I would fain have some private converse with thee, lady," said the Knight, solemnly. "Dost thou usually send forth thy page Tomkins on errands of charity so very early as several hours before sunrise?"

"No!—no!" replied the lady in a voice of hesitation. "Such are not indeed,—no, they are not his usual hours to be sent on such errands; but—but—the boy had some distance to go. And then—and—and—and then he hath so much to do ere we depart, that—that—But I wonder much that he is not returning by this time!"

"He is returning now!" said Sir Walter, looking hard and somewhat sternly at her. "But canst thou tell me what he did with a tinder-box, flint, and steel, and matches, concealed in his bosom?"

"Flin—flint—flint and steel saidst thou?" cried the lady, considerably agitated. "How can I say aught about it? Boys are ever full of tricks, and so, I doubt not, is Tomkins. But what hath he told thee himself? Didst thou not question him?"

"As yet he hath told us nothing," replied the Knight, ambiguously.

"Then all is yet right!" cried the lady, from an energetic impulse of satisfaction, which she could not control.

"What is right?" demanded Sir Walter, sternly.

"I would say that—that—that if the boy hath confessed no evil, then 'tis most likely that no evil hath been done."

"Yea," replied Sir Walter, gravely, and with deep feeling, "but the direst evil hath been done—a deed which is hardly to be matched in cruelty—the firing of the house, and the burning to death of an innocent lady and her woman!"

"An *innocent* lady!" exclaimed his wife, again forgetting herself for a moment. "But thou canst not suspect this boy of having done so foul a deed?"

"Most strongly do I suspect him," replied Sir Walter.

"Nay, nay, 'tis impossible," said the lady. "What could prompt *him* to so horrible an act?"

"What could prompt him!" exclaimed Sir Walter, "nothing, methinks, in his own bosom; but canst thou not guess who could have prompted him?"

"Nay, nay, how could I guess?" said the lady, in great trepidation.

"Lady!" said Sir Walter, with great solemnity, after having seated her in one chair and drawn one for himself close to her, where he sat for some moments looking steadily into her pallid and agitated countenance. "Lady! are these the charitable errands on which thou art wont to send this boy?"

"What mean ye, Sir Walter?" demanded the lady, in a state of trembling and alarm which she could not conceal. "The boy has not basely accused me of aught."

"Sir Walter, your pardon!" said Jane, the lady's bower woman, bursting at that moment most inopportunely into the room, "Ronald would fain know what you would have done with the corpse of poor Tomkins?"

"The *corpse* of Tomkins!" cried the lady, starting up and clapping her hands together in an ecstasy of joy, which she could not hide. "Then the boy is no longer alive!"

"He was found dead, it seems, my lady," said the maid, "and his corpse hath this moment been brought in by Ronald and the rest. 'Tis fearsome to look upon him. He hath got a deadly contusion and gash on his head."

"Alas, poor boy!" cried the lady, wiping her dry eyes with her pocket handkerchief, and mustering up all the symptoms of sorrow she could command. "Who can have murdered him? I shall never again meet with so faithful a page!"

"Faithful, indeed, madam," said Sir Walter, after showing the maid again out of the room, "faithful, indeed, readily to execute those most wicked and murderous orders with which thou didst charge him."

"Nay, nay, this is too much, Sir Walter," replied the lady, now gaining full boldness and command of herself from having been thus unexpectedly certified that her page was dead, and that he could now tell no tales; "how canst thou dare to insinuate anything against me?"

"Madam," said Sir Walter, in a hollow tone, and with considerable agitation of manner, "would it were so that thou couldst with truth speak thus boldly. But, alas! the words I heard thee utter last night to the page—the horrible catastrophe of this morning—the place where it pleased Providence that he should meet with his accidental death—the direction in which he was running when he received it, and the implements of destruction which were found in his bosom, can leave no rational doubt in my mind as to the person who conceived and directed this most cruel tragedy; and though evidence may be yet lacking to bring the crime fully home to thee, yet, convinced and satisfied as I am of the justice of this charge against thee, I can no longer suffer the head of so foul a murderess to rest upon this bosom. I leave thee to the stings of thine own conscience, and to that repentance which they may produce, believing that God, in his own good time, will make the truth appear, so that thou mayst be made to expiate thy guilt," and so saying Sir Walter Stewart left the apartment.

"Leave me to my conscience!" cried the lady, with a laugh of derision, after the door was closed, "my conscience will sit easy enough within me, I trow, since my good fortune hath thus got me so innocently rid of mine instrument after he had so well worked my will."

Sir Walter's heart was torn by a thousand afflictions. He felt that he would be better anywhere else than at Drummin. Having now no reliance in the fidelity of his wife, he resolved to leave her behind him, and having hastily packed up the important charters of his lands, and some other valuables, he added them to his other baggage. The time now left was just sufficient to enable him to obey the King's command to present himself before him on a certain day. His people were all waiting in readiness in the courtyard. Without more thought he flung himself into the saddle with a bleeding heart. He

was distracted by his feelings, but giving the word *"forward!"*
he dashed through the gateway at a furious pace, and his
troop of men-at-arms and attendants went thundering after
him.

Sir Walter Stewart was received in the kindest manner by
both the King and Queen. He was earnestly asked, especially
by James, why he had not brought his lady with him. As he
could not tell the whole truth without making a deadly
accusation against her, which he had no means of proving, he
was compelled to say that he had left her somewhat indisposed,
an answer that produced some good humoured raillery from
James, delivered in his wonted familiar manner, and left him,
for the time at least, sufficiently well satisfied.

The tournament took place in that beautiful tilting-ground
in the rocky valley close under the south-eastern side of the
crag upon which Stirling Castle stands, and which is still
pointed out by the citizens of the ancient town as the place
which was so used in those old times. Though few or none of
the discontented nobles appeared, it was yet a very glorious
spectacle. The singularity and grandeur of Sir Walter Stewart's
retinue, and their whole appearance, mounted as they were
upon the piebald horses, so richly caparisoned, presented by far
the finest feature of the royal procession, and swallowed up
every other theme of conversation. He was now perhaps the
only one to whom it gave but little pleasure, heavy as his
heart then was.

" We would know from our Queen who, in her mind, was
the prettiest gentleman that appeared at the show to-day," said
the King, after all was over, and that he was in private with
her.

" How can your Majesty hesitate one moment in coming to
a judgment upon so plain and palpable a question?" demanded
the Queen, with great animation. " The ornament of the
procession and pageant was undoubtedly Sir Walter Stewart.
Who was there who came within an hundred degrees of him?·
The number of his attendants—the beauty of the animals on
which they were mounted—creatures that would seem to have
been conjured forth out of the land of faery itself—creatures
that moved as if formed out of the rarer elements of nature—
and then the splendour of their housings—and, above all, the
rich and tasteful dress of the handsome and elegant owner of
so much bravery, who is so full of grace and skill in the
management of his steed that he bore off the applause of all
eyes and the love of all hearts! But what moves you, my

sovereign Lord? Methinks that something hath displeased you?"

"Your praises of Sir Walter Stewart would seem to us to be something extravagant," said the King, considerably disturbed. "Was there no one else there who might have demanded a like portion of your approbation?"

"If your Majesty would have an honest answer from me, I must reply,—no one," said the Queen. "Even the gorgeous and glittering retinue of Cochran, the budding Earl of Mar, who takes upon him as if your Majesty had already dubbed him by that title, was but as gilded clay compared to the well conceived arrangements of the accomplished Sir Walter Stewart, who outshone all others."

"*All* others, saidst thou, Margaret? Didst thou not think that we ourselves were of as fair a presence and appearance as thy minion Sir Walter Stewart?" demanded the King, with a pettish and perturbed air and manner.

"Nay, my liege Lord," replied the Queen, very much distressed to discover that she had thus so innocently offended her husband. "In speaking thus of Sir Walter Stewart, I never dreamed of bringing your royal person, or your royal retinue, into comparison with those of any subject, even with those of Sir Walter Stewart himself, whose individual splendour, was but as a part of that glorious magnificence which was all thine own. Do me not the injustice to judge me so harshly, or so hardly. Could you for one moment suppose that I could compare Sir Walter Stewart to thee, my royal liege and husband? Believe me, that although Sir Walter Stewart is much esteemed by me for his numerous merits, yet he is no minion of mine, and it were equally cruel and unjust of anyone to call him so."

"'Tis at least well to hear thee say so," replied the King, in a sort of half satisfied tone,—and then turning coldly away, he left the apartment, with such an air and manner, that Queen Margaret burst into tears, which it required some thinking and reasoning within herself to enable her to dry up.

Now it was that the facile mind of King James, became prepared to imbibe all the villanies which the designing Cochran could pour into it. Nay, his Majesty became the voluntary and the willing victim of them. He sent for Cochran, made him recapitulate all the particulars of the story of the hawk, shot with the birding-piece, together with that expression of Sir Walter's which he had formerly so repudiated, but which he now listened to and received as most true and convincing; and the royal ears being thus so unexpectedly open to him, Cochran now scrupled not to tell the King, that, to his certain knowledge, Sir Walter was faithless to his wife. To this story James listened with anxious attention and interest. He remembered the strange combination of Venus with the other planets, and he shuddered at the recollection, as he put it beside his Queen's declared approbation of Sir Walter Stewart. His Majesty's manner towards the Knight became again estranged and cold, and his treatment of him unkind; and this being quickly observed by those sordid and selfish wretches, who, with the sagacity of the sharks that follow a diseased ship, or the rats that leave one that is no longer seaworthy, are ever ready to watch and catch at such signs of a courtier's decaying influence, a regular bond of union was formed against him by all but Sir William Rogers, who could by no means be brought to see that he could benefit his niece by the ruin of her husband. This plot went on, for some considerable time, without producing the slightest suspicion on the part of Sir Walter Stewart, though he could not fail to be sufficiently sensible of the King's alienation from him.

He was sitting one night alone in his lodgings, when one, in the habit of a serving-man, was announced to him, as craving for a private audience of him, that he might deliver a particular message to him from a gentleman of the court. Having ordered him to be admitted, he was surprised to see enter a person who appeared to be a stranger to him, with a light handsome figure, but having a nose of most unnatural length, hugeness, and redness. He examined him narrowly, yet he still remained satisfied that he had never seen any such person before; but they were no sooner left alone, than the stranger began to speak, and Sir Walter recognised him immediately.

"Trust me, Stewart, it is not without some personal risk that I have thus adventured to hold communication with thee," said the stranger.

"Ramsay!" exclaimed Sir Walter Stewart, in amazement. "In such a disguise as this, I should never have discovered thee, but for thy voice."

"Then must I take care to keep that under," said Ramsay, in a half whisper. "But time is precious. Thy life is sought for! To-morrow, nay, even an hour hence, all attempt to escape may be unavailing, and I, even I, may suffer for this my attempt to save a friend."

"I well know the danger that attends such a duty," said Sir Walter, "and I would not for worlds that thou shouldst incur it."

"Aye, there thou hast said it," replied Ramsay. "I know well enough what thou wouldst hint at,—thy service to Albany! Nay, start not! Thy secret will never be the worse for me. But, nevertheless, that is one of the suspicions that is harboured against thee."

"Suspicions!" exclaimed Sir Walter, "What suspicions?"

"In the first place, the King hath taken up a jealousy against thee regarding the Queen," replied Ramsay. "Then some strange story hath reached his ears from Cochran, who, by the way, hath been this day created Earl of Mar, regarding some treasonable words thou didst drop in his hearing in the shooting of a hawk with a birding-piece. Besides this, Torfefan, the master of fence, hath said, that thou didst once step in to save the Earl of Huntly from his just vengeance, for speaking treasonably of the King and his courtiers; whence it is argued, that thou art in secret league with the discontented nobles. This is corroborated by that rascal, Hommil, the tailor, who says he was with Torfefan at the time. To this accusation, touching thy consorting with the nobles, Andrew, the Astrologer, bears his support, for he says that he one night found thee and the Earl in deep conference, alone in the hostel. And, finally, as I have already hinted, thou art, somehow or other, shrewdly suspected of having aided in, if not contrived the escape of the Duke of Albany from Edinburgh Castle. But besides all this, Sir William Rogers, who hath been long thy friend, hath at last gone over to those who are malcontent with thee, because he hath had letters from his niece, complaining that she had been disgracefully and cruelly treated by thee, and that, too, but a few days before she gave birth to thy son and heir; and that, in consequence of this thine evil treatment of her, she hath applied for divorce from thee. But what is all this, and why should I waste time in such a recapitulation of forgeries? Thy life, my dear Stewart, is sought for! Ere to-morrow's dawn thou wilt be a prisoner, and how soon afterwards thou mayest be numbered with the dead, the fate of the last Mar may teach thee. Fly then, my dear friend, for thy life! I dare not tarry here longer. Get into thy saddle with all manner of haste, and see that thou sparest not thy spurs! And so God give thee good speed till we meet in better times."

Ramsay gave him a warm embrace, and then hurried out of the room and the house. And Sir Walter Stewart, after packing up his writings and other valuables, cautiously and quietly summoned his people, and, getting into their saddles, they rode slowly out of the gate of the town and across the ancient bridge over the river Forth, the guards readily believing them when they said they were bound on the King's business. But they no sooner found themselves on the wide and flat carselands to the north of the river Forth than they made the hoofs of their steeds thunder across them with the rapid sweep of a whirlwind. Nor was this more than necessary either, for the distant shouts of people and the trampling of horses in pursuit were heard behind them. But the darkness of that night enabled them to throw them off, and, by forced journeys, they in a few days reached Huntly Castle, where they were joyfully and hospitably received by Sir Walter's friend the Earl. Although the people who pursued them very soon returned without success, they were enabled to carry back certain information as to Sir Walter Stewart's place of retreat ; and this was no sooner known than the newly made Earl of Mar, armed with the Royal authority, dispatched an especial messenger upon a fleet horse to go directly to Drummin as the bearer of certain royal letters to the Lady of Stradawn, together with a private communication from himself, which was conceived in these terms :—

"To the Lady Juliet Manvers, once called the Lady Stradawn, these, with speed.

" Most beauteous Lady, and my soul's idol ! Thou wilt herewith receive the dispensation of his Holiness Pope Sixtus the Fourth, annulling thy marriage with that traitor, Sir Walter Stewart of Stradawn, so that thou mayest now look forward to be speedily raised to the high title and dignity of Countess of Mar, as well as to those yet more elevated honours to which the growing edifice of my fortunes may yet uplift thee. But enough of this for the present. All will depend on thine own brave and steady deportment. Thou hast herewith sent thee, moreover, the King's royal letters, strictly enjoining thee to defend the Castle of Drummin against all comers, and to hold it for his sovereign Majesty ; and, above all, on no account to admit the traitor, Sir Walter Stewart, within its walls ; the which, seeing that I built and repaired them, I full well know, are stout enough to resist any engine which he or others may be able to bring against them when defended by so bold a heart as thine. To aid thee in this, and to enable thee to control the rebellious vassals of the Strath, a picked body of men are already on their march, and will be with thee in a very few days after these presents come to thy hand. So use thine authority like one who is destined to the great honours that await thee, and thus show thyself worthy of him who is the architect of thy fortunes—who is thy devoted adorer and slave, the deeply love-stricken

MAR."

Of all this the gallant Sir Walter knew nothing, save that the proclamation of his being declared traitor, and the public annunciation of the dissolution of his marriage had been so generally diffused that they came to him through the thousand mouths of common fame.

It was this last piece of intelligence that made him gather up his strength from that dejection to which he had for some time been disposed to yield. The very thought that his alliance with this now detested woman was thus severed and annihilated for ever gave him new life. But, alas! the recollection that she to whose wrongs, to whose sorrows, and to whose penitence he would now have wished to have held out the right hand of consolation was now no longer in life to receive it gave him fresh pangs of grief and despondency. He was resolved, however, to proceed to dispossess the murderess from the hearth of his fathers, and to take possession of his own fortress in defiance of the King's proclamation, being well aware that the same stout hands and sharp claymores in Stradawn which had ever proved so faithful to him would still enable him, if once in possession of his little place of strength, to laugh at all the King's heralds and parchments throughout broad Scotland.

It was after a long and tedious march that Sir Walter Stewart and his followers were seen winding up the valley of the Aven one beautiful afternoon. The shouts of the thinly scattered population rang through the woods from cottage to cottage as the news spread that their own knight and chieftain was returning. All turned out and crowded after him to welcome himself, to talk with their friends in the ranks of his retinue, and to glut their eyes with the splendid pageant presented to them by his gallant array, and his richly caparisoned piebald horses. The castle arose before them upon its level and elevated green terrace, and his troop was moving slowly forward to ford the river Livat, where it runs in a broad and shallow stream along the base of the promontory on which the fortress stands, when they, and especially their horses, were suddenly startled by the loud roar of a falconet fired from the walls, the echo from which ran thundering along the faces of the neighbouring mountains, whilst the bullet discharged from it whistled over their heads and went crashing through the boughs of a great tree behind them. A small plump of spears

16

appeared immediately afterwards without the walls, and ranged themselves along the edge of the terrace above. But although somewhat surprised by these warlike and hostile demonstrations, Sir Walter moved boldly onwards to the river side.

" Whosoever thou beest, thou hast already had one warning," cried a loud and hoarse voice from amid the spearmen on the terrace. " I bid thee beware of a second, till we know something of thee and of thy folk."

" We would hold parley," replied the Knight. " Friends, ye know not whom ye war against. Is Sir Walter Stewart to be held as an enemy before his own Castle of Drummin ?"

" We know naught of Sir Walter," shouted the other. " We know not Sir Walter Stewart, nay, nor any other Stewart save our liege lord and master, James Stewart, the third of that name, King of Scotland, in whose name we bid thee be warned and keep off."

" Who is he who so rudely challenges the Castle of Drummin ?" exclaimed a shrill woman's voice from the walls. " If anyone would have peaceful speech with us, let him advance with a moderate escort till he comes within earshot."

" By'r Lady, I would have thee beware, Sir Knight," said Ronald, the especial esquire of Sir Walter's body. " If thou art bold enough to go nearer, thou mayest come within something more than earshot. I will advance and hold parley with them, and I shall be safe enow too, for they will see that they can make nothing by any deed of traitory done against such an one as me."

" No, no, Ronald ; I will take my chance," said Sir Walter, in a melancholy tone. " My life is now but of little value to me. Let you and one more go with me, and let the rest stand fast here till we return to them."

Sir Walter Stewart and his two attendants now separated from their party—forded the river, and rode their horses up the steep diagonal path that led up to the terrace on the promontory, while the plump of spearmen were called in and the gates closed. On the outer wall of the barbican stood the Lady of Stradawn with her baby in her arms, and surrounded by a group of faces which were altogether strange to the Knight, or those who were with him.

" How comes it, lady, that I, Sir Walter Stewart, the rightful owner of this castle of Drummin, should be thus delayed in entering within mine own walls ?" demanded the Knight. " Give orders that instant entrance may be yielded to me and mine, that there may be no unseemly warring and blood between those who, if no longer one flesh, were at least once so united by the holy church."

"I no longer know Sir Walter Stewart!" cried the lady, in a lofty and imperious tone and manner. "I had indeed once the misfortune to be linked to him, of which union behold the sad fruits in this wretched babe! But my duty to my Sovereign, as well as my duty to the Earl of Mar, who is soon to be my husband requires that I should now know him no longer, save as a traitor to his King, as well as a traitor to me — alike disloyal to both. Begone, then! This fortalice is now held by me for James Third, King of Scotland, and entrance herein thou shalt never have, whilst I live to bar thee out."

"Lady, thou art bold," replied Sir Walter, coolly, "but remember, that stoutly garrisoned and well provisioned as thou doubtless art, we can soon raise willing hearts and hands enew in Stradawn, to force thee to a speedy surrender."

"Thou shalt do so then at the price of 'the murder of this thy child!" exclaimed the lady, lifting up the poor little innocent on high. "If but a single arrow be discharged against us, the tender flesh of this thy babe shall be the clout that shall receive it—and if but one burning brand be thrown, this shall be the very first food given to the conflagration. It is *thy* child. I hate it as being thine. No mother's feelings, therefore, shall hinder me from using its little body as the bulwark of our safety, and as the rampart of our security!"

"Fiend that thou art!" cried Sir Walter. "Let not harm fall on the innocent babe of thy womb! Give me but my child, and I shall retire and leave thee scaithless, and to such peace as thy guilty soul may command. Oh, harm not the babe, but let me clasp it in these arms!"

"Ha, ha, ha! a pretty nurse thou wouldst have me provide for the urchin!" cried the lady bitterly. "No, no, its body is our most potent shield, I tell thee, and thou shalt never win in here, till thou hast opened thy bloody way through the portal of its little heart. Shoot, if thou wilt, then, for this shall be thy mark."

"Oh, fiend! Oh, demon in woman's shape!" cried Sir Walter, in anguish. "How was I ever inveigled into thy toils? Terribly, indeed, am I punished for the sins of my youth! But thou wilt yet meet with thy reward! Fiend that thou art, I say thou shalt——"

"Nay, then, thou shalt have thy reward, and that straightway!" cried the lady, interrupting him. "Shoot, archers! let

him have his reward, promptly and powerfully delivered from
your well-strung bows! Shoot, I say, archers!"

A flight of arrows instantly came whizzing about them.
Several of these rang upon their mail-shirts, others slightly
wounded their horses, but one found its way through a faulty
link, to the very heart of Sir Walter Stewart's second attendant,
who fell lifeless from his horse. Again came the arrows thick
upon them, their barbed points prying about them, as it were,
like wasps, as if in search of any weaker part or interval, through
which they might most easily and certainly sting them to death.
There was no time to be lost. The faithful Ronald seized Sir
Walter Stewart's rein, and urging on the Knight's horse and
his own at full speed, he galloped straight off along the terrace,
and so he succeeded in placing his master entirely beyond all
hazard, ere yet the bewilderment of his keen and poignant
feelings permitted him very well to know what had befallen
him. And then, leading his horse in a slanting direction, down
the steep and grassy slope, and across the river, they joined
their party, and drew off under several ineffectual discharges of
the ill-served and ill-directed falconet.

With a heart depressed by grief and mortification, Sir Walter
Stewart had now nothing left for it, but to return on his way
to Huntly Castle. As he moved down the valley, the roofless
walls of poor Alice Asher's cottage arrested his eyes, rising
bare and blackened from among the wood, on the brow of the
isolated hill where they stood. The whole of the harrowing
scene of that murderous burning recurred to his recollection.
His soul was filled with affliction, and his heart became heavy,
and sank within him, from the poignant admonitions of that
conscience, which plainly and honestly told him, that if he had
sown more honourable and virtuous conduct in his youth, he
might now have been reaping pure and unalloyed happiness,
instead of that misery which threatened to cling to him, like a
poisoned garment, to the end of his days. He felt that he had
blighted the spring of his own life: that all sunshine had
departed from him for ever; and that all now before him was
dark and chilling winter. The only hope he could dare to
cherish now, was that of obtaining mercy, through the merits
of a blessed Saviour, and a deep and heartfelt repentance.
Giving way to the full indulgence of such thoughts as these,
his heart began to sicken at the world. In sorrow and in
silence he pursued his way towards Huntly Castle; and, long
ere he had reached the residence of his friend the Earl, he had
taken up his firm and unalterable resolution.

Acting upon this, he craved a private interview with the Earl that very evening; and, having retired to his apartment with him, he unfolded his mind fully to his friendly ear—gave over to him the charge of all his papers and charters, and prepared everything for executing a deed, by which his Lordship was made sole trustee over his estates, for the behoof of his infant son, with full powers to manage and direct all matters belonging to them, and, at the same time, making the Earl himself heir of all, in the event of the child's death. Some days afterwards, he put the last formal signature and seal to all this,—not without great, but vain expostulation on the part of Lord Huntly,—and, having done so, he declared his fixed determination to depart the very next morning for the Continent, where he had resolved to bury himself for ever within the cloisters of a monastery.

That night, previous to Sir Walter Stewart's departure, was a melancholy one for the two friends; and their parting next morning was still more sad.

The Knight's horses and attendants were already drawn up in the court-yard, and the Earl's men were thronging around them to bid them farewell, when a horseman rode into it, bearing a woman on a pad behind his saddle. The lady was veiled, and muffled up in a mantle; but, though the form was sufficiently light and delicate, and that of the youth also much more compact and athletic than gross or heavy, the good grey steed that bore this double weight, showed unequivocal symptoms of the long, rapid, and distressing journey he had undergone.

"Ha! we are yet in time?" cried the young man in a tone of enquiry. "Sir Walter Stewart is still here, is he not?"

"He is still here; but he is on the very eve of his departure for a foreign land," replied the esquire, in a grave and pensive tone and manner.

"I would fain speak a few words to him," said the youth, lighting down, and then lifting the lady from her pillion.

"I fear that may hardly be," said the esquire; "these last minutes of parting converse between Sir Walter Stewart and the Earl of Huntly, are, I warrant me, every one of them worth a purse of gold."

"So are they all the more valuable to me for the doing of mine errand," said the youth, with an air of command, which seemed naturally to belong to him. "Here, take this ring, so please thee. Take it to Sir Walter Stewart, and say that its owner bides without, and would fain have a short audience of him ere he goes."

"I will do your bidding, fair sir," said the squire, courteously; "though I know not well how mine embassage may be received; for, if I mistake not, the Earl and the Knight are shut up alone together in deep and important conference."

The esquire was in the right. The parting moments of these friends were precious, and occupied in most interesting talk. The Earl of Huntly had been using them in pouring out all his eloquence to induce Sir Walter Stewart, even yet, at this the eleventh hour, to abandon his resolution of going into a monastery, and to prevail on him to remain at home, and to resume the rights and the control of his estates. He urged it upon him, that he owed it to his country, as well as to his just vengeance against Cochran, and the King's other favourites, to join with him and the rest of the nobles in the plots which they were hatching for their destruction.

"It will be a sweet revenge for thee," said the Earl; "a most sweet revenge, I say, for thee, to have James suing to thee for mercy, for the lives of those very minions who have so conspired together for thy ruin."

"Nay, press me not, dear Huntly," replied Sir Walter Stewart; "though the King hath been blind and fickle, yet I cannot forget his long-exerted kindness to me. And as for vengeance, I trust that the exercise to which I have subjected my soul for these last few nights, hath conjured all such unholy and unchristian passions forth from my bosom. But to extinguish in thee all farther vain hope that I may be brought to yield to thy friendly entreaty, I will now tell thee that I last night took a solemn vow, on my knees, with mine eyes upon the blessed crucifix, and my right hand upon the open Evangile, that I would henceforth flee from the world, and dedicate myself to God."

"With such a vow upon thee," replied Huntly,—"with a vow so solemnly taken, I can urge thee no more."

"Then let my parting words entreat thee not to harm the King," said Sir Walter Stewart. "Harm not the King, and hurt not one hair of the head of Ramsay of Balmain, for he is a gentleman, and my very dear friend, and one indeed to whose friendly warning I have owed my life!"

"There is no intention of hurting James," said Huntly, coldly; "and as for Ramsay, thou hast said enough, in these last few words of thine, to make me sacrifice my life to save him, if he should be brought into peril."

"Thanks, thanks, my noble friend," said Sir Walter, "this

promise of thine gives me comfort in the certainty of Ramsay's safety."

"Who knocks there?" cried Lord Huntly. "Did I not say that we must be private?"

"A messenger with some errand of moment for Sir Walter Stewart," replied the Squire.

"Come in, and tell us who and what he may be," replied Lord Huntly.

"He desired me to deliver this ring into Sir Walter's own hand," said the Squire, entering and presenting it to the Knight.

"Ha!" cried the Knight, the moment he threw his eyes on it, "give him entrance without a moment's delay. My Lord, this is my boy Charley Stewart, who went abroad in the service of the royal Duke of Albany. I thank the saints that he is alive! I rejoice that I shall once more behold him, for I feared that something fatal had befallen him. It is well that he hath thus come, so opportunely, else, in my bewilderment, he might have lost his share of that which he hath so well deserved at my hands."

"It is well, indeed, that he hath come, then," replied the Earl, "for, if I mistake not, he is a young man worthy of the stock he hath sprung from. The Duke of Albany, I remember, spoke well of him from France, some little time after his arrival there."

"His Highness vouchsafed to do so," replied Sir Walter. "But it is so long since, that now I burn to behold the boy once more, and to see, with mine own eyes, what improvement foreign nurture hath done on him."

"And I," said the Earl, "am especially curious to hear how his royal master the Duke hath sped, and whether he may yet talk of returning to his country, and trusting his person to the protection of the Scottish nobles. But here comes the youth."

"Charley, my boy!—my son! thank God that thou art alive! I rejoice to behold thee again once more!" cried Sir Walter, hurrying forward to embrace him, with deep emotion. "I am glad, most glad, thou art come!"

"Your blessing, father!" cried Charley, who having entered the room with the veiled lady on his arm, quitted her at the door, and rushed forward to meet and to throw himself on his knees before Sir Walter.

"Thou hast it, boy!" replied the Knight, raising him up, and clasping him tenderly to his breast. "Thou hast it most sincerely. Recent melancholy events have now made thee

doubly dear to me. But say, why is it that I have heard
nought of thee for so long a time? Why is it that thou wert
as silent in thy communication as if thou hadst been dead?
Often did I of late seek tidings of thee of De Tremouille, but
so much in vain did I seek them, that I more than half
believed that some fatal calamity had befallen thee. Come,
say how hath it fared with thee and thy royal master, and
where, and wherefore, hast thou left him?"

"With your leave, dear father, and that of this noble Earl,"
replied Charley. "I shall hastily run over the outline of our
history.—A fair wind bore us to France, where we were soon
transported to Paris. There we were well received, and well
lodged, at the sign of the Cock, in the street of St. Martin, and
all manner of expenses were defrayed from the French treasury,
for the Duke and his attendants, to the number of twelve persons. We lived a merry life, mingling in all the shows and
pageants of the French court, and proving our horsemanship
with the French cavaliers, with no manner of disgrace on my
humble part, and with great honour on the part of my royal
master. But soon after this, some paltry jealousies and
suspicions broke out against us, fostered, no doubt, by certain
Scots, who had the secret ear of the King of France, and the
secret authority of James of Scotland. Prudence led the royal
Duke to travel in the provinces for a time, and under the
disguise of an errant knight, he wandered about, with me as
his esquire, doing feats of arms everywhere. Then it was that
De Tremouille could report nothing of me, for I was altogether
in disguise, doing the most agreeable service to my high and
most kind master."

"How camest thou to leave so good and honourable a
service then?" demanded the Knight.

"Simply on this ground," replied Charley. "A certain
correspondence began to arise between my royal master and
Edward of England. Whilst this was going on, the Duke,
who always showed most kindly towards me, took me one day
into his private apartment, and told me in confidential secrecy,
that a certain treaty was on foot between him and the English
king, with the intent of their uniting to make war upon Scotland. I was largely promised wealth and honours if I would
follow his Highness to England. But, albeit that I should
have been fain to have followed him all over the world, I could
in nowise bring myself to fight against the country of my birth,
or against that country which held my father, and whose king
I held to be my father's friend—that country which held her

—a—a—that country, I mean, which was a—dear to me from many a tender recollection—and that country, above all, which held my much loved and most affectionate and most revered mother."

"Poor, kind, and amiable boy!" murmured Sir Walter Stewart, groaning deeply, "little knowest thou what a shock thou hast yet to receive!"

"I could not fight against such a land," continued Charley, without observing this scarcely audible interruption. "And on my so declaring this, and setting forth my reasons before my royal master, he kindly, and, as he was well pleased to say, with regret, gave me his princely licence to depart; and as he had little to bestow, he honoured me by putting this massive gold chain around my neck, and I parted from him, after receiving his gracious thanks for the fidelity of my services, and with many friendly commendations on the Duke's part to you. I left him in the more honourable, yet not more faithful, hands of Monipeny and Concressault, who are now with him. Having taken ship and reached the shores of Scotland, I made the best of my way to my native Strath, and there, learning that thou hadst but recently left it, I hasted, with all speed, to follow thee hither."

"Thou hast well judged, and well acted, my dear boy!" said the Knight, embracing him. "By mine honour, but thou dost prove, by thy words, that thy head hath gained as much in solid sense as thy person and manners have gathered in strength and grace. My Lord of Huntly, since Charley hath thus, by God's mercy, turned up alive, thou must now see done for him, that which I, in such a case provided, as I already told thee. To thee then I leave it to see him duly enfeoffed in the place and lands of Kilmaichly, on a part of which he was born, and this I have bestowed upon him and his heirs in property for ever."

"Be assured I shall see this desire of thine most strictly executed," said Lord Huntly.

"Thanks, thanks, most gracious father!" cried Charles Stewart, throwing himself again upon Sir Walter's neck. "Yet would I consider it a far greater boon to be allowed to follow thee in whatever emprise thou mayest now be bound to."

"That which I am bound after, boy, is too solemn for thy years," replied Sir Walter Stewart, gravely. "Thou art as yet too young to quit the haunts of men, and sins hast thou but few to drive thee thence, unless mine be visited upon thee. But, hold! thou wouldst seem to have a fair companion there.

Tell me, I pray thee, hast thou brought a French wife with thee? Alas, rash youth, thou knowest not what perils are to be found within the silken meshes of the toils of matrimony! Hath not thine own past experience of the fickle nature of woman cured thee of love?"

"Nay, nay, my good and honoured father," replied Charley, "so far as I am concerned, I have learned, to my great joy, though to my sad remorse and contrition, that woman's love, when pure and virtuous, is inextinguishable by all the storms and tides of adverse fate. My Rosa was true, and she yet lives for me and me alone, and I was the rash insane tool of one who was more an evil spirit than a woman. Thanks be to God, too, that I have not the crime of murder on my conscience, for I have learned that my benefactor, Sir Piers Gordon, yet lives."

"Sir Piers Gordon!" exclaimed Huntly, in surprise, "Art thou then the youth who had so nearly deprived me of so valuable a kinsman and dependant? Trust me, young man, had the blow been fatal, I could not easily have forgiven thee."

"My Lord, I could never have forgiven myself," said Charley. "But now I hope to prove to Sir Piers my gratitude, as well as my penitence, if he will vouchsafe to pardon me, and to receive me again into his friendship."

"I think thou mayest safely reckon upon him," said Huntly, "especially with my intercession for thee."

"Is this thy Rosa then, boy?" demanded Sir Walter Stewart, pointing to the veiled lady. "And is she already thy wedded wife? Why all this mystery? Lead her hither, that we may see and become acquainted with her."

"It is not Rosa," replied Charley, solemnly, as he retired to the farther part of the room, and led forward the lady trembling beneath her veil. "It is not Rosa, nor is Rosa as yet my wife. She whom I would now introduce to you is no wife, nor hath she ever been bound by any such holy ties—yet would she crave thy blessing, and one kind word of comfort from thee," and with this he gently removed the veil from her head.

"Holy Virgin, and sacred ministers of Almighty Providence, what do I behold!" exclaimed Sir Walter Stewart, in amazement, "Alice Asher!—and in life! My beloved Alice, can it indeed be thee?" and then rushing forward to embrace her, he cried— "It is, it is my Alice!"

"Oh! this more than repays me for a life of wretchedness," said Alice, weeping, and warmly responding to his emotions. "A mother's pride, which I have in my boy, would not let me remain behind him; and the priest gave me licence. I wished to behold him in his father's arms, and my fond and foolish heart hath been gratified beyond its deserts. May blessings be showered down upon thee for what thou hast done!" continued she, sinking on her knees before him, "May blessings here, and eternal happiness hereafter, be thy portion!"

"Rise, my fair, my beloved, my much injured Alice!" cried the Knight, raising her gently up, and again tenderly embracing her. "This is indeed a day of joy! But tell me how it is that mine eyes thus gladly behold thee, when they have now so long wept for thy supposed death by that murderous and traitorous fire?"

"Providence interfered to save my worthless life," replied Alice. "It so happened, that on the very evening before the burning, I chanced to go up into Glen-Livat to visit the good widow MacDermot and her daughter Rosa, whose society was always balm to me, and especially so because their favourite talk was ever of mine absent Charley. As I was thus going away from home, my serving-maiden took in a girl, a friend of hers, to be company for her loneliness, and thus both these innocent creatures perished, whilst I escaped. But the ways of Heaven are inscrutable. Thus it was that two half-consumed corpses were discovered, which led to the belief of my death; and then it was that terror for the Lady of Drummin made me dread to contradict the rumour, and compelled me to live in concealment."

"Enough it is that thou art yet alive, my beloved Alice!" cried Sir Walter Stewart, carried altogether away by the wildest feelings of joy. "Dearest, we shall yet be happy!— Thou shalt yet be——"

"Oh, say!—speak!" said Alice, greatly agitated. "What— what wouldst thou say?"

"What—what have I said?" continued Sir Walter, sinking in tone and manner into those of deep despondency. "What! —said I that we should yet be happy?—that thou shouldst yet be my wife. Alas!—no, no, no—I forgot. It cannot be. My vow—my vow—my solemn vow, already registered in Heaven! Would that I had known all this ere I had made it! Would that I had but known that thou wert still alive! But now, even these regrets and repinings become sinful. The hand of Providence is in it, and God's holy will be done. The vow— the solemn vow which I recorded in Heaven must be fulfilled. Alice, dearest of human beings, I cannot now be thine! I have henceforth dedicated myself to the service of the Most High.

I depart this very day to make good my vow, by throwing myself into a foreign monastery."

"The will of the Lord be done!" said Alice Asher in a hollow voice of intense suffering, whilst, pale and trembling, she bowed her head and sank into a chair, where a deluge of tears gave vent to her emotions. "The will of the Lord be done! And why should it be otherwise? I have more than deserved all those sufferings and trials, which God, in his justice and wisdom, hath been pleased to bring upon me, and why should I wickedly murmur? As thou sayest, the finger of God is in it. May he sanctify his chastisement for our salvation, and so let me cheerfully kiss the rod of his fatherly correction."

"Angel that thou art!" cried Sir Walter, greatly moved. "Oh, what wouldst thou not have been, but for me, villain that I was! Thy sin was mine. On my head must fall the the whole of thy guilt. Thou wert young and pure, as a creature of heaven. On my head must fall all the wrath of an offended God; and mine, therefore, must be the penance. Return then to resume thine innocent and peaceful life. Thou hast a firm and able protector in thy son, whose strong arm, and upright heart, shall shield thee from all harm. In due time, he must marry Rosa MacDermot, and thou mayst yet live happily to see thy grandchildren growing up, like goodly plants, around thee. Pray for me in thy private hours of converse with the Almighty, that he may yet extend his mercy to me, a repentant sinner. My orisons shall never cease to rise for thee. And now, this last holy kiss may, without guilt, be permitted to us. May God for ever bless and preserve thee! And—now—now—farewell for ever!"

Alice flew into his arms with a frantic hysterical laugh; and after a long, a silent, and a last embrace, Sir Walter Stewart, gently unfolding himself from her, rushed with a broken heart from the apartment, followed by his son and Lord Huntly, leaving Alice Asher, who sank helpless into a chair, pale, motionless, and silent, as if death had suddenly fallen upon her. The Knight sprang into his saddle; Huntly silently but warmly squeezed his hand; Charley Stewart embraced his manly limb, as he put his foot into the stirrup—and his father stooped from his seat and tenderly kissed his brow and blessed him, ere he dashed his spur-rowels into the sides of his steed, and galloped out of the courtyard, with his followers behind him.

Let us now return to the Castle of Drummin. On that very

night in which the depressed and repentant Sir Walter was
solemnly dedicating himself at Huntly Castle to the service of
God, she who had been his lady retired to rest in her chamber,
with her infant child placed in a cradle beside her couch. A
lamp which burned on a table near her enabled her to read
over again the letter which she had received from Cochran, the
new Earl of Mar ; and, after she had done so, she laid her head
back upon the pillow to ruminate upon its contents, and to
resign herself to the enjoyment of those visions of ambition to
which it had given birth. By degrees sleep overpowered her,
and her waking thoughts began gradually to resolve themselves
into wild, floating, and ill-connected dreams. After many
strange and abrupt changes, she imagined that she was led to
the altar by the Earl of Mar. Both were dressed in all the
pomp that befitted the rank of such a bridegroom and bride.
The King and Queen were present, and all things were prepared for the nuptial ceremony. But when the marriage
service proceeded, both the Earl and Lady made vain and
ineffectual efforts to join hands. As she struggled to accomplish this, she suddenly perceived that the gorgeous golden
collar which surrounded the Earl's neck was changed into a
halter of horse hair. She stared with wonder upon him ; and, as
she did so, his coarse, ruddy features became pale and fixed and
corpse-like, and he was lifted slowly from before her, as if some
powerful and unseen hand had raised him from the ground by
the halter, until he disappeared altogether from her sight. She
struggled fearfully. The priests, the King, and the Queen,
and the other personages who were present at the bridal faded
away before her. Her heart grew cold within her from fear
and very loneliness. Suddenly the candles on the altar, and
the other lights in the church, blazed up miraculously till their
pointed flames were blunted and flattened on the vaulted roof.
She endeavoured to shriek aloud, but no utterance could she
give to her voice, whilst horrid laughter echoed through the
surrounding aisles, and demoniac faces mocked and gibbered at
her from behind the massive pillars. A complete and most
unaccountable change immediately took place, and she beheld
a burning cottage before her. Screams were heard from within
the walls, and she would have fain shut her eyes from the
sight, and stopped her ears from the sound ; but she could do
neither. She was in an agony which no human tongue can
describe. At length the figure of a woman of angelic beauty
and expression of countenance and ethereal airiness of form,
shot upwards as if borne to heaven by the rising column of

fire. The screams continued from within the burning walls. They pierced her ears horribly, and the flames darted around her on all sides, scorching her face and hands and setting fire to her garments ; and still all her efforts were vain to move herself from the spot so as to withdraw from their influence. Half suffocated, she struggled and toiled to escape them ; and being at last awakened by her efforts, she was for one moment conscious that she was in the midst of a real conflagration. In that one moment was concentrated the whole remorse of her wicked life—and it was terrible ! She heard the cries of her perishing babe ; and being herself so choked as to be unable for exertion, she speedily became an easy and helpless prey to the devouring element. The drapery of her bed, which she had put aside in order to read the letter, had fallen back into its place ; and having thus caught fire from the lamp, the flames had thence communicated to the cradle and to the bed ; and by the time the alarm of the conflagration had been given throughout the Castle and traced to its source, the lady and her innocent babe, and everything within the apartment, had been consumed to ashes.

After such an occurrence as this, it may easily be conceived that the gates of Drummin were thrown open to the Earl of Huntly the moment he appeared with a strong force before it. He stayed but a few days there to arrange such business as his new possessions demanded of him. The most prominent and important part of this was to see Charles Stewart regularly enfeoffed in his property of Kilmaichly, after which he bestowed knighthood upon him ; and having accomplished all this, the Earl hastened southwards to lend his powerful aid in perfecting those plots which were then ripening among the discontented nobles, and which terminated with the summary execution of Cochran and the other minions of King James the Third over the Bridge of Lauder. That the life or person of Ramsay was preserved untouched may have been in a great measure owing to the last parting injunctions of his friend Sir Walter Stewart.

The new Knight of Kilmaichly quickly proceeded to build himself a suitable dwelling, and that was no sooner in a habitable state, than he brought that courtship, which he began with Rosa MacDermot, before she was carried off from the harvest-rig by the eagle, to a proper period, by a mutual submission of the parties to that holy yoke, which was imposed upon them by the priest, who then lived at Dounan. The poor old Howlet's prophecy was thus verified, by Rosa MacDermot thus becoming a *landed lady*, and *marrying a man with a knight's spurs at*

his heels, and this, too, precisely according to the happy interpretation which the Lady Kilmaichly had herself put upon it.
Among the few people who were bidden to the marriage, and
certainly one who was by no means the least happy or jovial
among the company, was the good old knight, Sir Piers Gordon.
Nor was his niece, the Lady Marcella, absent; though, strange
to say, she was very much metamorphosed from what she once
was. Some time after those events which caused the flight of
Charley Stewart to Edinburgh, and which deprived her of all
further hope of him, she was one day riding with her uncle's
retainers, when they fell in accidentally with a party of
Catteranes. She charged them boldly at the head of her
people, and in the midst of the melée she had one eye scooped
out by the point of a lance, and half of her nose and a considerable portion of one cheek, carried off by the slash of a claymore;
and, had it not been for the intrepidity of an honest, stalwart,
broad-shouldered, and wide-chested man-at-arms, who came to
her rescue, beat off the enemy single-handed, and then carried
her off in his brawny arms, it is probable that she might have
died gloriously upon the battle-field. Recovering from her
wounds, the bravery of this hero touched her heart; and, notwithstanding the loss of so many of her charms the bold yeo-
man, declaring that there was quite enough left of her to make
a very fine woman still, and being altogether undeterred by her
Amazonian temper, he had no scruple in buckling with the
heiress of Sir Piers Gordon. Although a good-natured fellow,
he was by no means a man to be bullied. A very great
reformation was therefore speedily worked upon her disposition; and by the time she appeared as a guest at the marriage
of Sir Charles Stewart of Kilmaichly, she exhibited the countenance of a gorgon, with a temper and spirit subdued and
gentle as those of a lamb.

I have little to add now, gentlemen, to this true history, except to recount to you a very curious occurrence that took
place soon after Sir Charles Stewart and his lady were married
and comfortably settled at Kilmaichly, and which threatened
to interrupt the peacefulness of their lives for a time. A
dispute arose between Sir Charles's people and those of the
Laird of Ballindalloch, about the march between the farm of
Ballanluig, belonging to Kilmaichly, and Craigroy, which was
the property of his powerful neighbour. The House of Ballindalloch being likely to prove too strong for him in a matter
which he foresaw must probably be determined by the arm of
force, the prudent Sir Charles took the precaution to send a

messenger. into Athol, to his father's relative, the Laird of Fin-castle, craving his aid.   To his no small comfort, his petition was readily granted, and Fincastle sent him sixty well-armed men, and a capital piper, to stir up their souls to battle.   Sir Charles being now in every respect a match for his opponent, turned out bravely to make good his plea, whilst Ballindalloch came with an equal force to dispute the point.   Each of the two parties reached its respective ground at night, with the intent of joining battle by the earliest dawn.   That of Sir Charles Stewart took up its position in and about a kiln, whilst Ballindalloch's little army was similarly posted at or near a house at no great distance.   Both sides were breathing horrid war, and anticipating dreadful slaughter when daylight should enable them to see each other, for the night was dark as pitch. Some time before daybreak, the lightning flashed, and a fearful peal of thunder crashed suddenly over their heads, so that every man present was stricken with awe.   A waterspout then broke upon the hills, and came down upon them so tremen-dously as to produce a roaring noise as if a sea had been des-cending upon them.   Both sides were appalled, and sinking in terror upon their knees, they remained in that position until the morning dawned.   By that time the sky had cleared, and the sun rose smiling; and then it was that they beheld by his light that a large and frightful ravine had been cut out between them by the waterspout, where nothing of the sort had existed before.   Both parties felt that Providence had interfered to settle their dispute, and to save the effusion of human blood. Accordingly the two leaders at once agreed that the ravine thus strangely and miraculously opened by the sudden descent of this transient torrent from the hills should be the march between their properties in all time coming; and thus, they who came to the ground as deadly foes, separated as sworn brethren and allies.

Thus it seemed that Heaven itself had ruled that peace should be secured to those who so well merited it, and who so well knew how to enjoy it; and the felicity of Sir Charles Stewart and his lady was complete.   Years rolled on, and still the sunshine of their countenances—aye, and the sunshine of the faces of their merry children—would often conjure up an angelic smile of gratitude upon the pale and pensive features of Alice Asher.   Nor were the grateful feelings of this highly favoured family expended in barren expressions, for all around them were loud in praise of their hospitality, benevolence, and charity.

In the course of some generations Kilmaichly fell to an heiress, and the Laird of Ballindalloch having married her, she carried the estate into that family, where it now remains.

THE AUTHOR FLOORED.

Iт is not very easy to tell how we all bestowed ourselves after Serjeant Archy Stewart's story of Tàillear-Crubach, but it was no sooner brought to a close, than each of us proceeded to exert his own ingenuity, in making up a bed for himself. Some things there were indeed resembling beds in an upper room, but those who occupied them were perhaps not much more fortunate than those who chose a dry, and tolerably even corner of the floor, and there disposed of themselves, rolled up in their plaids. My own experience tells me, that sweeter, sounder, or more refreshing repose is nowhere to be enjoyed, than on such a bed as this, especially after fatigue ; and the great proof of its excellence, upon the present occasion, was, that five minutes did not elapse, ere we had all succeeded in our courtship of that sleep which our day's walk, and the lateness of the hour, had conspired to make it no very difficult matter for us to woo. Next morning, the roaring of the Aven, now turbid and discoloured, and flowing wide over the haughs, the rain still drizzling on, and the wet air and gloomy sky, and the plashy footing on the meadow where Clifford ventured out to experiment and explore, whilst we stood clustered within the door, with our heads out, to mark his proceedings, very speedily made us draw them back again, with a determined resolution to see a fairer promise of weather, before we should venture to thrust them forth to tempt our fate in travel.

Clifford (mincing his steps on tiptoe through a flock of ducklings rejoicing clamorously in the wet).—Fine weather for you young gentlemen, indeed ! Well, if the day will neither fish nor walk, we may be thankful that we are well provisioned with food for the body and the mind.

Dominie.—That is a great consolation indeed, Mr. Clifford, and leaves us little to be pitied.

Clifford.—Come then, let us have breakfast ; and, after that, let us resume our sitting of last night, and, since we cannot budge out, let us spend the day rationally, with legends and cigars, at Inchrory.

Author.—Pray, Mr. Serjeant, what is supposed to be the origin of the name of Inchrory?

Serjeant.—Why, sir, the place was so called from a certain Rory Mackenzie of Turfearabrad, or Fairburn, as it is called in modern language, who, about the sixteen hundred or so, was wont to drive great herds of cattle from his place in Ross-shire to the south country markets, by this way up Glen-Aven. His story is a sad one.

Grant.—Pray let us have it, Archy.

Serjeant.—With your leave, sir, I'll rather tell it to you on our way up the glen, when we come near to the place where the cruel deed was done. You will be the better able to understand some of its most important circumstances.

Author.—You are right, Serjeant.

Clifford (taking out his tablets).—Well, Mr. Serjeant, I'll book you for it, at all events.—Rory Mackenzie of Turfearabrad.

Serjeant.—I'll not forget it, sir. But, in the meanwhile, gentlemen, I may tell you, that as this Rory Mackenzie used to bring his beasts up this glen, which, as I formerly mentioned, was so full of woods at that time as to make an open patch of pasture a thing of great value, he was so tempted by the fineness and richness of the grass on the meadow that lies hereabouts, all produced, as you will naturally see, from the marly matter brought down upon it by the streams from the hill, that he used to make a regular practice of lodging himself and his animals here for some days, in order to rest and refresh them for their journey; and so, at last, the place got its name from him. But there was no house here in his day.

Dominie.—We have verra great reason to be thankful, Serjeant, that we have so good a house over our heads now, then.

Clifford.—House! why in such weather, a house like this in the wilderness is as good as a palace in a city. Soldier though I be, I by no means envy Rory, the laird of Turfearabrad, his sylvan bivouacs. What think you, Mr. Serjeant?

Serjeant.—Troth, sir, I can lie out when I am obliged to do it. But I am grown old enough now to think, that, in an ill day, the nearer to the fire-side the better, and still better it is in an ill night. What say you to that, Mr. Macpherson?

Dominie.—If my last night's scramble hither, and the deep mud of that filthy peat pot into which I fell, has not convinced me of that truth, Serjeant, I must be a stubborn bubo indeed.

Clifford.—Truth is generally found at the bottom of a well, but to find it, as you seem to have done, at the bottom of a peat pot, is a new discovery, Mr. Macpherson.

Clifford (after all are done with breakfast).—Come, then, gentlemen, shall we adjourn to the fire, and commence our sitting?

Grant.—Allons!

Author.—Now, my good woman, take away these things, and make the room a little tidy, and then bring us plenty of peats.

Clifford.—Aye, that will do.

Grant.—Who is to be story-teller?

Clifford.—Mr. Macpherson is the man. Now then, Mr. Macpherson, your Serjeant John Smith is the first for duty. He may mount guard as speedily as you please.

Dominie.—He shall obey the captain's orders without a moment's delay.

THE LEGEND OF SERJEANT JOHN SMITH'S ADVENTURES.

To understand my story the better, gentlemen, you must yemaygine to yourselves a snug well-doing Nairnshire farmer's onstead,* situated in the parish of Auldearn, with a comfortable dwelling-house, of two low stories, accurately put down, so as mathematically to face the twelve o'clock line,—with its crow-steppit gables, small windows, little out-shot low addition behind, tall chimneys, and grey-slated root—just such a house, to wit, as a man of his condition required in the middle of the last century—with two lines of strange-looking thatched or sod-covered stables, byres, barns, and other outhouses, projecting from its sides at right angles to its front, with divers out-riders, and isolated straggling edifices, of similar architecture and materials, dropped down here and there, as the hand of chance might have sown them—the smoke coming furth from some of their lumm-heads, and partly also from their low door-ways, proving to you, almost against your conviction, that they actually are the dwelling-places of human beings. Fancy the whole grouped (as Mr. Grant, the long painter lad of Grantown, would have said) with sundry goodly rows of peat and turf stacks, a number of corn ricks wonderfully formed, and bulging and hanging out of the centre of gravity, each in a different direction, like a parcel of drunken Dutch dancers;—in the midst of all a large midden—

* A Scottish farmer's house and offices.

(query whether the word *midden* may not be a mere corruption
of the words *middle-in,—the midden* being always *in the middle*
of all rural premises in Scotland? so that unlucky visitors not
unfrequently walk up to *the middle* into *the middle* of it).
Then picture to yourselves, behind the biggins, sundry kail-
yards, with a few very ancient ash trees, sycamores, and rowan
trees, rising from among their bourtree fences, or from the sides
of their dilapidated dry-stone dikes. At a little distance
below, a bog, with its attendant pools of dark moss-water,
which shine amidst the black chaotic mass around them, and
look blue by their reflection of the sky—with a half-ruined and
roofless killogie, or kiln for drying corn and malt, standing on
a slooping bank at no great distance from them. Then people
all this with the farmer himself, a stout, hale, healthy-looking
man, going bustling about from door to door among his folk,
his muck-carts, and his horses, with a hodden-grey coat upon
his back, a broad blue bonnet on his head, a hazle staff in his
hand, and a colley and one or two rough terriers and greyhounds at his heels, shouting every now and then in Gaelic to
his man, John Smith, a tall, handsome, strong-built Highlander, whilst the gudeman's wife, a very good-looking, round-
formed, trigly-dressed English woman, is seen appearing and dis-
appearing from under the wooden porch, over which some
attempts have been made to trail a plant or two of rose and
honeysuckle, but which attempts have been rendered abortive
by the epicurean taste of the browsing animals of the farm—
her south country tongue sounding quick and sharp in the ears
of Morag, or Mary, a clever, well-made, bare-footed, and short-
gowned Highland lass, with pleasing countenance, largish cheek
bones, black snooded hair, sparkling eyes, arched eyebrows,
and rosy cheeks, busied in washing out her milk cogues, with
her coats kilted up to her knees. To which add the herd of
cows, oxen, queys, stirks, and calves of all sorts and sizes, with
a due mixture of sheep and lambs, and pownys, sprinkled all
about, feeding among the whinny pasture-hillocks and baulks,
dividing the queer-shaped patches of the surrounding arable
land. Above all, I would have you particularly to remark a
verra large sow-beast, with a numerous litter of pigs, grubbing
up the ground about the old killogie, amid the ruins of which
her progeny first saw the light. In addition thereto, fancy,
in the words of our own Scottish pastoral poet, Allan Ramsay,
that

"Hens on the midden, ducks in dubbs are seen,"

and you will be in full possession of the first scene of my tale,

as well as acquainted with some of its more important *dramatis
personæ.*

Mr. MacArthur, the farmer, though a Highlander, was a
stanch Whig, which made him, as you may well suppose,
gentlemen, rather a

"Rara avis in terris, nigroque simillima cygno"

among his brother Celts. He had acquired his principles
during his residence in England, where he had fallen in with
and married his wife, who was a woman of good condition for
her rank of life, and of superior yeddication. She was
attached to the Hanoverian royal family, both by principle and
interest. Her brother was an officer in the Royal Regiment;
and as everything connected with England was dear to her,
because it was her country, so everything connected with the
English army was especially dear to her on her brother's
account.

During the year 1745, when the recruiting for the army of
the Prince of the Stuarts was going on, many of Mr.
MacArthur's servants, and John Smith in particular, manifested a strong disposition to enlist under his banners. But so
powerful were the influence and eloquence of this English lady,
that she succeeded in dissuading them, one by one, from following out the bent of their inclinations. This her zealous and
active opposition to the Prince's cause, soon began to attract
public attention, in a district where it was so generally
favoured. She became a marked object of dislike to the
Jacobites, and this all the more so, perhaps, that she was an
English woman. Oftener than once it happened, that, whilst
they spared some of her neighbours, whose politics were
dubious, and therefore obnoxious in their eyes, they plundered
her goodman's farm on her especial account. But these
depredations were comparatively trifling, and protected as she
was by her husband's fortitude, she bore these little evils with
the magnanimity of a martyr; nay, she even ventured to talk
of them with contempt, and there were many people who
believed that she actually gloried in them. As Mr. MacArthur
was a Highlander, and spoke the Gaelic language fluently, he
might perhaps have been able, by modest behaviour, kind
treatment, and smooth words, in some degree to have miti-
gated the prejudice which his countrymen had against his wife
as a *Pensassenach,* or English wife, as she was uniformly called
by way of reproach. But husbands cannot always restrain the
political enthusiasm of their ladies—and so it was with Mr.

MacArthur. With or without his approbation she scrupled
not, at times, when a good opportunity offered, to set the
Jacobites at defiance, to give them all manner of opprobrious
epithets, and, with all a woman's rashness, but with more than
feminine intrepidity, she dared them to do their worst.

It was after sunset on the evening of the 13th of April, 1745,
that the Pensassenach was seated in her elbow chair, by the
fire in her little parlour. She was alone, for her husband had
been called away from home, for some days, on very urgent
business, and as she felt herself slightly indisposed, she was
prepared to take particular care of herself for that night. A
small tall-shaped chased silver vessel of mulled elderberry
wine, with a close top to it to keep its contents warm, together
with a very tiny silver cup, were placed beside her on a little
round walnut-tree table, supported on a single spiral pillar with
three claws. She was about to pour out a little of this
medicinal fluid, to be taken preparatory to retiring to bed for
the night, when she was startled by a noise in the kitchen, and
immediately afterwards she was alarmed by the abrupt entrance
of her maid Morag.

" Mem!—Mem !" cried the girl, breathless with the importance of her intelligence, " tare's Wully Tallas, ta packman in
ta kitchen ! He's come a' ta way frae Speymouth sin yesterday. Ta Englishers are a' comin' upon us horse and futs !—
horse and futs an' mockell cannons, an' we'll be a' mordered an'
waur !—fat wull we do ?"

" What say you, girl ?" exclaimed the Pensassenach, starting
from her chair, and overturning all her meditated comforts in
her hurry. " But get out of my way, you senseless fool, I'll
speak to the man myself. Dallas ! Will Dallas !" cried she,
throwing her voice shrilly along the passage towards the
kitchen. " Come this way, Will Dallas, and let me hear your
news from your own mouth !"

" Comin' mem !" cried the travelling merchant, as he
appeared limping along the passage, by no means sorry to be
thus called on to unbuckle his budget of news, which he was
always ready to dispose of at a much cheaper rate than he
generally sold his goods.

" Where have you come from, Will Dallas ?" cried the Pensassenach ; " and what news have ye got ?"

" Weel, ye see, mem, I hae come straught frae Speymouth,
as fast as my heavy pack and this happity lamiter leg o' mine
wad let me," replied Dallas. " And my pack's very heavy yee
noo, for I've got a grand new stock o' gudes in't."

" Well, well, never mind your goods at present ! " cried the impatient Pensassenach : " quick ! quick ! what news have you ? "

" Od, mem, it wad at no rate do for me no to mind my goods at a' times and at a' saisins," said Dallas. " But touching the news, mem,—the Duke, mem—that is, the Duke o' Cummerland, I mean, crossed the Spey yesterday wi' a' his airmy."

" Is it possible ? " cried the Pensassenach, her eyes sparkling with delight."

" It's quite true, mem, for I seed the whole tott o' them yefeck the passage wi' my ain een," said Dallas.

" Ha ! tell me, good Dallas, how did they cross ? " demanded the lady.

" They just fuirded through the Spey, mem, in three grand deveesions, at three different pairts, just for a' the warld as gin ye had been rollin' aff three different pieces o' red ribban like, at yae time," replied Dallas.

" A glorious sight ! " cried the Pensassenach.

" Aye, truly, ye wad hae said sae had ye seen't, mem," said Dallas ; " gin ye had seen them wi' the sun glancin' on their airms, and on the flashin' faem o' the Spey ! Every bone o' them got safe across, exceppin' yae dragoon that had taen a wee thoughty ower muckle liquor, and fell fae his horse,—and four weemen fouk, wha were whamled out o' a bit cairty, and wha were a' carried down, and a' drooned outright."

" Poor wretches ! " said the Pensassenach. " But it was well they were not men : their lives were comparatively but little worth."

" I daur swear that you're right there, mem," said Dallas ; " little worth followers of the camp they were, nae doot ;—and yet the hizzies were weel pit on. I followed the bodies as they soomed down the water, and cleekit ane o' them ashore, and although her mutch was gane, she had a gude goon and a daycent rocklay on, and ither things forbye ; but they ware a' sae spiled wi' the water, that I selt them till a woman in Elgin for an auld sang. But I'll tell ye what it is, mem, weemen—that is, daycent weemen—have nae business——"

" You have no business with the women," Mr. Dallas," interrupted the Pensassenach, impatiently—" it is of the men —of the troops, and of their noble and gallant leader that I would hear. All across, said you ? and what became of the other Duke ? " continued she, in a contemptuous tone. " I mean the rebel Duke—the Duke of Perth, I mean ? Where was he, and where were his heroes, that they did not arrest the progress of the Royal army ? "

"Troth, mem, the Duke o' Perth and his men just came on their ways wast the country, and left the English airmy to cross at their ain wull," replied Willy.

"Bravo! bravo!" shouted the lady, waving her hand around her head. "The false knaves dared not to face them! Well, any more news, Dallas?"

"I ken nae mair that I hae to tell ye," said Dallas, "exceppin' that I was in the English camp yestreen mysel', and that I selled a wheen caumrick pocket-napkins, and three yairds o' black ribban, till yere brither, Captain John, and I promised to ca' in by this way aince eerant to tell ye that he was weel, and to drink his health."

"Thank ye, thank ye, good Bill Dallas!" cried the lady, clapping her hands in an ecstasy of joy; "you shall not fail to do that; but why did you not tell me this joyful news before? Stay, my good man—here is for your happy tidings!" and, running to a corner cupboard, she brought out a bottle of brandy, and filled him a tasse, that made his eyes dance in his head after he had tossed it off.

"My certy, that's prime stuff indeed," said Dallas, panting with the very strength of it. "And noo, mem, will ye look at my pack. I hae some o' the grandest jewels, rings, chains, watches, and brooches; the gayest ribbons, and, aboon a', the bonniest lace—ye never saw siccan lace. The captain said he was quite sure it wad tak' your ee, for that you had siccan a fine taste. Troth, says I till him, you're no far wrang there, captain; Mrs. MacArthur has the best taste and joodgement in lace o' a' my customers, north or sooth—north or sooth, said I. It's quite beautifou lace, mem, as ye'll say when ye see't; and sae cheap, too! Od, I'm sellin' it for half nothin'. Shall I bring the pack ben here, mem? Ye'll hae mair licht here."

"No — no — no! — not at present, Will," cried the Pensassenach, her patience quite exhausted with his prolixity. "Another time, Will—but I have other fish to fry at present. Morag!—Morag, girl! run! call out all the men! My stars, how unfortunate it is that MacArthur is from home! How he would rejoice! Call all the men, I say!"

"Fat vas she cryin' aboot?" said Morag, hurrying to answer her call.

"Run and call all the men, I tell you, girl!" cried the Pensassenach, bustling about, all life and activity, and her indisposition entirely forgotten. "Call all the men, I say; and John Smith in particular. I want John Smith here immediately. What glorious news! There won't be a rascally rebel knave of them left in the whole country. And my brother John coming too! Who knows but we may have the honour of being presented to his Royal Highness the Duke of Cumberland in person! How provoking it is that MacArthur is from home!"

"Fat wad ta leddy be wantin' wi' her?" said John Smith, at that moment putting his head into the room, his Kilmarnock cowl, and the disordered state of the covering of so much of the upper part of his person as was visible, sufficiently indicating that he had been roused from his bed. "Fat wad ta leddy be wantin'? We wus a' beddit."

"Run, John!" cried the impatient lady, "run and make all the people get out of their beds directly! collect every one, man and woman, about the farm. Make them yoke all the carts, and drive a whole peat-stack to the head of the knoll, and build up a large bonfire, and see that you mix your layers of peats with layers of moss-fir, and dry furze-bushes. I'll have a blaze that shall be seen from Forres to Inverness. Have we any tar-barrels left!"

"Ou aye!" replied John; "a tar-barrels tat was ower mockell fan we last tar ta sheeps."

"Then put the whole tar-barrel in the midst of all," cried the Pensassenach. "Come, John, why do you stand staring so? Run, man, and do as I bid you, without a moment's delay."

"Ou aye, aye, she's runnin' fast," replied John, slowly moving away. "Fod, but she's thinks tat ta Pensassenach be gaen taft awtagedder."

"Morag! bring a basket here directly," cried the Pensassenach, as she hurried down stairs with the large key of the cellar in her hand. "Now," said she, putting a number of bottles into the basket, "take care of these; and make haste, and bring a cheese, and some loaves of bread, and follow me quickly out to the knoll with the basket."

In a very little time an enormous pile of fuel was built up on the summit of the knoll, with the tar-barrel in the centre of it, to which an opening was at first left from the external air, which was afterwards partially filled with dry furze-bushes dipped in tar, so as to afford the flame a ready communication inwards. When everything was prepared, the Pensassenach seized a lighted candle from a lantern, and, as Dryden hath it, she

"Like another Helen, fired another Troy!"

that is to say, she set fire, not to a city, indeed, but to the whin-bushes, and the flame running inwards, to the tar-barrel, the whole mighty fabric of fuel was instantaneously in such a blaze, that anyone might have thought that it was Troy itself that was burning.

"Now," said the Pensassenach, "draw me one of those stone bottles of brandy, and fill me a tasse of it. I drink to those to whom I have dedicated this bonfire—I drink, in the first place, to the health of my brother John, captain in the Royal Regiment, whom I hope soon to see here!" and, putting the cuach to her lips, she sipped a modest lady's share of the contents.

"Come, Bill Dallas," continued she, addressing the travelling merchant, who, tired as he was with his long tramp, had yet sneaked out to secure his share of the liquor, as well as of the fun. "Come, Bill, you must drink next; you have the best right to do so, as the bearer of the good news."

"Weel, here's to Captain John, and wussin' him health, and muckle happiness, and a gude wife till him, wi' plenty o' siller," said the packman, tossing off the full contents of the tasse. "I'm sure there's no a bonnier man, nor a better man, nor a gallanter sodger—eh, beg his honour's pardon, I meant offisher—in the hail land o' the British Isles, be the ither wha he may."

"Well spoken, Bill," cried the lady. "Now, John Smith, come it is your turn next."

"Here's helss, an' mokel o't, to her broder Captain Shon, and mokel gude wifes and gude sillers!" cried John Smith, draining the cuach to the last drop.—"Oich, but she's goot trinks!" added he.

The cup and the toast went round a large and increasing party; for the bonfire, sending up sharp pointed flames, as if it meditated piercing the very clouds, spread wonder and speculation all over the country far and wide, and brought all manner of idlers, like flies and moths, about it. A considerable space of time, as well as a tolerable quantity of brandy, was expended, before the health had been drank by everyone.

"Now," said the Pensassenach, filling the cuach again to the brim, "I drink health and success to his Royal Highness the Duke of Cumberland, and confusion to all his enemies!"—and, kissing the cup merely, she handed it to the packman.

"Weel, mem, here's wussin' that same wi' a' my heart!" cried Mr. Dallas, and off went every drop of his brimmer.

"Now, John," said the Pensassenach, filling the cuach again to the lip, "now, John Smith, it is your turn. Come, man, drink the toast—health and success to the Duke and his brave fellows."

"Na!" said John,—turning away as if the cup had contained vinegar or verjuice—"na! Teel be on her an' she do!"

"What do you mean, John?" demanded the Pensassenach, in a mingled tone of surprise and displeasure. "Will you refuse to drink my toast?"

"Hoot, man, dinna refuse to drink the leddy's toast," said the packman. "That gude brandy would wash down ony toast ava, let alane siccan' a grand man, and a hero like the Duke o' Cummerland. Od, man, an' ye had seen him as I hae seen him, ridin' at the head o' his men, wi' as muckle gold lace and reyal Genowa velvet aboot him as might serve to cover a papish pulpit wi', ye wad say he was the grandest man that ever ye seed. Come, man, drink success till him, and confusion till a' his yennemies!"

"Surely you will not refuse to drink success to that brave army in which my brother John serves?" said the Pensassenach, "and to that noble and gallant Prince who commands it?"

"She'll no grudge to drink hail bottals till ta helts o' Captain Shon, because she's her broder," said Smith, in a positive manner; "but fint ae drops wull she tak' to wuss ony helts to ta titter man an' his fouks!"

"Tuts, nonsense man," said the packman; "ye're just a reyal guse. Come awa! drink the Duke's health—the brandy's just parteeklar gude."

"Why should you hesitate?" said his mistress. "Come, drink the Duke's health."

"Tamm hersell an' she do ony siccan' a sing!" said John Smith, doggedly, and with powerful emphasis and action. "She'll as soon eat ta cuach!"

"What! are you a loyal subject, and refuse to drink the health of the Duke of Cumberland—the King's own brother!" exclaimed the Pensassenach, energetically.

"Ou troth—ou aye,—she be loyals eneugh till her ain Kings," said John, "an' she'll no grudge to trink gallons till her. But for ta titter mans, fod but she's wussin' her nasins ava but a good clink on ta croon;" and with that John walked off with a countenance so expressive of dissatisfaction and determination as rendered it evident that it would be quite hopeless to call him back.

"He is an obstinate disloyal mule!" cried the Pensassenach, giving full way to her anger.

"A reyal dour ass as I ever cam' across," said the packman. "An' siccan' reyal fine speerits too. The cheild thought naething o' hammerin' awa' and keepin' a' huss loyal folk frae our drap drink. It's weel that he's awa'. My certy, I rauken that there's nae ither body here that'll be sae dooms foolish as to refuse that gude brandy, let what toast there may be soomin' on the tap o' the brimmer."

"I trust that that fellow is the only disloyal man about the place," said the Pensassenach. "If it be otherwise, I'll have all such Jacobite knaves turned off this farm. We shall have none other but good loyal subjects here, I promise you, now that the Duke and his gallant army are coming among us."

This hint was not lost on the rest of the company; for whatever their private political opinions might have been, they preferred swallowing the good brandy in peace, let the tasse be prefaced by whatsoever toast the Pensassenach pleased, rather than be martyrs like John Smith, and risk the loss of the liquor and their places by any heroic and straightforward declaration of their sentiments. We sometimes see such folk in common life even at the present time, gentlemen. Many, then, were the toasts of the same character that went round. Liberally did the Pensassenach make her enlivening eau-de-vie to circulate. The huge bonfire was again and again supplied by the willing revellers. They were wise enough to see that the endurance of the joviality of the night must, in all probability, be measured by that of the fire, and so they laboured and sweated like horses to keep it going. Loud were the shouts, and many were the antic tricks performed around its blazing circle, all of which were to be attributed to the mirth-inspiring spirit. The packman was particularly joyous and hilarious, and his loquacity increased as he became elevated with the liquor. At last the Pensassenach, wishing gradually to wind up the festivities of the night, proposed another toast.

"Now, come," said she, filling the cuach, "Let us drink confusion to the rebels!"

"Hurrah! a capital toast!" cried the packman, whilst his cheer was blindly echoed by the more than half-intoxicated crowd around him.

"Then here I drink it as my most cordial wish," said the Pensassenach, sipping a little of the liquor in token of her earnestness and sincerity.

"Tamm! but she'll rue tat wuss!" cried a hoarse voice, which came from the shadow beyond the circle of the revellers.

"Who spoke?" demanded the Pensassenach, in vain endeavouring to dart her eyes into the impenetrable darkness by which the bright field of light was surrounded.

"Tamm her, but she'll ken tat soon eneugh!" replied the same voice; but the Pensassenach could see nothing but a pair of eyes, that, for the fraction of an instant, caught a strong reflection of the red light from the bonfire, glared fearfully at her, and then were gone.

"Lord hae a care o' huss! I wus that I had had naething ado wi' this matter," exclaimed Mr. Dallas, very much fear-stricken.

"Seize that man, whoever he may be!" cried the Pensassenach. But he was nowhere to be found. All the feeble and unsteady attempts of the drunken people to catch him were thrown away. The Pensassenach was vexed and mortified. The voice was sterner than John Smith's; but she could by no means banish the idea that it was his. She inquired and found that he was nowhere about the place, and she retired home to her chamber, filled with doubt regarding him, or rather more than half convinced that she nourished a traitor in her house.

Appearances on the following morning were by no means such as to overcome these suspicions.

"Is that you, Morag?" demanded the Pensassenach, as awakened at a later hour than usual by her maid she started up from that profound sleep which the extraordinary fatigue and excitement of the previous evening had thrown her into, and began to huddle on such parts of her clothes as lay nearest at hand.

"Aye, mem, it's me," replied Morag. "Fat wull she be doin' for mulks? Shon Smiss has driven awa' a' ta wholl kye lang or it was skreichs o' tay."

"What said you?" demanded the Pensassenach. "John Smith has driven away all our cows! Traitorous thief and robber that he is, I thought as much!"

"Toot na! Shon's nae fiefs nor rubbers neither," replied Morag, in anything but a pleased tone.

"He is a thief and a traitor to boot," cried the enraged Pensassenach.

"He is no fiefs!" rejoined Morag, with great energy, both of voice and of action. "Not a bone o' him but is as honest as yoursel'."

"I tell you he is a thief and a traitor, and for aught I know, an assassin too!" replied the Pensassenach; "and you are an impudent baggage for daring to contradict me."

"She canna stand and hear Shon Smiss misca'ed," exclaimed Morag, bursting into tears of mingled grief and rage, excited

by the unextinguishable love for John which had long secretly
possessed her; "an' war she no the mistress," continued
Morag, with very violent action, "war she no the mistress,
Fod but she wad pu' tat cockernony aff her head for saying as
mockell! But och mercy be aboot huss a'!" cried the girl,
darting a look out at the window and hurrying away as she
spoke; "mercy be aboot huss a'! yonder comes Shon himsel',
rinnin' like ony rae-buck!"

"God be merciful to me, can the traitor mean murder!" cried
the Pensassenach, hastily shutting, locking, and bolting the
chamber door, and with great exertion moving a chest of
drawers against it, whilst her very heart almost ceased to beat
from the terror that fell upon her.

"Far is she, Morag? Is she oot o' her bed!" cried John, in
a loud and hurried voice as he came flying up the stair and
began thundering like a madman at the lady's bed-chamber
door. "Come, come, let her in direckly!"

"No one can come here," said the lady, trembling; "I am
not half dressed."

"Dress be tamm!" cried John, furiously; "come away fast
—open ta toor or she be killed!"

"You shall find no entrance here, you murdering bloodthirsty villain, whilst I have power to defend my life," cried
the Pensassenach, driven to desperation, and as, with immense
labour, she was dragging a heavy trunk of napery across the
floor, which she reared on end against the chest of drawers.
"Oh, why did MacArthur leave me thus to be murdered?"

"Let her in, or she see her sure murdered," cried John, in a
voice of thunder, and kicking terribly at the door.

"God help me, I'm gone!" muttered the Pensassenach, in
an agony of fear. "Oh, why did my husband leave me? The
door never can stand such kicks as these. I see it yielding.
Murder! murder! murder!"

"Tamm her nane sel', but she has no more time for nonsense!" cried John, in a voice that seemed to betoken the
climax of fury, and with that he drove the whole weight of his
body with the force of a battering-ram against the door, forcing
it out from its hinges and tumbling it and the chest of drawers
and the huge trunk into the very middle of the room with a
violence that burst them open and scattered their contents in
all directions.

"Villain!" cried the Pensassenach, now suddenly excited to
an unnatural boldness by despair of life, and standing with her
back to the farther wall, armed with her husband's broadsword

which she had snatched from the bed-head, and drawn in her own defence, and which she now flourished with great activity and determined resolution, altogether regardless of the imperfect state of her attire. "Villain that you are, come but one step nearer to me and this sword shall drink your life's blood from your heart."

"Ou fye! ou fye!" cried John, standing considerably abashed at this spectacle; "far got she tat terrible swoord?"

"Villain, you tremble!" cried the Pensassenach, roused still more, and advancing towards John Smith step by step as she spoke; "fly villain, or I will put you to instant death!"

"Fye, fye!" said John; "but Fod she mauna mind it noo; tere's nae mair time for ceremonies. She maun e'en tak' her as she is."

"Attack me as I am!" cried the Pensassenach; "if you do, death, instant death, shall be your portion."

"We sall see tat," said John, lifting his hazel rung; "we sall soon see tat," and springing suddenly over the obstructing obstacles, John, with one blow of his stick, sent the sword spinning from the feeble grasp of the delicate hand that held it.

"Oh, mercy, mercy!" cried the Pensassenach, throwing herself on her knees before him with the horrible dread of impending death upon her. "You would not murder your mistress, John, and all for asking you to drink an idle toast? Oh, spare me! spare me! Do not murder me in cold blood!"

"Shon Smiss murder!" cried he, with horror and astonishment on his countenance. "Foo! foo! fat could gars her sinks tat o' Shon Smiss? Shon wad fichts to ta last trop o' her blots for her, futher she be King Charles's man or futher she be ta titter bid body o' a sham king's man. Foo! foo!—hoo could she sinks tat Shon Smiss wad do ony ill to ta Pensassenach tat has aye been sae kind till her, aye, and to Morag an a'," and the poor fellow began blubbering and crying.

"God be praised that I am safe, then!" cried the lady, immeasurably relieved. "But what is the meaning of all this violence, John? Are you mad?"

"Na," cried John, starting from the melting fit into which he had been thrown. "She no mad a bit. But ta Hillant-mens comin'! Swarrants ta Hillantmens no liket ta bonfires!"

"The Highlanders!" cried the Pensassenach. "Heaven defend me, what shall I do without the protection of my husband? What!—what shall I do?" and she burst into a flood of tears, from the nervous excitement to which she had been subjected.

"Troth, she be sinkin' tat its as weel tat ta master's no at hame," said he. " But fat need she fear as lang as Shon Smiss be here ?"

" Will you protect me ?" cried the Pensassenach, eagerly. " Will you really be true to me ?"

" Fat has Shon Smiss toon to mak ta Pensassenach sink tat she'll no be true till her ain mistress ?" cried Smith, in a whimpering tone, betokening vexation, so sincere, as, in a great measure, to restore the lady's confidence in him.

" Why did you drive away the cattle this morning, and what have you done with them ?" demanded she.

" Trots she was dootin', a' nicht, tat ta Hillantmen wad come after a' yon mockel fires," replied John, " an' sae she just trave tem coos, cattal, sheeps, an' staigs, an' awtegitter, a' awa' ower to ta glen, whaur she's sinking tat tey'll no be gettin' tem at 'tis turn."

" Faithful creature, after all, then !" cried the Pensassenach. " How can I sufficiently thank you ?"

" Did she no tell her tat Shon Smiss was nae feefs nor rubbers neither," said Morag, entering triumphantly at that moment. " Is she no a prave ponny man ? But uve, uve, mem, fat way is tat to be stannin' ? Fye, Shon Smiss ! hoo could ye stand glowerin' tere ?—get oot, man, till she gets ta leddy dressed."

" Fod, she has nae time, noo !" cried John. " Fod, but she hears ta pipes 'tis blesset moment. Hoot, toot ! Hurry, hurry ! Fod, but ta Hillantmens comin' noo !" and snatching a blanket from the bed, he threw it over his mistress, and whipping her up in his arms ere she wist, he strode down stairs with her in a moment. " Where are you carrying me ? Where are you carrying me to, John Smith ?" cried the Pensassenach, much alarmed.

" Dis she no hear ta pipes ?" cried John. " She be carrying her to hide her in ta auld killogie to be sure. Dinna be fear. She mak' her safe enough, she swarrants her o' tat."

John accordingly ran with the Pensassenach to the old kiln, as fast as his legs could carry him and his burden. He found it already occupied by the great sow and her numerous progeny, who, from their unwillingness to quit it, seemed to consider it, both by birthright, and by long possession, as their own particular castle, from which no one could lawfully remove them. John Smith used no great ceremony with them, but serving them all with an instantaneous process of ejectment, delivered by divers rapid and severe blows of his hazel cudgel, he forthwith dislodged them from the pond, or fire-place of the kiln, where they were used to find a dry and snug lair, and from which both mother and children retreated with manifest dissatisfaction, and with all manner of sounds and signs of extreme ire. To these John Smith gave but small heed, but, shoving the Pensassenach, blanket and all, with as much tenderness and delicacy as he could, into this their vacant bed-chamber, he concealed her as much as possible by covering her up with straw, and he had hardly accomplished all this, and made his retreat good from the killogie, when a large body of armed Highlanders, under the command of a certain Captain M'Taggart, appeared filing over the neighbouring brow, and with what intent might easily be guessed, from the numerous horses they brought with them, some harnessed in rude carts, and some fitted with panniers or crooked saddles, for carrying off plunder. The men themselves displayed infuriated countenances, and ceased not, as they drew nearer, to give vent to the most horrible denunciations of vengeance against the Pensassenach.

"Ta Pensassenach! ta Penassenach!" cried the same stern voice that had spoken from amid the darkness that surrounded the blazing bonfire of the preceding night. "She sall soon ken fat it is to trink confusion to ta reypells! Far be ta Pensassenach?—ta Englis wife?"

"Ta Pensassenach!—ta pensassenach!—ta heart's blott o' ta Pensassenach!—hang her!—purn her!—troon her!—far is she?—her heart's blott!—her heart's blott!" vociferated some thirty or forty rough and raging voices, coming from men that thirsted revengefully for her blood.

The poor woman's heart almost died within her through fear, as these murderous sounds reached her, where she lay half suffocated under the straw in the killogie. Most active and particular was the search which the Higlanders then commenced. First of all, the captain and some of them proceeded to examine the dwelling-house, and there they were met at the very door by Mr. Dallas the packman. This worthy having been altogether overpowered by his last night's debauch, had thrown himself down in his clothes on the bed hospitably provided for him by his hostess in the room contained in the little out-shot behind, and there he had slept, with his pack as usual under his head, until awaked by the noise made by John Smith and the Pensassenach. He had then witnessed enough to make him aware of the place where the lady was secreted. Seeing that the Highlanders came so suddenly upon them as to

18

make it quite hopeless for him to attempt a retreat, with his lame leg, he hurried away out to the kail-yard and hid his pack under a gousberry bush, an operation which John Smith, as he was flying with his mistress on his back, chanced, with the tail of his eye, to observe him performing. After having done this, Mr. Dallas returned into the house, and, making a virtue of necessity, he stepped boldly forth to meet the leader, when the party came to the door.

" Muckle prosperity till you and your cause, noble captain," said he, making his reverence. " There's a bonny mornin'."

"Who the devil are you, sir?" said Captain M'Taggart, sharply.

" Troth, captain, I'm a poor travellin' chapman," replied Dallas. " I chanced to come here last night, and the guidewife gied me ludgings for Charity's sake."

" Where's your pack, sir ?" demanded Captain M'Taggart."

" Troth, I left it yesterday at Inverness to get some fresh guides pit intil't," replied Dallas.

" You are rather a suspicious character, methinks," said the captain. " See that you search every corner of the main house for this woman," continued he, turning to his men, " and if you find this fellow's pack bring it forth to me."

" There's nae pack o' mine there, captain, an' that's as fack as death," said Dallas. " But ye need hae nae jealousy o' me, for I'm a reyal true and loyal subject o' the Prince."

" Ta Prince ! " cried the same man who had watched the last night's proceedings at the bonfire. " Ta Prince !—ta teevil ;— tat is ta vera chield tat wanted to mak' honest Shon Smiss trink ta helss o' tat teevil ta Tuke o' Cummerlant. He's a reyal and blotty whugg, and weel deserves till hae his craig raxit."

" Hang up the villain directly, then," cried M'Taggart, carelessly.

" Oh ! spare my life, good captain, and I'll tell ye whaur the P—p—p——." *Pensassenach is hid,* were the words that the villain would have uttered, but they were arrested by the ready hand of John Smith, who sprang upon him with the pounce of an eagle, and clutched him up as that noble bird might clutch up a rat, his left arm being half round his middle, and his right hand gripping his throat, in such a manner as to stop all utterance, and nearly to choke him.

" Ta tamm scounrel would fain puy her life for tellin' her fare her pack is," said John, laughing heartily. " But she need na mak' nae siccan pargains wi 'her, for her nane sell saw her hide it under a perry-puss in ta kail-yaird, and a rich

pack it is, she kens tat weel eneugh. See, captain, tats ta way
till ta yaird, and Shon Smiss 'ill tak care o' tis chiel, and pit
her past tooin' ony mair harms, she'll swarrants tat."

Off went the captain and those about him, greedy upon the
scent of the pack, and caring little what became of its owner.
John called to Morag to bring him a sack and some bits
of rope, and he had no sooner got them under one arm than he
ran off with the sprawling Mr. Dallas under the other, who,
having his wind-pipe still tightened by the fearful grasp of him
who bore him, was now kicking in the agonies of death. John
dived through among some peat-stalks, and so managed to get
clear off without observation, to the side of a deep pond or pool,
in a retired spot, where the Pensassenach was wont to steep
her flax. There laying his, by this time, semi-animate burden
at length upon the brink, he put some heavy stones into the
bottom of the sack, and then began to draw it on, like an
under-garment, over the limbs of the unfortunate Mr. Dallas,
inserting his arms therein, and tying the mouth of it tight
round his neck, just as if he had been preparing him for running
in a sack race, though it must be premised, that for such
a purpose the heavy stones might have been well enough left
out of the bottom of the sack.

"Hae mercy on my sowl, Maister Smith, ye're no gawin'
till droon me!" groaned out Mr. Dallas, in a faint, hollow, and
semi-suffocated voice. "Oh, mercy! mercy! what a horrible
death! I'm no fit till dee, Maister Smith. I've been a
horrible sinner. God forgee me for cheating the puir fowk?
Oh, hae mercy, Maister Smith—mercy!—mercy!—for I'm no
fit till dee."

"She no be gawn till mak' her dee," said John, coolly,
"though she wad pe weel wordy o't. But she only be gawn
ta hide her in ta watter tat ta Hillantmen mayna hangit
her."

"Hide me in the water? and is na that droonin'?" cried the
terrified wretch. "Oh, mercy! mercy!"

"Foots, na, man!" said John. "Hidin's no troonin' ava,
ava. She'll come back an' tak' her oot again fan a' is dune,
an' she'll no be a hair ta waur o't. But she maun stop her
gab frae speakin' about ta Pensassenach; an' trots an' she had
been hangit or droonit either, aye, or baith tagedder, she had
been weel wordy o't a', for fat she was gaein' to hae tell't on
ta puir Pensassenach."

By this time John had prepared an effectual gag for his
patient's mouth, which he had made him gape and receive

between his jaws, and then he secured it firmly by tying it behind his neck. He then lifted him up bodily, and while the poor man "aw awed" and "yaw yawed," from the dreadful fear that still possessed him that John's intention, after all, was certainly to drown him, he gradually let down Mr. Dallas's feet into a part of the water, the exact depth of which he perfectly knew would just admit of his immersion up to the neck, he left him, with his head resting safely against the bank on the side of the pool, with some dry rushes and sedges and flax scattered carelessly both over the bank and the water where he was, so as perfectly to conceal him.

Great as was the time that all this occupied, John found, on his return to the farm-house, that it had not been more than sufficient to satisfy Captain M'Taggart and his friends, in their examination of Mr. Dallas's pack, and in the' division of the rich booty it contained. Meanwhile, the search for the Pensassenach was going on keenly and most unremittingly, and John was relieved to find that it was so, since he was thereby satisfied that, as yet at least, her place of concealment had not been discovered. They opened every door, and looked into every corner, for the unfortunate lady, still swearing all the time the bloodiest oaths of vengeance against her. Not a house upon the premises, not a hole nor crevice about the whole place did they pass unexamined, save and except only the eye of the ruined killogie itself, where the object of their search was in reality concealed. Frequently, to the almost complete annihilation of the action of the pulses of her heart, did she hear the footsteps of some of them passing close beside the place where she lay, as well as their curses, as they went. But so completely were they deceived by the ruined appearance of the roofless killogie, that they never once thought of the possibility of any one being concealed there. Wearied at length with their ineffectual search, and believing that the Pensassenach had fled, they began to wreak their rage, and to glut their rapacity, by plundering her effects. Meal, butter, cheese, beef, and bacon, were crammed indiscriminately into sacks, with articles of wearing apparel, and the blankets, and the webs of cloth and linen which the thrifty housewife had prepared for her household. Articles of silver plate were not forgotten, as well as all other valuables upon which they could lay their rapacious hands. The cellar was broken open and ransacked, and its contents, as well as many other pieces of plunder of a bulky nature, were stowed away to be carried off in the carts belonging to the farm. A general assault then

commenced upon the live stock. John Smith's zealous precaution had secured the greater part of the larger animals
from their clutches, but the attack on the poultry was simul-
taneous and terrific. Loud was the cackling, gobbling, and
quacking of the fowls, turkeys, ducks, and geese, as they were
caught, one after another; and fearful was it to hear their
music suddenly silenced, by their necks being drawn, and
melancholy to behold their inanimate bodies thrown into the
hampers that hung on the crook-saddled horses. The good
Morag's heart was rent, as she beheld these ruthless murders
committed upon the innocent creatures whom she had delighted
to rear. But honest John Smith comforted himself with the
reflection, that he had saved all the weightier and more valuable stock, and therefore he witnessed all these ravages among
the feathered folk with tolerable composure, until a circumstance occurred which renewed all his apprehensions for the
safety of his mistress, and again excited him to the full exertion
of all his energies.

War had not been long commenced against the poultry,
when the large sow, alarmed by the murders she beheld going
on around her, and terrified by the loud hurrahs of the plun-
derers, as well as scared by the sudden striking up of the
bagpipes, took to flight in good time, and made straight for the
eye of the killogie, at the head of her troop. The quick-sighted
John Smith at once perceived the risk which his mistress, the
Pensassenach, ran of being discovered, by the animals making
this attempt to find shelter there. Off he flew like the wind
to intercept them; and cutting in before them with great
adroitness, he turned them right away towards the fragment
of meadow, which lay in the close vicinity of the black bog.
John played his part so well that this manœuvre of his had all
the appearance as if he had been merely making a dash at them
for the purpose of catching some of them, and that the creatures
had for the present foiled him. There they were accordingly
left at peace for a time, during which John's mind also remained
in some degree tranquil and at ease.

But the sow and her inviting family were not long in being
descried by the Highlanders, after every other living thing had
been sacked by them, and a most eventful, hazardous, and very
ludicrous chase after them immediately took place. Full of
the most anxious apprehensions as to the result, John planted
himself in front of the killogie, and between it and the scene of
action; and as all the old sow's efforts were directed towards
her stronghold in the kiln, it was with the greatest difficulty

that he repeatedly succeeded in driving her from the dangerous
post. At length, by one exertion, greater than the rest, he
had the good fortune to force the sow once more fairly a-field
again, with all her grunting young ones running scattering
after her, whilst the Highlanders, deceived by his shouting to
them in Gaelic, and encouraging them to the pursuit, believed
that he had no other object in view than honestly to aid them
in catching her. To bind them still more, he now started off
full tilt at the head of them, and soon outran the swiftest of
them. With amazing dexterity, he first clutched up one pig,
and then another, until he had one in each hand, swinging by
the tail, and squeaking so fearfully as to excite the maternal
anxiety and rage of the sow mother, to so great an extent, that
she followed him, fast and furiously grunting, wheresoever he
turned. John inwardly chuckled at the thought of having
thus got so easily and so perfectly the command of her motions.
But a sudden onset from the Highlanders speedily dispersed
the remainder of her progeny; and the pursuers naturally
scattered themselves to follow after individual grunters, so that
the race was seen to rage over all parts of the field. This
distracted the attention of the old sow, and she went cantering
about, hither and thither, like a frantic creature, until; by
degrees, she found herself at the very farthest end of the bog.
There, seized by a panic, she suddenly turned, and bolted
desperately back again, with her snout pointed directedly
towards the kiln. Winged by terror, she pushed wildly on at
a bickering pace, and running her head right between John's
legs ere ever he wist, she carried him off for several yards,
horsed upon her back, with his face to the tail; and in the
blindness of her alarm, she ran headlong with him into a
great peat-pot, where he was instantly launched all his length
among the black chaotic fluid which it contained. John
scrambled out of the hole with some difficulty, and, starting to
his legs, and shaking his ears like a water-spaniel, and clearing
the dirt from his eyes, he, to his great horror, beheld the sow
scouring away as hard as she could gallop, in a direct course
for that chamber in the killogie, which prescriptive right had so
long made her believe to be her own. John saw her hurrying
thither, pursued by one or two of the Highlanders. It was
evident that she must soon reach it; and he felt certain that
she would instantly dart in among the straw where the Pensassenach was lying, and that so the lady must be exposed to
certain discovery, and consequently to instant death. What
was to be done? Not a moment was to be lost. Taking

With amazing dexterity he first clutched up one Pig and then another.—Page 262.

advantage of a double which the sow was compelled to make, in consequence of some one having headed her course, and which forced her to swerve considerably from the straight line of the chase, John seized a gun from the hand of a Highlander near him, and aiming at the animal as she thus presented her great broadside to him, he fired at her, and rolled her over and over, by a bullet that passed through her very heart. There she lay dead before her pursuers, within some thirty or forty yards of her perilous place of refuge. A shout of applause at so wonderful a shot arose from all who witnessed it.

"Tat's ta learn her, mockel fusome beast tat she is, for tummelin Shon Smiss inta ta peat-hole!" cried John, infinitely relieved from all his terrors.

The pigs were now very speedily secured in detail, and the great sow was dragged up to the farm-house, and quietly deposited, with her slaughtered family, in one of the carts.

"My brave fellow!" said Captain M'Taggart, the leader of the party, now advancing towards John, and shaking him heartily by the hand, "you must come along with us. A young man, so handsome, so active, so spirited, and so soldierly-looking,—and, above all, so capital a shot as you are,—was never intended by nature to hold the stilts of a plough, or to fill dung-carts. You were born to be an officer at the very least, and, for aught I know, to be a colonel or a general. We are already aware that you are staunch to the righteous cause of the true Prince. Now is the time for you to raise yourself in the world, by joining his royal standard. Come, then, and lend us your powerful aid in placing our lawful King upon the throne of his ancestors! Come along with us, and I shall forthwith introduce you to Prince Charles, who may yet make a lord of you before you die."

John Smith was, in truth, all that M'Taggart had called him, being a handsome, good looking man, as brave as a lion, and not altogether devoid of a certain natural ambition. But he was ignorant, thoughtless, and credulous, owing to his having been, up to that day, entirely without experience. He had never before seen anything like military array, and irregular and deficient, in many respects, as that was which he now beheld, still it was enough to captivate his unpractised eye. John had a strong attachment to his master and mistress, who had always been very kind to him. But his devotion to the Prince, whom he had never seen, was of a higher and holier order. Bestowing a few moments of reflection on the ceaseless and profitless plodding, and slavish drudgery of his present duties, all, in themselves, absolutely repugnant to the very nature of a Highlander, and comparing them with the ideal picture he had drawn to himself, of the gallant, gentlemanlike service of the Prince, whose soldiers, he believed, had not only daily opportunities of enriching themselves with honourable plunder,—a small specimen of which he had just witnessed—but who had the prospect opened to them of one day becoming great men, the contrast was by far too flattering in favour of the latter not to dazzle him. But if it had not had that effect, the promise which M'Taggart made him of introducing him to Prince Charles, the son of the true and legitimate King of Scotland, was enough of itself to have gained John's consent in a moment.

"Ou, troth, she'll no be lang o' gangin' wi' her," said John, "an she'll but stop till she clean hersel' a wee frae ta durt o' ta fulthy bog, tat ta soo beast pat her intill,—and syne bids fareweel to ta leddy."

"Whoo!" exclaimed M'Taggart. "The lady! What, then, the Pensassenach is somewhere about the place after all, and you know where she is? By holy St. Mary, but I will burn every house here, and force the rancorous whig she-devil to unkennel out of her hiding place!"

"Teel purn her nanesell's fooliss tongue for namin' ta leddy ava ava!" said John bitterly. "But she may e'en purn ta hale toon gin she likes—fint a bit o' ta leddy can she purn."

"Ha, my good fellow," said M'Taggart, "since you have the secret knowledge of her place of concealment locked up in your bosom, what is to hinder me to use a thumbikin as a key to unlock it. I have a great mind to try."

"She may e'en puts ta toomkin on her nanesell's neck, and she'll no tell after a'," said John resolutely. "And ponny pounties tat wad be surely for Shon Smiss to serve ta Prince."

"Nay, my good fellow, I was only joking," said M'Taggart, afraid to lose so good a volunteer; "trust me I meant you no harm."

"Gin she purns ta toon, or gin she do ony mair ill aboot ta place, fouk wull be sayin' tat Shon Smiss bid her do it," continued John—"an tat wad be doin' Shon mockell harm. Teevil ae stap wull Shon be gangin' wi' her at a' at a', and she do ony mair bad sings here."

"Well well," said M'Taggart, soothing him, "go in and dress yourself, and make your mind easy; and the sooner we are away from here the better."

John thought so too.   He ran to the stable for his *breachcan;**
put on his best coat, kilt, and hose ; tied up his only two shirts,
and a spare pair of hose, in a napkin, and placed the bundle
into the fold of his plaid ; and then seizing a trusty old broad-
sword, he put on his new Sunday's bonnet, smartly cocked up,
—and he strode so erectly forth to M'Taggart, and with so
martial an air, that, added to the wonderful change created in
his personal appearance by his dress, made the captain hesitate
for a moment in believing him to be the same man.

"She be ready noo," said John ; "put fare be ta rest o' ta
men, Captain?"

"They are hunting the Pensassenach," replied M'Taggart
with a careless laugh.

"She pe verra idle loons tan," said John, "for gin she wad
seek a' tay she wad na' find her."   And then, by way of
diverting the Captain's attention from the search by a joke, he
pointed to Morag, who stood at the door, weeping bitterly at
the prospect of his departure, and added,—"see, tat pe ta
Pensassenach."

"That the Pensassenach!" said M'Taggart.   "That's a good
joke truly.   I know well enough that's not the Pensassenach
that we are after."

"She pe a verra ponny Pensassenach," said John, going up
to Morag, and hastily delivering to her, in a Gaelic whisper,
directions how and when she should relieve her mistress from
her confinement, and also where she was to look for the packman, that she might get him taken out of the water.

"That Pensassenach seems to be a favourite of yours, John,"
said the Captain.

"She wunna say put she is," replied John, his heart filling a
little with sympathy for Morag's tears, and at the prospect of
leaving her.   "Petter tak tiss Pensassenach wi' huss,"—and
then, rather as a parting word of kindness than anything else,
he added, "Will she go, Morag?"

This was too much for poor Morag.   Her heart was too full
for her to command words to reply.   She rushed forward, and
threw her arms around John.   She fixed her hands into the
folds of that breachcan, in which, in their days of *herding*, when
she was but a lassie, and he but a boy, she had been so often
wrapped by her lover as a shelter from the stormy elements,
and she gave way to a burst of grief that at length enabled her
to find utterance for her feelings.   She implored him, in all the

* Plaid.

anguish of despair, not to leave her. John's heart was softened by her words, and her tears, and he blubbered like a child. M'Taggart, fearing that the martial influence in John's soul might be overpowered and extinguished by that of love, and setting a much greater value on him as a recruit, than on the capture of the Pensassenach, he thought it advisable to put an end to this tender interview as speedily as might be. He ordered the piper to play up therefore, and the men, abandoning their fruitless search after the English wife, were speedily gathered around him. The train of carts and horses, with the plunder, were driven on—the order of march was formed. John, after a severe struggle with his heart, rent himself away from the arms of Morag, and followed M'Taggart, without daring to speak, or to look behind him ; whilst the poor girl, bereft of her support, fell upon the green—where she lay beating her breast and tearing her hair in utter despair, till the sound of the distant pipe died away, and the presence of some of her fellow-servants brought her back to her reason.

Morag was no sooner sufficiently calm and collected, than she hastened to execute John Smith's last injunctions. The poor Pensassenach was taken from the killogie more dead than alive. Morag would have had her to go to bed, but, having recovered herself a little, she became too much excited to rest; and, having arranged her dress, she began to bustle about her affairs, and to take a full note of her loss. It was, indeed, severe. But she felt that she endured it for a glorious cause, and that reflection made her bear it with wonderful philosophy. She was grieved, and even angry to learn that John Smith had enlisted with the Prince's men, but she felt deeply grateful to him for having saved her life ; and especially so, when she heard from Morag the story of the packman's treachery, and John's ingenuity in defeating it, as well as of the whole of his exertions for her preservation.

" Where has John bestowed the villain ?" demanded the Pensassenach.

" Toon in ta lint pot, mem," replied Morag ; " I maun gang toon an get him oot o' ta hole noo."

" I'll go with you, Morag," said the Pensassenach ; and so mistress and maid proceeded together towards the pond. " What noise is that ?" cried the Pensassenach, as they drew near to it.

" Aw—yaw !—yaw—aw !" cried the packman from the pool.

" Where are you, wretched man ?" cried the Pensassenach.

" Yaw—aw !—yaw—aw !" replied Mr. Dallas.

" Why don't you speak distinctly ?" demanded the lady.

" Aw—aw !—yaw—aw !" replied Dallas again.

" The sound would seem to come from under that loose heap of rushes at the margin of the pool yonder," said the Pensassenach.

Oich aye, she's here mem," cried Morag, removing the covering from the packman's head.

" Yaw—aw !—aw—aw !" cried Dallas, raising his eyes with an expression of intense agony.

" Ah, I see how it is," said the Pensassenach ; " John has gagged him, to prevent his vile tongue from betraying me. Loosen that string, Morag, and take out the gag."

" Oh, Heeven be praised that I hae fand freends at last," cried the packman in a hoarse voice. " Hech, my jaws are stiff, stiff, and sair, sair, wi that plaguit bit o' a rung that John Smith pat into my mooth. Hech me ! kind souls that ye are, pu' me oot, pu' me oot o' this, or I maun e'en drap awthegither owerhead into the pool, for I haena mair poor to stand on this ae leg o' mine, and I canna rest ony at a' on the short ane, mind ye, without sinkin' my mooth below the water. Och, mem, pu' me oot !"

" How can you ask me to assist you, base wretch that you are ?" cried the Pensassenach ; " you who would have sold my life to have saved your own. I shall push you as gently under the water as I can, but drowned you must be."

" Oh, for the love o' Heeven hae mair charity !" cried the packman most piteously. " I'm a sad sinner, nae doot. But I'm a puir, wake, nervish craytur,—and fan that deevil incarnate, Captain M'Taggart, spak o' hangin' me, my brains whurled sae i' my head, that I didna ken what I was sayin'. But I'm sure I never thocht o' doin' harm till you or ony o' your hoose. Pu' me oot, mem ; pu' me oot for the love o' Heeven, or the very life 'll leave my legs wi' cauld."

" Pull you out," exclaimed the Pensassenach ; " pull you out,—you who would have helped the Highlanders to my murder : pull you out, who wilfully spoke treason, to aid, abet, and comfort the rebel Captain. My loyalty to my King and my country forbids me to assist you, and compels me to make a sacrifice of you immediately. So, prepare for instant death."

" Och, hae mercy on my puir sowl," cried the packman in despair ; " surely, surely, ye're no gawin' till droun me ?"

" What can you say in exculpation of your treason ?" demanded the Pensassenach, laying hold of the upper part of the sack with both her hands, and giving Mr. Dallas a gentle shake.

"Och, naething—naething ava," cried Mr. Dallas. "Oh, I'm a dead man—a dead man : hae mercy—hae mercy upon me. I'm a great sinner—a wicked, and hardened sinner."

"Perhaps it were well to allow you a few moments, wretch that you are, to confess your sins and repent, before you are sent into the other world," said the Pensassenach. "So make haste—lose not the fleeting space of time which I thus mercifully grant to you, and lighten your soul of as much load as you can."

"Oh, hae mercy—hae mercy on me!" cried Dallas.

"I'll have no mercy on you, more than this," cried the Pensassenach in a terrible voice. "If you will not confess yourself, your last moment is at hand;" and so saying, she ducked Mr. Dallas's head under the water.

"O! O! O! Oh!—hech! ech!" cried Mr. Dallas, panting for breath; "I'm a dead man! I'm a dead man! Oh, Lord forgie me for sellin' pastes for precious stanes."

"Come! is that all?" cried the Pensassenach, shaking him again.

"Hae mercy on me for sellin' rock crystal for diamunts," cried Dallas.

"Come! out with it all!" said the Pensassenach.

"Och! Och! Forgie me for sellin' bits o' ayster shells for pearls," cried Dallas again, "and pinchbeck for gold; and watches wi' worn out auld warks for new anes."

"Come! nothing else to confess?" said the Pensassenach.

"Oh, yes. Heaven help me, and hae mercy on me, for keepin' fause weights and a fause ell-wand," cried Dallas.

"Are these all your sins, villain?" exclaimed the Pensassenach.

"Oh, hey, aye, aye," said Dallas piteously, "and ower muckle, gude kens."

"Well, then," said the Pensassenach, taking a more determined grasp of the sack; "now, that you have duly confessed, here goes."

"Oh, stop, stop!" cried Dallas, in great fear. "Stop, stop! no yet! no yet! I hae mair to tell o' yet. I hae noo an' then picked up an odd silver spoon, or sae, or ony siccan wee article whan it came in my way, just tempin' me like, in ony o' the hooses whaur I had quarters. But I never was a great tief—no, no."

"'Twas you belike who stole my silver punch-ladle," said the Pensassenach. "I missed it immediately after you were last here."

"I canna just charge my memory wi' the punch-ladle," said Mr. Dallas, unwilling to admit that he had in any way wronged the Pensassenach.

"Nay, then, your thefts must have been too numerous for you to note such a trifling item as that," said the Pensassenach; "but it is clear you did steal my punch-ladle, so now you shall die for not confessing. Now!"

"Oh, stop, stop, for mercy's sake!" cried Dallas, in livid apprehension. "I mind noo! I mind noo! I did tak' it— I did tak' the ladle! It shined sae tempin' through the glass door o' the bit corner cupboard, and the door was open, sae that I may amaist say that the devil himsel' handed it oot till me, and pat it intil my very pack. But I'll never wrang you ony mair."

"I'll take good care you shall not," said the lady; "you shall never wrong me, nor any one else more. So now, prepare, for this is your last moment."

"Oh, mercy, mercy," cried the packman again. "I hae mair yet to confess! Oh, dinna droun me just yet!"

"Well, be quick," said the Pensassenach; "what more have ye to tell?"

"Oh, mercy, mercy!" cried Dallas. "That woman that I telled ye o' yestreen; that woman that I clippit out o' the Spey wasna just awthegither dead ——"

"What!" exclaimed the Pensassenach, in horror; "wretch that you are, did you murder the woman?"

"Eh, na, na!" cried Dallas; "ill as I am, I didna do that. I just took her roklay and her gown, and some ither wee things aperteenin' till her, and syne I gaed aff wi' mysel', leaving her to come roond to life at her nain leisure and convenience."

"Leaving her to die without help you mean, you murdering thief!" said the Pensassenach, shrinking back with horror from the very touch of him. "Wretch, you are unworthy of life! But I shall not be your executioner. You will grace a gallows yet, I'll warrant you. I shall now leave Morag to pull you out of the way. But hark ye, Mr. Dallas, before I leave you I may as well tell you that though I have spared your life, as indeed I never had the least intention of taking it, I advise you never to darken my door again; for, if you do, I promise you that you shall have another and a deeper taste of this lint-pot."

"Oh, bless you, mem!" cried Mr. Dallas, with an earnestness which showed how much he was relieved by her words; "I'll never come within five miles o' your farm. Noo, Morag, my dawty," continued he, addressing the maid after the mistress was gone; "gudesake, woman, be quick an' pu' me oot; or, as sure as death, I'll dee o't awthegither."

"Fawse loons tat she is," said Morag, looking terribly at him. "She will no pu' her oot; she wull pit her toon in ta hole, an' troon her! She is a wicked vullian—she wull pit her toon in ta hole an' troon her wissout nae mercy at a' at a'."

"Oh!" cried the terrified Dallas, with his eyeballs again starting from his head with apprehension. "Oh, dinna droun me, noo that your mistress has spared me! I was ragin' fu' wi' brandy last nicht, and I didna ken what I was doin'; and maybe I was a wee unceevil till ye, or the like. But oh, hae mercy, hae mercy on me!"

"She'll no be ta waur o' a gude tooky tan," said Morag, seizing the sack and plunging the gasping Mr. Dallas two or three times successively under the water; "tat 'll cool ta hot speerits in her stamick, or she pe far mistane."

"Oh! O! O! Och! hech! och! oh!—O!" cried Dallas, gasping and panting. "O, mercy, mercy! an' I hadna drucken a' yon oceans o' brandy yester nicht I had assuredly been a dead man this day, just frae very cauld itsel'. But the brandy o' yestreen has saved me frae a' the water that my body has imbibit frae this nasty lint-pot by actuwully makin' a kind o' wake punch o' me. Oh, gude lassie that ye are, pu' me oot, pu' me oot!"

"Its mair nor she's weel deservin'," said Morag, now putting forth all her strength to pull the sack and its contents up out of the water; "but Morag canna let a man be trooned an she can help it, pad man so she pe."

Having hauled up the sack, she laid it upon the grass, undid the fastenings of its mouth, and with some difficulty extricated Mr. Dallas from its durance vile. The worthy packman arose to his feet, and, shaking himself heartily, and stretching out first his short and then his long leg two or three times alternately, to relieve that killing cold cramp which possessed them, he hobbled off without uttering a word of thanks, and shivering so that his teeth were rattling in his head as if his jaws had contained a corps of drummers beating the rogue's march. Morag looked after him with a hearty laugh, and then picking up the wet sack she hastened to join her mistress.

Let us now follow the march of John Smith.

COMFORTS OF A LONDON CLUB-HOUSE.

Author.—Pray, stop for one moment, Mr. Macpherson, if you please. Let me throw a few more peats on the fire. With the rain still beating thus without, and the picture of the half-drowned shivering chapman brought so vividly before our mind's eyes by your description, we shall have our teeth rattling in our jaws from very sympathy if we don't keep up the caloric we have already generated.

Grant.—It is right not to allow it to be too much reduced, certainly; but I declare I am as comfortable here in Inchrory as if I were in my club-house in London.

Clifford.—Much more so, my good fellow, take my word for it. Where is the London club-house in which we could have been so quiet as we are here, especially in such weather as this. Think of the noise in the streets; think, I say, of the eternal thunder of the carriages of all kinds, the hackney-coaches, stage-coaches, omnibuses, and cabs, with the Cherokee yelling and whooping of the drivers, uttering strange and horrible oaths; and, to complete the instrumental part of this mechanical concert, to have it grounded with the grating double bass of the huge carts, drays, and waggons. The mellow rear of the Aven is like the soft music of a flute compared to so terrific a combination of ear-rending sounds. Then think of the crowd of dull and damp fellows, dry to talk to but wet enough to the touch, who are continually coming in and going out, restless and unhappy—miserable when condemned to the house, and yet more wretched when out in the rain—giving you hopes of enjoying a glimpse of the fire at one moment, and then shutting you out entirely from it at the next, with persons so steeped as to make the very evaporation from their bodies by the heat fill the room with clouds of steam—talking and chattering and recognising each other—disputing about politics, or the merits of the last opera, or opera singer, or ballet, or dancer. In vain you try to have some rational talk with some sensible man, or to listen to something of the greatest possible interest which he has to tell you—for you have hardly begun so to do when up comes some fool of a fellow who, at some unfortunate time or another, has sworn eternal friendship to you, and who now, to your great discomfiture as well as to the imminent peril of your good temper and manners, breaks boisterously in upon your *tête-a-tête* to prove to you how well he keeps his oath by nearly shaking your hand off, or perhaps dislocating your shoulder, by loudly protesting how rejoiced he is to see you, and by most heroically sacrificing himself and his own valuable time in kindly bestowing his fullest tediousness upon you that he may give you the whole history of his life since he last saw you. Then suppose you sit down to read some important speech, or leading article, in your favourite newspaper, or something which you wish to devour out of some much-talked-of pamphlet or review of the day, it is ten to one but you experience a similar interruption from some such kind and much attached friend. But the height of your misery is only attained when you come to take refuge in the writing-room in order to write a letter of more than ordinary importance, and requiring great care in the arrangement of its subject as well as in the choice of its expressions. Then it is that among those employed at the different tables you are certain to find some two or more idle scribblers, who go not there really to write, but who, notwithstanding, waste more of the writing materials belonging to the club than all the rest of its members put together in order to give themselves importance by an affectation of much business and high correspondence. Amongst these there is probably one who, after allowing you to get down to the bottom of your first page and fairly into your subject, suddenly, and as if accidentally, descries you, and rushing across to salute you, rivets himself on the floor close to your chair, and goes on ear-wigging you with his important secrets, whilst he is all the time curiously drinking in your's from your half-written letter which lies open before him. Or, if you should have the good fortune to escape from such a jackal as this, then you may find the other men of his kidney, who may be sitting at the different tables with the affectation of writing, carrying on such a battery of loud talk across the room as altogether to distract your attention. In vain do you try to control your thoughts within their proper current. They are continually jostled aside by some half-caught sentence, which sets your mind working in some wrong direction, merely to have it again driven off at a tangent into some other which is equally foreign to that subject to which you would confine it. In vain do you rub your brow, cover your eyes, and gnaw your pen; every thought but the right thought is forced upon you, until at last, in utter despair, you start to your feet, snatch up your blotted and often corrected letter, tear it into shreds, commit it to the flames, and, seizing your hat, you abruptly hurry homewards, duly execrating, as you go, all club-houses, and those many men of annoyance with which clubs are so universally afflicted.

Grant.—Your picture is a lively one, Clifford, and in its general features most just. Though our London clubs have many advantages this lonely house of Inchrory is certainly better for our present purpose.

Author.—Gentlemen, unless you mean to enact here the part of some of those London club-annoyance-givers, which you, Clifford, have so well described, I think you had better drop your conversation and allow Mr. Macpherson to proceed with his story.

Clifford.—I stand corrected ;—then allow me to light a fresh cigar ; and now, Mr. Macpherson, pray go on with Serjeant John Smith.

THE LEGEND OF SERJEANT JOHN SMITH'S ADVENTURES CONTINUED.

You will remember, gentlemen, that when I was interrupted I was about to follow John Smith on his march with Captain M'Taggart. Well, you see, Prince Charles Edward chanced to be at this time at Kilravock Castle, the ancient seat of the Roses. Thither the sagacious captain thought it good policy to present himself with the motley company, the greater number of the individuals of which he had himself collected. There he received his due meed of praise for his zeal, with large promises of future preferment for his energetic exertions in the Prince's cause. But although the Captain thus took especial care to serve himself in the first place, he made a point of strictly keeping his own promise to John Smith, for he did present him to the Prince along with some five or six other recruits whom he had cajoled to follow him somewhat in the way he had cajoled John. But this their presentation was more with a view of enhancing the value of his own zeal and services for his own private ends than for the purpose or with the hope of benefiting them in any way. The Prince came out to the lawn with M'Taggart and some of his own immediate attendants. The men were presented to him by name, and John Smith was especially noticed by him. He spoke to each of them in succession, and then clapping John familiarly on the shoulder—

" My brave fellows," said he, " you have a glorious career before you. The enemy advances into our very hands. I trust we shall soon have an opportunity of fighting together

19

side by side. Meanwhile, go, join the gallant army which I have so lately left at Culloden, eagerly waiting the approach of our foes. I shall see you very soon, and I shall not forget you." So saying he took off his Highland bonnet, and, whilst a gentle zephyr sported and played with his fair curls, he bowed gracefully to the men, and then retired into the house.

"She's fichts to ta last trap o' her bluids for ta ponny Princey!" cried John, with an enthusiasm which was cordially responded to by shouts from all present.

M'Taggart then gave the word, and the party wheeled off on their march in the direction of Inverness, in the vicinity of which town the Prince's army was encamped. Their way lay down through the parish of Petty, and past Castle-Stuart. As they moved on, they were everywhere loudly cheered by the populace—men, women, and children, who turned out to meet them, and showered praises and blessings upon them; and this friendly welcome seemed to await them all along their route, till they joined the main body of their forces, which lay about and above the mansion house of Culloden.

John Smith would have much preferred to have placed himself under the standard of the Macintosh, whom the Smiths or Gows, the descendants of the celebrated Gowin Cromb, who fought on the Inch of Perth, held to be their chief, as head of the Clan-Chattan. But M'Taggart was unwilling to lose the personal support of so promising a soldier. Perhaps also he began to feel a certain interest in the young man; and he accordingly advised him to stick close to him at all times.

"Stick you by me, John," said he—"stick you close by my side; I shall then be able to see what you do, as well as to give a fair and honest, and I trust not unfavourable report of the gallant deeds which your brave spirit may prompt you to perform. Depend upon it, with my frequent opportunities of obtaining access to the Prince, I can do as much good for you, at least, as any Macintosh."

On the night of the 14th of April then, John Smith lay with M'Taggart and his company, among the whin and juniper bushes in the wood of Culloden, where the greater part of the Jacobite army that night disposed of themselves. Whatever might have been the ill-provided state of the other portions of the Prince's troops, that with which John was now consorted, had no reason to complain of any want of those refreshments which human nature requires, and which are so important to soldiers. Large fires were speedily kindled; and the Pensassenach's great sow, with all her little pigs, and the poor woman's poultry of all kinds, together with some few similar delicacies which had elsewhere been picked up here and there, were soon divided, and prepared to undergo such rude cookery as each individual could command; and these, with the bread and cheese, and other such provisions, which they had carried off from the Pensassenach, as well as from some other houses, enabled them to spread for themselves what might be called a verra liberal table in the wilderness. But the savoury odour which their culinary operations diffused around, brought hungry Highlanders from every quarter of the wood, like wolves upon them, so that each man of their party was fain to gobble up as much as he could swallow in haste, lest he should fail to secure to himself enough to satisfy his hunger, ere the whole feast should disappear under the active jaws of those intruders. The liquor was more under their own control. The flask was allowed to circulate through the hands of those only to whom it most properly belonged by the right of capture. John, for his part, had a good tasse of the Pensassenach's brandy; and the smack did not seem to savour the worse, within his lips, because it was prefaced with the toast of—"Success to the Prince, and confusion to the Duke of Cumberland!"

After this their refreshment, the men and officers disposed themselves to sleep around the fires of their bivouac, each in a natural bed of his own selection, John Smith, being a pious young man, retired under the shelter of a large juniper bush, and having there offered up his evening prayer to God, he wrapped himself up in his plaid, and consigned himself to sleep. How long he had slept he knew not; when, as he turned in his lair to change his position, his eye caught a dim human figure, which floated, as it were, in the air, stiff and erect, immediately under the high projecting limb of a great fir tree, that grew at some twenty paces distant from the spot where he lay. The figure seemed to have a preternatural power of supporting itself; and as the breeze wailed and moaned through the boughs, it appeared alternately to advance and to recede again with a slow tremulous motion. John's heart, stout as it was against everything of earthly mould, began to beat quick, and finally to thump against his very ribs, with all manner of superstitious fears. He gazed and trembled, without the power of rising, which he would have fain done, not for the purpose of investigating the mystery, but to take the wiser course of looking out for some other place of repose, where he might hope to escape from the appalling contemplation of this strange and most unaccountable apparition. He lay staring then at it in a cold sweat of fright, whilst the faint glimmering light from the nearest fire, as it rose or fell, now made it somewhat more visible, and now again somewhat more dim. At length, an accidental fall of some of the half burnt fuel, sent up a transient gleam that fully illuminated the ghastly countenance of the spectre, when, to John's horror, he recognised the pale and corpse-like features of Mr. William Dallas, the packman, whom he had left so ingeniously inserted into the sack, and deposited in the Pensassenach's lint-pot. Though the gag was gone, the mouth was wide open, and the large, protruded, and glazed eye-balls, glared fearfully upon him. Though the light was not sufficient to display the figure correctly, John's fancy made him vividly behold the sack. He would have spoken if he could ; but he felt that the apparition of the murdered man was floating before him. His throat grew dry of a sudden. He gasped—but could not utter a word. He doubted not that the packman had been forgotten by Morag, and that, having fallen down into the water through cold and exhaustion, the wretch had·at last miserably perished ; and he came very naturally to the conclusion that he who had put the unfortunate man there, was now doomed to be henceforth continually haunted by his ghost. Fain would he have shut out this horrible sight, by closing his eyes, or by drawing his plaid over them ; but this he was afraid to do, lest the object of his dread should swim towards him through the air, and congeal his very life's-blood by its freezing touch. Much as he loved Morag, he had some difficulty in refraining from inwardly cursing her for her supposed neglect of his express injunctions to relieve the packman from the pool. As he stared on this dreadful apparition, the flickering gleam from the faggot sunk again, and the countenance again grew dim ; but John seemed still to see it in all its intensity of illumination. No more rest had he that night. Still, as he gazed on the figure, he again and again fancied that he saw it gradually and silently gliding nearer and nearer to him. The only relief he had was in fervent and earnest prayers, which he confusedly murmured, from time to time, in Gaelic. He eagerly petitioned for daylight, hoping that the morning air might remove all such unrealities from the earth. At length, the eastern horizon began to give forth the partial glimmer of dawn ; but John was somewhat surprised to find, that, instead of the apparition fading away before it, the outlines of its horrible figure became gradually more and more distinct as it advanced, until ·even the features were by degrees rendered visible. But although John, by this time, began to discover that his fancy had supplied the sack, he now perceived something which he had not been able to see before, and that was a thin rope which hung down from the horizontal limb of the fir tree, and suspended, by its lower extremity, the body of the poor packman by the neck. John was much shocked by this discovery. But he could not help thanking God that he was thus acquitted of the wretched man's death; and after the misery that he had suffered from the supposed presence of the apparition of a man who had been drowned through his means, however innocently, the relief he now experienced was immense. He called up some of his comrades to explain the mystery; and from them he learned that Mr. Dallas had been caught in the early part of the night, in the very act of attempting to carry off Captain M'Taggart's horse from its piquet, and that he had been instantly tucked up to the bough of the fir tree, without even the ceremony of a trial.

The young Prince Charley was in the field by an early hour on the morning of the 15th, and being all alive to the critical nature of his circumstances, and by no means certain as yet how near the enemy might by this time be to him, he judged it important to collect, and to draw up his army on the most favourable ground he could find in the neighbourhood. He therefore marched them up the high, partly flattish, and partly sloping ridge, which, though commonly called Culloden Moor, from its being situated immediately above the house and grounds of that place, has in reality the name of Drummossie. He led them to a part of this ground, a little to the south eastward of their previous position in the wood of Culloden, and there he drew them up in order of battle. There they were most injudiciously kept lying on their arms the whole day, and if Captain M'Taggart's men had feasted tolerably well the previous night, there commons were anything but plentiful during the time they occupied that position. It was not in the nature of things that subordination could be so strictly preserved in the Prince's army, as it was in that of the Duke of Cumberland. I, who am well practeesed in the discipline of boys, gentlemen, know very well that it would be impossible to bring a regiment of them under immediate command, if the individuals composing it were to be collected together all at once, raw and untaught, from different parts of the district, It is only by bringing one or two at a time, into the already great disciplined mass, that either a schoolmaster or a field-

marischal can promise to have his troops always well under
control. By the time evening came, the officers, as well as the
men of the Prince's army, began to suffer under the resistless
orders of a commander to whom no human being can say nay.
Hunger, I may say, was rugging at their verra hearts, and as
they all saw, or supposed that they saw, reason to believe that
there was no chance of the enemy coming upon them that night,
many of them went off to Inverness and elsewhere, in search
of food. M'Taggart himself could not resist those internal
admonitions, which his stomach was so urgently giving him
from time to time, and accordingly John Smith conceived he
was guilty of no great dereliction of duty, in strictly following
the first order which his captain had given him, viz., to "stick
by his side," which he at once resolved to do, as he saw him go
off to look for something to support nature.

But the captain and his man had hardly got a quarter of a
mile on the road to Inverness, when they, with other stragglers,
were called back by a mounted officer, who was sent, with all
speed, after them, to tell them that they must return, in order
to march immediately. The object of their march was that ill-
conceived, worse managed, and most unlucky expedition for a
night attack on the Duke of Cumberland's camp at Nairn,
which had that evening been so hastily planned. Hungry as
they were they had no choice but to obey, and accordingly they
hurried to their standards. The word was given, and after
having been harassed by marching all night, without food or
refreshment of any kind, they at last got only near enough to
Nairn just to enable them to discover that day must infallibly
break before they could reach the enemy's camp, and that consequently no surprise could possibly take place. Disheartened
by this failure, they were led back to their ground, where they
arrived in so very faint and jaded a condition, that even to go
in search of food was beyond their strength, so that they sank
down in irregular groups over the field, and fell asleep for a
time. Awakened by hunger after a very brief slumber, they
arose to forage. M'Taggart, and some of his party, and John
Smith amongst the rest, went prowling across the river Nairn,
which ran to the south of their position, and there they caught
and killed a sheep. They soon managed to kindle a fire, and
to subdivide the animal into fragments, but ere each man had
time to broil his morsel, an alarm was given from their camp.
Like ravenous savages they tore up and devoured as much of
the half raw flesh as haste would allow them to swallow, and
hurrying back they reached their post about eight o'clock in

the morning, when they found that the Duke of Cumberland was approaching with his army in full march.

The position chosen by the Prince as that where he was to make his stand on that memorable day, the 16th of April, was by no means very wisely or very well selected. It was a little way to the westward of that which his army had occupied on the previous day. Somewhat in advance, and to the right of his ground, there stood the walls of an enclosure, which the experienced eye of Lord George Murray soon enabled him to perceive, and he was at once so convinced that they presented too advantageous a cover to the assailing enemy, to be neglected by them, that he would fain have moved forward with a party to have broken them down, had time remained to have enabled him to have effected his purpose. But the Duke of Cumberland's army was already in sight, advancing in three columns, steadily over the heath, from Dalcross Castle, the tower of which was seen rising towards its eastern extremity. The Highlanders were at this time dwindled to a mere handful, and some of the best friends of the cause of the Stewarts who were present, and perhaps even the young Prince himself, began to believe that he had been traitorously deserted. But the alarm had no sooner been fully spread by the clang of the pipes, and the shrill notes of the bugles, than small and irregular streams of armed men, in various coloured tartans, were seen rushing towards their common position, like mountain rills towards some Highland lake, and filling up the vacant ranks with all manner of expedition. Many a brave fellow, who had gone to look for something to satisfy the craving of an empty stomach, came hurrying back with as great a void as he had carried away with him, because he preferred fighting for him whom he conscientiously believed to be his king, to remaining ingloriously to subdue that hunger which was absolutely consuming him. No one was wilfully absent who could possibly contrive to be present, but yet the urgent demands of the demon of starvation, to which many of them had yielded, had very considerably thinned their numbers, and, in addition to this source of weakness, there was another obvious one, arising from the physical strength of those who were present being woefully diminished by the want they had endured, and the fatigue they had undergone. But with all these disadvantages the heroic souls of those who were on the field remained firm and resolute.

John Smith's military knowledge was then too small to allow him to form any judgment of the state of affairs, far less to enable him to carry off, or to describe, anything like the general arrangement of the order of battle on both sides. He could not even tell very well what regiments his corps was posted with : he only knew this, that according to the order he had received he stuck close to Captain M'Taggart. He always remembered with enthusiasm, indeed, that the Prince rode through the ranks with his attendants, doing all that he could to encourage his men, and that when he passed by where John himself stood, he smiled on him like an angel, and bid him do his duty like a man.

"Och, hoch !" cried John, with an exultation, which arose from the circumstance of his not being in the least aware that every individual near him had, like him, flattered himself that he was the person so distinguished,—" Fa wad hae soughts tat ta ponny Princey wad hae mindit on poor Shon Smiss? Fod, but she wad fichts for her till she was cut to collops !"

But John had little opportunity of fighting, though he appears to have borne plenty of the brunt of the battle. There were two cannons placed in each space between the battalions composing the first line of the Duke of Cumberland's army, and these were so well served as to create a fearful carnage among the Highland ranks. To this dreadful discharge John Smith stood exposed, with men falling by dozens around him, mutilated and mashed, and exhibiting death in all his most horrible forms, till, to use his own very expressive words,—" She was bitin' her ain lips for angher tat she could not get at tem." But before John could get at them, the English dragoons, who, under cover of the walls of the enclosure I have mentioned, had advanced by the right of the Highland army, finally broke through the fence, and getting in behind their first line, came cutting and slashing on their backs, whilst the Campbells were attacking them in front, and mowing them down like grass. Then, indeed, did the *melée* become desperate, and then was it that John began to bestir himself in earnest. Throwing away his plaid, and the little bundle that it contained, he dealt deadly blows with his broad-sword everywhere around him. He fought with the bravery and the perseverance of a hero. At length his bonnet was knocked from his head, and although he was still possessed with the most anxious desire to obey Captain M'Taggart's order to stick to his side, he was surprised on look-ing about him to find that there was no M'Taggart, no, nor anyone else left near him to stick to but enemies.

John Smith's spirit was undaunted, so that, seeing he had no one else to stick to, he now resolved to stick to his foes, to the last drop of life's blood that was within him. Furiously and fatally did he cut and thrust, and turn and cut and thrust again, at all who opposed him; but he was so overwhelmed by opponents, that in the midst of the blood, and wounds, and death which he was thus dealing in all directions, he received a desperate sabre cut, which, descending on him from above, entirely across the crown of his bared head, felled him instantaneously to the ground, and stretched him senseless among the heather, whilst a deluge of blood poured from the wound over both his eyes.

When John began partially to recover, he rubbed the half-congealed blood from his eyelids with the back of his left hand, and looking up and seeing that the ground was somewhat clear around him, he gripped his claymore firmly with his right hand, and raising himself to his feet, he began to run as fast as his weak state would allow him. He thought that he ran in the direction of Strath Nairn, and he ran whilst he had the least strength to run, or the least power remaining in him. But his ideas soon became confused, and the blood from the terrible gash athwart his head trickled so fast into his eyes, that it was continually obscuring his vision. At length he came to a large, deep irregular hollow hag, or ditch, in a piece of moss ground, which had been cut out for peats, and there, his brain beginning to spin round, he sank down into the moist bottom of it to die, and as the tide of life flowed fast from him, he was soon lost to all consciousness of the things or events of this world.

Whilst John was lying in this senseless state, he was recognised by one of the fugitives, who, in making his own escape, chanced to pass by the edge of the ditch in the moss where the poor man lay. This was a certain Donald Murdoch, who had long burned with a hopeless flame for black-eyed Morag. With a satisfaction that seemed to make him forget his present jeopardy in the contemplation of the death of his rival, he looked down from the edge of the peat hag upon the pale and bloody corpse, and grinned with a fiendish joy.

"Ha! there you lie!" cried he in bitter Gaelic soliloquy. "The fiend a bit sorry am I to see you so. You'll fling or dance no more, else I'm mistaken. Stay!—is not that the bit of blue ribbon that Morag tied round his neck, the last time that we had a dance in the barn? I'll secure that, it may be of some use to me;" and so saying he let himself down into the peat hag, hastily undid the piece of ribbon,—and then continued his flight with all manner of expedition.

Following the downward course of the river Nairn, running at one time, and ducking and diving into bushes, and behind walls at another, to avoid the stragglers who were in pursuit, he by degrees gained some miles of distance from the fatal field, and coming to a little brook, he ventured to halt for a moment, to quench his raging thirst. As he lay gulping down the crystal fluid, he was startled by hearing his own name, and by being addressed in Gaelic.

" Donald Murdoch !—Oh, Donald Murdoch, can you tell me is John Smith safe? Oh, those fearful cannons how they thundered !—Oh, tell me, is John Smith safe?—Oh, tell me! tell me !"

" Morag !" cried Donald, much surprised, but very much relieved to find that it was no one whom he had any cause to be afraid of,—" Morag ! What brought you so far from home on such a day as this ?"

" Oh, Donald !" replied Morag, " I came to look after John Smith ;—oh, grant that he be safe !"

" Safe enough, Morag," replied Donald, galled by jealousy. " I'll warrant nothing in this world will harm him now."

" What say you ?" cried Morag. " Oh, tell me ! tell me truly if he be safe ?"

" I saw John Smith lying dead in a moss hole, his skull cleft by a dragoon's sword," replied Donald, with malicious coolness.

" What !" cried Morag, wringing her hands, " John Smith dead ? But no ! it is impossible !—and you are a lying loon, that would try to deceive me, by telling me what I well enough know you would wish to be true. God forgie you, Donald, for such cruel knavery !"

" Thanks to ye, Morag, for your civility," replied Donald Murdoch, calmly ; " but if you won't believe me, believe that bit of ribbon—see, the very bit of blue ribbon you tied round John Smith's neck, the night you last so slighted me at the dance in the barn. See, it is partly dyed red in his life's blood."

" It is the ribbon !" cried Morag, snatching it from his hand with excessive agitation, and kissing it over and over again, and then bursting into tears. " Alas! alas! it must be too true ! What will become of poor Morag ?—why did I not go with him ? What is this world to poor desolate Morag now? And yet he may be but wounded after all. It must be so—he cannot be killed. Where did you leave him ?—quick, tell me ! oh, tell me, Donald. Why do we tarry here ? let us forward and seek him !—there may be life in him yet, and whilst there is life there is hope. Let me pass, Donald ; I will fly to seek him !"

"I love you too well to let you pass on so foolish and dangerous an errand," said Donald, endeavouring to detain her. "I tell you that John Smith is dead; but you know, Morag, you will always find a friend and a lover in me. So think no more ——"

"I will pass, Donald," cried Morag, interrupting him, and making a determined attempt to rush past him.

"That you shall not," replied Donald, catching her in his arms.

"Help, help!" cried Morag, struggling with all her might, and with great vigour too, against his exertions to hold her.

At this moment the trampling of a horse was heard, and a mounted dragoon came cantering down into the hollow. His sabre gleamed in the air—and Donald Murdoch fell headlong down the bank into the little rill, his skull nearly cleft in two, and perfectly bereft of life.

"A plague on the lousy Scot!" said the trooper, scanning the corpse of his victim with a searching eye. "His life was not worth the taking, had it not been, that the more of the rascally race that are put out of this world, the better for the honest men that are to remain in it, and therefore it was in the way of my duty to cut him down. There is nought on his beggarly carcase to benefit any one but the crows. And so the knave would have kissed thee against thy will, my bonny black-eyed wench. Well, 'tis no wonder thou shouldst have scorned that carotty-pated fellow; you showed your taste in so doing, my dear: and now you shall be rewarded by having a somewhat better sweetheart. Come!" continued he, alighting from his charger, and approaching the agitated and panting girl—"Come, a kiss from the lips of beauty is the best reward for brave deeds; and no one deserves this reward better than I do, for brave deeds have I this day performed. Why do you not speak, my dear? Have you no Christian language to give me? Can it be possible that these pretty pouting lips have no language but that of the savages of this country? Come, then, we must try the kissing language; I have always found that to be well understood in all parts of the world."

"Petter tak' Tonald's pig puss o' money first," said Morag, pointing to the corpse in the hollow.

"Ha! money saidst thou, my gay girl?" cried the trooper. "Who would have thought of a purse of money being in the pouch of such a miserable rascally savage as that? But the best apple may sometimes have the coarsest and most unpromising rind; and so that fellow, unseemly and wretched

as he appears, may perchance have a well-lined purse after all.
If it be so, girl, I shall say that thy language is like the talk of
an angel. Then do you hold the rein of this bridle, do you
see, till I make sure of the coin in the first place—best secure
that, for no one can say what mischance may come; or
whether some comrade may not appear with a claim to go
snacks with me. So lay hold of the bridle, do you hear, and
don't be afraid of old Canterbury, for the brute is as quiet as a
lamb."

Morag took the bridle. The trooper descended the bank,
and he had scarcely stooped over the body to commence his
search for the dead man's supposed purse, when the active girl,
well accustomed to ride horses in all manner of ways, vaulted
into the saddle, and kicking her heels into Canterbury's side,
she was out of the hollow in a moment. Looking over her
shoulder, after she had gone some distance, she beheld the
raging dragoon puffing, storming, and swearing, and striding
after her, with, what might be called, that dignified sort of
agility, to which he was enforced by the weighty thraldom of
his immense jack-boots. Bewildered by the terror and the
anxiety of her escape, she flew over the country, for some
time, without knowing which way she fled. At length she
began to recover her recollection, so far as to enable her to
recur to the object which had prompted her to leave home. On
the summit of a knoll she checked her steed—surveyed the
country,—and the whole tide of her feelings returning upon
her; she urged the animal furiously forward in the direction
of the fatal field of Culloden.

She had not proceeded far, when, on coming suddenly to the
edge of a rough little stony ravine, she discovered five
troopers refreshing themselves and their horses from the little
brook that had its course through the bottom. She reined back
her horse, with the intention of stealing round to some other
point of passage; but as she did so, a shout arose from the
hollow of the dell. She had been perceived. In an instant
the mounted riders rushed, one after another, out of the
ravine, and she had no chance of escape left her, but to ride as
hard as the beast that carried her could fly, in the very
opposite direction to that which she had hitherto pursued, for
there was no other course of flight left open to her.

The five troopers were now in full chase after Morag,
shouting out as they rode, and urging on their horses to the
top of their speed. The ground, though rough, stony, and
furzy, was for the most part firm enough, and the poor girl,

now driven from that purpose to which her strong attachment to John Smith had so powerfully impelled her, and being distracted by her griefs and her fears, spared not the animal she rode, but forced him, by every means she could employ, either by hands, limbs, or voice, to the utmost exertion of every muscle.

"Lord, how she does ride!" said one trooper to the others; "I wish that she bean't some of them witches, as, they say, be bred in this here uncanny country of Scotland."

"Bless you no, man," said another; "them devils as you speak of ride on broomsticks. Now, I'se much mistaken an' that be not Tom Dickenson's horse Canterbury."

"Zounds, I believe you are right, Hall," said another man; "but that bean't no proof that she aint a witch, for nothing but a she-devil, wot can ride on a broom, could ride ould Canterbury in that 'ere fashion, I say."

"Witch or devil, my boys, let us ketch her if we can," shouted another. "Hurrah! hurrah!"

"Hurrah! hurrah! hurrah!" re-echoed the others, burying their spurs in their horses' sides, and bending forward, and grinning with very eagerness.

For several miles Morag kept the full distance she had at first gained on her pursuers, but having got into a road, fenced by a rough stone wall upon one side, and a broad and very deep ditch on the other, the troopers, if possible, doubled their speed, in the full conviction that they must now very soon come up with her, and capture her. Still Morag flew,—but as she every moment cast her eyes over one or other of her shoulders, she was terrified to see that the troopers were visibly gaining upon her. The road before her turned suddenly at an angle,—and she had no sooner doubled it, than, there, to her unspeakable horror—in the very midst of the way—stood Tom Dickenson, the dismounted dragoon from whom she had taken the very charger, called Canterbury, which she then rode. The time of the action of what followed was very brief. For an instant she reined up her horse till he was thrown back on his haunches. Tom Dickenson's sword-blade glittered in the sun.

"By the god of war, but I have you now!" cried he in a fury.

The triumphant shouts of Morag's pursuers increased, as they neared her, and beheld the position in which she was now placed. No weapon had she, but the large pair of scissors that hung dangling from her side, in company with her pincushion. In desperation she grasped the sharp-pointed

implement dagger fashion, and directed old Canterbury's head
towards the ditch.   Dickenson saw her intention, and making to
counteract it, he rushed to the edge of the ditch.   The hand of
Morag which held the scissors descended on the flank of the
horse, and in defiance of his master, who stood in his way,
and the gleaming weapon with which he threatened him, old
Canterbury, goaded by the pain of the sharp wound inflicted
on him, sprang towards the leap with a wild energy, and
despite of the cut, which deprived him of an ear, and sheared a
large slice of the skin off one side of his neck, he plunged the
unlucky Tom Dickenson backwards, swash into the water, and
carried his burden fairly over the ditch.

Morag tarried not to look behind her, until she had scoured
across a piece of moorish pasture land, and then casting her
eyes over one shoulder, she perceived that only two of the
troopers had cleared the ditch, and that the others had either
failed in doing so, or were engaged in hauling their half-
drowned comrade out of it.   The two men who had taken the
leap, however, were again hard after her, shouting as before,
and evidently gaining upon her.   The moment she perceived
this, she dashed into a wide piece of mossy, boggy ground, a
description of soil with which she was well acquainted.   There
the chase became intricate and complicated.   Now her pursuers
were so near to her, as to believe that they were on the very
point of seizing her, and again some impassable obstacle would
throw them quite out, and give her the advantage of them.   Various
were the slips and plunges which the horses made ; but ere she
had threaded through three-fourths of the snares which she met
with, she had the satisfaction of beholding one of the riders
who followed her, fairly unhorsed, and hauling at the bridle of
his beast, the head and neck of which alone appeared from the
slough, in which the rest of the poor animal was engulfed.
The man called loudly to his comrade, but he was too keenly
intent on the pursuit, to give heed to him.   The hard ground
was near at hand, and he pushed on after Morag, who was now
making towards it.   She reached it, and again she plied the
points of her scissors on the heaving flanks of old Canterbury.
But she became sensible that his pace was fast flagging,—and
that the trooper was rapidly gaining on her.   In despair she
made towards a small patch of natural wood.   She was already
within a short distance of it.   But the blowing and snorting of
the horse behind her, and the blaspheming of his rider, came
every instant more distinctly upon her ear.   Some fifty or an
hundred yards only now lay between her and the wood.

Again, in desperation, she gave the point of the scissors to her steed—when, all at once he stopped—staggered—and, faint with fatigue and loss of blood, old Canterbury fell forward headlong on the grass.

"Hurrah!" cried the trooper, who was close at his heels, "witch or no witch, I think I'll grapple with thee now."

He threw himself from his heaving horse, and rushed towards Morag. But she was already on her legs, and scouring away like a hare for the covert. Jack-booted and otherwise encumbered as he was, the bulky trooper strode after her like a second Goliath of Gath, devouring the way with as much expedition as he could possibly use. But Morag's speed was like that of the wind, and he beheld her dive in among the underwood before he had covered half the distance.

"A very witch in rayal arnest!" exclaimed the trooper, slackening his pace in dismay and disappointment. And then turning towards his comrade, who, having by this time succeeded in extricating his horse from the slough, was now coming cantering towards him, "Hollo, Bill!" shouted he, "I've run the blasted witch home here. Come away, man, do; for if so be that she don't arth like a badger, or furnish herself with a new horse to her own fancy out of one of 'em 'ere broom bushes, this covert aint so large, but we must sartinly find her. So come along, man, and be active."

But we must now return to poor John Smith, whom we have too long left for dead in the bottom of a peat-hag. The cold and astringent moss-water flowing about his head, by degrees checked the effusion of his blood, and at length he began to revive.

When his senses returned to him, he gathered himself up, and leaning his back against the perpendicular face of the peat bank above him, he drank a little water from the hollow of his hand, and then washed away the clotted blood from his eyes. The first object that broke upon his newly recovered vision was an English trooper riding furiously up to him, with his brandished sword. John was immediately persuaded that he was a doomed man, for he felt that, in his case, resistance was altogether out of the question. He threw himself on his back in the bottom of the broad deep cut in the peat-hag. The trooper came up, and having no time to dismount, he stooped from his saddle and made one or two ineffectual cuts at the poor man. The horse shied at John's bloody head as it was raised in terror from the peat-hag, and then the animal reared back as he felt the soft mossy ground sinking under him. The trooper was determined,—got angry, and spurred the beast forward, but the horse became obstinate and restive. At length the trooper succeeded in bringing him up again to the edge of the peat-hag; but just as he was craning his neck over its brink, John, roused by desperation, pricked the creature's nose with the point of his claymore. It so happened that he accidentally did this, at the very instant that the irascible trooper was giving his horse a dig with his spurs, and the consequence of these double, though antagonist stimuli, was, that the brute made a desperate spring, and carried himself and his rider clean over the hag-ditch, John Smith and all, and then he ran off with his master through the broken moss-ground, scattering the heaps of drying peats to right and left, until horse and man were rolled over and over into the plashy bog.

Uninjured, except as to his gay clothes and accoutrements, which were speedily dyed of a rich chocolate hue, the trooper arose in a rage, and could he have by any means safely left his horse so as to have secured his not running away, he would have charged the dying man on foot, and so he would have very speedily sacrificed him; but dreading to lose his charger if he should abandon him, he mounted him again, and was in the act of returning to the attack, with the determination of putting John to death, at all hazards, either by steel or by lead, when he was arrested by the voice of his officer, who was then passing along a road tract, at some little distance, with a few of his troop, and who called out to him in a loud authoritative tone, " Come away you, Jem Barnard ! Why don't you follow the living ? Why waste time by cutting at the dying or dead ?"

On hearing this command, the trooper uttered a half-smothered curse, and unwillingly turned to ride after his comrades, throwing back bitter execrations on John Smith as he went. John's tongue was otherwise employed. He used it for the better purpose of returning thanks to that Almighty Providence who had thus so wonderfully protected him.

After this pious mental exercise, John thought that he felt himself somewhat better. He made a feeble effort to rise, but it was altogether abortive. The blood still continued to flow from his head—he began to feel very faint, and a raging thirst attacked him. Turning himself round in the peat-hag, he contrived to lap up a considerable quantity of the moss water, which, however muddy and distasteful it might be, refreshed him so much as to give him strength sufficient to raise himself up a little, so as to enable him to extend the circuit of his view. He had now a moment's leisure to look about him, and to consider, as well as the confusion of his ideas would allow him, what he had best to do. But what was his surprise and dismay to see, that although many were yet flying in all directions, and many more pursuing after them, whole battalions of the enemy still remained unbroken in the vicinity of the field of battle, and that some were marching up, in close order, both to the right and left of him. There was but little time left him for farther consideration, as one of these battalions was so near to him, that he saw, from the course it was holding, that it must soon march directly over the spot where he was. The first thought that struck him was that his best plan would be to lie down and feign that he was dead. But it immediately afterwards occurred to him that a thrust from some curious or malicious person, who might be the bearer of one of those bayonets, which already glittered in his eyes, might do his business even more effectually than the sword of the trooper might have done. He became convinced that he had nothing left for it but to run. But although he was now somewhat revived, and that the dread of death gave new strength to exhausted nature, he felt persuaded of the truth, that if his wound should continue to bleed, as it had already again began to do, his race could not be a long one in any sense of the word, even if he should have the wonderful luck to escape the chance of its being shortened by the sword, bayonet, or bullet of an enemy. To give himself some small chance of life, John, though he was no surgeon, would have fain tried some means of staunching the blood, but he lacked all manner of materials for any such operation, and he could only try to cover the wound very ineffectually with both hands, whilst the red stream continued to run down through his fingers. At length, necessity, that great mother of invention, and wisest of all teachers, enabled him to hit off, in a moment, a remedy, which, as it was the best he could have possibly adopted in his present difficult and distressing situation, might perhaps, even on an occasion where no such embarrassment exists, be found as valuable and effective as any other which the most favourable circumstances could afford, or the most consummate skill devise. Stooping down, he picked up a large mass of peaty turf, of nearly a foot square, and two or three inches thick. This had been regularly cut by the peat-diggers, but having tumbled by chance into the bottom of the peat-hag, it had been there lying soaking till the soft unctuous matter of which it was composed was completely saturated with water like a sponge. John proceeded upon no certain *ratio medicandi*, except this, that as his life's blood was

20 ·

manifestly welling fast away from him, he thought that the wet peat would stop the flow of it, and as his head was in a burning fever, every fibre of his scalp seemed to call out for the immediate application of its cold and moist surface. John seized it then with avidity, and clapping it instantly on his head, with the black soft oleaginous side of it next to the wound, and the heathery top of it outwards, he pressed it down with great care all over his skull, and then quickly secured it fast, by tying a coarse red handkerchief over it, the ends of which he fastened very carefully under his chin. The outward appearance of this strange uncouth headgear may be easily imagined, with the heatherbush rising everywhere around his head over the red tier that bound it on, and surmounting a countenance so rueful and bloody ; but the effect within was so wonderfully refreshing and invigorating, that he felt himself almost immediately restored to comparative strength. He started to his feet ; and, being yet uncertain as to which way he should run, he raised his head slowly over the peat-hag to reconnoitre.

Now, it happened that at this very moment, a couple of English foot soldiers came straggling along, thirsting for more slaughter, and prowling about for prey and plunder. Ere John was aware of their proximity to him, they were within a few yards of the peat-hag. As he raised his head, he beheld them approaching with their muskets and their bayonets reeking with gore. Believing himself to be now utterly lost, a deep groan of despair escaped from him. The soldiers had halted suddenly on beholding the bloody face and neck of what scarcely seemed to be a human being, with a huge overgrown forest of heather on the head instead of hair, appearing, as it were by magic, out of the very earth. They started back, and stood for an instant transfixed to the spot by superstitious fear.

" Waunds, Gilbert, wot is that ?" cried one, his eyes staring at John with horror.

Seeing, that as he was now discovered, his only chance lay in working upon that dread which he saw that he had already excited, John first gradually drew down his head below the bank, and then again raised it slowly and portentously, and uttered another groan more deep and ghostly and prolonged than the first. The effect was instantaneous.

" Oh Lord ! oh Lord ! one of them Highland warlocks of the bog, wot devours men, women, and children !" cried Gilbert. " Fly—fly, Warner, for dear life !"

Off he ran, and his comrade stayed not to question farther, but darted away from him, and John had the satisfaction to see the two heroes, from whom he had looked for nothing but sudden death, scouring away over the field, and hardly daring to look behind them.

John Smith was considerably emboldened by the discovery that his appearance was so formidable to his foes. He again applied himself to the consideration of the question as to which way it was best for him to fly. He cast his eyes all over the field of action around him; and, much to his satisfaction, he perceived that the officer at the head of the red regiment of Englishmen, which had previously given him so much alarm, had been so very obliging as to determine this difficult question for him. Some movement of the flying clans, who had retreated on Strath Nairn, had induced the officer to alter his line of march; and, in a very short time, John had the happiness of seeing himself very much in the rear of the red battalion, instead of being immediately in its front, as he had formerly been. Looking to the north-eastward, he perceived that all was comparatively clear and quiet, so far as he could see. There were now no longer any regular masses of men on the field, neither were there any signs of flight or pursuit in that direction. A few stragglers were to be seen, it is true, moving about like evil spirits among the killed, and perhaps performing the office of messengers of death to the wounded. Strange, indeed, was the change that had taken place upon that which had been so lately a scene of stormy and desperate conflict. A few large birds of prey were soaring high in air, in eager contemplation of that banquet which had been so liberally spread for them on the plain by ferocious man. But, in the immediate neighbourhood of the spot where John Smith was, the terrified pewitt had already settled down again with confidence on her nest, the robin had again begun to chirp, and to direct his sharp eye towards the earth in search of worms; and the lark was again heaving herself up into the sky, giving forth her innocent song as she rose,—all apparently utterly unconscious that any such terrible and bloody turmoil had taken place between different sections of the human race. John therefore made up his mind at once; and, scrambling out of the peat-hag, he darted away over the moor, and flying like a ghost across the very middle of the field of battle, through the heaps of dead and dying, to the utter terror and discomfiture of those wolves and hyenas in the shape of men—aye, and of women too—who were preying, as well upon those who had life, as upon those who were lifeless, he scattered them to right and left in terror at his appalling appearance, and dived amid the thick woods of Culloden.

Having once found shelter among the trees, John stopped to breathe awhile, and then he again set forward to unravel his way. It so happened that as he proceeded, he chanced to come upon the very spot where he had feasted with M'Taggart and his comrades on his mistress the Pensassenach's sow, and the other good things which the Highlanders had taken from her. The gnawing demon of hunger that possessed him, inserted his fell fangs more furiously into his stomach, from very association with the scene. What would he not have now given for the smallest morsel of that goodly beast, the long and ample side of which arose upon his mind's eyes, as he had beheld her carcase hanging from the bough of a tree, previous to the rapid subdivision which it underwent. Alas! the very thought of it was now an unreal mockery. Yet he could not help looking anxiously around, though in vain, among the extinguished remains of the fires of the bivouacs; and he figured to himself the joy and comfort and refreshment he would have experienced, if his eyes could have lighted even on a half-broiled fragment of one of the pettitoes, which he might have picked at as he fled. John's eyes were so intently turned to the ground, that he saw not the unfortunate Mr. Dallas, who still dangled from the bough of the fir tree above him.

Whilst John was poking about in this manner, earnestly turning over the ashes, and looking amongst them as if he had been in search of a pin, he suddenly heard the tramp of horses at some little distance. The sound was evidently coming towards him; and he could distinguish men's voices. He cast his eyes eagerly around him, to discover some ready place of concealment; and now, for the first time, he caught sight of the wasted figure of Mr. Dallas, swinging at some distance above him, with the dull glassy eyeballs apparently fixed upon him. His heart sank within him; for the corpse of the wretched man seemed to typify his own immediate fate. He was paralysed for a moment. But the sound drew nearer; and, spying a holly-tree with a reasonably tall stem, and a very thick and bushy head, which happened to grow most fortunately near him, he ran towards it, reached up his hands, seized hold of its lower branches, and, weak though he was, the energy of self-preservation enabled him very quickly to coil himself up amongst its dense foliage, where he sat as still as death, and scarcely allowing himself to breathe. The holly-tree stood by the side of a horse-track that led through the wood, and which crossed the small open space where most of the fires of Captain M'Taggart's bivouac had been kindled. Two troopers came riding leisurely up through the wood along it, their horses considerably jaded by the work of the day.

"Ha !" said one of them to the other, reining up his steed as he spoke, just on entering the open space,—" What have we here, Jack ?"

"I should not wonder now if 'em 'ere should be the remains of the fires of some of them rebel rascals," said Jack, with wonderfull acuteness. "Them is a proper set of waggabones, to be sure. How we did lick the rascals ! Did'nt we, Bob ?"

"To be sure we did, Jack," replied Bob.

"But you and I ain't made much on it arter all. I wish the captain at the devil—so I do—for sendin' us a unting arter that officer he was a wanting to ketch."

"Aye," said Jack ; "so do I, from the bottom of my soul. But if we had ketcht him, I think we should a' gained a prize, seeing that he wur walued at twenty golden pieces by his Highness the Duke. Whoy, who the plague could he be ? Not the chap they calls Priuce Charles Stuart himself surelye ? I should think that his carcase would fetch a deal more money."

"A deal more money indeed !" said Bob.

"Lord bless thee, I would not sell my share of him for an underd. But why may we not ketch him yet, Jack ? Look sharp ; do—and see if you can spy ere an oak in this wood, with a head so royal as to hide this Prince Charles Stuart iu it, as that 'ere one did King Charley the Second arter the great battle of Worcester. Zounds ! what a fortin you and I should make, an' we could only ketch him !"

"Pooh !" replied Jack, moving so close to the little holly, that his head and that of John Smith were within two yards of each other—"Pooh, man ! there bean't no oaks bigger than this here holly, in all this blasted, cold, and wretched country." And, at the same time, he gave its bushy head a thwack with the flat of his sword that set every leaf of it in motion, and John's heart, body, muscles, and nerves, shaking in sympathy with them.

"Beg your pardon," said Bob. "I was in a great big wood yesterday—that same, I mean, that spreads abroad all over the country, above that 'ere ould castle wot they calls Cawdor Castle. And sitch oak trees as I seed there ! My heyes, some on 'em had heads as would cover half a troop ! But, hark ye,

Jack! Is there no tree, think ye, fit to have a man in't but an oak? Dost not think that a good stout fir-tree now might support a man?"

"Oh," replied Jack, "surelye, surelye. This here holly, for instance, might hide a man in its head;"—and, as he said so, he gave the holly another thwack, that, for a few moments, banished every drop of blood from the heart of John Smith. "But your oak is your only tree for concealing your King or your Prince; for, as the old rhyme has it,

'The royal oak is not a joke.'

As for your firs, they may be well enough for affording a refuge to your men of smaller mark."

"Then you don't think that 'ere feller, wot hangs from yonder fir tree, can be a King or a Prince, do you, Jack?" demanded Bob, laughing heartily at his own joke.

"My heyes!" exclaimed Jack, rubbing his optics, and looking earnestly for some time at the corpse of Mr. Dallas; "sure I cannot be mistaken? As I'm a soldier, that 'ere is the very face, figure, clothes, and, above all, short leg and queer shoe, of the identical feller wot sould me an ould watch, wot was of no use, because you know it never went, and therefore it stands to reason that it could only tell the hour twice in the twenty-four. I say surelye, surelye, that 'ere is the very feller as sould me this here ould useless watch, for a bran new great goer. Well, if it bean't some satisfaction to see the feller hanging there, my name aint Jack Blunt!"

"Them rascally rebels has robbed and murdered the poor wretch," said Bob.

"Well," replied Jack, "I am a right soft arted Christine; and therefore most surely do I forgive 'em for that same hact, if they'd never ha' done no worse. But come Bob, my boy; an' we would be ketching kings or princes, I doubt we mun be stirrin'."

"Aye, aye, that's true—let's us be joggin'," replied Bob.

You may believe, gentlemen, that it was with no small satisfaction that John Smith beheld them apply their spurs to the sides of their weary animals. He listened to their departing footsteps until they were beyond the reach of his hearing; and then, conscious as he felt himself, that he was in much too weak a state to have maintained an unequal combat against two fresh and vigorous men, with the most distant chance of success, he put up a fervent ejaculation of thankfulness for their departure, and his own safety.

He was in the act of preparing himself to drop from the tree, that he might continue his flight, and was just putting down his legs from amid the thick foliage, when he met with a new alarm, that compelled him to draw them up again with great expedition. Some one on foot now came singing along up the path, and John had hardly more than time to conceal himself again, when he beheld the person enter upon the open space, near the holly tree where he was perched. And a very remarkable and striking personage he was. He wore an old, soiled, torn, and tarnished regimental coat, which, though now divested of every shred of the lace that had once adorned it, seemed to have once belonged to an English officer; and this was put on over a tattered Highland kilt, from beneath which his raw-boned limbs and long horny feet appeared uncased by any covering. A dirty canvas shirt was all that showed itself where a waistcoat should have been, and that was all loose at the collar, fully exhibiting a thin, long, scraggy neck, that supported a head of extraordinary dimensions, and of the strangest malconformation, having a countenance, in which the appearance of the goggle eyes alone, would have been enough to have satisfied the most transient observer of the insanity of the individual to whom they belonged. An old worn-out drummer's cap completed his costume. He came dancing along, with a large piece of cheese held up before him with both hands, and he went on, singing, hoarsely and vehemently,—

> "Troll de rol loll—troll de loll lay :
> If I could catch a reybel, I would him flay—
> Troll de roll lay—troll de roll lum—
> And out of his skin I wud make a big drum.

Ho! ho; ho; that wud be foine. But stay; I mun halt here, and sit doon, and munch up my cheese that I took so cleverly from that ould woman. Ho! ho! ho! ho! How nice it is to follow the sodgers! Take what we like—take what we like! Ho! ho! This is livin' like a man! They ca'ed me daft Jock in the streets o' Perth; but our sarjeant says as hoo that I'm to be made a captain noo. Ho! ho! A captain! and to have a lang swurd by my side! Ho! ho! ho! I'll be grand, very grand—and I'll fecht, and cut off the heads o' the reybel loons! Ho! ho! ho!

> Troll de roll loll—troll de roll lay—
> If I could catch a reybel I wud him ——"

"Hoch!"—roared out John Smith, his patience being now quite exhausted, by the thought that his chance of escaping with life was thus to be rendered doubly precarious, by the provoking delay of this idiot. Hoch!" roared he again, in a yet more tremendous voice, whilst at the same time he thrust his head—and nothing but his turf-covered head—with his bloody countenance, partially streaked with the tiny streams of the inky liquid that had oozed from the peat, and run down here and there over his face ;—this horrible head, I say, John thrust forth from the foliage, and glared fearfully at the appalled songster, who stopped dead in the midst of his stave.

"Ah—a-ach—ha—a-ah—ha!" cried the poor idiot, in a prolonged scream of terror that echoed through the wood, and off he flew, and was out of sight in a moment.

John Smith lost not another instant of time. Dropping down from the tree, he hastily picked up a small fragment of the cheese which the idiot had let fall in his terror and confusion, and this he devoured with inconceivable rapacity. But although this refreshed him a little, it stirred up his hunger to a most agonizing degree, so that if he had had no other cause for running, he would have run from the very internal torment he was enduring. Dashing down through the thickest of the brakes of the wood, so as to avoid observation as much as possible, he at last traversed the whole extent of it in a north-easterly direction, and gained the low open country beyond it, whence he urged on his way, until he fell into that very line of road, in the parish of Petty, which he had so lately marched over in an opposite direction, and under circumstances so different, with Captain M'Taggart and his company, on the afternoon of the 14th, just two days before.

Remembering the whole particulars of that march, and the benedictions with which they had been everywhere greeted, John Smith flattered himself that he had now got into a country of friends, and that he had only to show himself at any of their doors, wounded, weary, an' hungered and athirst, as he was, to ensure the most charitable, compassionate, and hospitable reception. But, in so calculating, John was ignorant of the versatility and worthlessness of popular applause. He forgot that when he was passing to Culloden, with the bold Captain M'Taggart and his company, they had been looked upon as heroes marching to conquest; whilst he was now to be viewed as a wretched runaway from a lost field. But he still more forgot, that the same bloody, haggard countenance, and horrible head-gear, which had been already so great a protection to him by terrifying his enemies, could not have much chance of favourably recommending him to his friends.

John stumped on along the road, therefore, with comparative
cheerfulness, arising from the prospect which he now had of
speedy relief. At some little distance before him, he observed
a nice, trig-looking country girl, trudging away barefoot, in the
same direction he was travelling. He hurried on to overtake
her, in order to learn from her where he was most likely
to have his raging hunger relieved. The girl heard his footstep
coming up behind her, whilst she was yet some twenty paces
a-head of him;—she turned suddenly around to see who the
person was that was about to join her, and beholding the
terrible spectre-looking figure which John presented, she
uttered a piercing shriek, and darted off along the highway,
with a speed that nothing but intense dread could have produced. Altogether forgetful of the probable cause of her
alarm, John imagined that it must proceed from fear of the
Duke of Cumberland's men, and, with this idea in his head, he
ran after her as fast as his weak state of body would allow him,
earnestly vociferating to her to stop. But the more he ran,
and the more he shouted, just so much the more ran and
screamed the terrified young woman. Another girl was
seated, with a boy, on the grassy slope of a broomy hillock,
immediately over the road, tending three cows and a few sheep.
Seeing the first girl running in the way she was doing, they
hurried to the road side to enquire the cause of her alarm, but
ere they had time to ask, or she to answer, she shot past them,
and the hideous figure of John Smith appeared. Horror-
struck, and so bewildered that they hardly knew what they
were doing, both girl and boy leaped into the road, and fled
along it. A little farther on, two labourers were engaged
digging a ditch, in a mossy hollow below the road. Curiosity
to know what was the cause of all this shrieking and running,
induced these men to hasten up to the road-side. But ere they
had half reached it, they beheld John coming, and turning
with sudden dismay, they scampered off across the fields, never
stopping to draw breath till they reached their own homes.
John minded them not,—but fancying that he was gaining on
the three fugitives before him, and perceiving a small hamlet of
cottages a little way on, he redoubled his exertions.

Some dozen of persons, men, women and children, were
assembled about a well, at what we in Scotland would call the
town-end. They were talking earnestly over the many and most
contradictory rumours that had reached them of the events of
that day's battle, their rustic and unwarlike souls having been
so sunk with the trepidation occasioned by the distant sound

of the heavy cannonade, that they as yet hardly dared to speak but in whispers. Suddenly the shrieking of the three young persons came upon their ears. They pricked them up in alarm and turned every eye along the road. The shrieking increased and the two girls and the boy appeared, with the formidable figure of John Smith in pursuit of them.

"The Duke's men! the Duke's men! with the devil at their head!" cried the wise man of the hamlet in Gaelic. "Run or we're all dead and murdered!"

In an instant every human head of them had disappeared each having burrowed under its own proper earthen hovel, with as much expedition as would be displayed by the rabbits of a warren, when scared by a Highland terrier. So instantaneously, and so securely, was every little door fastened, that it was with some difficulty that the three fugitives found places of shelter, and that, too, not until their shrieks had been multiplied ten-fold. When John Smith came up, panting and blowing like a stranded porpus, all was snug, and the little hamlet so silent, that if he had not caught a glimpse of the people alive, he might have supposed that they were all dead.

John knocked at the first door he came to.—Not a sound was returned but the angry barking of a cur. He tried the next—and the next—and the next—all with like success;—at last he knocked at one, whence came a low, tremulous voice, more of ejaculation than intended for the ear of any one without, and speaking in Gaelic.

"Lord be about us!—Defend us from Satan, and from all his evil spirits and works!"

"Give me a morsel of bread, and a cup of water, for mercy's sake!" said John, poking his head close against a small pane of dirty glass in the mud wall, that served for a window.

"Avoid thee, evil spirit!" said the same voice.—"Avoid thee, Satan!—O deliver us from Satan!—Deliver us from the Prince of Darkness and all his wicked angels!"

"Have mercy upon me, and give me but a bit of bread, and a drop of water, for the sake of Christ your Saviour!" cried John earnestly again.

"Avoid, I say, blasphemer!" replied the voice, with more energy than before. "Name not vainly the name of my Saviour, enemy as thou art to him and his. Begone, and tempt us not!"

John Smith was preparing to answer and to explain, and to defend himself from these absurd and unjust imputations against him, when he heard the sound of a bolt drawn in the

hovel immediately behind him. Full of hope that some good
and charitable Christian within, melted by his pitiful petitions,
had come to the resolution of opening his door to relieve him,
he turned hastily round. But what was his mortification,
when, instead of seeing the door opened, he beheld the small
wooden shutter of an unglazed hole in the wall, slowly and
silently pushed outwards on its hinges, until it fell aside, and
then the muzzle of a rusty fowling-piece was gradually projected,
levelled, and pointed at him. John waited not to allow him
who held it to perfect his aim. He sprang instantly aside
towards the wall, and fortunately the tardy performance of the
old and ill constructed lock enabled him to do so, just in time
to clear the way for the shower of swan-shot which the gun
discharged in a diagonal line across the way. Luckily for
John, he had thus no opportunity of judging of the weight of
the charge in his own person, but he was made sufficiently
aware that it was quite potent enough, by its effects on an
unfortunate sheep-dog, that happened to be at that moment
lying peaceably gnawing a bone on the top of a dunghill, some
fifty yards down the road, on the opposite side of the way to
that where the hovel stood from which the shot had been fired.
The poor animal sprang up, and gave a loud and sharp yelp,
when he received the shot, and then followed a long and dismal
howl, after which he rolled over on his back and died. After
such a hint as this, John stayed not to make further experiments
on the hospitality of the little place, but, getting out at the farther
end of its street with all manner of expedition, he slowly
proceeded on his way, weary, faint, and heart-sunken.

Just as sunset was approaching, he came to the door of a
small single cottage, hard by the way-side. There he knocked
gently, without saying a word.

"Who is there?" asked a soft woman's voice in Gaelic, from
within.

"A poor man like to die with hunger and thirst," replied
John in the same language. "For the love of God give me
a piece of bread, and a drink of water."

"You shan't want that," said the good Samaritan woman
within, who promptly came to undo the door.

"Heaven reward you!" said John fervently, as she was
fumbling with the key in the key-hole, and with an astonishing
rapidity of movement in his ideas, he felt, by anticipation, as if
he was already devouring the food he had asked for.

"Preserve us, what's that?" cried the woman, the moment
the half-opened door had enabled her to catch a glimpse of his
fearful head and bloody features.

The door was shut and locked in an instant; and whether it was that the poor young lonely widow, for such she was, had fainted or not, or whether she had felt so frightened for herself and her young child, that she dared not to speak, all John's farther attempts to procure an answer from her were fruitless. It was probably from the cruel and unexpected disappointment that he here had met with, just at the time when his hopes of relief had been highest, that his faintness came more overpoweringly upon him. He tottered away from the widow's door, with his head swimming strangely round, and he had not proceeded above two or three dozen of steps, when he sank down on a green bank by the side of the road, where he lay almost unconscious as to what had befallen him.

He had not lain long there, when the tender hearted widow, who had reconnoitred him well through a single pane of glass in the gable end of her house, began to have her fears overcome by her compassion. Seeing that he was now at some distance from her dwelling, she ventured again to open her door, and perceiving that he did not stir, she retired for a minute, and then reappeared with a bottle of milk and two barley cakes, with which she crept timorously, and therefore slowly and cautiously, along the road. Her step became slower and slower, as, with fear and trembling, she drew near to John. At last, when within three or four yards of him, she halted, and looking back, as if to measure the distance that divided her from her own door, she turned towards him, and ventured to address him.

"Here, poor man," said she, setting down the cakes and the bottle of milk on the bank. "Here is some refreshment for you."

John Smith raised his eyes languidly as her words reached him, and spying the food she had brought him, he started up and proceeded to seize upon it with an energy which no one could have believed was yet left in him; and, as the benevolent widow was flying back with a beating heart to her cottage, she heard his thanks and benedictions coming thickly and loudly after her. John devoured the barley cakes, and drank the milk, and felt wonderfully refreshed, and then, placing the bottle on the bank in view of the cottage, he knelt down and offered up his thanks to God for his mercy, and prayed for blessings on the head of her who had relieved him. He then arose, and having waved his hand two or three times towards the cottage in token of his gratitude, he proceeded with some degree of spirit on his journey. I may here remark, gentlemen, that however those worthies who denied John admittance to their houses may have passed the night, I may venture to pronounce, and that with some probability of truth too, that the sleep of that virtuous young widow, with her innocent child in her arms, was as sweet and refreshing as the purity and balminess of her previous reflections could make it.

John Smith had not gone far on his way till the sun went down; but, as the moon was up, and he knew his road sufficiently well, he continued to trudge on without fear, until he approached the old walls of an ancient church, the burying yard of which had an ugly reputation for being haunted, and then he began to walk with somewhat more circumspection. As he drew nearer to it, he halted under the shadow of a bank, and stood for a time somewhat aghast, for, in the open part of the grave-yard, between the church and the high road, he beheld three figures standing in the moonlight which then prevailed. At first John quaked with fear, lest they should prove to be some of the uncanny spirits which were said to frequent the place. But he soon became reassured, by observing enough of them and of their motions to convince him that they were men of flesh and blood, yea, and Highlanders too, like himself.

As John Smith had no fear of mortal man, he would have at once advanced. But there was something so suspicious in the manner in which the three fellows hung over the wall, as if they were watching the public road, that he became at once convinced that they were lying in wait for a prey; and although he had nothing to lose, he did not feel assured as to the manner in which they might be disposed to accost him; and in his present weak state, he felt prudence to be the better part of valour. Availing himself of the concealment of the bank, therefore, until he had entered a small opening in the church-yard wall, he crept quietly across a dark part of the churchyard itself, by which means he got into the deep shadow that fell with great breadth all along the church wall, between the moon and the three figures who were watching the road, and who consequently had their backs to the old building. Having succeeded in accomplishing this, John was stealing slowly and silently along the wall, with the hope of passing by them, altogether unnoticed, when, as ill luck would have it, one of them chanced to turn round, so as dimly to descry his figure.

"What the devil is that gliding along yonder?" cried the man, in Gaelic, and in a voice that betrayed considerable fear.

"Halt you there!" cried another, who was somewhat bolder. "Halt, I say, and give an account of yourself."

John saw that there was now no mode of escaping the danger but by boldly bearding it. He halted therefore, but still keeping deep within the shade, he drew out his claymore, and placed his back to the church wall to prepare for defence.

"Ha! steel!" cried the third fellow; "I heard it clash on the stones of the wall, and I saw it bring a flash of fire out of them too. Come, come, goodman, whoever you are—come out here, and give us your claymore."

"He that will have it, must come and take it by the point,' said John, in Gaelic, and in a stern, hoarse, hollow voice; "and he had better have iron gloves on, or he will find it too hot for his palms."

"What the devil does he mean?" said the first.

"We'll detain you as a runaway rebel," said the third.

"The boldest of men could not detain me," replied John, now recognising the last speaker, by the moonlight on his face, as well as by his voice. "But for a base traitor like you, Neil MacCallum, better were it for you to be lying dead, like your brave brother, among the slain on Drummossie Moor, than to encounter me here in this churchyard, at such an hour as this!"

"In the name of wonder, how knows he my name?" exclaimed MacCallum in a voice that quavered considerably.

"Oh, Neil! Neil!" cried the first speaker, in great dismay, "it is no man! it is something most uncanny: For the love of God, parley with it no farther!"

"Pshaw—nonsense!" exclaimed the second speaker. "It's a man, and nothing else. Let us all rush upon him at once. Surely, if he were the devil himself, three of us ought to be a match for him."

"I am the devil himself!" cried John Smith in a terrible voice, and at the same time stalking slowly forth from the shadow, with the bloody blade of his claymore before him, he strode into the moonlight, which at once fully disclosed his hideous head-gear and ghastly features, to which at the same time it gave a tenfold effect of horror.

"Oh, the devil!—the devil!—the devil!" cried the fellows, the moment they thus beheld him; and, overpowered by their terror, they rushed forward towards the churchyard wall, and threw themselves over it pell-mell, tumbling higgledy-piggledy into the road, and scampering out of sight and out of hearing in a moment, leaving John Smith sole master of the field.

In the midst of all his miseries, John could not help laughing heartily at the suddenness of their retreat. But gravity of mood came quickly over him again, when he heard his laugh re-echoed—he knew not how, as it were in a tone of mockery, from the old church walls. He began to recollect where he was, and he half repented that he had.so indiscreetly used the name of Satan in the manner he had done.

"The Lord be about us !" ejaculated John most fervently, whilst his knees smote against each other violently, and his jaws were stretched to a fearful extent.

He felt that the shorter time he tarried in that uncanny place the better it would be for his comfort; and, accordingly, he began to move forward as quickly as he could towards a wicket gate, which he well knew gave exit to the footpath at the other end of the churchyard.

John, now proceeding at what might rather be called an anxious pace than a quick one, had very nearly reached the wicket, when his eye caught a tall white figure standing within a few yards of it, and posted close by the path which he must necessarily pursue. The moonshine enabled him to see a terrible face, with a huge mouth.; and, so far as his recollection of his own natural physiognomy went, derived as it was from his shavings on Saturday nights ever since his chin required a razor, he felt persuaded that the countenance before him was a fac-simile of his own. It was, moreover, very ghastly, and very bloody. His eyes fixed themselves it upon with unconquerable dismay, and he shook throughout every nerve, like the trembling poplar. But that which most astonished and terrified him, as he gazed on this apparition, was the strange circumstance that he could distinctly perceive, that it had already assumed a head-gear precisely similar to the very remarkable one which he had been so recently compelled from necessity to adopt. On the summit of its crown appeared a huge sod, with all its native plants upon it, and these waved to and fro before him with something like portentous omen. John felt as if he had only fled from the battle-field of Culloden to meet both death and burial in this most unchancy churchyard, and if his knees smote each other before, they now increased their reciprocal antagonist action in a degree that was tenfold more striking. John felt persuaded beyond a doubt, that the devil had been permitted thus to assume his own appearance, and to come thus personally to reprove him for the indiscreet use which he had made of his name. Sudden death seemed to be about to fall.on him. The grave appeared to be about to open to receive his wounded and worn-out body. But these were evils which, at that dreadful moment, John hardly recognised, for the jaws of the Evil Spirit himself seemed to him to be

slowly and terribly expanding themselves to swallow up his
sinful soul. Fain would John have fled, but he was riveted
to the spot. No way suggested itself to his distracted mind
by which he could escape, and he well knew that he had no
way that led homewards to that spot where he looked for concealment and safety, save that which went directly by the
dreaded object before him. For some time he stood trembling
and staring, in a cold sweat, until at length, overpowered by
his feelings, he dropped upon his knees, and began putting up
such snatches of prayer to Heaven, for help against the powers
of darkness, as his fears allowed him to utter.

As John thus sat on his knees, praying and quaking, his
animal courage so far returned to him as to permit him to
observe that the object of his terror remained unchanged and
immovable. At length his mind recovered itself to such an
extent, as to enable him to revert to that night of misery which
he had so recently experienced, in beholding that which he had
believed to be the spirit of Dallas the packman, and remembering how that matter had been cleared up by the appearance
of daylight, he began to reason with himself as to the possibility
of this being a somewhat similar case. Having thus so far
reduced his fears within the control of his reason, he summoned
up resolution to raise himself from his knees, and to advance
one step nearer to the phantom which had so long triumphed
over the courage that was within him. And, seeing that,
notwithstanding this movement of his, it still maintained its
position, and uttered no sound, he ventured to take a second
step—and then a third step, until the truth, and the whole
truth, began gradually to dawn upon his eyes and his mind,
and then, at last, he discovered, to his great relief, that the
horrible and much-dreaded demon whose appearance had so
disturbed and discomposed his nervous system, was no other
than a tall old tombstone, with a head so fearfully chisselled
on the top of it, as might have left it a very doubtful matter,
even in the day-time, for any one, however learned in such
pieces of art, to have determined whether the rustic sculptor had
intended it for a death's-head or a cherubim. Some idle artist
of the brush, in passing by that way with a pot full of red
paint, prepared for giving a temporary glory to a new cart
about to be turned out from a neighbouring wright's shop, had
paused as he passed by, and exhausted the full extent of his
small talents in communicating to the countenance that bloody
appearance, the effect of which had so much appalled John
Smith, and some waggish schoolboy had finished the figure, by

For some time he stood trembling and staring in a cold
sweat.—Page 304.

tearing up a sod covered with plants of various kinds, and clapping it on its top, so as thereby very much to augment its artificial terrors. John Smith drew a long breath of inconceivable relief on making this discovery, and then darting through the wicket, pursued his journey with as much expedition as his weakness and fatigue permitted him to use.

John walked on for some hour or twain with very determined resolution, but at length the great loss of blood he had experienced, brought on so unconquerable a drowsiness, that he felt he must have a little rest, were it but for a few minutes, even if his taking it should be at the risk of his life. John was never wont to be very particular as to the place where he made his bed, but on the present occasion it happened, probably from the blood-vessels of his body having been so much drained, that he had a most upleasant chill upon him. He felt as if ice itself was shooting and crystallizing through every vein and artery within him. Then the night had become somewhat raw, and he had left his plaid, which is a Highlander's second house, on the fatal field of battle. Under all these circumstances, John was seized with a resistless desire to enjoy the luxury of sleep for a short time, under the shelter of a roof, and in the vicinity of a good peat fire. Calling to mind that there was an humble turf-built cottage in a hollow a little way farther on, by the side of a small rushy, mossy stream, he made the best of his way towards it.

The house consisted of three small apartments, one in the middle of it, opposite to the outer door, and one at either end, which had their entrances from that in the centre. When John came to the brow of the bank that looked down upon this humble dwelling, he was by no means sorry to perceive that the middle apartment had a good blazing fire in it, as he could easily see through the window and outer door, which last chanced to be invitingly open. John, altogether forgetful of his uncouth and terrific appearance, lost not a moment in availing himself of this lucky circumstance. But he had no sooner presented his awful spectral form and visage within the threshold, than he spread instantaneous terror over the group assembled within.

"Oh, a ghost! a ghost!" cried out in Gaelic a pale-faced girl of some eight or nine years of age as she dropped on her knees, shaken by terror in every limb and feature.

"Oh, the devil! the devil!" roared an old man and woman, who also sank down before John, bellowing out like frightened cattle. "Och, och! we shall all be swallowed up quick by the Evil One!"

21

"Fear nothing," said John Smith, in a mild tone, and in the same tongue. "I am but a poor wounded and wearied man. I only want to lie down and rest me a little, if you will be so charitable as to grant me leave."

"Wounded!" said the old man, rising from his knees, somewhat reassured; "where were you wounded?"

"In the head here," said John, with a stare that again disconcerted the old man; "and if it had not been for this peat that I clapped on my skull, I believe my very brains would have been all out of me."

"Mercy on us, where got ye such a mischance as that?" exclaimed the old woman.

"At Culloden, I'll be sworn," said the old man.

"Aye, aye, it was at Culloden," replied John. "But, if ye be Christians, give me a drink of warm milk and water to put away this shivering that is on me, and let me lie down in a warm bed for half an hour."

"Och aye, poor man, ye shall not want a drop of warm milk and water, and such a bed as we can give you," said the old woman, moving about to prepare the drink for him.

"Thank ye—thank ye!" said John, much refreshed and comforted by swallowing the thin but hot potation. And then following the old man into the inner apartment on the right hand, he sank down in a darksome nook of it on a pallet among straw, and covering himself up, turf, nightcap, and all, under a coarse blanket, he was sound asleep before the old man had withdrawn the light and shut the door of his clay chamber.

"Oh that our boys were back again safe and sound!" cried the old woman, wringing her hands.

"Safe and sound I fear we cannot expect them to be, Janet," replied the old man. "But oh that we had them back again, though it was to see them wounded as badly as that poor fellow! Much do I fear that they are both corpses on Drummossie Moor."

"What will become of us!" cried the old woman, weeping bitterly; "what will become of this poor motherless lassie now, if her father be gone?"

But, leaving this aged couple to complain and John Smith to enjoy his repose, we must now return to poor Morag whom, as you may recollect, gentlemen, we left hunted into covert by the two dragoons who had so closely pursued her. The patch of natural wood into which she dived was not large. It chiefly consisted of oaks and birches, which, though they had grown to a considerable size in certain parts, so that their wide-spread ing heads had kept the knolls on which their stems stood, altogether free from the encumbrance of any kind of brushwood,—had yet in most places risen up thinner and smaller, leaving ample room and air around them to support thickets of the tallest broom and juniper bushes.

It chanced that Morag was not altogether unacquainted with the nature of the place, having at one time in earlier life been hired to tend the cows of a farmer at no great distance from it. She was well aware that a rill, which had its origin in the higher grounds at some distance, came wimpling into the upper part of the wood, and thence, during its descent over the sloping surface of the ground, from its having met with certain obstructions, or from some other cause, it had worn itself a channel through the soft soil to the depth of some six feet or so, but which was yet so narrow that the ferns and bushes growing out of the undermined sods that fringed the edges of it almost entirely covered it with one continued tangled and matted arch. Towards this rill Morag endeavoured to make her way through the tall broom, and as she was doing so she heard the dismounted trooper, who had by this time entered the wood after her, calling to his comrade, who sat mounted outside :

"Bill! do you padderowl round the wood, and keep a sharp look out that she don't bolt without your seeing her. I'll follow arter her here, and try if I can't lay my hands on her ; and if I do but chance to light on her, be she witch or devil, I'll drag her out of her covert by the scruff of the neck."

Morag heard no more than this. She pressed forward towards the bed of the rill, and having reached it, she stopped, like a chased doe, one moment to listen, and hearing that the curses, as well as the crashing of the jack-boots of her pursuer, as yet indicated that he was still at some distance behind her, and evidently much entangled in his progress, she carefully shed the pendulous plants of the ferns asunder, and then slid herself gently down into the hollow channel. There finding her feet safely planted on the bottom, she cautiously and silently groped her way along the downward course of the rill through the dark and confined passage which it had worn out for its tiny stream. In this way she soon came to the lower edge of the wood, where the hollow channel became deeper, and where it assumed more of the character of a ravine, but where it was still skirted with occasional oaks, mingled with thickets of birches, hazels, and furze bushes.

Morag was about to emerge from the obscurity of this

subterranean arch into the more open light when, as she looked out, she beheld the mounted trooper standing on his stirrups on the top of the bank eagerly gazing around him in all directions. The furze there grew too thick and high for him to be able to force his way down to the bottom of the ravine even if he had accidentally observed her. But his eyes were directed to higher and more distant objects, and seeing that she had been as yet unperceived, she instantly drew so far back as to be beyond all reach of his observation, whilst she could perfectly well watch him, so long as he maintained his present position. She listened for the crashing strides of him who was engaged in searching the wood for her. For a time they came faint and distant to her ear, but by degrees they began to come nearer, and then again the sound would alternately diminish and increase as he turned away in some other direction, fighting through the opposing boughs, and then came beating his way back again in the same manner with many a round oath. At length she heard him raging forward in the direction of the rill, at some forty yards above the place where she was, blaspheming as he went.

"Ten thousand devils!" cried he; "such a place as this I never se'ed in all my life afore. If my heyes bean't nearly whipt out of my head with them 'ere blasted broom shafts, my name aint Tom Wetherby! Dang it, there again! that whip has peeled the very skin off my cheek, and made both my heyes run over with water like mill-sluices—I wonder at all where this she-devil can be hidden? Curse her! Do you think, Bill, that she can raaly have ridden off through the hair, as they do say they do? But for a matter of that, she may be here some-where after all, for my heyes be so dimmed, that, dang me an' I could see her if she were to rise up afore my very face. How they do smart with pain! Oh! Lord, where am I going?" cried he, as he went smack down through the ferns and brush into the concealed bed of the rill, and was laid prostrate on his back in the narrow clayey bottom of it, in such a position that it defied him to rise.

"Hollo, Bill!" cried he, from the bowels of the earth, in a voice which reached his comrade as if he had spoken with a pillow on his mouth, but which rang with terrible distinctness down the hollow natural tube to the spot where Morag was concealed. "Hollo!—help!—help!"

"What a murrain is the matter with ye?" cried Bill, very much astonished.

"I've fallen plump into the witches' den!—into the very

bottomless pit!—Hollo!—hollo! Help!—help!" cried the fallen trooper from the abyss.

"How the plague am I to get to ye if so be the pit be bottomless?" cried Bill, in a drawling tone, that did not argue much promise of any zealous exertion of effective aid on the part of the speaker.

"Curse ye, come along quickly, or I shall be smothered in this here infernal, dark, outlandish place," cried Tom Wetherby.

"Well,—well," replied Bill, with the same long-drawn tone of philosophic indifference, "I'm a coming—I'm a coming. But you must keep chaunting out from the bottom of that bottomless pit of yours, do you hear, Tom, else I shall never find you in that 'ere wilderness. And how the devil I am to get into it is more than I know."

The dragoon turned his horse very leisurely away, to look for some place where he could best quit his saddle, in order to make good his entrance on foot into the thicket. The moment the quick eyes of Morag perceived that he had disappeared from his station on the brow of the bank, she crept forth from her concealment, and keeping her way down through the shallow stream, that her footsteps might leave no prints behind them, she stole off, until she was beyond all hearing of the two dragoons. Then it was that Morag began to ply her utmost speed, and, after following the ravine until it expanded into a small and partially wooded glen, she hurried on through it, until at length she found herself emerging on the lower and more open country. Afraid of being seen, she made a long circuitous sweep through some rough broomy waste ground of considerable extent, towards a distant hummock, with the shape of which she was familiar, and having thus gained a part of the country with which she was acquainted, though it was still very distant from her present home, she hailed the descent of the shades of night with great satisfaction.

Under their protection she proceeded on her way with great alacrity, and without apprehension, though with a torn heart, that made her every now and then stop to give full vent to her grief for John Smith, of whose death she had so little reason to doubt, from all the circumstances she had heard. At length fatigue came so powerfully upon her, that she was not sorry to perceive, as she was about to descend into a hollow, the light of a cheerful fire, that blazed through the window of a turf-built cottage, and was reflected on the surface of a rushy stream that ran lazily through the bottom near to it. The door was shut, but Morag descended the path that led towards it, and knocked without scruple.

An old man and woman came immediately to open it, and looked out eagerly, as if for some one whose coming they had expected, and disappointment seemed to cloud their brows, when they found only her who was a stranger to them. Morag, addressing them in Gaelic, entreated for leave to rest herself for half an hour by their fireside. She was admitted, after some hesitation and whispering between them, after which she craved a morsel of oaten cake, and a draught of water. A little girl, of some eight or nine years old, waited not to know her granny's will, but ran to a cupboard for the cake ; and brought it to her, and then hastened• to fill a bowl with water from a pitcher that stood in a corner. The old couple would have fain pumped out of Morag something of her history, and they put many questions to her for that purpose. But she was too shrewd for them, and all they could gather from her was, that she had been away seeing her friends a long way off, and that she had first rode, and then walked so far, that she was glad of a little rest, and a morsel to allay her hunger, after which she would be enabled to continue her journey, with many thanks to them for their hospitality.

Morag had not sat there for many minutes when there came a rap to the door. The old man sprang up to open it, and immediately three Highlanders appeared, full armed with claymores and dirks, but very much jaded and soiled with travel. Morag retired into a corner.

"Och, Ian ! Ian !"—"Och, Hamish ! Hamish !" cried the old couple, embracing two of them, who appeared to be their sons ; and, "Oh, father ! father !" cried the little girl, springing into Ian's arms.

"Tuts, don't be foolish, Kirstock !" cried Ian, in a surly tone, as he shook off the little girl ; "What's the use of all this nonsense, father ?"—Better for you to be getting something for us and our comrade MacCallum here to drink. We are almost famished for want ;" and with that he threw himself into the old man's wooden arm-chair.

"Aye, aye, father," said Hamish, occupying the seat where his mother had sat, and motioning to MacCallum to take that which Morag had just left; "we have had a sad tramp away from the battle. Would we had never gone near it ! Aye, and we got such a fright into the bargain."

"Fright !" cried the old man much excited; "surely, surely, my sons are not cowards ! Much as I love you, boys, I would rather that you had both died than run away."

"Oh!" said MacCallum, now joining in the conversation, " we all three fought like lions in the battle. But it requires nerves harder than steel to look upon the Devil, and if ever he was seen on earth, we saw him this precious night."

"Preserve us all!" said the old woman; "what was he like?"

"Never mind what he was like, mother," said Ian gruffly; "let us have some of your bread and cheese, and a drop of Uisge-beatha to put some heart in us."

"You shall have all that I have to give you, boys," said the old man; "but that is not much. I would have fain given a sup out of the bottle to the poor wounded man that came in here, a little time ago; but I bethought me that you might want it all, and so we sent him to his bed with a cup of warm milk and water."

"Bed, did you say?" cried Ian. "What!" one of Prince Charley's men?

"Surely, surely!" said the old man. "Troth, I should have been anything but fond of letting in anyone else but a man who had fought on the same side with yourselves."

"Don't speak of our having fought on Charley's side, father," said Ian; "that's not to be boasted of now. The fruits of fighting for him have been nothing but danger and starvation, so far as we have gathered them; and now we have no prospect before us but the risk of hanging. Methinks you would have shown more wisdom if you had sent this fellow away from your door. To have us three hunted men here, is enough to make the place too hot, without bringing in another to add to the fire."

"Never mind, Ian," said MacCallum; "why may we not make our own of him? You know very well that John MacAllister told us that he could make our peace, and save our lives, if we could only prove our loyalty to the King, by bringing in a rebel or two."

"Very true," said Hamish; "and an excellent advice it was."

"Most excellent," said Ian; "and if we act wisely, and as I advise, this fellow shall be our first peace-offering."

"Oh, boys, boys!" cried the old man; "would you buy your own lives by treachery of so black a dye?"

"Oh, life is sweet!" cried the old woman—"and the lives of my bairns ——"

"Hould your foolish tongue, woman!" interrupted the old man. "No, no, boys! I'll never consent to it."

"Oh, life is sweet! life is sweet!" cried the old woman again; "and the lives of both my bonny boys—the life of Ian, the father of this poor lassie! ——"

"Oh, my father's life!" whimpered the little girl.

"This is no place to talk of such things," said the old man, leading the way into the apartment at the opposite end of the house, to that where John Smith was sleeping, and followed by all but Morag, who, having slipped towards the door, to listen after he had closed it, heard him say, "What made you speak that way before the stranger lass?"

"Who and what is she at all?" demanded Ian.

"A poor tired lass, weary with the long way she has been to see her friends," said the old woman; "but she'll be gone very soon."

"If she does not go of her own accord, we must take strong measures with her too," said Ian.

"God forgive you, boys, what would you do?" said the old man. "Let not the Devil tempt you thus. Would you bring foul treason upon this humble, but hitherto spotless shed of mine, by violating the sacred rights of hospitality to a woman, and by giving up a man to an ignominious death, who, upon the faith of it, is now soundly sleeping under my roof, in the other end of the house? Fye, fye, boys! I tell you plainly I will be a party to no such wickedness."

"So you would rather be a party to assist in hanging Hamish and me, your own flesh and blood?" said Ian. "But you need be no party to either; for we shall take all the guilt of this fellow's death upon ourselves."

"You shall never do this foul treason, if I can prevent it," said the old man, with determination.

"Poof!" said Ian, "how could you prevent us?"

"By rousing the man to defend himself," said the father rather unguardedly.

"Ha! say you so?" cried Ian. "What! would you rouse up an armed man to fight against your own children? Then must we take means to prevent your so doing."

"Oh, Ian!" cried the old woman. "Oh, Hamish! Oh, boys! boys!"

"What! what! what boys!" cried the old man with great excitement, whilst there was a sound of feet as of a struggle. "Would you lay your impious hands upon your own father?"

"Oh, don't hurt poor granny!" cried the little girl, in the bitterest tone of grief.

"Be quiet, I tell you, Kirstock!" cried Ian, in an angry

tone. "Hold out of my way, mother! We'll do him no harm! we are only going to bind him that he may not interfere."

"Boys, boys!" cried the old man; "you have been tempted by the Devil! There is no wonder that you should have seen him once to-night? and I should not wonder if he was to appear to you again, for you seem resolved to be his children, and not mine."

"Sit down—sit down quietly in the chair," said Ian; "sit down, I say quietly, and let MacCallum put the rope about you. By the great oath you had better!"

"Oh, boys!" cried the old woman; "Och, Hamish! Och, Ian."

Morag hardly waited to hear so much of this dialogue as I have given, when she resolved to be the means, if possible, of saving the life of the poor wounded man, whom the wretches had thus determined so traitorously to give up to the tender mercies of the Duke of Cumberland. She had her hand upon the door of the chamber where he slept, in order to go in and rouse him, when she remembered that, in this way, her own safety was almost certain to be compromised. She therefore immediately adopted a plan, which she considered might be equally effectual for her purpose as regarded the stranger, whilst it would leave to herself some chance of escape. Slipping on tiptoe to the outer door, she quietly opened it, and, letting herself out, she moved quickly round the house, towards a little window belonging to the room at that end of it, where she knew the wounded man was lying. It consisted of two small panes of glass, placed in a frame that moved inwards upon hinges. She put her ear to it, but no sound reached her save that of deep snoring. Morag pushed gently against the frame, and it yielded to the pressure. Having inserted her head, and looked eagerly about, in the hope of descrying the sleeper, by the partial stream of moonlight that was admitted into the place, she could discover nothing but the heap of straw in the bedstead in a dark corner, where, wrapped in a blanket, he lay so buried as to be altogether invisible. She called to him, at first in a low voice, and afterwards in a somewhat louder tone, till at length she awaked him.

"Who is there?" demanded he in Gaelic.

"Rise! rise, and escape!" said she, in a low but distinct voice, and in the same language; "Your liberty! your life is in danger! Up, up, and fly from this house!" Having said this, she retreated her head a little from the window, to watch the effect of her warning, so that the moon shone brightly upon her countenance, and completely illuminated every feature of it.

There was a quick rustling noise among the straw, and then she heard the slow heavy step of the man within. Suddenly a head was thrust out of the window, and the moonbeam falling fully upon it, disclosed to the terrified eyes of Morag, the features of John Smith—pale, bloody, and death-like, with all the fearful appendages which he bore, the whole combination being such as to leave not a doubt in her mind that she beheld his ghost. With one shrill scream, which she could not control, she vanished in a moment from before the window. John Smith, filled in his turn with superstitious awe, as well as with the strangeness of the manner in which he had been roused from the deep sleep into which he had been plunged,—and struck by the well-known though hollow voice in which he had been addressed—the solemn warning which he had received, and, above all, the distinct, though most unaccountable appearance of Morag, with whose features he was so perfectly acquainted — together with the wild and sudden manner in which the vision had departed—all tended to convince him that the whole was a supernatural visitation. For some moments his powers of action were suspended; but steps and voices in the outer apartment speedily recalled his presence of mind. He drew his claymore, summoned up his resolution, and banging up the door with one kick of his foot, he took a single stride into the middle of the floor. The fire was still blazing, and it threw on his terrible figure the full benefit of its light. The three villains having tied the old man into his chair, and locked him and his wife and grandchild into the place where the conference was held, had been at that moment preparing to steal in upon the sleeping stranger. Suddenly they beheld the same apparition which they had seen in the churchyard, burst from the very room which they were about to enter. The threatening words of the old man recurred to them all.

"Oh, the devil! the devil! the devil" cried the terrified group, and bearing back upon one another, they tripped, and in one moment, all their heels were dancing the strangest possible figures in the air, to the music of their own mingled screams and yells. You will easily believe, gentlemen, that John Smith tarried not a moment to inquire after their bruises, but pushing up the outer door, and slapping it to after him, he again pursued his way towards the farm of the Pensassenach.

Winged by her fears, and in dreadful apprehension that the ghost of John Smith was still following her, Morag flew with an unnatural swiftness and impetus. She was quite unconscious of noticing any of the familiar objects by the way; yet, by a species of instinct, she reached home, in so short a time, that she could hardly believe her own senses. But still in dreadful fear of the ghost, she thundered at the door, and roared out to her mistress for admittance. The kind-hearted Pensassenach had been sitting up in a state of the cruellest anxiety regarding Morag, of whose intended expedition she had received no inkling, nor had she been informed of her departure until long after she was gone. She no sooner heard her voice, and her knock, than she hastened to admit her.

"Foolish girl that you are!" said she, "I am thankful to see you alive. My stars and garters, what a draggled figure you are!—But come away into this room here, and let me hear all you have to tell me about the battle. The rebels were defeated, were they not?—eh?—Why, what is the matter with the girl? she pants as if she was dying. Sit down, sit down, child, and compose yourself; you look for all the world as if you had seen a ghost."

"Och, och, mem!—och, hoch!" replied the girl, very much appalled that her mistress should thus, as she thought, so immediately see the truth written in her very face. "Och, hoch! an' a ghaist Morag has surely seen. Has ta ghaist put her mark upon her face?—Och, hoch! she'll ne'er won ower wi't!"

"The poor girl's head has been turned by the horrible scenes of carnage she has witnessed," said the Pensassenach.

"Och, hoch!" said Morag, with her hands on her knees, and rocking to and fro with nervous agitation; "terrible sights! terrible sights, surely, surely!"

"Here, my poor Morag," said the Pensassenach, after she had dropped into a cup a small quantity of some liquid nostrum of her own, from a phial, hastily taken from a little medicine chest, and added some water to it, "drink this, my good girl!"

"Och, hoch!" said Morag, after she had swallowed it; "she thinks she sees ta ghaist yet."

"What ghost did you see?" demanded the Pensassenach.

"Och, hoch! Och, hoch, mem!" replied Morag, trembling more than ever; "Shon Smiss, ghaist; Shon Smiss, as sure as Morag is in life, an' ta leddy stannin' in ta body tare afore her een."

"John Smith's ghost!" cried the Pensassenach. "Pooh, nonsense! But again I ask you, how went the battle? The rumour is, that the rebels have been signally defeated, and all cut to pieces."

"Och, hoch! is tat true?" said Morag, weeping. "Och, hoch, poor Shon Smiss!"

"Did you not see the rout?" demanded the Pensassenach. "Did you not witness the battle, and behold the glorious triumph of the royal army?"

"Och, hoch, no!" replied the girl! "Morag saw nae pattals, nor naesin' but hearin' terrible shots o' guns, an' twa or sree red cotted sodgers tat pursued her for her life."

"Well, well!" replied the Pensassenach; "come now I tell me your whole history."

Morag's nerves being now somewhat composed, she gave her mistress as clear an outline as she could of all that had befallen her. The Pensassenach dropped some tears, to mingle with those which Morag shed, when she recounted the evidence of John Smith's death, which she felt to be but too probably true. But when she came to talk of the ghost, she did all she could to laugh the girl out of her fears, insisting with her that she had been deceived by terror and weakness, and seeing how much the poor girl was worn out, she desired her to take some refreshment, and to go to bed directly; and she had no sooner retired, than the Pensassenach prepared to follow her example.

Morag, overcome with the immense fatigue she had undergone, had not strength left to undo much more than half her dress, when she dropped down on her bed, and fell over into a slumber. She had been lying in this state for fully half an hour or more, during part of which she had been dreaming of John Smith, mixed up with many a strange incident, with all of which his slaughter, and his pale countenance and bloody figure were invariably connected, when she was awaked by a tapping at the window of her apartment, which was upon the ground floor. She looked up and stared, but the moon was by this time gone down, and all without was dark as pitch.

"Morag! Morag!" cried John Smith, who knowing well where she slept, went naturally to her window to get her to come round and give him admission to the house, and yet at the same time half doubting, after the strange visitation which he had had, from what he believed to be her *wraith*, that he could hardly expect to find her alive. "Morag! Morag!" cried he again in his faint hollow voice.

"Och, Lord have mercy upon me, there it is!" cried Morag,

in her native tongue, and shaking from head to foot with terror. "Who is there?"

"It's me, your own Ian," cried John, in a tender tone. "Let me in, Morag, for the love of God!"

"Och, Ian, Ian!" cried Morag. "Och, Ian, my darling dear Ian! are you sure that it is really yourself in real flesh and blood?—for I have got such a fright already this night. But if it really and truly be you, go round to the door and I'll be with you in a minute. Och, och, the Lord be praised, if it really be him after all!"

Trembling, and agitated with the numerous contrary emotions of hope, fear, and joy, by which she was assailed, Morag sprang out of bed, lighted her lamp, hurried on just enough of her clothes as might make her decent in the eyes of her lover, and with her bosom heaving, and her heart beating, as if it would have burst through her side, she ran to unlock the outer door. Her lamp flashed on the fearful figure without. She again beheld the horrible spectre which had so recently terrified her, and believing that it was John Smith's ghost which she saw, and that it had followed her home to corroborate the fatal tidings she had heard regarding his death, which had been already so much strengthened by her dreams, she uttered a piercing shriek, and fainted away on the floor. The shriek alarmed the Pensassenach, who was not yet in bed. Hastily throwing a wrapper over her deshabille, she seized her candle, and proceeded down stairs with all speed, and was led by John's voice of lamentation to the kitchen, whither he had carried Morag in his arms, and where the lady found him tearing his hair, or rather the heathery turf which then appeared to be doing duty for it, in the very extremity of mental agony. It is strange how the same things, seen under different aspects and circumstances, will produce the most opposite effects. There being nothing now about John Smith, or his actions, that did not savour of humanity, but his extraordinary head-dress, the Pensassenach had no doubt that it was the real bodily man that she saw before her; she perceived nothing but what was powerfully ludicrous in his strange costume, the absurdity of which was heightened by his agonising motions and attitudes, and exclamations of intense anxiety about Morag, whose fainting-fit gave no uneasiness to a woman of her experience. The Pensassenach laughed heartily, and then hurried away for a bunch of feathers to burn under Morag's nose, by which means she quickly brought her out of her swoon, and by a little explanation she speedily restored her to the full possession of her reason. This accomplished, the Pensassenach entirely forgot John Smith's wretched appearance, in the eagerness of her inquiries regarding the result of the engagement.

"How went the battle, John?" demanded she. "We heard the guns, but the cannonade did not last long. The victory was soon gained, and it was with the right cause, was it not?"

"Woe, woe! Oich, oich!" cried John, in a melancholy tone, and shaking his head in utter despair. "Oich, oich, her head is sore, sore."

"Very true, very true!" cried the compassionate Pensassenach. "I had forgotten you altogether, shame on me! Ah! poor fellow, how bloody you are about the face! You must be grievously wounded."

"Troth she be tat," said John Smith. "She has gotten a wicked slash on ta croon, tat maist spleeted her skull. An' she wad hae peen dead lang or noo an it had na peen for tiss ponny peat plaister tat she putten tilt. Morag tak' her awa' noo, for she has toon her turn, and somesing lighter may serve."

"Och, hoch, hoch, tat is fearsome," said Morag, after she had removed the clod from John's head. "She mak's Morag sick ta vera sight o't."

"Och, but tat be easy noo," said John. "Hech, she was joost like an if she had been carryin' a' ta hill o' Lethen Bar on her head."

"Poor fellow, poor fellow!" cried the Pensassenach, "that is a fearful cut indeed. But I don't think the skull is fractured. How and where did you get this fearful wound?"

"Fare mony a petter man's got more," replied John, yielding up his head into the affectionate hands of Morag, who was now so far recovered as to be able to look more narrowly at it.

"Oich, oich, fat a head!" cried the affectionate and feeling girl, shuddering and growing pale, and then bursting into an agony of tears, as she looked upon his gaping wound. "Oich, oich, she'll never do good more! She canna leeve ava, ava!"

"Tut, tut!" cried John, with a ghastly smile that was meant to reassure Morag. "Fat nonsense tat Morag pe speak! An' she pe traivel a' ta way hame so far, fat for wad she pe deein' noo tat she is at hame?"

"Alas, poor fellow!" said the Pensassenach, as she was directing Morag to bind up his head, "I wish I may be able to

make this your home. After all our losses and sufferings for
our loyalty by those marauding rascals three days ago, we
shall next run the risk of being punished for harbouring a
rebel. But no matter. Happen what may, you have large
claims upon me, John, and as long as Morag can conceal you
here you shall be safe. You have been so short a time away
that few people can be aware of it, and still fewer can know
the cause of your absence."

What the Pensassenach said was true, for as most of her
people had run away when the Highland party appeared, there
were few who certainly knew the cause of John Smith's absence,
and those few who did know were not very likely to tell anything about it. Trusting to this she gave out that she had
sent him after the rebels to keep an eye on her husband's
horses, and to endeavour to recover them if he could, and that
in making this attempt he had received his wound. To give
the better colour to this story, she called her people together,
and offered a handsome reward to such of them as would go
immediately and try to find and bring back the horses, telling
them that John Smith could describe to them whereabouts
they were most likely to fall in with them, he having at one
time actually got possession of most of them, but that they had
escaped from him, having been scared away by the thundering
of the artillery. But not a man of them would venture upon
such a search among the gibbets, where, as they were told, so
many of their murdered countrymen were still hanging, and
where without much inquiry or ceremony anyone who might go
on such an errand might be tucked up to swing in company
with them. Every hour increased this terror by bringing
accounts of fresh executions, and indeed the fears of the
Pensassenach's men turned out to be by no means groundless,
for it is a truth but too well known that many innocent
servants who were sent to seek their master's horses never
returned.

The Pensassenach did not suffer for her kindness in thus
protecting John Smith; and she and her husband were
ultimately no losers from the havoc which the Highlanders
committed on their farm. Their damage was reported to the
Duke of Cumberland, and the lady's conduct having been
highly extolled as that of a very loyal Englishwoman, who had
been thus persecuted for the open expression of her sentiments,
the most ample remuneration was assigned to her by the
government.

John Smith, nursed as he was by Morag, soon recovered.

After he was quite restored to health, he only waited until he could scrape a little money together to enable him to furnish a cottage ere he should make her his wife. The penetration of the Pensassenach soon enabled her to discover how matters stood between them, and she found means to make all smooth for them in the manner which was most flattering to John, that is, by presenting him with a very handsome purse of money as a reward for the eminent services he had rendered her. John was so proud of the purse that he did not know whether most to value it or the gold pieces it contained, and much as he loved Morag, and eager as he was for their union, he had some doubt whether he could ever bring himself to part even with one of those pretty pieces which he so respected for the Pensassenach's sake. And, alas, as it so happened, he was never called upon to spend them as it was intended they should have been spent. Fain would I have made my story end happily, gentlemen; but, as I am narrating a piece of actual history, I must be verawcious. John had made all preparation for their marriage when, alas, Morag was seized with some acute complaint about the region of the heart and lungs, which all the medical attendants that the Pensassenach could command could not fathom or relieve. John watched her with the tenderest and most remitting solicitude. But it pleased God that his unwearied care of her should not be blessed with the same happy result which hers had been with regard to him, for after a long and lingering illness poor Morag died on the very day she should have been his bride. The probability was that the unheard of fatigue of body and agitation of mind which she underwent during her heroic expedition in search of her lover had produced some fatal organic change within her.

John Smith was inconsolable for the loss of Morag. For some time he was more like a walking clod than a man. Even the kind attempts of his master and mistress to rouse him were unavailing. When at length he was able to go about his usual duties on the farm, to do which his honest regard for his employer's interest stimulated him, he suffered so much mental agony from the painful recollections which every object around him suggested to his mind that he felt he could no longer go rationally about his master's affairs. Being at last convinced that he was in danger of falling into utter and hopeless despair, he came to the resolution of enlisting in the army, and having once formed this determination, he went through a very touching scene of parting with the kind Pensassenach and her husband, and shouldering his small kit he went and joined the gallant Forty-Second, then the Black Watch. He served with distinguished approbation in all the actions in which that brave corps was in his time engaged. He was made a serjeant at Bunker's Hill; and after time had in some degree assuaged his affliction, he married a very active, intelligent, and economical woman, with whose aid·he undertook to keep the regimental mess. John could neither read nor write, and he always spoke English imperfectly. But his clever wife enabled him to carry on the business for so many years, with so much credit to himself, and so successfully, that he ultimately retired with her at an advanced period of life with the enjoyment of his pension and such an accumulation of fortune as made him perfectly comfortable.

I knew John well. He was a warm-hearted man, and always remarkable for his uprightness and integrity, and especially for a strict determination to keep his word, whatever it might cost him so to do. As an instance of this, I may mention, that having on one occasion had a serious illness, in which he was given up by the doctor, he made a will, in which he left many small legacies to poor people. John recovered, but he thought it his duty to keep his word, and he paid the legacies. To me, and to my brother, who lived in one of his houses while we were at the school of Nairn, he acted the part of a kind friend and guardian. He was perhaps too kind and indulgent to us, indeed. No one dared to him to impute a fault to us, even when we were guilty. I remember that he had a large garden, well stocked with fruit trees and gooseberry bushes. Often has the good old man sent me into it to steal fruit for myself and brother, whilst he watched at the door, lest his wife might surprise and detect me. Many is the time that I have listened to him, with boyish wonder, as, with lightning in his eye, he fought over again his battles of Culloden, Bunker's Hill, and Ticonderoga.

As John had no children, his intended heir was a nephew. His greatest desire in life was to marry him to a grand-daughter of his old departed benefactress, the Pensassenach. He offered to settle his whole fortune, which was not small, on the young lady, if she would only marry his nephew; and John's wife did all in her power to back up the proposal. But although the nephew was a good, well-doing lad, he was not the man to take the young woman's fancy; and so the match never took place.

22

CRUELTY OF THE DUKE OF CUMBERLAND AFTEI
THE BATTLE OF CULLODEN.

Clifford.—Is it possible that the Duke of Cumberland coul have authorised such atrocities, as the hanging up innocen servants in the way you describe, Mr. Macpherson ?

Dominie.—I am afraid that what I have asserted is but to true, sir.

Author.—I am sorry to say, that I am in possession of document which but too satisfactorily proves, that he did gi most cruel orders. It is an orderly book of the thirty seventh regiment, which was called Cholmondeley's Regiment and in that I find, in the general orders, dated "*The Camp a Enverness April,* 17*th,* 1746," the following entry :—"*A captain and fifty foot to march directly, and vizt all th cothidges in the naberhod of the field of battal, and to search fo rebbels, the officers and men will take notiss, that the pubilick orders of the rebbels yesterday was to give us no quarters.*' This, I think, was a pretty broad hint to the men and th officer commanding them, what it was that the Duke expected of them.

Grant.—Very distinct, indeed.

Author.—Not to be mistaken, I think.

Clifford.—Is there anything existing to establish that any such order was given by the Prince, previous to the battle, as that to which the Duke here alludes !

Author.—Not a vestige of anything that I am aware of. But if such orders had been given by the Prince, that circum- stance would have afforded no apology for him to have issued the order I have now repeated to you, after the battle was over, and the enemy so effectually cut to pieces in the field. Noth- ing, I think, could more mark a sanguinary temper than his thus letting loose a body of men, to visit all the neighbouring cottages, and to put to death, in cold blood, all whom his ignorant and bloodthirsty myrmidons might choose to con- sider as rebels. The slaughter in this way, of the innocent as well as of the guilty, was said to have been immense.

Clifford.—The picture is horrible !

Grant.—It is horrible to think of it, even at this great distance of time, seated comfortably, as I am at this moment, in this great oaken arm chair.

Serjeant.—And a comfortable arm-chair that is, sir; and many a good day and queer night has it seen. If I am not

mistaken, that was old Allister Shaw of Inchrory's very
chair.

Author.—Ay—who was Alister Shaw, Archy?

Serjeant.—Faith, sir, he was a queer tough little fellow,
Inchrory—for by that name he was always best known in the
country—as proud as a bantam cock on his own midden-head.
The body cared not for the King. I have two or three
curious little anecdotes about him, which I can tell you and the
gentlemen, if you have no objections.

Clifford.—Objections, Mr. Serjeant! I, the secretary,
desire that you shall tell them, without another moment's
delay.

Serjeant.—Aweel, aweel, sir! I'll do that at your bidding.
I'm not accustomed to disobey the adjutant.

<hr>

ALISTER SHAW OF INCHRORY.

IT happened one day, gentlemen, that the Earl of Fife was
travelling up this glen on his way over to his house of Mar
Lodge in Braemar, and having stopped at Caochan-Seirceag
over by yonder, he sent one of his people across the meadow
here to tell Inchrory that he meant to honour him with a visit.
The gentleman knocked at the door, was admitted by the good-
wife, and ushered into Inchrory's presence. He found him
seated in his arm-chair in the position which he always
occupied, that is, on the most comfortable side of the fire.

" Good day to you, Inchrory," said the gentleman, bowing.

" The same to you sir," said Inchrory, bowing his head very
grandly and ceremoniously, but without stirring.

"My Lord the Earl of Fife, who is halting at Caochan-
Seirceag, on his road to Braemar, has sent me over to tell you
that he means to step aside from his way to visit you," said the
gentleman.

"Well, sir," said Inchrory, proudly, "what of that? Tell
him he is welcome."

The gentleman, astonished with his reception, bowed and
retired as an ambassador might have done from a royal presence.

" Well, sir," said Lord Fife to him, after he had rejoined
him, " is Inchrory at home?"

" He is at home, my Lord," replied the gentleman; " but he
is the surliest churl I ever came across."

" As how?" demanded the Earl.

"Why, my Lord, the little wretch never rose from his chair," replied the gentleman; and then he repeated the conversation he had had with Inchrory. "If your Lordship would take my counsel, you would e'en continue your journey and leave the bear to suck his own paws in his own den."

"Why do you not flit* that insolent fellow," said Lord Fife to James MacGrigor of Pitiveach, his factor, who happened to be with him; "you are tacksman of this farm, and so you have it in your power to turn him out."

"Why, my Lord," replied MacGrigor, "he and his forbears† have been there for generations; and, though he certainly is a great original, he is no bad fellow for all that."

"So, so," replied the Earl, laughing, "the fellow is an original, is he? Then I must see him. It is something to discover so great a potentate, holding his undisputed reign in wilds like these, so many miles from any other human dwelling. I must visit him directly."

The fact was that the Earl had but recently become possessed of these Highland estates, and Inchrory looked upon him as a new man—a Lowlander—whom it was his duty, as it was very much his inclination, to despise; whilst the Earl, for his part, knowing that such was a feeling which naturally enough pervaded the minds of the Highlanders even on his own newly-acquired lands, was determined to do it away by using all manner of courtesy to everyone with whom he might come into contact. Above all things he felt that the opportunity which he now had of overcoming the prejudice of such a man as Inchrory was by no means to be lost. To Inchrory, therefore, he went without a moment's delay, was admitted into the house, and ushered into the presence.

"Good day to you, Inchrory," said the Earl, bowing.

"Good day to you, Lord Fife," replied Inchrory, bowing with the same formality as formerly, but still keeping his seat. "Sit down, my Lord—sit down. Here is a chair beside me; for I always keep the *benmost*‡ seat in my own house."

"Very right, Inchrory," said the Earl, smiling, and seating himself accordingly beside his host; "and a very comfortable seat it seems to be."

"Very comfortable," said Inchrory, setting himself more firmly into it; "and I hope that one is easy for your Lordship."

"Very easy indeed," said Lord Fife; "a long ride, such as I have had, would make a hard stone feel easy, and much more

---

* Remove.   † Ancestors.   ‡ Innermost.

this chair beneath your hospitable roof of Inchrory and before
your good fire in this bitter cold day."

"Well, well, my Lord," replied Inchrory, for the first time
shaking the Earl heartily by the hand, and very much pleased
with the familiar manner in which his visitor had so unexpectedly comported himself,—"well, all I can say is, that you
are heartily welcome to it. Here, gudewife! Bring out the
bottle. Lord Fife must taste Inchrory's bottle; and bestir
yourself, do you hear, and see what you can give his Lordship
to eat."

The whisky bottle was brought, and Inchrory drank the
Earl's health, who without any ceremony hobernobbed with
him in turn. Mutton, ham, cheese, broiled kipper salmon,
bannocks and butter, were produced and put down promiscu-
ously. The Earl ate like a hill farmer, and partook moderately
of the whisky, which Inchrory swallowed in large and repeated
bumpers to his Lordship's good health. He talked loud and
joyously, and the Earl familiarly humoured him to his full
bent. They were the greatest friends in the world. The Earl
particularly delighted Inchrory by praising, caressing, and
feeding a great rough deer-hound, which, roused from his lair
in front of the fire by the entrance of the eatables, put his long
snout and cold nose into his Lordship's hand, and craved his
attention. But this dog had very nearly ruined all; for the
Earl was so much taken with the animal that, having left the
house after a very warm parting with Inchrory, he sent back
his factor to him to offer to purchase the animal at any price.

"What!" cried Inchrory, drawing himself up in his chair,
and looking thunderbolts,—"what! does Lord Fife take me
for a dog-dealer? I would not sell my dog to any Lord in the
land. I would not sell my dog to the King on the throne.
Tell his Lordship I would as soon sell him my wife!"

"What a stupid fellow I am, Inchrory!" said the factor.
"Did I say that it was the Earl that sent me? If I did, I was
quite wrong. No! no! his lordship did no such thing. He
only admired the dog so much, that he could speak of nothing
else as he crossed the meadow to join his people. It was my
mistake altogether. Hearing him admire your dog so much, I
thought it would be a kind act from me to you, my old friend,
just to ride back quietly, and give you a hint of it. 'I thought
I had the best dogs in all Scotland,' said the Earl, 'but that
dog of Inchrory's beats them all clean. He is worth them all
put together. He is a prince among dogs, as his master is a
prince among men. Where could you find a master worthy of

such a dog but Inchrory himself—the best fellow I have met with in all this country.'"

"Did the Earl of Fife say that?" cried Inchrory, "Here, bring me a leash. Now," added he, after having fastened it about the hound's neck, "take hold of that, and lead the dog to the Earl, and tell him that Inchrory begs he will accept of him as a present."

The Earl was delighted with the dog, as well as with the able conduct of his ambassador who brought him; and he was no sooner fairly established in his own house at Mar Lodge, than he sent an especial messenger over the hill to Inchrory, with a letter from himself, thanking him for his noble present, and requesting him to come and pay him a visit. Inchrory most graciously accepted the invitation; and the Earl took care to be prepared to give him a proper reception.

Inchrory, dressed in his best Highland costume, accoutred with sword, dirk, and pistols complete, mounted his long tailed garron, and rode over to Mar Lodge. When he arrived, two grooms of the Earl's were ready, one to hold his horse's head, and the other his stirrup while he dismounted, and he was ushered into the house by the house-steward, and through an alley of footmen, all richly attired in the Earl's livery, till he was shown into the room where his Lordship was seated. Inchrory had never seen anything the least like this before. But he was too proud to manifest the smallest surprise—and holding up his head, he strode in with a dignified air, and took all this pomp as if it had belonged to him of course. The Earl was seated, amidst all his magnificence, in a great arm-chair next the fire, with an empty one placed at his left hand.

"Good day to you, Inchrory," said the Earl to him as he entered, and at the same time nodding his head familiarly as he spoke, but without rising from his seat.

"Good day to you, my Lord," said Inchrory, strutting forward like a turkey cock.

"Come away, and sit down beside me here, Inchrory," said the Earl, "for I always keep the benmost seat in my own house."

"Right!—right, my Lord!" said Inchrory, seating himself beside the Earl, and taking his hand and shaking it heartily, without any sort of ceremony; "you are quite right, my Lord; that is exactly my rule. Every man should have the benmost seat in his own house."

"You see that Luath hath not forgotten you," said the Earl, as the great dog was manifesting his joy at seeing his old master.

"By my faith you have him in good quarters here!" said Inchrory, observing that a quadruple fold of carpet had been spread for the animal close in front of the fire.

"The best I can give him, Inchrory," said the Earl; "as, next to his late master, he deserves the best at my hands. Here, bring the bottle! Inchrory must taste the Earl of Fife's bottle! And, do you hear, bring something for Inchrory to stay his hunger with after his long ride!"

Immediately, as if by magic, several footmen entered with a table covered with the richest viands and wine, which was placed close to Inchrory's chair and that of the Earl. By especial order a bottle of whisky appeared among the other liquors.

"Here's to ye, Inchrory!" said the Earl, after filling himself a glass of whisky, and drinking to his guest with a hearty shake of his hand. And,—

"Here's to you, my Lord," cried Inchrory, following his example in a bumper of the same liquor.

Inchrory had no reason to complain of his entertainment during the time he was at Mar Lodge. The Earl gave orders that everything should be done to please him; and the little man was *highly* pleased, and as proud as a peacock. Amongst other things, hunting parties were made in all directions through the neighbouring forests; and although these were by no means expressly got up for him, yet he was always brought so prominently forward on all such occasions, that in his pride, he believed, like the fly on the pillar, that the very world was moving for him, and for him alone.

It happened that a *Tenchil,* or a driving of the wood for game of all kinds, was one day held at Alnac. Inchrory was posted in a pass with Farquharson of Allargue and Grant of Burnside in Cromdale, who was one of Lord Fife's factors. This last mentioned gentleman, having only arrived at Mar Lodge that morning, knew nothing of Inchrory personally, though Inchrory knew something of him. So that, whilst Farquharson, who was by this time well acquainted with Inchrory and all his peculiarities, was treating him with all that respect, which was at all times paid him by a universal agreement among Lord Fife's friends then assembled as his guests, the little man was left quite unnoticed by Burnside, and treated by him as nobody. Inchrory was severely nettled at this apparently marked neglect on the part of Burnside towards him. As usual on such occasions, the people who had surrounded a large portion of the forest, gradually contracted their circle, and their shouts increasing, and the dogs beginning to range through the coverts, and to give tongue, game of all kinds came popping singly out through the different passes where the hunters were stationed. A short-legged, long-bodied, rough, cabbage-worm-looking terrier, of the true Highland breed, came yelping along towards the point where Burnside, Allargue, and Inchrory were posted near to each other. All was anxiety and eager anticipation. A hart of the first head was the least thing looked for. When,—lo and behold, out came an enormous wild-cat, the very *tigger* of our Highland woods. Burnside had a capital chance of him, but fired at him, and missed him. Inchrory immediately levelled his piece, and shot him dead.

"There's at you, clowns of Cromdale!" cried Inchrory, leering most triumphantly and provokingly over his shoulder at Burnside.

"What do you mean by that, you rascal?" cried Burnside, firing up at this insult, and at the same time striding towards Inchrory with every possible demonstration of active hostility. "What do you mean by that, you little shrimp?"

"Sir," said Inchrory, standing his ground boldly and proudly, "what do *you* mean? I know nothing of *you;* and, it appears by your insolent manners, that *you* know nothing of *me.*"

"Stop, stop, gentlemen!" cried Allargue, running in between them; "the fault is mine for having neglected to introduce you to each other. Burnside, this is Inchrory, the particular friend of the Earl of Fife;—and, Inchrory, this is Burnside, also a particular friend of your friend, the Earl. This, I hope, is enough to put a stop to anything unpleasant between you."

Oh!" said Burnside, who had caught the intelligent wink of the eye which Allargue had secretly conveyed to him, whilst going through this pompous introduction, and who had heard enough of Inchrory to enable him to guess at the case and the character of the animal he had to deal with, as well as to pick up his cue as to the proper way in which he should treat him— "Oh, that is altogether another affair! Had I only known the person in whose company I had the good fortune to be, I should not have presumed to have fired a shot before him. But if I have said anything amiss, I am sure Inchrory will have the magnanimity to forgive me, seeing that I have been already sufficiently punished by the exhibition of bad gunning which I have unwittingly ventured to make in presence of him who is by all acknowledged to be the best marksman in Scotland."

"Sir," said Inchrory, rising full a couple of inches higher in his brogues, and coming forward to Burnside with extended palm, and with a manner full of dignified condescension,—"you are a gentleman of the first water! I beg you will forget and forgive any expression which in my ignorance I may have let fall, that may by chance have given you offence."

"Sir, I am proud to shake hands with you," said Burnside, advancing to give him a cordial squeeze.

"Sir," said Inchrory with a proud air, but at the same time shaking him heartily by the hand, "any friend of my friend the Earl of Fife, is *my* friend. Henceforth, sir, I am your sworn friend."

I daresay, gentlemen, I have given you enough of Inchrory to make you sufficiently well acquainted with his character. But I have yet one more anecdote of him, which I think brings it out more than all the others. His wife, Ealsach, was one morning occupied in tending the cattle at the *shieling* of Altanarroch. Lonely as you already know this place of Inchrory to be, its loneliness was nothing when compared to that of the shieling of Altanarroch, where even the cattle themselves could only exist for a month or two during the finest part of the year. Now, it happened that Ealsach, being in the family way, became extremely anxious and unhappy as her time of confinement approached, and her anxiety went on increasing daily, till at last she began to think it very expedient to go home to Inchrory. The distance was considerable, and the way rough enough in all conscience. But, having the spirit of a Highland woman within her, she set out boldly on foot, and arrived at Inchrory at an early hour in the morning. Her husband met her at the door of the house, where she looked for a kind welcome from him, and modestly signified the cause of her coming.

"Ha!" exclaimed he proudly, and with anger in his eye. "How is this that you come on foot? How dared you to come home till I sent a horse for you, that you might travel as Inchrory's wife ought to do?"

"No one saw how I came," replied his wife meekly. "I met nothing but the moor-cocks and the pease-weeps on the hill."

"No matter," said Inchrory, "even the moor-cocks and the pease-weeps should not have it to say, that they saw the wife of Inchrory tramping home a-foot through the heather. Get thee back this moment every foot of the way to Altanarroch, that I may send for thee as Inchrory's wife ought to be sent for."

The poor woman knew that argument with him was useless.

Without entering the house, therefore, she was compelled to turn her weary steps back to Altanarroch; and she was no sooner there, than a servant appeared, leading by the bridle a horse, having a saddle on its back covered with a green cloth, on which she was compelled to mount forthwith, in order to ride home over the barren and desert moors and mosses, in such style, as might satisfy the moor-cocks and the pease-weeps, that she was the wife of Inchrory.

DRUM-HEAD COURT-MARTIAL AND SENTENCE ON INCHRORY.

Dominie.—What a vain windy-wallets of a body the creature must have been! My humble opinion is, that he would have been much benefited by a gentle tasting of my tawse.

Clifford.—Or the drummer's cat-o-nine-tails, Mr. Macpherson. But come, gentlemen, who tells the next tale? I have nothing now on my book but old Stachcan, and Turfearabrad, both, as I understand, adjourned to time and place more fitting. Come, I must beat up for a volunteer.

Author.—The circumstance of Mr. Macpherson having incidentally mentioned Ticonderoga, towards the end of his account of the adventures of Serjeant John Smith, has brought to my mind a legend of the family of Campbell of Inverawe, which I had from a friend of mine, the story of which is intimately connected with that most disastrous affair. If you like I shall be happy to give it to you.

Clifford.—Andiamo dunque, Signore mio!—let's have it without more delay.

THE LEGEND OF THE VISION OF CAMPBELL OF INVERAWE.

PERHAPS you are all acquainted with the history of the Black Watch, which, as Mr. Macpherson has already told you, was afterwards formed into that gallant corps now immortalised by its actions as the Forty-Second Highlanders? General Stewart of Garth, in his interesting account of the Highland Regiments, tells us that it was originally composed of independent companies, which were raised about 1725 or 1730. These were stationed in small bodies in different parts of the country, in order to preserve the peace of the Highlands. It was, in some sort, a great National Guard, and it was considered so great an honour to belong to it, that most of the privates were the sons of gentlemen or tenants. Most of them generally rode on horseback, and had gillies to carry their arms at all times, except when they were on parade or on duty. They were called Freiceadan Dubh, or the Black Watch, from the dark colour of their well-known regimental tartan, in opposition to the Seider-Deargg, or Red Soldiers, who were so named from the colour of their coats. You may probably remember the circumstance of their having been most unfairly marched to London, under the pretence that they were to be reviewed by the King,—of their having been ordered abroad,—of their refusal to go,—of their having been moved, as if by one impulse pervading every indignant bosom among them, to make that most extraordinary and interesting march of retreat which they effected to Northampton,—of their having been ultimately brought under subjection,—and, finally, of their brave conduct in Flanders, from which country they returned in October 1745.

After their return to Great Britain, the Black Watch were ordered into Kent, instead of being sent into Scotland with the troops under General Hawley, to act against those who had risen for Prince Charles. This arrangement probably arose entirely from great consideration and delicacy on the part of the government, who, fully aware of the high honour of the individuals of the corps, never entertained the smallest doubt of their loyalty, but who felt the cruelty of exposing men to the dreadful alternative of fighting against their friends and relatives, many of whom were necessarily to be found in the ranks of the insurgents. There were, however, three additional companies raised in the Highlands, a little time before the return of the regiment from abroad. These were kept in Scotland, and however distressing to their feelings the duty was which they were called upon to perform, on the side for which they were enlisted, they did that duty most honourably. One of these was recruited and commanded by Duncan Campbell, laird of Inverawe.

After various services in their own country during the period that the rest of the corps was abroad for the second time, these three companies were ordered to embark, in March 1748, to join the regiment in Flanders. But the preliminaries of peace having been soon afterwards signed, the order was countermanded, and they were reduced.

During the time that Campbell of Inverawe's company was occupied in the unpleasant duty to which I have alluded, he had been on one occasion compelled to march into the district of Lorn, and to burn and destroy the houses and effects of a few small gentlemen, who were of that resolute description that they would have sacrificed all they had, and even life itself, rather than yield to what they held to be the government of an usurper. Having been thus led to pursue his route, in a certain direction, for many a mile, he happened, on his return, to be detained behind his men by some accidental circumstance, and having lost his way after night-fall, he wandered about alone for several hours, until he became considerably oppressed with hunger and fatigue. With the expectation of gathering some better knowledge of his way, he left the lower grounds, where the darkness of night had settled more deeply and decidedly down, and he climbed the side of a hill with the hope of benefiting, in some degree, by the half twilight which lingers longer upon these elevations, continuing to rest upon them sometimes for hours after it has altogether deserted their lower regions. With the dogged perseverance of one who labours on because he has no other alternative, he blindly pursued his hap-hazard course in a diagonal line along the abrupt face, always rising as he proceeded, until his way became every moment more and more difficult. The side of the hill became steeper and steeper at every step, until he began to be satisfied that he had no chance of reaching its brow, except by retracing his steps, in order to discover some other means of ascending to it. To any such alternative as this he could by no means make up his mind. He cursed his own folly for allowing his company to march on without him. He uttered many a wish that he was with them. He felt sufficiently convinced that he had acted imprudently in having thus exposed himself alone, in the midst of a district which was yet reeking with the vengeance which his duty had compelled him so unwillingly to pour out upon it. But his courage was indomitable, and his way lay onwards, and onwards he without hesitation resolved to go.

He had not proceeded far, until high cliffs began to rear themselves over his head, whilst, from his very feet, perpendicular precipices shot down into the deep night that prevailed below. The goat or deer track that he followed became every moment more and more blocked up with stony fragments, until at length it offered one continuous series of dangerous steps, requiring his utmost care and attention to preserve him from a slip or fall that might have been fatal.

Whilst he was thus proceeding, with his whole attention occupied in self-preservation, he was suddenly challenged in Gaelic by a rough voice in his front.

"Who comes there?"

"A friend," replied Inverawe, in the same language in which he was addressed.

"I am not sure of that," said the same voice hoarsely and bitterly. "Is he alone?"

"He *is* alone," said a voice a little way behind Inverawe; "we are quite safe."

"Come on then, sir," said the voice in front, "you have nothing to fear."

"Fear!" cried Inverawe, in a tone which implied that any such feeling had ever been a stranger to him; "I fear nothing."

"I know you to be a brave man, Inverawe!" said the man who now appeared in front of him. "Come on then without apprehension. You need not put your hand into the guard of your claymore, for no one here will harm you. But what strange chance has brought you here?"

"The loss of my way," replied Inverawe. "But how do you come to know me so well?"

"It is no matter how I know you," replied the other. "It is sufficient that I do know you, and know you to be a brave man, to whom, as such, I am prepared to do what kindness I can. What are your wants then, and what can I do for you?"

"My wants are, simply to find my lost way, and then to procure some food, of which I stand much in need," replied Inverawe.

"Be at ease then, for I shall help you to both," replied the person with whom he was conversing; "but methinks your last want requires to be first attended to, as the most urgent; so follow me, and look sharply to your footing." Then, speaking in a louder tone to some individuals, who, though unseen, were posted somewhere in the obscurity to the rear of Inverawe, he said, "Look well to your post, lads, I shall be with you by-and-bye." And then again turning to Inverawe, he added—"Come on, sir, you must climb up this way; the ascent is steep, and you will require to use hands as well as feet. Goats were wont to be the only travellers here, and even they must have been hardy ones. But troublous times will often people the desert cliffs themselves with human beings, and scare the very eagle from her aerie, that she may yield her lodging to weary man."

Inverawe now began to clamber after his guide up a steep,

tortuous, and dangerous ascent, where in some places they were compelled to pull up their bodies by the strength of their hands and arms. It lasted for some time; and he of the Black Watch, albeit well accustomed to such work, was beginning to be very weary of it, when at length they landed on a tolerably wide natural ledge, where Inverawe perceived that the cliffs that arose from the inner angle of it so overhung their base as to render it self-evident that all farther ascent in this direction was cut off by them. Rounding a huge fallen mass of rock, which lay poised on the very edge of the precipice, they came suddenly on a ravine, or rift, in the face of the cliff above, on climbing a few paces up which, they discovered the low, arched mouth of a cave, whence issued a faint gleam of light, and an odour of smoke. His guide stooped under the projection of the cliff that hung over it, and let himself down through the narrow entrance. Inverawe followed his example without fear, and found himself in a cavern of an irregular form, from ten to twenty feet in diameter. This he discovered partly by the light of a fire of peats that smouldered near the entrance, and partially filled the place with smoke, but more perfectly by a torch of bog-fir which his guide immediately lighted. But he felt no curiosity about this, in comparison with that which he experienced in regard to the figure and features of his guide, with which he was intensely anxious to make himself acquainted.

He was a tall and remarkably fine looking man, considerably below middle age. He was dressed in a grey plaid and kilt, betokening disguise, but with the full complement of Highland armour about him. His hair hung in long black curls around his head. His face was very handsome, his nose aquiline, his mouth small and well formed, having its upper lip graced by a dark and well-trimmed moustache. His eyes, and his whole general expression, were extremely benignant. After scanning his face with great attention, Inverawe was satisfied that he never had seen him before, and he had ample opportunity of ascertaining the reverse, if it had been otherwise, for the man stood with the bog-fir torch blazing in his hand, as if he wished to give his guest the fullest advantage of it in his scrutiny of him, and then, as if guessing the conclusion to which that scrutiny had brought him, he at last began to speak.

"Aye," said he calmly, "you are right, Inverawe. Your eyes have never beheld me until this moment. But I have seen you to my cost. I was looking on all the while that you and your men were burning and destroying my house, goods, and gear, this blessed morning, and *I* can never forget *you.*"

"I know you not, that is certain," replied Inverawe; "and the cruel duty we were on to-day was so extensive in its operation, that I cannot even guess whom you are."

"You shall never know it from me, Inverawe," replied the other.

"And why not?" demanded Inverawe.

"From no fear for myself," replied the stranger; "but because I would not add to that remorse, which you must feel, from being compelled to execute deeds which are as unworthy of you, as I know they are contrary to your generous and kindly nature. I have suffered from you deeply—deeply indeed have I suffered. But I look upon you but as an involuntary minister of the vengeance of a cruel Government, and perhaps as an agent in the hand of a just God, who would punish me for those sins and frailties which are inherent in my human nature. I blame not you, and I can have no feeling of anger against you, far less of revenge. Give me, then, the right hand of fellowship."

"Willingly, most willingly!" said Inverawe, cordially shaking hands with him. "You are a noble high-minded man; for certainly I can imagine what your feelings might have very naturally been against me, and I know that I am now in your power."

"All I ask, Inverawe, is this," continued the stranger; "that as I have been, and will continue to be honourable towards you, you will be the same to me; and in asking that, I know that I am asking what is sure to be granted. The confidence in your honour which I have shown by bringing you here, will not be betrayed."

"Never!" said Inverawe, with energy. "Never while I have life!"

"I know I can rely upon you," said the stranger; "and now let me hasten to give you such refreshment as I possess. Sit down, I pray you, as near to the ground as possible, you will find that the smoke will annoy you less."

Inverawe did as his host had recommended, and, seating himself on some heather which lay on the floor of the place, the stranger opened a wicker pannier that stood in a low recess, and speedily produced from it various articles of food, of no mean description, together with a bottle of French wine, and, spreading the viands before his guest, he seated himself by him, and they ate and drank together. They had little conversation;

and the stranger no sooner saw that Inverawe's hunger was satisfied, than he arose, and proposed that he should now guide him on his journey. Creeping from the hole, therefore, they descended the crags together, with all that care which the steepness of the declivity rendered necessary, until they came to the spot where they had first encountered each other, and then the stranger began to guide Inverawe onwards in the same direction he had been formerly pursuing.

They had not proceeded far, until they were challenged by voices among the rocks, showing that his host's place of retreat was protected by sentinels in all quarters. His guide answered the challenge, and they then went on without molestation. After about an hour's walk over very rugged ground, during which they wound over the mountain, and threaded their way through various bogs and woods, that completely bewildered Inverawe, his guide suddenly brought him out upon a road which he well knew, and then shaking hands with him, and bidding him farewell, he dived again into the wood, and disappeared.

Inverawe rejoined his company at their night's quarters. They had spent an anxious time, regarding him, during his absence, and they were clamorous in their enquiries as to what had become of him. He gave them an account of the circumstance of his losing his way; but he told them not a syllable of his adventure with the stranger, resolving that it should be forever buried in his own bosom. There, however, it produced many a thought; and often did he earnestly hope, that chance might again bring him into contact with the man who had taken so noble a revenge of him—to whom he felt as an honest bankrupt might do towards his generous and forgiving creditor; and whose person and features he had engraven so deeply on his recollection, to be embalmed there amidst the warmest and kindliest affections of his heart.

It was soon after the disbanding of his company, that Campbell of Inverawe returned to his own romantic territory, and to his ancient castle, standing in the midst of beautiful natural lawns, surrounded by wooded banks and knolls, lying at the north-western base of the mighty Ben-Cruachan. Speaking in a general way, the country around was thickly covered with oak and birch woods, giving double value, both in point of beauty and utility, to the rich, glady pastures, which were seen to spread their verdant surface to the sun, along the course of the river Awe. Behind the grey towers of the building, broken rocks arose here and there, in bare masses, in the direction of the mountain,—whilst the blue expanse of Loch Etive stretched away from the eye towards the north-east, as well as to the west. To the south-west, the groves, and grassy slopes, were abruptly broken off by the perpendicular crags of the romantic ravine through which the river makes its way, to pour itself across the open haughs of Bunawe, and into Loch Etive. To sketch out the remainder of the neighbourhood, so that you may be fully aware of the nature of the country, which was the scene where one of the most important circumstances of my tale took place, I may add, that about a mile above the ravine, the river has its origin from a long narrow arm of Loch Awe, which presents one of the most romantic ranges of scenery in Scotland. The lake in the bottom, is there everywhere about eighty or an hundred yards wide only ; and whilst a bare, rocky mountain front, furrowed by many a misty cataract, rises sheer up out of the water on its western side, the steep, lofty, and rugged face of Cruachan shuts it in on the eastern side, forming the grand and wild pass of Brandera. Here the mountain exhibits every variety of picturesque form,—of prominent crag, and half-concealed hollow, among which the grey mists are continually playing and producing magical effects; together with deep torrent beds, and innumerable waterfalls, thundering downwards unseen, save in glimpses, amid the thick copse which, generation after generation, has sprung from the stools of those giant oaks, which were once permitted to rear their spreading heads, and to throw their bold arms freely abroad athwart the rocky steeps that rear themselves so high up above, as to be softened by distance and air, till they almost melt from human vision.

Having thus put you in possession of the scenery, I shall now proceed to tell you, that Campbell of Inverawe, after his long absence from home on military duty, felt all the luxury of enjoyment which these his own quiet scenes could bestow. And his mind expanding to all his old friendships, he largely exercised all the hospitalities of life. Frequently did he fill the hall of his fathers with gay and merry feasters, and his own hilarious disposition always made him the very soul of the mirth that prevailed among them.

On one occasion, it happened that he had congregated a large party together. The wine circulated freely. The fire bickered on the hearth, and threw a cheerful blaze over the walls of the hall, reddening the very roof, and gleaming on the warlike weapons that hung around. The wine was good,—the jests were merry,—and the conversation sparkling, so that the guests

23

were as loath to depart as their kind host was unwilling to let them go. His lady had retired to her chamber—but still they sat on, making the old building ring again with their jocund laughter. But all things must have an end. The parting cup, to their host's rooftree, was proposed by a certain young man called George Campbell, and it was filled to the brim. But as all were on their legs to drain it, with heart and good will, to the bottom, a rattling peal of thunder rolled directly over their heads. There was not a man of them that did not feel that the omen was appalling. Some hardy ones tried to laugh it off, as a salvo from heaven in homologation of their good wishes to the house of Inverawe. But the pleasantry went ill down with the rest. Servants were called for,—horses were ordered, and out poured their owners to mount them,—when they were all surprised to see the heavens quite serene and tranquil. But not a word of remark was ventured by any one on this so very strange a circumstance. Their hospitable entertainer saw every man of them take his stirrup cup; and they galloped away, one after the other.

After they were all gone, Inverawe paced about in the court-yard for some time, in sombre thought, which stole involuntarily upon him. He then sought his way upstairs, and lifting an oaken chair towards the great hearth, where the billets had by this time begun to burn red, and without flame, he sat down in it for a while, listlessly to ponder over the events of the evening. The weary servants had gladly stolen away to bed, and the whole castle was soon as silent as the grave. Not a sound was to be heard within the walls but the dull, drowsy buzzing of a large fly, when the flickering light of a solitary lamp, left on the table, had prevented from retiring to some cranny of repose. The master of the mansion smiled for a moment, as the whimsical idea crossed him, that this tiny insect was perhaps the only thing of life which, at that time, kept watch with him within the castle.

Inverawe's thoughts reverted to the last toast which had been given by his young friend Campbell, and the strange circumstances by which it had been accompanied. He had an only son, called Donald, a promising young man, who was the prop of his house, and to whose future career in life he looked forward with all a father's anxiety. He had been long accustomed to weave a silken tissue of anticipated happiness and honours for the young man, and to view him, in his mind's eye, as the father of many generations to come. The youth was at that time from home; and this was the very first moment of his life that the notion of there being any chance of his being one day left childless had ever occurred to him. He tried to shake off these gloomy presentiments, but still they returned, and clung to him with a force and pertinacity that no reason could conquer. He would fain have risen to go to his chamber, but he felt as if some powerful, though unseen, hand had held him down to his chair,—and he continued to sit on, absorbed in contemplative musings on these gloomy and painful dreams, till the billets on the hearth had consumed themselves to their red embers.

Suddenly all such thoughts were put to flight from his mind. He distinctly heard the great outer door of the castle creak upon its hinges. He remembered, that although he had not locked it, he had shut it behind him when he came him. It now banged against its doorway, and sent a hollow sound echoing up the long turnpike stair. Faint, quick, and stealthy foot-steps were then heard ascending. One or two other doors were moved in succession. The footsteps approached with cautious expedition. And as Inverawe listened with breathless attention, the door of the hall was thrust open,—a human countenance appeared for an instant in the dusky aperture—and then a man, with a naked dirk in his hand,—his clothes dripping wet, — his long hair hanging streaming over his shoulders, and half veiling his glaring eyes and pale and haggard countenance, rushed in, and made straight up to him.

Inverawe started to his feet, drew his dirk, and prepared to defend himself from the unlooked for attempt at assassination. But ere he had well plucked it forth from its sheath, the intruder assumed the attitude of a suppliant.

" For mercy's sake pardon my unceremonious entrance, Inverawe !" said the stranger, in a hollow, husky, and exhausted voice. " And be not alarmed, for I come with no hostile intention against you or yours. I am an unfortunate wretch who, in a sudden quarrel, have shed the blood of a fellow-creature. He was a man of Lorn. I have been hotly pursued by his friends, and though I have thrown those who are after me considerably out during the long chase they have kept up, yet they are still pressing like blood-hounds on my track. To baffle them, if possible, I threw myself into the river, and swam across it, and I now claim that protection, and that hospitality, which no one ever failed to find within the house of Inverawe."

" By Cruachan !" cried Inverawe, sheathing his dirk, and

slapping it smartly with the open palm of his hand—" By
Cruachan, I swear that you shall have both !"

Now, I must tell you, that this was considered as the most
solemn pledge that a Campbell of Inverawe could give.   Their
war-cry was, " *Coar-a-Cruachan,*" that is, " *Help from Cruachan.*"   And this expression had a double meaning, inasmuch
as the word Cruachan had reference both to the mountain
of that name and to the hip where the dirk hung.   To
swear by Cruachan, therefore, and to strengthen the oath
by slapping the dirk with the open palm, was to utter an
oath which must, under all circumstances, be for ever held
inviolable.

"·But tell me," said Inverawe, " how happened this unlucky
affair ?"

" We were all met to make merry at a wedding," replied the
stranger, " when, as I was dancing with—— But hold !—I
hear voices ! They approach the castle ! I am lost if you do
not hide me immediately."

" This way," said Inverawe, leading him to a certain obscure
part of the hall.   " Aid me to lift this trap.—Now, down with
ye and crouch there.—They come."

Inverawe had barely time to drop the trap-door into its place,
to resume his seat at the fire, and to affect to be in a deep sleep,
when the voices and the sound of human footsteps were heard
ascending the stairs.   Three men entered the hall in reeking
haste—claymores in hand.   They rushed towards the fire-place,
where he was sitting.   Inverawe started up as if just awaked
by the noise they made, and drew his dirk, as if to defend
himself from their meditated attack.

" Ha !" cried he with well-feigned surprise.   " Assassins !
Then must I sell my life as dearly as I can."

" Not assassins !" cried they.   " We are not assassins,
Inverawe.   We crave your pardon for this apparently rude
intrusion, but we are in pursuit of an assassin.   We come to
look for a man who has murdered another.   Have we your
permission to search for him ?"

" Certainly," said Inverawe, " wherever you please."

" He cannot be here," said one of the men.   " I told you
that he could not be here.   Don't you see plainly that he could
not have come in here without awaking Inverawe.   We lose
time here.   We had better be on after our friends."

" Depend on't he has run up Loch Etive side," said another
of them.

" What are all these wet foot-steps on the floor ?" said the first of them that spoke. "He might have been here without Inverawe's knowledge."

"Don't you see that Inverawe has had a feast, and that wine, and water, and whisky too,' have been flowing in gallons in all directions?" said the second man. "See there is a large pool of lost liquor. I verily believe that some of these footsteps are my own, made this moment, by, walking accidentally through it. I tell you he never could have come here."

"It is true that I have had a feast," said Inverawe, carelessly, "as you may see from the wrecks of it that still remain on the table."

"I told you so," said the second man. "We only lose time here. If you had only been guided by my counsel we might have been hard at his heels by this time, as well as the rest."

"Haste then, let us go!" said the first man.

"Away! away!" cried his companions, and, without waiting for further parley, they rushed out of the hall, and Inverawe heard with some satisfaction, their footsteps hurrying down stairs, and the shouts which they yelled forth after their companions, growing fainter and fainter, until they were altogether lost in the direction of Loch Etive.

Inverawe was no sooner certain that they were fairly gone, without all risk of returning, than he proceeded, in the first place, to secure the outer door of the castle, and then returning to the hall he went to the trap-door, and calling softly to the man concealed below it, he desired him to aid him in raising it, by applying his strength to force it upwards, and thus their united strength enabled them speedily to open it, and to lift it up.

"Come forth now, unfortunate man, said Inverawe; "your pursuers are gone."

"I come," said the stranger, in his husky hoarse voice, and as he raised himself from the trap-door, his haggard countenance, and his blood-shot eyes, that glared with the horror of his situation, half seen as they were through his long moist locks, chilled Inverawe's very heart as he looked upon him.

"Now, sir," said Inverawe, "you are safe for the present, your pursuers have passed on."

"Thanks! thanks!" replied the man; "I know not how sufficiently to thank you."

"Aye—all is so far well for you," said Inverawe; "but concealment for you here is impossible. You must remove into a place of more certain safety, and no time is to be lost. At present you may remove without observation or suspicion;

but no one can say how soon the search for you hereabouts may be renewed. Here," continued he, setting before him some of the remains of the feast, which the tired servants had not removed from the sideboard; "take what refreshment circumstances may allow, whilst I go for a basket, in which to carry food enough to last you during to-morrow. We must go to Ben-Cruachan, with as much secrecy and expedition as we can."

The stranger, thus left for a few minutes by himself, hastily devoured some of the viands, of which he had much need, and having swallowed a full cup of wine, he was rejoined by Inverawe with a basket, into which he hastily packed some provisions, and, without a moment's delay, they quietly and stealthily quitted the hall and the castle, and the moment they found themselves in the open air, Inverawe led the way diagonally up the slope on the western side of Ben-Cruachan.

Their way was long, and their path rough, and they moved on through woods, and over rocks, without uttering a word. Many a half expressed exclamation, indeed, burst involuntarily from the stranger, betraying a mind ill at ease with itself, and many a start did he give, as if he apprehended surprise from some lurking pursuer; and Inverawe shuddered to think that the haggard appearance of the man, and these his guilty-like apprehensions, were more in accordance with the accusation of murder, or unfair slaughter, which seemed to have been made against him, by the expressions of some of those who had come into the hall in search of him, than with the chance-medley killing of a man in an affray, which was the complexion he had himself wished to put on the matter. Be this as it might, however, his most solemn pledge had been given for his security, and accordingly he determined honourably to fulfil it, at all hazards to himself. His reflections, as he went with this man, were of anything but a pleasing nature.

After a long and painful walk, or rather race, for their pace had been more like that than walking, Inverawe began to climb up the abrupt face of Cruachan, till he came to that part of it which hangs over the northern entrance of the Pass of Brandera, where the river Awe breaks away from the end of the narrow branch of the lake, and there, after some scrambling, he led the stranger high up the face of the mountain, to a cave that yawned in the perpendicular cliff. The concealment here was perfect, for its mouth was masked in front by a cairn of large stones, which might have been accidentally accumulated by falling during successive ages from the rocks above, or perhaps artificially piled up there in memory of some person or event long since forgotten. It was moreover surrounded by trees of all sorts of growth; indeed, the universal wooding which prevailed over the surrounding features of nature, of itself rendered any object on the ground of the mountain side difficult to be discovered by any creature that did not, like an eagle, mount into the sky. In addition to this, the great elevation of the position added to the security of the place, and the ravine-seamed front of the perpendicular mountain of rock that guarded the western side of the pass, immediately opposite to the face of Cruachan, precluded all chance of observation from that quarter.

"This is not exactly the place where Campbell of Inverawe would wish to exercise his hospitality, to anyone who deigns to ask for his protection," said the Laird, whilst he was engaged in striking a light; "but in your circumstances it is the best retreat in which I can extend it towards you. Here is a lamp; and I will leave this tinder-box, and this flask of oil with you. The cave is dry enough, and there is abundance of heather to be had around you. Use your lamp only when you may find it absolutely necessary so to do; for its light might betray you; and take care to show yourself as little as possible during the daylight of to-morrow. I have promised you protection by Cruachan, and by Cruachan you shall have it. You must be contented with this my assurance for the present, for your safety demands that I shall not see you again, until I can do so without observation, under the veil of to-morrow-night's darkness. Till then, you must e'en do with such provisions as this basket contains, and you may reckon on my bringing a fresh supply with me when I return. Farewell, for I must hurry back, so as to escape discovery."

"Thanks! thanks! kind Inverawe!" said the man, in a state of extreme agitation and excitement,—"a thousand thanks! But, must you—must you leave me thus alone? Alone, for a whole night, on this wild mountain side, with that yawning hole for my place of rest, and with nothing but the roar of these eternal cataracts, mingled with the wild howl of the wind through the pass to lull me to repose! That cairn, too!—may not that be a cairn which marks the spot where— where—where some murder has been done? Can you assure me that no ghosts ever haunt this wild place?"

"The soul that is free from all consciousness of guilt may hold patient, solitary, and fearless converse with ghost or goblin, even on such a wild mountain side as this," said Inverawe, somewhat impatiently. "But surely you cannot expect that my hospitality to you should require my sharing this mountain concealment with you? If you do, I must tell you, what common prudence ought to teach you, that if I were disposed to do so, nothing could be more unwise, as nothing could more certainly lead to your detection. My absence from home would create so much surprise and anxiety, that the whole country would turn out to seek for me, and their search for me, could not fail to produce your discovery. Even now, I may be risking it by thus delaying to return."

"True, true, Inverawe!" said the stranger, in a desponding tone, and apparently making a strong effort to command his feelings. "There is too much truth in what you say. I must steel myself up to this night. My safety, as you say, demands it. Yet, 'tis a terrible trial! Would that the dawn were come! Is it far from day?"

"I hope it is, indeed," replied Inverawe, "else might my absence and all be discovered. It cannot, as yet, as I suppose, be much after midnight; but even that is late enough for me. I must borrow the swiftness of the roebuck to carry me back. So again I say farewell till to-morrow-night."

Inverawe tarried not for an answer, but, darting off through the wood, he rapidly descended among the rocks, and then bounded over all the obstacles in his way, with a swiftness almost rivalling that of the animal he had alluded to; and so he reached his own door, in a space of time so short, as to be almost incredible. The fire in the hall had now sunk into white ashes. The lamp, which he had left burning, was now flickering in its last expiring efforts. He swallowed a single draught of wine to restore his exhausted strength, and then he stole to his chamber, and crept into bed, happy in the conviction that his lady, who was in a deep sleep, had never discovered that he had been absent.

The sleep that immediately fell upon Inverawe himself was that of the most perfect unconsciousness of existence. He knew not, of course, how long it had lasted, nor was he, in the least degree, sensible of the cause or manner of its interruption. But he did awake, somehow or other; and then it was that he discovered, to his great wonder and astonishment, that the chamber which, on going to bed, he had left as dark as the most impenetrable night could make it, was now illuminated with a lambent light, of a bluish cast, which shone through the very curtains of his bed. A certain feeling of awe crept chillingly over him; for he was at once convinced that the light was something very different from the dawn of morning. It became gradually more and more intense, till, through the thick drapery that surrounded him, he distinctly beheld the shadow of a human figure approaching his bed. He was a brave man; but he felt that every nerve and muscle of his frame was paralysed, he knew not how. He watched the slow advance of the figure with motionless awe. The shadowy arm was extended, and the curtain was slowly and silently raised. The bluish light that so miraculously pervaded the chamber, then suddenly arose to a degree of splendour that was dazzling to his sight, and clearly defined the appalling object that own presented itself to his eyes. The face and figure were those of the very man who had formerly entertained him in the hole in the cliff on the mountain side, in Lorn. He was wrapped in the same grey plaid, too. But those handsome features, which had made so deep an impression on the recollection of Inverawe, were now pale and fixed, as if all the pulses of life had ceased, and the raven locks, which hung curling around them, and the moustaches which once gave so much expression to his upper lip, now only served to increase the ghastliness of the hue of death that overspread his countenance, as well as that of the glaze of those immoveable eyes which had then exhibited so much generous intelligence. Inverawe lay petrified, his expanded orbs devouring the spectacle before them. With noiseless action, the figure dropped one corner of the shadowy plaid in which it was enveloped, and displayed a gaping wound in its bosom, which appeared to pour out rivers of blood. Its lips moved not; yet it spoke,—slowly, and in a sepulchral tone.

"Inverawe!—blood must flow for blood! Shield not the murderer!"

Slowly did the spectre drop the curtain; and its shadow, seen through it, gradually faded away in the waning light, ere Inverawe could well gather together his routed faculties to his aid. He rubbed his eyes, started up in bed, leaned on his pillow, and brushed the curtain hastily aside. All was again dark and silent. Again he rubbed his eyes, and looked; but again he looked into impenetrable night.

"It was a dream," *thought*, rather than *said*, Inverawe; "a horrible dream—but nevertheless it *was* a dream—curious in its coincidences, but not unnatural. Nay, it was most natural, that the strangest adventure of my past life, should be recalled by the yet stranger occurrences of this night, and that both should thus link themselves confusedly and irrationally together during sleep. Pshaw! It is absurd for a rational man to think of this illusion more. I'll to sleep again."

But sleep is one of those blessed conditions of human nature, which cannot be controlled or commanded by the mere will. On the contrary, the very resolution to command it, is almost certain to put it to flight. The vision, or whatever else it might have been, haunted his imagination, and kept his thoughts so busily occupied, that he could not sleep. When his lady awaked in the morning, she found him lying fevered, restless, and unrefreshed. Her inquiries were anxious and affectionate; but, by carelessly attributing his indisposition to the prolonged revelry of the previous evening, he at last succeeded in ridding himself of farther question, and springing from his couch, he tried to banish all thought of the unpleasant dilemma into which he had been brought, by occupying himself actively in the business of the day.

He was so far successful for a time; but as night approached, his uncomfortable reflections and anticipations began again to crowd into his mind. He must fulfil his promise of visiting his guest of the cave, a guest whom he now could not help looking upon with horror as a foul murderer; and yet, if he disbelieved the reality of the previous night's visitation, there was no reason that he should so regard him more now, than he had done before. The difficulty of contriving the means of managing his visit, so that it should escape observation or suspicion on the part of his lady, or his domestics, was very considerable. His lady was that evening more than ordinarily solicitous about him, from the conviction that pressed upon her, that he had had little or no sleep the previous night, and remarking his jaded appearance, she eagerly urged him to retire to bed at an early hour.

"My dearest," said he affectionately, "I shall; but before I can do so, I have some otter-traps to set. Perhaps I had better go and finish that business now, while there is yet some twilight. Go you to your chamber, and retire to rest. I shall sleep all the sounder by and by, after breathing the fresh air of this balmy evening for an hour or so."

The lady yielded to his persuasion, and she had no sooner left him, than he took an opportunity of filling his basket, with such provisions as he could appropriate for the stranger, with the least possible chance of detection; and putting a few of his otter-traps over all, by way of a blind, he sallied forth in the direction of the river. There he first most conscientiously made good his word, by planting his traps, and then, as it was by that time dark, he turned his steps up the side of Ben-Cruachan, and made the best of his way towards the cliffs where the cave was situated. As he drew near to its mouth, he was, in some degree, alarmed by observing a light proceeding from it. He approached it with caution, and, on entering it, he beheld the stranger sitting in the farthest corner of it on the bed of heather, with his figure drawn up and compressed together, and his features painfully distorted, whilst his eyes were intently fixed on vacancy. For a moment Inverawe doubted whether some fit had not seized upon him; but he started at the noise made by the entrance of his protector, and sprang up to meet him.

"Oh, Inverawe," said he, "what a relief it is to behold you! Oh what a wretched weary time I have passed since you left me!"

"I have brought you something to comfort you," said Inverawe, so shocked with his haggard appearance, and conscience-worn countenance, as almost to recoil from him. "You know that I could not come sooner. You seem to be exhausted with watching. You had better take some of this wine."

"Oh, yes, yes, give me wine—a large cup of wine!" cried the stranger, wildly seizing the vessel which Inverawe had filled, and swallowing its contents with avidity. "Oh, such a time as I have spent!"

"This place is quite secure," said Inverawe. "You have no cause for such anxiety, if you will only be prudent. But why do you keep this light burning? Did I not tell you it was most dangerous to do so. Some wandering or belated shepherd or huntsman might be guided hither by it, and if your retreat should be once discovered, your certain destruction must follow."

"I could not remain in darkness, replied the stranger, with a cold shudder; "it was agonising to do so! Horrid shapes continually haunted me,—horrid, horrid shapes! Even the shutting of my eyes could not exclude them. Oh, such a night as last! never have I before endured anything so horrible."

"You must take your own way then," said Inverawe, as he spread out the contents of the basket before him; "I am sorry that I can do nothing better for you, but this is the best fare I could provide for you, without exciting suspicion in my own house. Stay—here is a blanket to help to make your bed somewhat more comfortable. And now, I must hurry away. Yet, before I go, let me once more caution you about the light.

Perhaps I had better make all secure, by taking the lamp with me."

"Oh no! no! no! no!" cried the stranger, his eyes glaring like those of a maniac, while he rushed towards the lamp and seized it up, and clasped it within his arms. "No, nothing shall rend it from me! I will sacrifice my life to preserve it. What! would you leave me to another long, long, and dreadful night? Would you leave me to utter darkness and despair?"

"Leave you I must," replied Inverawe; "and if you will keep the lamp, you must do so at your own risk. But your thoughts must be dreadful thoughts indeed, so to disturb you. If conscious guilt be the cause of them, I can only advise you to confess yourself humbly to your Creator, and to pray for his forgiveness."

Without waiting for a reply, Inverawe left the cave, and made the best of his way home. On reaching his apartment, he found his lady awake.

"You have been a long time absent, Inverawe," said she anxiously.

"I have, my love," replied he carelessly; "the delicious air of this night induced me to stay out longer than I had intended; but I hope I shall sleep all the better for it."

Exhausted as he was by fatigue of body and mind, as well as worn out by want of rest, Inverawe did fall asleep immediately, and his sleep was sound and deep. For aught he knew, it might have lasted for some hours, when again, as on the previous night, he was awaked, he could not tell how. The curtains of his bed were drawn close, but the same uncouth blue light which pervaded the apartment on the former night, now again rendered them quite transparent. To convince himself that he was awake, Inverawe looked round upon his wife. Even at this early stage, the light was sufficiently bright to enable him distinctly to see his lady's features as her head lay in calm repose on the pillow beside him. He turned again towards the side of the bed, and his eyes were dazzled by the sudden increase of light, produced by the curtain being raised as before, by the extended hand of the spectre. The same well remembered features were there, pale, fixed, and corpse-like, but the expression of the brow, and bloodless lips, was more stern than it was on the previous night. Again the spectre dropped the fold of the filmy plaid that covered the bosom, and displayed the yawning gash, which continued to pour out rivers of blood. The spectacle was horrible, and Inverawe's very arteries were frozen up. Again it spoke in a deep hollow tone, whilst its lips moved not.

"Inverawe! My first visit has been fruitless!—Once more I come to warn you that blood must flow for blood. No longer shield the murderer! Force me not to appear again, when all warning will be vain!"

Inverawe made an effort to question it. His parched mouth, and dried and stiffened tongue, refused to do their office. The curtain fell, and the light in the room, as well as the shadow of the figure, began to wane away. He struggled to spring out of bed, but his nerves and muscles refused to obey his will, until it was gone, and all was again darkness. The moment that his powers returned to him, he dashed back the curtain, threw himself from the bed, and searched through the room, with outstretched arms, yet, bold and desperate as he was, he almost feared that they might embrace the cold and bloody figure which he had beheld. His search, however, was vain, and, utterly confused and confounded, he returned to bed with his very heart as cold as ice. Fortunately, his lady had lain perfectly undisturbed, and amidst his own horror, and amidst all his own agonising agitation of thought, he felt thankful that she had escaped sharing in the terrors to which he had been subjected. As on the former night, he tried to persuade himself that all that had passed was nothing more than a dream,—but all the reasoning powers he possessed were ineffectual in removing from his mind the conviction that now laid hold of it, that it really was a spirit that had appeared to him. Sleep was banished from his eyelids for the remainder of the night; and never before had he so anxiously longed for daybreak. It came at last; and soon afterwards his lady awaked.

"Inverawe," said she, tenderly and anxiously addressing him, "you are ill—very ill. What, in the name of all goodness, is the matter with you? Your worn-out looks tell me that something terrible has occurred to you. Your late excursion of last night has something mysterious about it. You were not wont thus to have concealment from me—from me your affectionate wife!—What is it that preys upon your mind?—I must know it."

"Promise me, upon the honour of Inverawe's wife," said he, now seeing that concealment from her was no longer practicable; "promise me on that honour which is pure and unsullied as the snow, that you will not divulge what I have to tell you, and your curiosity shall be satisfied."

With a look of intense and apprehensive interest, the lady

promised what he desired, and then Inverawe communicated to her every circumstance that had occurred to him. She was struck dumb and petrified by the narration; but she had no sooner gathered sufficient nerve to speak, than she earnestly entreated him to have nothing to do in concealing the guilty stranger.

"Let not this awful warning, now given you for the second time, be neglected," said she. "Send for the officers of justice without delay, and give up the murderer to be tried by the offended laws of his country. You know not what curse may fall upon you, for thus trying to arrest Heaven's judgment on the guilty man. Oh, Inverawe, it is dreadful to think of it!"

"All this earnestness on your part, my love, is natural," said Inverawe calmly. "But think of the solemn oath I have sworn;—you would not have Inverawe—you would not have your husband—break a pledge so solemnly given? Whatever may befal me *here*, I cannot so dishonour myself. Besides," added he, "whilst, on the one hand, I know that he to whom I am so pledged is like myself, a man of flesh and blood, who, for anything I know to the contrary, may, after all, be really less guilty than unfortunate; I cannot even yet say with certainty, that I have not been the sport of dreams, naturally enough arising out of the strange circumstances to which I have been exposed. But were it otherwise, and that, contrary to all our accustomed rational belief, I have indeed been visited by a spirit, what proof have I that it is a spirit of health? What proof have I that it may not be a spirit wickedly commissioned by the Father of lies to take this form, in order to seduce me into that breach of my pledge, which would forever blacken the high name of Campbell of Inverawe, and doom myself to ceaseless remorse during the rest of my days?—No, no, lady!—I must keep my solemn vow, whatever may befal me."

The lady was silenced by these words from her husband, but her anxiety was not thereby allayed. It increased as night approached; and especially when Inverawe told her that he must again visit the man in the cave. During that day, various rumours had reached him, of people being afoot in search of a murderer, who was supposed to have found a place of concealment somewhere in that neighbourhood; and it was with some difficulty that he could suppress a hope that unconsciously arose within him, that he might be relieved from his pledge, and from his present most distressing and embarrassing position, by the accidental capture of him for whom they were searching. The duty of visiting the wretched man had now become oppressively painful to Inverawe,—and the painfulness of it was not decreased by the additional risk which he now ran of being detected. But Inverawe was not a man to abandon any duty for any such reasons. Having again privately made up his basket of provisions therefore, and put his otter traps over its·contents, as formerly, he left the castle as twilight came on, and making his circuit by the river side with yet more care and caution than before, he climbed along the side of Cruachan, and in due course of time reached the mouth of the cave. The light was burning as before, and on entering the place, its inmate was sitting with a countenance and expression if possible more haggard and terrific than he had exhibited on the previous night.

"Welcome!—welcome!" cried he, starting wildly up, and speaking in a frantic tone, as he rushed forward to seize Inverawe's cold hand in both of his, that felt like heated iron, —"welcome, my guardian angel! All other good angels have fled from me now!—And the bad!—Oh!—But you will not leave me to-night?—Oh, say that you will not leave me to-night!"

"I grieve to say, that, for your own sake, I cannot gratify you," replied Inverawe, withdrawing his hand involuntarily from the contamination of his touch, and shrinking back with horror from the glare of his phrenzied and blood-shot eyes, though with a heart almost moved to pity for the wretch before him, whose very manhood seemed to have abandoned him. "It is vain to ask me to stay with you, as I have already frequently explained to you; but much more so, now that I have learned that there are men out searching for you in this neighbourhood, brought hither by the strong conviction that you are concealed somewhere hereabouts. This circumstance renders it imperatively necessary that you should no longer persevere in the perilous practice of burning your lamp, which exposes you to tenfold danger."

"Talk not to me of danger!" exclaimed the man, in a dreadful state of excitement, and in a tone and words that seemed more like those of a raving madman than anything else—"I must have light—I should go distracted if I had not light. Darkness would drive me to self-destruction! I tell you it is filled with horrible shapes. Even when I shut my eyes the horrible spectre appears. Have pity!—have mercy on me, and stay with me but this one single night!—for even the light of the lamp itself cannot always banish the terrific spectre from before me!"

"Spectre!" cried Inverawe, shuddering with horror,—"what spectre?"

"Aye, the horrible spectre," replied the man. And then suddenly starting back, with his hands stretched forth, as if to keep off some terrific shape that had instantaneously risen before him, and with his eye-balls glaring towards the dark opening of the cave, he shrieked out—"Hell and torments! 'tis there again,—there—there—see there!"

"I see nothing," said Inverawe, with some difficulty retaining a proper command of himself. "But this is madness—absolute insanity. See, here is your food;—I must leave you immediately."

"Oh, do not go!" said the stranger, following Inverawe for a few steps towards the mouth of the cave, and entreating him in a subdued and abject tone. And then, just as his protector was about to make his exit, he again started back, and stood as if he had been transfixed, whilst, with his hands stretched out before him, and his eyes fearfully staring on the vacancy of the darkness that was beyond the cavern's mouth, he again yelled out—"There! there!—see there!"

It must be honestly confessed, that it was with no very imperturbed state of nerves, that Inverawe committed himself to the obscurity of that night, to hurry homewards, and though no spectre appeared before his visual orbs, yet the harrowing spectacle which the guilty man had exhibited, and the allusion which he had made to the supposed spectre which he had seen in his imagination, kept that which he had himself beheld constantly floating before his mind's eye, during the whole of the way home; and he was not sorry, when he reached his own hall, to find his lady sitting by the fire waiting for his return. She was lonely, and cheerless, and full of anxious thoughts regarding him; but her eye brightened up at his entrance, and she filled him a goblet of wine. Inverawe swallowed it greedily down,—gave her a brief and bare account of his evening's expedition,—and then they retired to their chamber.

On this occasion Inverawe silently took the precaution of bolting the door of the apartment; and, on going to bed, the lady, with great resolution of mind, determined within herself to keep off sleep, and to watch, so that she too might behold whatever apparition might appear; hoping that if the spectre which had so disturbed Inverawe, should, after all, prove to be nothing but a dream, she might be able, from her own observation, to disabuse him of his phantasy. But it so-happened, that, notwithstanding all her precautions, and all her mental exertions to prevent it, she fell immediately into a most unaccountably deep sleep; and Inverawe himself, in spite of all his harassing and distressing thoughts, was speedily plunged into a similar state of utter unconsciousness.

Again, for this the third night, he was awaked by the same light streaming through the apartment, and rendering the curtain of his bed transparent by its wonderful illumination. Again he looked round on his wife, and beheld every feature of her face clearly displayed by its influence. She lay in the soundest and sweetest repose. His first impulse was to awake her,—but he instantly checked himself, and felt grateful that she was thus to be saved from the contemplation of the terrific spectral appearance, the shadow of which he now observed gliding slowly towards the bed. The curtain was again raised. The same well-remembered figure and face appeared under the usual increased intensity of light. Again the filmy plaid was partially dropped, and the fearful gash in the bosom was exposed, as before, pouring out blood. Again the deep, hollow voice came from the motionless lips, but it was accompanied by a yet sterner expression of the eyes, and of the pale countenance.

"Inverawe! My warnings have been vain. The time is now past. Yet blood must flow for blood! The blood of the murderer might have been offered up—now your blood must flow for his! We meet once more at Ticonderoga!"

This last visitation of the apparition, accompanied as it was by a denunciation so terrible, had a yet more overwhelming effect upon Inverawe than either of those that preceded it. Bereft of all power over himself, he lay, conscious of existence it is true, but utterly incapable of commanding thought, much less of exercising action. Ere he could rally his intellect, or his nervous energy, the spectre was gone, and the apartment was dark. When his thoughts began to arise within him, they were of a more agonising character than any which he had formerly experienced—"*Your blood must flow for his.*" These dreadful words still sounded in his ears, in the same deep, sepulchral tone in which they had been uttered. Do not suppose that one thought of himself ever crossed his mind. He thought of his son—that son, for whose welfare every desire of his life was concentrated—that was *his blood*, against which he conceived this dread prophecy to be directed —that was *his blood* which he dreaded might flow. He shivered at the very thought. He recalled the strange circum-

24

stances which had attended the drinking of the toast to his roof-tree. His anxiety about his son was raised to a pitch, that converted his bed, for that night at least, into a bed of thorns. He slept not,—yet all his tossings failed to awaken his lady, who slept as if she had been drenched with some soporiferous drug. The sun had no sooner darted his first rays through the casement, however, than she awaked as if from a most refreshing sleep. She looked round upon her husband— observed his haggard and tortured expression—and the whole recollection of what she previously knew having come upon her at once, she began vehemently to upbraid herself.

" I have slept," said she, in a tone of vexed self-reprehension. "After all my determination to the contrary, I have slept throughout the whole night; and you have been again disturbed. Say !—what has happened ! Have you seen him again ?"

" I have seen him," replied Inverawe in a subdued tone and manner—" I have seen him, and his appearance was terrible."

" Say—tell me—what passed ?" exclaimed the lady, earnestly. " Inverawe, I must know all."

Inverawe would have fain eaten in his words. He would have especially wished to have left his wife in ignorance of the denunciation to which the apparition had given utterance. But he had not as yet recovered sufficient mastery over himself, to enable him to baffle the questioning of an acute woman. In a short time the whole truth was extracted from him ; and now the lady, in a state of agitation that very much exceeded his, began to press upon him the necessity of giving up the criminal to justice. Her argument was long and energetic ; and during the time that it occupied, he gradually resumed the full possession of himself.

" I have heard you, my love," replied he, calmly ; " yet you have urged, and you can urge nothing which can persuade me to break my solemn pledge. The hitherto spotless honour of Inverawe shall never be tarnished in my person. Dreadful as is the curse which has been denounced upon me, I am still re- solved to act as an honourable man. Yet I will do this much. I will again visit the man in the cave, and insist with him that he shall seek some other place of refuge. I have done enough for him. I have suffered enough on his account. He must go elsewhere. Perhaps I should have come to this resolve yesterday—the time, alas ! *may now be past.* But, come what come may, I am determined that the visit of this night shall be the last that I shall pay to him. He must go elsewhere.

Even his own safety requires that he shall do so—and mine! But no matter, he must seek some other asylum."

Even this resolve—late though it might be, was, for the time, some consolation to the afflicted mind of his wife. Nay, it was in some degree matter of alleviation to his own sufferings. The broad sunlight of Heaven, and the bustling action of the creatures of this world while all creation is awake, produces a wonderful effect upon the human mind, in relieving it from all those phantoms of anticipated evil which the silent shades of night are so apt to conjure up within it. Inverawe and his lady were less oppressed with gloomy thoughts during that day than might have been supposed possible. It is true, that he often secretly repeated over the denunciation of the apparition, but even yet he would have fain persuaded himself, as he tried to persuade his wife, that he had been the sport of dreams, resulting from some morbid state of his system.

"Ticonderoga!" said he, "where is Ticonderoga? I know of no such place; nay, I never heard of any such; and, in truth, I do not believe that any such place really exists on the face of this earth. Ticonderoga! A name so utterly unknown to me, and so strangely uncouth in itself, would lead me to believe that it is the coinage of my own distempered brain; and, if so, then the whole must have been an illusion. Yet it is altogether unaccountable and inexplicable."

Thus it was that Inverawe reasoned during that day; but as night again approached, it brought all its phantoms of the imagination along with it.

Inverawe, however, wound himself up to go through with that which he now considered as his last trial. Having filled his basket as before, he set off on his wonted circuitous route to the cave. As he went thither, he endeavoured to steel up his mind to assume that resolute tone with the stranger which he now felt to be absolutely necessary to rid himself of so troublesome and distressing a charge. Much as it did violence to his innate feelings of hospitality to come to any such determination, he resolved to insist on his departure from the cave that very night, and he had no difficulty in persuading himself that his doing this would be the best line of safety he could prescribe for the stranger, seeing that by the active use of his limbs during the remaining portion of it, he might well enough reach some distant place of concealment before daybreak. Full of such ideas, he pressed on towards the cave, that he might get him off with as little delay as possible. The light which had shone from its mouth upon former occasions was now absent, and Inverawe hailed the circumstance as a proof that the wretched man had at last become more rational. He approached the orifice in the cliff, and gently called him. His own voice alone was returned to him from the hollow bowels of the rock. All was so mysteriously silent, that an involuntary chill fell upon Inverawe. He repeated his call in a louder voice, but still there was no reply—no stir from within. A cold shudder crept over him, and for a moment he half expected to see issue from the black void before him, that appalling apparition which had now three several times appeared by his bedside. A little thought enabled him to get rid of this temporary weakness. He recalled the last words of the spectre, and the strange uncouth name of Tigonderoga. If such a place had existence at all, it was there, and there only, that he could expect to behold him again. He became reassured, and all his wonted manliness returned to him. He struck a light, and crept into the cave. A short survey of its interior satisfied him that the stranger was gone. The blanket, the extinguished lamp, and some other things lay there, but no other vestige of its recent inmate was to be seen. Inverawe felt relieved; he was saved from even the semblance of inhospitality. But the recollection of the apparition's last words recurred to him, and then everything around him seemed to whisper him that indeed *the time might now be past.* He began, most inconsistently, to wish that the stranger had still been there—nay, he almost hoped that he might yet be lingering about the neighbouring rocks or thickets. He sallied forth from the cave, and abandoning all his former caution, he shouted twice or thrice in succession, at the very top of his voice, but without obtaining any response, except that which came from the echoes of the cliffs, muffled as they were by the roar of the numerous cataracts of the mountain side, and the howling blast that swept downward through the pass far below. For a moment he felt that if the stranger had been still in his power, he could have given him up to justice, to be dealt with as a murderer; but reason made him blush, by bringing back to him his high and chivalric sense of honour in its fullest force, so that he turned to go homewards possessed with a very different train of thought. When his lady met him, she was eager in her enquiries, and deeply depressed when she learned that Inverawe had now lost all chance of delivering up the murderer.

"Alas!" said she, in an agony of tears, "*the time is now past.*"

"Do not allow this matter to distress you so, my love," said Inverawe, endeavouring to soothe her into a calm, which he could by no means command for himself. "The more I think of it, the more I am persuaded that the whole has been a phantasm of the brain. Let us have a cup of wine, and laugh all such foolish fancies away ere we go to bed. This perplexing and distressing adventure has now passed by, and this night I hope to shake off all such vapours of the imagination."

Inverawe had little sleep that night, but he was undisturbed by any re-appearance of the apparition. Unknown to his wife, he made a circuitous excursion next day to Ben-Cruachan, where a more accurate examination of the cave and its environs satisfied him that the stranger was indeed gone. And he was gone for ever, for Inverawe never afterwards saw him,—nor, indeed, did he ever again hear the slightest intelligence regarding him.

Days, weeks, and months rolled away, and by degrees the gloom which these extraordinary and portentous events had brought upon Inverawe, as well as upon his lady, began to be in a great degree dissipated. His son had long since returned home in full health and vigour, and things fell gradually into their natural and usual course.

Inverawe was one night sitting in social converse with his wife and his son, and their friend, young George Campbell— the same individual who, as you may remember, was the giver of the toast of the roof-tree of Inverawe—when a packet of letters was brought in, and handed to the laird.

"What is all this?" exclaimed he, quickly breaking the seal, and hastily examining the contents. "Ha! the old Black Watch again! this *is* news indeed!"

"What?—What is it?" cried his lady.

"Glorious news!" cried Inverawe, rubbing his hands. "I am appointed to the majority of the Highlanders; and here is an ensign's commission for you, young gentleman," said he, addressing George Campbell. And my friend Grant, who writes to me, tells me that he has got the lieutenant-colonelcy. What can be more delightful than the prospect of serving in such a corps, under the command of so old a friend?"

"Glorious!—glorious!" cried young George Campbell, jumping from his chair, and dancing through the room with joy.

"A bumper to the gallant Highlanders, and their brave commander!" cried Inverawe, filling the cups.

The toast was quaffed with enthusiasm. Young Inverawe alone seemed to feel that there was no joy in the cup for him.

"Would I had a commission too!" said he, in a tone of extreme vexation.

" Boy," said Inverawe, gravely, " Your time is coming. It will be well for you to stay at home to look after your mother. One of us two is enough in the field at once."

" Am I then to be doomed to sloth and idleness at home ?" said Donald, pettishly; " better put petticoats on me at once, and give me a distaff to wield."

" Speak not so, Donald," said his mother, in a trembling voice. " You are hardly old enough for such warlike undertakings; and, indeed, your father says what is but too true— for what could I do, were both of you to be torn from me ?"

Donald said no more. The cup circulated. George Campbell was in high spirits, and full of happy anticipations.

" I hope we may soon be sent on service," said he, exultingly.

" You may have service sooner than you dream of," said Inverawe, going on to gather the remainder of the contents of his packet. " Grant writes me here, that in consequence of the turn which matters are taking in America, he hopes every day for the arrival of an order for the regiment to embark. George, you and I must lose no time in making up our kitts, for we must join the corps with all manner of expedition."

The parting between Inverawe and his lady was tender and touching. Donald bid his father farewell with less appearance of regret than his known affection for him would have led any one to have anticipated. There was even a certain smile of triumph on his countenance as he saw them depart. But his mother was too much overwhelmed by her own feelings, to notice anything regarding those of her son.

The meeting between Inverawe and his old brother officers was naturally a joyous one, and nothing could be more delightful than the warmth of the reception he met with from his long-tried friend Colonel Grant, now the commanding-officer of the corps.

" My dear fellow, Inverawe !" said he, cordially shaking him by the hand, " this happy circumstance of having got you amongst us again, is even more gratifying to me than my own promotion, and yet, let me tell you, the peculiar circumstances attending that were gratifying enough."

" I need not assure you that the news of it were most gratifying to me," replied Inverawe. " It doubled the happiness I felt, in getting the majority, to find that I was to serve under so old and so much valued a friend. But to what particular circumstances do you allude ?"

" When the step was opened to me, by the promotion of Colonel Campbell to the command of the fifty-fourth regiment," replied Colonel Grant, in a trembling voice, and with the tears beginning to swell in his eyes, "I was not a little surprised, and, as you will readily believe, pleased also, to be waited on by a deputation from the non-commissioned officers and privates of the corps, to make offer to me of a purse containing the sum necessary to purchase the lieutenant-colonelcy, which they had subscribed among themselves, and proposed to present to me, with the selfish view, as the noble fellows declared to me, of securing to themselves as commanding-officer a man whom they all so much loved and respected! Campbell!—Inverawe!" continued he, with his voice faltering still more from the swelling of his emotions, "I can never forget this, were I to live to the age of Methuselah—I can never deserve it all—but—but pshaw! my heart is too full to give utterance to my feelings—and I must e'en play the woman."

"Noble fellows indeed!" cried Inverawe, fully sympathising with him in all he felt; "but by my faith they looked at the matter in its true light, when moved by selfish considerations, they were led so to act—for they well knew that you would be as a father to them."

"I shall ever be as a father to them whilst it pleases God to spare me," said the Colonel warmly, "and if ever I desert them while life remains, may I be blown from the mouth of a cannon!"

"What was the result of this matter then?" demanded Inverawe.

"Why, as it happened," replied the Colonel, "the promotion went in the regiment without purchase, so that I enjoyed all the pleasure of receiving this kind demonstration from my children, without taxing their pockets, or laying myself under an unpleasant pecuniary obligation to them, which might at times have had a tendency in some degree to paralyse me in the wholesome exercise of strict discipline. And we shall require to stick the more rigidly to that now, seeing that we are going on service."

"We *are* going on service then?" said Inverawe.

"We have this very evening received our orders for America," replied Colonel Grant; "and never did commanding-officer go on service with more confidence in his men and officers than I do."

"And I may safely say that never did officers or men go on service with greater confidence in their commander than we shall do," replied Inverawe, again shaking the Colonel heartily by the hand.

George Campbell was introduced by Inverawe to the particular notice of Colonel Grant, and by him to the rest of the officers, among whom he soon found himself at his ease. The time for their embarkation approached, and all was bustle and preparation amongst them. George had much to do, and it was with some difficulty, but with great inward delight, that he at last found himself complete in all his arms, trappings, and necessaries. The night previous to their going on board of the ships appointed to convey them to their place of destination, was a busy one for him, and he was still occupied, at a late hour, in his quarters, when he was surprised by a knock at his door.

"Come in!" cried George Campbell.

The door opened, and a young man entered, whose fatigued and soiled appearance showed that he had come off a long journey.

"Donald Campbell of Inverawe!" cried George, in utter astonishment; and the young men were instantly in one another's arms. "My dear fellow, what strange chance has brought you hither?"

"I come to throw myself on your honour," said Donald. "I come to throw myself on the honour of him whom I have ever held to be my dearest friend;—on the honour of one who has never failed me hitherto, and who, if I mistake not, will not fail me now. Give me your solemn promise that you will keep my counsel, and do your best to assist me in my present undertaking."

"Methinks you need hardly ask for my solemn promise," replied George Campbell; "for you might safely count on my best exertions to oblige you at all times. But what can I do for you? It would need to be something that may be quickly and immediately gone about, else cannot I stay to effect it. We embark to-morrow morning."

"You will not require to stay behind the rest, in order to do what I require of you," said Donald of Inverawe.

"I could not if I would," replied George Campbell.

"Do you go in the same ship with my father?" demanded young Inverawe.

"I wish I did," replied George Campbell; "but I regret to say that I go in a different vessel."

"So much the better for my purpose," replied young Inverawe eagerly. "You will be the better able to take me with you without my being discovered."

"Take you with me!" cried George Campbell, in great astonishment. "What in the name of wonder would you propose?"

"That which is perfectly reasonable," replied young Inverawe. "Do you think that I could sit quietly at home, whilst my father, and you, and so many of my friends, are earning honour and glory abroad? Ask yourself, George, what would you have done under my circumstances?"

"I have never thought as to how I might have acted had I been so placed," replied George Campbell, much perplexed. "But I have no relish for having any hand in aiding you to oppose the will of your father."

"No matter now, George, whether you have any relish for it or not," replied young Inverawe, smiling. "You have given me your promise that you will aid me, and you must now make the best of it. So come away. Let me see how you can best manage to get me aboard. I must not be seen by my father till we land in America, and then I shall enter as a volunteer."

"What will your father say then?" demanded George Campbell.

"Why, that the blood of Inverawe was too strong in me to be restrained," replied Donald. "Why, man, it is just what he would have done himself. He will be too proud of the spirit inherent in his house, which has impelled me to this act, ever to think of blaming me for it. Come, come, you have given me your word."

"I *have* given you my word," said George Campbell; "and I must honestly tell you that I wish I had been less precipitate. But having given it, I must in truth abide by it. It may be as you say, that your father will have more pride than pain in this matter, when he comes to know it. And then, as for myself, I shall be too happy to have you as my companion in so long a voyage. But come, let us have some refreshment, and then we can talk over the matter, and consider how your scheme may be best carried into effect."

The thing was easily enough arranged. Many of the privates of the corps were gentlemen who had attendants of their own. There was nothing extraordinary, therefore, in an officer being so provided. A slight disguise was employed to alter Donald's appearance, so that he might escape detection from anyone who had seen him before. Next morning he went on board in charge of some of Ensign George Campbell's baggage, and there he remained snugly, until the expedition sailed.

The Highland regiment embarked full of enthusiasm, and it was ultimately landed at New York in the highest health and spirits. Colonel Stewart of Garth, in his interesting work, tells us, that they were caressed by all ranks and orders of men, but more particularly by the Indians. Those inhabitants of the wilds flocked from all quarters to see the strangers, as they were on their march to Albany, and the resemblance which they discovered between the Celtic dress and their own, inclining them to believe that they were of the same extraction as themselves, they hailed them as brothers. Orders were issued to treat the Indians kindly; but, although these were most generally and most cheerfully obeyed, instances did occur where gross acts of impropriety and harshness were exhibited towards them, and one of these I shall now mention.

A young Indian, of tall and handsome proportions, with that conscious air of equality which they all possess, came up to a group of the Highlanders who were resting themselves round a fire. An ignorant and mischievous fellow of the party, who much more merited the name of savage than him of the woods, having heated the end of the stalk of a tobacco-pipe, handed it, full of tobacco, with much mock solemnity, to the young Indian, who, in ignorance of the trick, was just about to take it into his hand, and to apply the heated end of it to his lips, when a young Highlander who was present, dashed it to the ground. The Indian started—looked tomahawks at the Highland youth, and might have used one too, had not he, with his glove on, taken up a portion of the broken pipe-stalk, and signing to the Indian to feel it, made him sensible of the kind and friendly service he had rendered him. The ferocious rage that lightened in the eye of the Red Man was at once extinguished. A mild and benignant sunshine succeeded it. He took the hand of the young Highlander, and pressed it to his heart; and then, darting a look of dignified contempt upon the poor creature who had been the author of this base and childish piece of knavery against him, he slowly, solemnly, and silently withdrew.

Whilst Major Campbell of Inverawe was on the march, his noble appearance seemed to make a strong impression on their Indian followers. For his part, he was peculiarly struck with the fine figure and graceful mien of a heroic-looking young warrior of the woods, who seemed to keep near to him, as if earnestly intent on holding intercourse with him. He encouraged his approach; and, conversing with him, as well as the young man's imperfect knowledge of English permitted him to do, he invited him, when they halted for refreshment, to partake of his hasty meal. The young Eagle Eye—for such was the Indian's name in his own tribe—carried a rifle; and Major Campbell having put some questions to him as to his skill in using it, his curiosity was so excited by all that the red man

said of himself, that he resolved to put it to the proof. Having
loaded his own piece, therefore, he proposed to his new Indian
ally, to take a short circuit, to look for game, during the brief
time that the men were allowed for rest, and one or two of the
officers arose to accompany them. The Eagle Eye moved on
before them with that silence, and with that dignified air, which
marked the confidence which he had in his own powers. A
walk of a few hundred yards from their line of march, brought
them into a small open space of grassy ground, surrounded by
thickets. Inverawe stopped by chance to adjust the buckle of
his bandoleer, when the Eagle Eye, who happened at that
moment to be some paces to the right of him, sprang on him
like a falcon, and threw him to the ground. As he was in the
very act of doing so, an arrow from the thicket in front of them
pierced the Indian's shoulder, whilst he, almost at the same
moment, levelled his rifle, fired it in the direction from whence
the arrow came, and, rushing forward with a yell, plunged
among the bushes. The whole of these circumstances passed
so instantaneously, that Major Campbell's brother officers were
confounded. But having assisted him to rise from the ground,
they congratulated him on his escape from a danger which
neither he nor they could as yet very well comprehend or
explain. They were not long left in suspense however, for the
Eagle Eye soon reappeared, dragging from the thicket the body
of an Indian belonging to a hostile tribe. In an instant, the
Eagle Eye exercised his scalping-knife, and possessed himself of
the bloody trophy of his enemy. On examination, the ball
from his rifle was discovered to have perforated the brain
through the forehead of his victim. The mystery was explained.
The young Eagle Eye had suddenly descried the lurking foe,
deeply nestled among the bushes, and in the act of taking a
deliberate aim at Inverawe. He had saved the Major's life at
the imminent risk of his own, and that quick sight from which
he had his name, had enabled his ready hand to take prompt
and deadly vengeance for the wound he had received in doing
so. The grateful Inverawe felt beggared in expression of thanks
to his Indian preserver. He and his friends extracted the
arrow from the shoulder of the hero, poured spirits into the
wound, and bound it up; and then, as they hastened back to
join the troops, he entreated the Eagle Eye to tell him how he
could recompense him.

"It is enough for me," replied the young Indian warrior,
with dignified gravity of manner, mingled with becoming
modesty, and in his broken language, the imperfections of

which I shall not attempt to give you, though I shall endeavour to preserve the finer peculiarities of its poetical conceptions,— "it is enough for my youth to be suffered to live within the shadow of a chief, broad as that which the great rock spreads over the grassy surface of the prairie.. A chief among those who have come over the waters of the great salt lake, in number like that of the beavers of the mohawk, whose fathers were the brethren of our fathers, though their hunting grounds are now so far apart. The tribe of the Eagle Eye has been broken. The pride of the foes of the Eagle Eye is swelled by a thousand scalps of his kindred. He is like a solitary tree that has escaped from the whirlwind that has levelled the forest. The Eagle Eye has no father—he is alone—make him thy son."

"You shall be as a son to me!" said Inverawe, deeply affected by the many tender recollections of home which this appeal had awakened in his mind. "You shall never want such fatherly protection as I can give you. But I would fain have you ask some more instant and direct recompense from me, for having thus so nobly saved my life at the peril of your own. Is there nothing immediate that I can do for you? Gratify me by asking something."

"The Eagle Eye will obey his father," replied the Indian, calmly. "One of your pale-faced tribe has deeply insulted your red son."

"Ha!" exclaimed Inverawe, "find him out for me, and you shall forthwith see him punished to your heart's content."

"The cunning and cowardly kite is beneath the vengeance of the Eagle," replied the Indian. "But there was a youth among your pale faces, who stood the red man's friend. Him would I hold as my brother. Him would I bring with me beneath the shelter of my father, the great chief, that he may grow green and lofty under his protection."

"You shall search me out that youth," replied Inverawe, "and be assured he shall find a friend in me for your sake."

The Eagle Eye, with great dignity, took the right hand of Inverawe between both of his, and pressed it forcibly to his heart. When they reached the ground where the men were halting, the major despatched a non-commissioned officer with the Indian, to find out the young man, and to bring him immediately before him. They soon reappeared with him; and what was Inverawe's astonishment, when he lifted up his eyes, and beheld—his son!

It was exactly as Donald had himself prognosticated.

Inverawe's heart was so filled with joy, in thus so unexpectedly beholding and embracing his boy, at the very moment when he had been dreaming that he was so far from him; and with pride in thinking of that brave spirit which had impelled him to follow him to America; as well as with deep gratification at the kind-hearted act which had thus caused him to be so strangely brought before him, that no room was left within it for those gloomy thoughts which might have otherwise arisen there. He clasped him again and again to his bosom, whilst the Indian stood by as a calm spectator of the scene, his countenance unmoved by the feelings of sympathy that were working within him. Their first emotions were no sooner over, than Inverawe hurried Donald away to introduce him to the commanding-officer, and he was speedily admitted into the corps as a gentle-man volunteer, with the promise of the first vacant ensigncy. It will easily be believed, that the strict ties which were thus formed between the Campbells of Inverawe and the noble Eagle Eye, were destined to increase every day. Under the direction of his European friends, his wound was treated with the most tender care, and he was soon perfectly cured. The Eagle Eye deeply felt the kindness of his Highland father and brother; but, whether in happiness or in pain, in joy or in grief, his lofty countenance never betrayed those feelings which are so readily yielded to in civilised life. It was in vain that they tried to induce him to adopt European habits, or to domesticate him so far as to make him regularly participate in those comforts which are the fruits of civilisation. He adhered with pertinacity to his own customs, and looked down with barbarian dignity upon those of his hosts, which so widely differed from them; and when at any time he was induced to partake of them, it was with a lofty native politeness, which seemed to indicate that he did so more in compliment to those with whom he was associated, than from any gratification he received in his own person.

Circumstances, with which they or their commanding-officer had nothing to do, had kept the Highlanders altogether out of action during the campaign of 1757, which had done so little for the glory of the British arms. But in the autumn of this year, Lord Loudon was recalled, and Lieutenant-General Abercromby succeeded to the command of the army. By this time, the Highlanders had received an accession of strength, by the arrival of seven hundred recruits from their native mountains; and the corps now numbered no less than thirteen hundred men, of size, figure, strength, and courage, not easily to be matched. The British army in America now consisted altogether of above twenty-two thousand regulars, and thirty thousand provincial troops, which last could not be classed under that character. The hopes of all were high, therefore, and active operations were immediately contemplated.

It was some little time before this, that Inverawe was spending an evening, *tête-a-tête*, with his friend, Colonel Grant. The bottle was passing slowly, but regularly, between them, when, by some unaccountable change in their conversation, the subject of supernatural appearances came to be introduced. Colonel Grant protested against all belief in them. The recollection of the apparition which had three several times visited Inverawe, came back upon his mind, in form and colours so strong and forcible, that his cheeks grew pale, and a deep gloom overspread his brow; so much so, indeed, that it did not escape the observation of his friend. Colonel Grant rallied him, and asked him, jocularly, if *he* had ever seen a ghost.

" I declare I could almost fancy that you saw some spectre at this moment, Inverawe," said he.

" Where ?—how ?—what ?" cried Inverawe, darting his eyes into every corner of the room, with a degree of perturbation which the Colonel had never seen him display before.

" Nay," said the Colonel, surprised into sudden gravity, " I cannot say either where or what; but I must confess that you seem to me as much disturbed at present as if you saw a spectre."

" I cannot see *him* here," said Inverawe, with an abstracted solemnity of tone and manner, that greatly increased his friend's astonishment—" I cannot see *him* here. This is not the place where I am fated to behold *him*."

" *Him !*" exclaimed Colonel Grant, with growing anxiety— " him !—who, I pray you ? For heaven's sake tell me who it is that you are fated to behold !"

" Pardon me," replied Inverawe, at length in some degree collecting his ideas, but speaking in a solemn tone. " An intense remembrance which came suddenly upon me, regarding strange circumstances which happened to myself, has betrayed me to talk of that which I would have rather avoided, and— which cannot interest you, incredulous as you have declared yourself to be regarding all such supernatural visitations."

" Nay, you will pardon *me*, if you please," said the Colonel, eagerly; " for you have so wonderfully excited my curiosity, that I must e'en entreat you to satisfy me. What were these circumstances that happened to you?—tell me, I conjure you."

"It is with great pain," said Inverawe, gravely, "that I enter upon them at all; for, although they still remain as fresh upon my mind as if they had happened yesterday, I would fain bury them, not only from all mankind, but from myself. And yet, perhaps, it may be as well that you should know them,— for strange as they are in themselves, they would yet be stranger in their fulfilment. Listen then attentively, and I shall tell you everything, even to the very minutest thought that possessed me." And so he proceeded to narrate all that I have already told.

"Strange!" said the Colonel, after devouring the narrative with breathless attention—"wonderfully strange indeed! But these are airy phantoms of the brain, which we must not—nay, cannot allow to weigh with us, or to dwell upon our minds—else might we be bereft of reason itself, by permitting them to get mastery over us, and so might we unwittingly aid them in working out their own accomplishment. Help yourself to another cup of wine, Inverawe, and then let us change the subject for something of a more cheerful nature."

But all cheerfulness had fled from Inverawe for that night, and the friends soon afterwards separated, to seek a repose, which he at least in vain tried to court to his pillow for many hours; and when sleep did come at last, the figure of the murdered man floated to and fro in his dreams. But it did so, only the more to convince him of the wonderful difference between such faint visions of slumber, and that vivid spectral appearance, which had formerly so terribly and deeply impressed itself upon his waking senses, in his own bed-chamber at Inverawe.

The conversation I have just repeated, together with Inverawe's narrative, remained strongly engraven upon the recollection of Colonel Grant. The whole circumstances adhered to him so powerfully, that he almost felt as if he too had seen the apparition, and heard him utter his fatal words. He could not divest himself of a most intense solicitude about his friend's future fate, which he could in no manner of way explain to his own rational satisfaction. But the active and bustling duties which now called for his attention, in consequence of the approaching campaign, very speedily banished all such thoughts from his mind.

It was not long after this that Colonel Grant was summoned by General Abercromby to meet the other commanding officers of corps in a council of war. The council lasted for many hours, and when the Colonel came forth from it after it had broken up, he was observed to have a cloud upon his brow, and a certain air of serious anxiety about him, which was very much augmented by his meeting with his friend Inverawe.

"Well," said Inverawe cheerfully to him, as Colonel Grant joined him and his other officers at mess—"I hope you have good news for us, Colonel, and that at last you can tell us that we are to march out of quarters on some piece of active service."

"We are to march to-morrow," replied the Colonel, with unusual gravity.

"Whither?" cried Inverawe, eagerly. "Whither, if I may be permitted to ask?"

"We march to Lake George," replied the Colonel, with a very manifest disposition to taciturnity.

"Pardon me," said Inverawe; "perhaps I push my questions indiscreetly,—if so, forgive me."

"No," replied the Colonel, with assumed carelessness. "I have nothing which the good of the service requires me to conceal from you, Inverawe, nor, indeed, from any one here present. We march for Lake George, as I have already said; and there we are to be embarked in boats to proceed up the lake. Our object," added he, in a deeper and somewhat melancholy tone,—"our object is to attack Fort Defiance."

"What sort of a place is it?" demanded one of the officers.

"A strong place, as I understand from the engineer who reconnoitred it," replied the Colonel. "But these American fastnesses are so beset with forests, that no one can well judge of them till he is fairly within their entrenchments."

"Then let us pledge this cup to our speedy possession of them!" exclaimed Inverawe joyously.

"With all my heart," said the Colonel, filling his to the brim,—but with a solemnity of countenance that sorted but ill with the cheerful shouts of mutual interchange of congratulation that arose around the table. "With all my heart I drink the toast, and may we all be there alive to drink a cup of thanks for our success."

"Father," cried young Inverawe, in his keenness overlooking the Colonel's ominous addition to the toast; "now, father, these Frenchmen shall see what stuff Highlanders are made of!"

"They shall, my boy," replied Inverawe. "Come, then, as I am master of the revels to-night, I call on you all to fill a brimmer. I give you *Highlanders shoulder to shoulder!*"

"Hurrah!—hurrah!—hurrah!" vociferated the whole officers present.

This was but the commencement of an evening of more than usual jollity. The spirits of all were up,—and of all, none were so high in glee as those of Inverawe and his son. There was something, indeed, which might have been almost said to have been strangely wild in the unwonted revelry of the father. Colonel Grant was the only individual present, who did not seem to keep pace with the rest. The flask circulated with more than ordinary rapidity and frequency,—but as the mirth which it created rose higher and higher, and especially with Inverawe and young Donald, Colonel Grant's thoughts seemed to sink deeper and deeper into gloomy speculation. He retired from the festive board at an early hour, leaving the others, who kept up their night's enjoyment as long as they could do so with decency. Inverawe and his son sat with them to the last; and all agreed, at parting, that they had been the life and soul of that evening's revel.

The next morning, the officers of the Highlanders were early astir, to get their men into order of march. Major Campbell of Inverawe was the most active man among them. General Abercromby's force upon this occasion consisted of about six thousand regulars, and nine thousand provincial troops, together with a small train of artillery. Before they moved off, the General rode along the line of troops, giving his directions to the field officers of each battalion in succession. When he came up to the Highlanders, he courteously accosted Colonel Grant and Major Campbell.

"Gentlemen," said he, "we shall have toughish work of it; for though the enemy have not had time to complete their defences, yet, I am told, that, even in its present state, there are few places which are naturally likely to be of more troublesome entrance than we shall find ——"

"Than we shall find *Fort Defiance*," somewhat strangely interrupted Colonel Grant, with an emphasis which not a little surprised Inverawe, as coming from a man usually so polite. "Aye, I have heard, indeed, that Fort Defiance is naturally a strong place, General. But what will not Highlanders accomplish! You may rely on it you shall have no cause to complain of the Black Watch!"

"I have no fear that I shall," replied the General, betraying no symptoms of having taken offence at the Colonel's apparently unaccountable interruption. "I know that both you and your men will do your duty against Fort Defiance, or any other fort."

"Fort Defiance is a bold name, General," said Major Campbell, laughing.

25

" It is a bold name," said the Colonel, gravely.

" It is a vaunting name enough," replied the General. "Yet I hope to meet you both alive and merry as conquerors within its works. Meanwhile, gentlemen, pray get your Highlanders under march for the boats with as little delay as possible."

Not another word but the necessary words of command were now uttered. The regiment moved off steadily, and the embarkation on Lake George was speedily effected, with the most perfect regularity and order, on the 5th of July, 1758.

It must have been a beautiful sight indeed, to have beheld that immense flotilla of boats moving over the pellucid surface of that lovely sheet of water—not a sound proceeding from them save that of the oars,—the unruffled bosom of the lake everywhere reflecting the serene sky of a July evening, together with all the charms of its bold and varied shores, and its romantic islands ;—its stillness affording a strange prelude to that tempest of mortal contest which was about to ensue. Its breadth is about two miles—so that the boats nearly covered it from side to side. They moved on, while snatches of scenery, and many little circumstances in the features of nature around them, called up the remembrance of their own Loch Awe to both the Laird of Inverawe and young Donald, as the sun went down ; and the pensiveness arising from these home recollections, at such a time, kept both of them silent. At length, after a safe and easy, and, on the part of the enemy, an unobserved navigation, the boats reached the northern end of the lake early on the ensuing morning ; and the landing having been effected without opposition, the troops were formed by General Abercromby into two parallel columns.

The order was given to advance ; and the troops speedily came to an outpost of the enemy, which was abandoned without a shot. But as they proceeded, the nature of the ground, encumbered as it was with trees, rendered the march of both lines uncertain and wavering, so that the columns soon began to interfere with each other ; and great confusion ensued. Whilst endeavouring to extend themselves, the right column, composed of the Highlanders, and the Fifty-fifth Regiment, under the command of Lord Howe, fell in with a detachment of the enemy, which had got bewildered in the wood, just as they themselves had done. The British attacked them briskly, and a sharp contest followed. The enemy behaved gallantly ; and the Highlanders especially distinguished themselves. Young Donald of Inverawe, his bosom bounding with excite-

ment, from the shouts of those engaged in the skirmish, rushed
into the thickest part of the irregular melée, and performed
such feats of prowess with his maiden claymore, that they might
have done honour to an old and well-tried soldier. Excited yet
more by his success, he became rash and unguarded, and being
too forward in the pursuit among the trees—which had already
broken the troops on both sides into small handfuls—he found
himself suddenly engaged with three enemies at once. As he
was just about to be overpowered by their united pressure upon
him, a ball from a rifle stretched one of them lifeless before
him, and in an instant afterwards, the Eagle Eye, whose
accurate aim had directed it to its deadly errand, was flourish-
ing his tomahawk over the head of another of his foes. It fell
upon him—the skull was split open—the man rolled down on
the ground a ghastly corpse; and the third, that was left
opposed to young Inverawe, began to give way in terror before
him. Urging fiercely upon this last foe, however, the youth
ran him through with one tremendous thrust, and he too
dropped dead.

Flushed with success, Donald Campbell was now about to
continue the pursuit, after some fugitives of the enemy, who
came rushing past him, when, turning to call on his red brother
and preserver, the Eagle Eye, to follow him, he beheld him
stooping over one of his dead foes, in the act of scalping him.
At that very moment, he saw a French soldier approaching his
Indian brother unperceived, with sword uplifted, and with the
fell intent of hewing him down. Springing before the Eagle
Eye, the young Inverawe prepared himself to receive the meditated stroke—warded it skilfully off, and then following in
on his foe with a thrust, he penetrated him right through the
breast, with a wound that was instantaneously mortal. The
Eagle Eye was now as sensible that he owed his life to young
Donald, as Donald could have been that his had been preserved
by the Indian warrior. They stood for a moment gazing at
each other, and then they embraced, with an affection, which
the stern Eagle Eye had difficulty in veiling, and which young
Inverawe could not conceal.

By this time the enemy were all cut to pieces, or put to
flight. The joy of this unexpected victory was turned into
mourning, by the death of Lord Howe, who had been unfortunately killed in the early part of this random engagement.
His loss, at such a time, was greater than anything they had
gained by this partial overthrow of the enemy. And you will
easily understand this, when I tell you, that it was said of this

young nobleman, that he particularly distinguished himself by his courage, activity, and rigid observance of military discipline; and that he had so acquired the esteem and affection of the soldiers, by his generosity, sweetness of manners, and engaging address, that they assembled in groups around the hurried grave to which his venerated remains were consigned, and wept over it in deep and silent grief.

The troops having been much harassed by this engagement, as well as by the troublesome nature of their march, General Abercromby, in consideration of the lateness of the hour, deemed it prudent, to deliver them from the embarrassment of the woods, to march them back to the landing-place, which they reached early in the morning. They were then allowed the whole of the ensuing day and night for repose. But on the morning of the 8th of July, he rode up to the lines of the Highlanders, and saluting Colonel Grant and Major Campbell of Inverawe, "Gentlemen," said he, "I have just obtained information from some of the prisoners, that General Levi is advancing with three thousand men to reinforce, or succour,—a—a—a—to succour, I say,—the garrison I wish to attack."

"What!" exclaimed Colonel Grant,—"to succour *Fort Defiance*, General? Then I presume you will move on directly, to strike the blow before they can arrive."

"That is exactly my intention," replied General Abercromby.

"And now I must tell you confidentially, gentlemen, that the present garrison consists of fully five thousand men, of whom the greater part are said to be French troops of the line, who, I am informed, are stationed behind the traverses, with large trees lying everywhere felled in front of them. But I have sent forward an engineer to reconnoitre more strictly, and I trust I shall have his report before we shall have advanced as far as—as—"

"As Fort Defiance," interrupted Colonel Grant. "Well, General, are we to be in the advance?"

"No," replied the General. "As you and the Fifty-fifth have had all the fighting that has as yet fallen to our lot, I mean that you shall be in the reserve upon this occasion. The picquets will commence the assault, and they will be followed by the grenadiers,—which will be in their turn supported by the battalions of the reserve.—Nay, do not look mortified, Colonel;—you and your men will have a bellyfull of it before all is done, I promise you."

With these words the General left them, and the columns moved on through the wood in the order he had signified to them. They had now possessed themselves of better guides, and they were thus enabled to make their march more direct, and as they had already cleared their front of enemies, the leading troops were soon up at the entrenchments. Here they were surprised to find a regular breast-work, nine or ten feet high, strongly defended with wall-pieces, and having a very impregnable *chevaux de frieze*, whilst the whole ground in front was everywhere strewed thickly over with huge newly felled oak trees, for the distance of about a cannon-shot from the walls. From behind the *chevaux de frieze*, the enemy, in strong force, commenced a most galling and destructive fire upon the assailants, so as to render the works almost unapproachable, without certain destruction, especially without the artillery, which, from some accident, had not as yet been brought up. But the very danger they had to encounter seemed to give the British troops a more than human courage. Regardless of the hailstorm of bullets discharged on them, with deliberate aim from behind the abattis, whilst they were fighting their laborious and painful way through the labyrinth of fallen trunks and branches that opposed their passage, they continued, column after column, to advance, dropping and thinning fearfully as they went.

The Highlanders beheld this slaughter that the enemy was making of their friends—their blood boiled within them. In vain Colonel Grant and Major Campbell galloped backwards and forwards along the line, using every command and every argument that official authority or reason could employ to restrain and to soothe them, till their time for action should arrive. With one tremendous shout they rushed forward from the reserve, and cutting their way through the trees with their claymores, they were soon showing their plumed crests among the very foremost ranks of the assailants. But so murderous was the fire that fell upon them, that their black tufted bonnets were seen dropping in all directions, never to be again raised by the brave heads that bore them. Their loss before they gained the outward defences of the fort was fearful; but the onset of those who survived was so overwhelming that it drove the enemy from these outworks, and compelled them to retreat within the body of the fort itself.

Now came the most dreadful part of this work of death. The garrison, protected by the works of the fort, mowed down the ranks of the besiegers with a yet more certain and unerring aim. Under the false report that these works were as yet incomplete, scaling ladders had been considered as unnecessary. The Highlanders, gnashing their teeth like raging tigers caught in the toils, endeavoured to clamber up the front of them, by rearing themselves on each other's shoulders, and by digging holes with their swords and bayonets in the face of the intrenchments. Some few succeeded, by such means, in gaining a footing on the top. But it was only to make themselves more conspicuous, and more certain marks for destruction; and they were no sooner seen, than their lifeless bodies, perforated by showers of bullets, were swept down upon their struggling comrades below. By repeated and multiplied exertions of this kind, Captain John Campbell succeeded in forcing his way entirely over the breastwork, at the head of a handful of men; but they also were instantly despatched by the multitude of bayonets by which they were assailed. Four hours did these gallant men persevere in the repetition of such daring attempts as I have described—all, alas! with equal want of success, and with increasing slaughter, till General Abercromby ordered the retreat to be sounded. To this call, however, the Highlanders were deaf; and it was not until Colonel Grant, after receiving three successive orders from the General, which he had failed in enforcing, threw himself among them, and literally drove them back from the works with his sword, that he could collect and bring away the small moiety that yet remained alive, of that splendid regiment with which he had marched to the attack. More than one-half of the men, and two-thirds of the officers, were lying killed or wounded on that bloody field.

Colonel Grant had hardly gathered this remnant of his men together, when he hastened back over the ground where the contest had raged, to search eagerly for some of those whom he most dearly loved, and for the cause of whose absence from this hasty muster he trembled to inquire or investigate. The enemy, though victorious, had been too roughly handled to be tempted to a sally, for the mere purpose of annoying those who were peacefully engaged in the sad duty of carrying off their wounded or dying comrades. The Colonel was therefore enabled to make his way over the encumbered field without molestation, and with no other interruption than that which was presented to him by the prostrate trees, which, however, seemed to him to offer greater obstruction to his present impatience, than they had done during his advance with his corps to the attack. The scene was strangely terrible! It might have been imagined by anyone who looked upon that field, that all Nature, even the elements themselves, had been at strife. Slaughtered, and mutilated, and dying men lay in confused heaps, or scattered singly among the overthrown giants of the forest, those enormous trees which had been so recently rooted in the primeval soil, where they had stood for ages. Colonel Grant looked everywhere anxiously around him. Many were the familiar faces that he recognised, but their features were now so fixed by the last agonising pang of a violent death, as cruelly, yet certainly, to assure him, that *they* could never again in this world recognise him. The last spirited words of high and courageous hope, so recently uttered by many of them to him in their anticipation of triumph, still rang in his recollection, and as he tore his eyes away from them, the tears would burst over his manly cheeks as the thought arose in his mind, that words of theirs would never again reach his ears. He moved hurriedly on, endeavouring to suppress his feelings, but every now and then compelled to give way to them, till his attention was absorbingly attracted by descrying the dark form of an Indian, who was seated on his hams, beneath the arched trunk and boughs of a huge felled oak. It was the Eagle Eye.

He sat motionless as a bronze statue, with the drapery of his blanket hanging in deep folds from his shoulders. His features were grave and still, and apparently devoid of feeling; but his eyes were turned downward, and they were immoveably fixed on the countenance of a young man who lay stretched out a corpse before him. His head was supported between the knees of the red man, whilst the cold and stiffened fingers of him who was dead were firmly clasped between both his hands. The body was that of young Donald Campbell of Inverawe.

"God help me!" cried the Colonel, clasping his hands and weeping bitterly. "God help me, what a spectacle!"

"Why should you weep, old man?" said the Eagle Eye, with imperturbable calmness. "My young brother has gone to the Great Spirit, like a great warrior as he was. Who among his tribe shall be ashamed of *him?* Who among warriors shall call *him* a woman? I could weep for him too did I not know that the Great Spirit has taken him to happiness, from which it were wicked in me to wish to have detained him for my own miserable gratification. But he is happy! He has gone to those fair, boundless, and plentiful hunting-grounds that lie beyond the great lake, where he will never know want, and where we, if our deeds be like his, will surely follow him. But till then the sunshine of the Eagle Eye has departed, and night must surround his footsteps, since the light of his pale-faced brother has departed!"

"This is too much!" said the Colonel, quite overwhelmed by

his feelings. "Help me to bear off the body. It must not be left here."

The Eagle Eye arose in silence, and gravely and solemnly assisted the Highlander who attended the Colonel to lift and bear away the body, and they had not thus proceeded more than a few paces in their retreat from the works when the weeping eyes of the Highland commanding-officer and the eagle gaze of the red warrior were equally arrested at the same moment by one and the same object. This was the manly and heroic form of Major Campbell of Inverawe. He sat on the ground desperately wounded, with his back partially supported against the body of his horse, which had been killed under him. His eye-balls were stretched from their sockets, and fixed upon vacancy, with an expression of terror greater than than that with which death himself, riding triumphant as he was over that field of the slain, could have filled those of so brave a man. Colonel Grant was so overcome that he could not utter a word. He was convulsed by his emotions. The Eagle Eye laid down the body of Donald opposite to his father, and silently resumed his former position, with the youth's head between his knees. The father's eyes caught the motionless features of his son, and he started from his strange state of abstraction.

"My son!" murmured the wounded Inverawe. "So, it is as I supposed,—he is gone! But I shall soon be with you, boy. God in his mercy help and protect your poor mother!"

"Speak not thus, my dearest friend!" said Colonel Grant, making an effort to command himself, and hastening to support and comfort the wounded man; "trust me you will yet do well. You must live for your poor wife's sake."

"No!" replied Inverawe, with deep solemnity. "My hour is come. In vain was it that your kind friendship and that of the brave Abercromby, succeeded in deceiving me,—for I have seen *him*—I have seen *him* terribly,—and this is Ticonderoga!"

"Pardon me, my dear Inverawe, for a deception which was so well intended," said the Colonel, much agitated. "It is indeed Ticonderoga as you say, but—but—believe me,—that which now disturbs you was only some phantom of your brain, arising from loss of blood and weakness. Cheer up!—Come, man!—Come!—Inverawe!—Merciful Heaven, he is gone!"

Hay Nisbet & Co., Printers, Stockwell Street, Glasgow.